Seasoned Rookie

To:
Conley Cheer
Look forward to doing
great things together
in the future!
9-9-2013

This book is for those people, both good and bad,
who played a role in shaping my destiny.
Thank you.

PART I

CHAPTER ONE HOMECOMING

"Rain, the call's for you. I think you'd better take it."

Those words echoed through Rain Henry's mind as he emerged from the private jet and descended the stairs onto the runway at Key Field in Meridian, Mississippi. Once his dress shoes hit the hard concrete, he checked the watch his father had given him as a congratulatory gift only a few weeks before; it was 1:30 A.M. local time. As Rain began the short walk to the terminal, his eyes ached and his mind swam like a drunken catfish in a pond of tequila.

The faint sound of a calling voice, which barely transcended the whine from the idling jet engines, caused Rain to stop and turn. The pilot, halfway down the ladder, waved hesitantly from twenty yards away. Rain noted how his thin tie fluttered slightly in the cool, early morning autumn breeze. He still wore his black captain's hat with its golden "NOC" insignia spelled diagonally across the front. Rain felt a sharp pang of guilt. In his haste to get to the bottom of the stairs and on to the hospital, he had forgotten to thank Charlie for flying him down.

Charlie Dobbs, the pilot, jogged to his former passenger.

Charlie grinned reassuringly while he extended his hand. He spoke at a moderate shout over the singing turbines. "Rain, I know you're a little out of sorts, and I don't want to hold you up. Just wanted to say how sorry I am about your father. We all wish you the best."

With a forced smile, Rain connected palms with the pilot. "Thanks, Charlie. I really do appreciate you and Bob working overtime tonight. Tell everyone I'll be back as soon as I can."

Charlie pumped Rain's arm vigorously. "You bet, Rain. Once everything turns out okay, give me a call and I'll be back here in a flash. That's a promise. We wouldn't want you to miss the celebrations when we all get home to New Orleans!"

His sendoff delivered, Charlie Dobbs briskly returned to the jet. Rain, still tingling with guilt, watched as the pilot ascended the stairs and disappeared into the belly of the slender flying tube.

After Charlie gave him an encouraging salute from the cockpit, Rain resumed his walk for the poorly lit terminal. He inhaled deeply as he approached the only passenger waiting area Key Field offered. Behind him, his ears detected the increasing pitch of the plane's engines as their fan blades spun faster and faster. The shrill whistle rose briefly, leveled off, and then faded as the aircraft taxied for the runway.

Finally, after an incredibly long night, Rain was home. Though Charlie had called New Orleans "home," Rain disagreed. His true home would always be East Mississippi, a lesson learned about eleven months before. Besides, Rain believed a person had to live in the same place for more than six months to call it home. He had been in New Orleans only since mid-May.

In the distance, the rear door of the terminal pushed open, breaking Rain's thoughts and birthing a shadowy figure that slowly ambled forward. Instantly, he recognized Wayne LeRoy, his childhood best friend and the one who had placed that fateful telephone call. As the two men approached one another, Rain contemplated the philosophical postulation that one man's triumph is often counterbalanced by another man's tragedy. The two friends, who had tipped each end of both scales, shook hands and hugged.

"Sorry I had to track you down when I did, Rain. I had a heckuva time getting through. I guess they thought it was a prank call or somethin'. Anyways, I'm glad you made it. How you holdin' up?"

"I'm a little tired. Did Railroad come with you?"

Wayne put his hand on his friend's shoulder and gently prodded him toward the terminal entrance. "Railroad's outta town, 'member? He's in Florida, but I left a message on his cell phone."

"Oh yeah, Florida," Rain answered blankly.

Because of past injuries to his knees, Wayne walked by rotating thrusts of each leg that emanated from the hips. Just when it appeared he would lose balance and fall, the other leg would shoot out and not only stabilize Wayne's body, but also propel him forward. His gait closely resembled a wobbling horseshoe, and Rain remembered how, under Wayne's faded jeans, his legs still bore dark, painful scars that would never fully heal.

"How are the knees, Wayne?"

Wayne chuckled. "Not so bad. They only hurt when I squat."

Upon entering the building, a lone security guard delivered a quick greeting and Rain heard the guard's keys jingle as he relocked the door behind them. While they made their way through the museum part of the terminal, an oversized picture of two men standing by an antiquated, single-prop airplane triggered a vivid memory of an unforgettable boyhood field trip.

They soon reached Wayne's Ford 150 pickup, the same vehicle he had received as a high school graduation present more than fifteen years before. The once proud red paint had significantly faded over time. Scrapes and dings along the outside combined with scars lining the inside of the truck's bed to indicate that it had seen more than its fair share of work.

Wayne opened his door and gingerly swung under the steering wheel while Rain slid onto the bench seat from the passenger side entrance. Wayne offered his friend a thin smile, but said nothing. He took the keys from his windbreaker's pocket and, with a minimum of searching by feel, found the one he needed and plugged it into the ignition. After the third try, the engine cranked and the truck rumbled from the parking lot.

They turned left onto Highway 11, which would take them to the western edge of Meridian. Rain rolled his window down about a quarter of the way, precisely enough to allow his nostrils to quench their thirst for the crisp and pure October air.

"So, what's the latest?" Rain asked.

Wayne visibly squirmed. "I'd better let the doctor explain. He said he'd wait up at the hospital no matter how late you got in."

About ten minutes north of the airport, they reached the intersection of Highway 11 and 8th Street. Straight ahead lay College Park Shopping Center, the western edge of the small city. With the back of his left hand, Wayne flipped the blinker and they headed east on four-lane 8th Street, which would guide them directly into the heart of downtown Meridian. Although it was close to two on a Sunday morning, several cruisers lingered from the previous night, and Rain and Wayne melted into their flowing streams of exhaust and dreams.

Once Wayne and Rain reached downtown, 8th Street ended and Wayne turned north onto 22nd Avenue. A few blocks later, 22nd Avenue fed directly into the main entrance for Landerson Medical Center. Wayne eased the truck to a stop, reached up to the dashboard, and tore off a piece of dingy paper from a "stick-on" notepad. Grabbing a pencil from the console, Wayne Leroy scribbled down seven numbers. He offered the paper with a slow southern drawl. "Rain, if you need anythin', give us a call. Here's our new number, in case you don't have it with you. I'm sure everythin' will be fine with your old man. He's a pretty tough guy. I'll stop by later today and see how ya'll are doin'."

Rain took the phone number, folded it twice, and stuffed it in his shirt pocket. "Thanks again for the ride, Wayne. Give the missus a kiss from me when you sneak back into bed." With a parting handshake, Rain stepped from the pickup and closed the door.

Through the windshield, Wayne offered a final wave before pulling off into the night. Rain was glad the trip from the airport had been a quiet one; it had given him precious time to think. Besides, he felt confident he would get to see more of Wayne over the next day or so and they could have a chance to catch up then. It seemed that no matter how long they had been apart, each could read the other's mind. Rain was not in a talkative mood for obvious reasons, and he knew Wayne understood. On some level, best friends will always be best friends, and that thought brought Rain courage to face the road immediately ahead.

Rain consciously put one foot in front of the other and headed up the walkway to the entrance of the medical center. The electronic eye registered his approach and the sliding glass doors hummed to life, opening with a well-oiled swish. Rain entered a dim and completely empty lobby. The hospital was as much asleep as the rest of Meridian, excluding 8th Street, which still kept one eye open. The silence and lack of light cast him even further into a somber mood, as if that were possible. He stopped at the information desk and the receptionist on duty, a middle-aged woman in her mid-forties, picked up a phone from the inside of her wood-paneled work cube and placed it on the shelf that greeted all visitors to the main entrance.

"Rain Henry, I reckon?"

"Yes, ma'am."

"Thought so. We've been expecting you. Dr. Littleton's probably asleep down in the doctor's lounge, but he wanted me to call him when you got here." Her fingers swiftly dialed a number, and she handed the receiver to Rain.

After the fifth ring, a groggy voice answered, "Littleton."

"Sorry to wake you, Dr. Littleton. This is Rain Henry."

The doctor cleared his throat. "Oh, yes. Henry. James Henry's son. I'll be right down."

Rain heard a click, hung up the receiver, and then settled into an overly cushy 1970's-styled couch. Less than a minute later, a cough from behind broke the room's silence. Rain leapt to his feet and spun to face the doctor, a short and stout man with a thin mustache and even thinner, blond hair.

"Hello, Rain. I'm Dr. Littleton."

"Rain Henry," the much taller of the two replied as they shook hands. "What can you tell me about my father's condition?"

"I'll brief you once we get to the ICU. Let's head on up there now."

They passed the information desk where the receptionist had returned to reading some sort of romance novel under the hazy light from a banker's lamp. Her jaws moved quietly as her fingers fed her mouth a new piece of chewing gum.

Upon rounding the corner, Rain and Dr. Littleton reached the elevator. Dr. Littleton hit the up button, and a muffled bell rang a tired "bing." They entered once the doors parted and when Dr. Littleton pushed the third-floor button, the elevator hummed skywards. Rain kept hoping the doctor would say something, but nothing came from his lips; he simply stared straight ahead at the closed elevator doors, his hands clasped neatly behind his back. Shortly thereafter, the worn bell rang again, the double doors parted on cue, and the physician and the son of the patient exited and headed down the hallway to the left. As they hurried past, three nurses working the night shift offered short, sympathetic smiles.

When Rain and the doctor reached the intensive care unit, Dr. Littleton stopped at room 304. Rain anxiously returned Dr. Littleton's narrow-eyed, weighty stare.

"Rain, I'm your father's here due to his heart attack, but that's only one of his problems. A few hours ago, we discovered something else. During a CT scan of the heart cavity region, we found several lung tumors. A cranial MRI revealed six small tumors growing a few millimeters below the surface of his brain. Your father's entire body is riddled with cancer, which most likely started in the lungs and was quite probably a result of his life-long smoking habit. I'm afraid the window of opportunity to medically treat your father has passed. Today's medicine can do little to help him now."

Rain opened his mouth to say something, but Dr. Littleton raised his hand like a police officer halting traffic. "I know what you're thinking, but you could take your father to the best hospital in the world and they would tell you the same thing."

The doctor licked his lips and swallowed hard before he resumed. "Rain, your father's heart attack was not a mild one. He's still with us, but I'm afraid we've only bought him a brief reprieve from the inevitable. But, even if his heart miraculously healed, the cancer would take his life within a few months. Are you his only living relative?"

"Yes," Rain mumbled.

"It's never easy to say, but as a physician I have an obligation to tell you the truth. Your father doesn't have much time left. I don't think he'll make it out of the hospital alive."

Because he so badly wanted to rush into the room and be with his father, Rain had only vaguely listened. Something told Rain that his mere presence possessed some sort of magical power that would make everything okay again. The doctor's last sentence, however, awakened Rain like a hard slap in the face. For a moment, he had trouble breathing and it felt as though someone ripped his already queasy stomach from his body and dropped it straight down from the top of a skyscraper.

Rain paused for a moment and gathered his thoughts. He steadied his legs and gaped at Dr. Littleton. *He won't make it out of the hospital alive?*

"Are you sure?" Rain asked in a low, controlled voice.

"Yes. I'm afraid both of your father's conditions are inoperable. His fate rests in God's hands now."

Dr. Littleton stepped aside and allowed Rain to push open the door. Rain looked through the glaze of tears that had formed in his eyes and saw his father lying on the hospital bed. His father's nose and mouth were covered by a clear, plastic mask connected to the wall by a long tube, and multiple machines beeped as they projected digital readouts that glowed all colors in the faint light of the room.

The doctor pulled even with Rain. "Right now your father is resting. We've put him into a medically induced coma to ease the strain on his heart. The longer your father rests and can regain some strength, the longer he'll be able to talk with you if and when he wakes up. At this point, that's the best we can do. I'll come back and check on him later this morning. If anything unusual happens, pull this cord and one of the nurses at the station will come to offer assistance." Littleton's hand motioned at a vinyl chair against the far wall. "It's not much, but try to get some sleep if you can."

Littleton quietly retreated and closed the door, leaving Rain and his father alone. Rain moved quickly to the edge of the bed. While Rain stood six feet, eight inches and was filled out nicely at 240 pounds, his father at his healthiest was only five feet, eleven inches and 175. Now, Jim Henry appeared to be trapped in a paper shell of a body that had yellowed with the passage of time, his addiction to nicotine, and his most recent brush with death.

Ever so softly, Rain placed the back of his hand on his father's sunken sallow cheek and held it there. Rain knew his father would leave him alone in the world eventually, but he was not prepared to let go this soon. His father meant the world to Rain. Growing up, Jim Henry fed his son strong doses of love tempered by hard work and discipline, the latter of which the father believed would create an independent man of strong character. Because of this philosophy, father and son once experienced a terrible rift in their relationship, when all communication ceased between the two. Yet fate had given them a second chance, and they embraced it, although it came at a high cost. The dark years had proven lonely and difficult times for both men, but they had since recreated their unbreakable bond. It transcended even the loving relationship Rain remembered from his childhood.

He removed his hand from his father's cheek and softly sat down in the vinyl chair. Rain's head hung low, and he held it with his moist palms in an effort to shield his face and mind from this horrific turn of events. For a moment, he controlled the wrenching sobs that wanted to explode from deep inside, but the tears he could not. They leaked from his eyes as water seeps from a stripped water faucet. The salty liquid trickled down his fingers and wrists to the sleeves of his dress shirt. He tried to slow the process by shutting his eyelids even tighter, but before long, the wet sleeves of his dress shirt clung to the skin of his arms like soggy plaster of Paris strips applied by an invisible, sadistically voyeuristic sculptor.

Rain collected his thoughts and searched for something, anything that might bring him solace. He stared at his father's expressionless face and contemplated the life of the man before him. Jim Henry had faced many extraordinary hurdles, especially during early adulthood. He had lost his true love, Rain's mother, in a car accident when Rain was only six months old. That same car accident had crippled Jim Henry's left arm, leaving the limb so grotesquely mangled and scarred that his father wore only long-sleeve shirts, even during Mississippi's hottest summer months. The ruined appendage served as a constant reminder of that tragic day God sent for Sarah Henry, and now, like a testament to its owner's state of health, it lay naked and limp and vulnerable. For the first time Rain could remember, the arm lay in full view for anyone to see. Rain debated covering the ugliness with the sheet, but decided against it. His father had nothing to hide at this point.

Rain's thoughts turned to the ironic fates of Jim Henry's father and mother. Frank Henry had been dead from a heart attack for more than 33 years, and his mother, Rain's grandmother, had passed away only last December as a result of metastatic breast cancer. In a cruel twist of irony, while nature once created Jim Henry based on the genetic combination of both parents, it now sought to destroy him with a combination of their fatal diseases.

Solace. Solace. Rain forced his mind to keep searching. He remembered how his father had lived a second life through him, his only son. Jim Henry beamed with pride at his son's accomplishments as if they were his own. Rain pondered whether or not his most recent achievements could ever make up for the time that had been lost during the dark years. As his father lay dying before him, Rain sadly realized that they could not.

Rain rubbed his watery eyes with the tips of his fingers and pushed his tired brain again, but nothing came. Gradually, Littleton's prognosis sunk in and a strange, yet comforting sensation took hold. Rain's father would soon die and Rain was powerless to prevent it. Maybe the time had truly come for his father to move on to a better life, Rain thought. He had always believed that heaven existed – it served as a gathering point for those who lead honest and unselfish lives, helping others along the way. Despite his own personal tragedies, Jim Henry certainly exemplified those virtues. And in heaven, Rain knew his father would finally reunite with his beloved Sarah, the girl who stole his heart and gave him a son to love and cherish.

Visualizing his father and mother in a warm embrace became the wrench that repaired the leaky faucets. Rain's tears ebbed as Sarah Henry's hugs and kisses welcomed her husband to eternity, exactly the way his father had always told him it would be. The image brought him comfort and granted him his needed solace.

He fell asleep from sheer exhaustion.

CHAPTER TWO
FIELD TRIP

On the flight to Meridian, Rain had dreaded the nightmares he anticipated from visiting the hospital and seeing his father in the ICU. However, the Sleep Spirits, as his father called them when Rain was a little boy, granted a reprieve. Instead, he dreamt of his childhood. He was a young boy awakening on the Henry family farm.

Rain could hear the birds announcing the spring morning in the pine trees outside his bedroom window. In the distance, Mackel barked incessantly. Mackel had been named after macaroni, which was Rain's favorite food when the family adopted the shepherd mix from the Meridian Humane Society. The brown-and-yellow-spotted dog had been part of the Henry family for almost four years and Rain guessed that Mackel had probably been out early hunting squirrels and now had one treed. Half asleep, eyes closed, and still comfortably curled under several layers of bedding, Rain imagined the squirrel trying to hide its existence from the predator barking below. He pictured the furry creature pasted flat and motionless high against the trunk of an old oak desperately proclaiming, "No squirrels up here!"

While Rain twisted under the blankets, rolling from his back to his side, the early morning rays of the sun peered through his small window and onto the edge of his bed. He pulled the pillow over his head and waited for the approaching footsteps he knew would soon come. Every morning those footsteps served as an alarm clock. Any minute now, his father would enter his room and drag him, if necessary, out from under the nice warm covers for chores before school. As fast as that thought registered, he heard the solid thumps on the stairs and the corresponding creaks of Jim Henry's work boots as they strained the wooden slats.

James Charles Henry paused momentarily before entering his son's room. He enjoyed this part of his day more than any other. Gently, he opened the door and approached the long, motionless lump under the blankets. He suspected Rain feigned sleep, as usual. With a right hand calloused from years of farm work, he reached down under the pillow and tussled Rain's hair.

Rain wiggled away and a muffled, "C'mon Dad, it's Saturday," drifted up through the pillow.

Jim Henry straightened his posture and laughed tenderly. "Son, you know today's not Saturday. Now wake up, Rumplestiltskin. It's time to rise and shine. You've got your chores to do before Mrs. LeRoy comes to get you for school. Granny's already got your breakfast waiting, so let's get a move on."

Rain turned his body from his side to his back and threw off the fluffy cushion, revealing his face. He kept his eyes closed. "Dad, I don't feel good. I don't think I'll be able to go to school today."

"Son, first of all, if you're sick, you don't feel *well*. You know we speak proper English in this family. Secondly, as for missing school because you're sick, that's fine with me, but you'll still have to do your chores, so you might as well get started early. Chores have to be done whether a person's sick or not. Besides, Granny could use your assistance canning some of those spring vegetables for us to eat this winter. You can help her with that today, if you don't feel well enough to go to school."

Rain gave a tired stretch, like a tomcat stirring from a long nap, then sat up and leaned against the headboard. His hands found his eyes, and he rubbed them hard. He stared intensely at the fuzzy blob that had been speaking to him. After a few blinks, his father came more into focus. He wore a big smile on his face, one that seemed permanently etched, especially at this time of the morning. Jim Henry had won a father-son battle of wits with Rain for the thousandth time. Rain knew if it got out to his friends at school, especially Wayne LeRoy, that he had stayed home and canned vegetables all day, he would undoubtedly have to endure taunts of "little girl" and "sissy" for weeks to come. Every boy knew that canning vegetables was women's work. He unscrewed the rest of the sleep from his eyes with a final twist of his fists and let out a great yawn. His day had begun, and he couldn't go back now.

"One more thing," his father said as he turned and started to leave Rain's room. "It's too bad you won't be going to school. As I recall, today your class is going on that field trip to the airport in Meridian. I guess Wayne can tell you if the trip was any fun."

Suddenly, electricity shot through Rain's body. He and Wayne had looked forward to visiting the airport for months. With great haste, he leapt to the floor and bounded down the stairs like a jackrabbit with its tail on fire. As he shouted, "Hey, Dad, wait up! I was just kiddin'!" he could already smell sweet aroma emanating from the morning's southern-style breakfast.

Seconds later, Rain arrived at the kitchen's small breakfast table and slid into a vacant seat. In front of him stood a mound of crispy bacon (just the way he liked it), a small tub of buttered grits, a plate of steamy fried eggs, and a huge pan of buttermilk biscuits. A large, long-necked glass jug of cold, fresh milk he had taken yesterday from Tonla, their dairy cow, stood on the table next to the breakfast cornucopia.

The muscular black man seated to his left glanced up from his plate and greeted him with his mouth still full of biscuit. "Good mornin' mista Rain, suh." His jaws worked effortlessly as two well-oiled, food-crushing machines and the muscles that operated them visibly moved within the depths of his cheeks.

"Good mornin' Mr. Williams. You having breakfast with us today?" This arrangement was not uncommon, but it usually meant that Mr. Williams and his father had been up working early. While waiting for a response from his chewing dining companion, Rain filled his plate with food. Bacon came first, as always, because he considered the salty meat the most precious and tasty of anything on the table.

Before the black man could respond, Rain's father entered the kitchen through the creaky screen door that led to the back porch. "Mr. Williams and I were out by the pond cutting down some trees that we'll use for new fence posts. As hot as it's going to be today, you've got to beat the heat by working the early mornings. Otherwise, we'll end up as crispy as that bacon you like so much."

As Jim Henry joined them, he chuckled, then added matter-of-factly, "When you get a little older you'll be out there with us."

Rain's face unsuccessfully hid his disappointment at the thought of having to leave his cozy bed at dawn to go cut down trees.

Mr. Williams suspended the two food crushers and washed down any remnants of their work with a chug of milk. Inspired by the pouting look on the young boy's face, he added his good-natured, two-cent's worth. "That's right, Mr. Rain. You's just 'bout big enough to help." His black eyes shined like polished glass whenever he looked at Rain; not even a pupil was visible. "An' to answer your question, since we's started workin' so early, I's snuck out of the house so's not to wake Mrs. Williams or L'il Cent b'fow they gets up and eats breakfass. Dat's why I'm a eatin' with ya'll."

Rain smiled and the conversation ended as the three took the task at hand more seriously. Soon, they had consumed all but the crumbs of what was once a veritable mountain of food.

Rain stole a peek at Mr. Williams as the black man finished the last of his milk. The Williams family lived in a tiny bungalow on a corner of the Henry Farm. In exchange for Mr. Williams' work, he received a small salary and the family lived in the house rent-free. Mr. Williams had also worked for Rain's grandfather, as well as for the family who had owned this farm before them, the Braygens. He essentially served as the farm's foreman and possessed an uncanny ability with the land. Jim Henry said over and over that Mr. Williams was like a more accurate, living edition of the *Farmer's Almanac.* Rain remembered being told once that Mr. Williams had been born in that bungalow a long time ago. At the age of twelve, like Mr. Williams' own father, he dropped out of school to work the land fulltime. He was barely literate, but could read the earth, sky, and wind as if he'd read and analyzed thousands of books on each.

When Rain's grandfather purchased the farm, the Williams family conveyed with the property like the barn and storage shed. Mr. Williams's farm duties kept him occupied enough until both his parents died and he grew lonely from lack of companionship. Religion emerged in his life for the first time, and he began attending the all-black Baptist church in Whynot, as it was the closest. Before long, he took a bride eighteen years his junior. He was thirty-four, she was sixteen and just old enough to marry, everyone reckoned. Ten months after the marriage, Mrs. Williams gave birth to Cynthia. However, the young mother experienced a difficult pregnancy and an even tougher delivery. Afterwards, the doctor explained to Mr. and Mrs. Williams that there could be no more babies. While Mr. Williams loved his wife with all of his heart, he loved his daughter with his heart *and* his soul. He called her his little brown sugar angel and proclaimed

Cynthia the greatest gift God, or anyone else, had ever given him.

It amazed Rain how much the father and daughter contrasted. While Mr. Williams's skin was wrinkled, leather-like and black as coal from decades of working under the scorching Mississippi sun, his daughter's appeared soft and silky brown like a perfect glass of chocolate milk. Masculinity oozed from his pores with each drop of perspiration and femininity emanated from her skin like the aroma of a spring rose.

Mr. Williams spoiled Cynthia openly and shamelessly. He told anyone who would listen that, "One day, L'il Cent gonna do somethin' special." Currently in the first grade, she was four years younger than Rain. However, the two children did not attend the same school. Cynthia went to the local public school that was mostly black and he went to the nearby private school, which was all white. Once, Rain had asked his father why. By the look on his father's face, Rain could immediately tell that he had posed a tough question. Jim Henry had answered, "Politics, Son." As soon as Rain heard the "P" come out in his father's "politics" responses, he knew from past experience to probe no further.

Although they lived less than a mile apart, Rain seldom saw Cynthia as she mostly stayed close to home except on the occasion when she briefly visited the Henry house on a holiday or when Rain would deliver something to their bungalow. Whenever Rain did see Cynthia, he always came away thinking she looked cute and seemed smart for her age.

Finished with breakfast, Rain slid his chair back and stood. "How's Little Cent doing, Mr. Williams? Ain't she in the first grade now?"

"*Isn't she,*" his father rolled his eyes.

"Why, yes, suh, she is, Mr. Rain. I thank ya' for askin' 'bout her. You know's she's done learned readin' an writin'! Her teacher says she's 'bout as smart as them young 'uns come!"

"Well, that's great. Please tell her I said hello." Rain caught his father's eye as he pushed away from the table and his dad gave him a wink of approval. Rain then shuffled for the living room, where he knew his grandmother would be sitting on the sofa, pouring over the morning edition of *The Meridian Star*.

Rain admired Mildred Henry's intelligence. Because she read for several hours each day, she could thoroughly discuss almost any subject. Granny also possessed an uncanny ability to make people come around to her point of view no matter how strongly they felt the opposite at the beginning of the discussion. Her hair had turned snow white some time ago, before Rain could even remember, and she relied on thick reading glasses to help her absorb her beloved articles, newspapers, and books. She doted on her grandson constantly, but seemed to sometimes have a strained relationship with her son, Rain's father. Rain's young mind believed that this friction might have been due to the circumstances that ultimately brought the three together.

Rain's grandfather had died shortly after he moved the family south from Chicago to begin a career as a farmer and rancher. During a mid-life crisis, Franklin Scott Henry abruptly relinquished his position as an executive vice president of the First Chicago Bank. On a Wednesday, he quit the bank and by the following Friday, he had purchased the Braygen's farm, or so the story went. Neither Rain's grandmother nor his father openly discussed his grandfather's queer career change. Rain had simply been told that he did it because his professional life fell into a rut. This explanation confused Rain until he remembered that deer got in ruts, which he knew resulted in more deer. Rain deduced that his grandfather had probably brought some deer with him from Chicago and planned on raising them like cattle. What Rain decided his grandfather should have known, but didn't, was that deer can easily jump over barbed wire fences. Shortly thereafter, they all escaped, Rain guessed. The deer must have liked the area, though, because Rain still saw them roaming around the farm quite frequently.

Ultimately, however, a banker to farmer and rancher transition for Frank Henry was not meant to be. The physical strain on a man who had sat behind a desk for twenty-five years proved too much for someone accustomed to mild summers with gentle breezes blowing in from Lake Michigan. On a Sunday in June, during the very first summer at his new profession, Rain's grandfather suffered a massive heart attack and fell from his tractor while tilling the fields under an unusually smothering sun. Most likely, he was dead before he hit the freshly overturned earth, or so the doctor conjectured.

And yet, Frank Henry's unexpected passing served as the *second* death the Henry family suffered that same weekend. Unbeknown to Frank and Mildred, the night before Frank's heart attack, their son and daughter-in-law were involved in a deadly car accident while visiting friends outside New Orleans. Jim barely clung to life at a hospital on the northeastern shore of Lake Pontchartrain. Sarah had been killed. After the authorities tracked down Mildred and explained what had happened, Mr. Williams took on the responsibility of burying Frank while Rain's grandmother traveled to Slidell to pray at her son's bedside, make arrangements for her daughter-in-law's burial, and care for her six-month-old grandson. Like all families that face tragedies somehow do, they picked up the remaining pieces of their shattered lives and moved forward as best they could. Mildred and her son, Jim, jointly decided he should give up his career teaching high school English and history in Beaumont, Texas, and return to Mississippi to help Mildred run the farm. Their plan allowed what remained of the Henry clan to lean on one another for desperately needed emotional support and provide Rain a stable home-life. Despite the tragedies that occurred when he was an infant, Rain felt lucky to be a part of such a loving family.

Rain picked up speed as he sprinted through the living room to the stairs that led up to his room. As he rushed by his grandmother, Rain called out his daily greeting. "Mornin', Granny, thanks for cooking breakfast. It was great as usual!"

"You're welcome, young man. Now you'd better hurry and get dressed. Don't forget your books for school. A man with an education is a man without limitations." With that, the matriarch of the Henry family pushed her bifocals a few millimeters up the bridge of her nose to regain optimal focus. With a well-practiced snap of both wrists and spreading of her arms, as if conducting the Chicago Symphony, she opened the paper fully again. This action smoothed whatever creases or wrinkles had crept in when she lowered the pages to address her grandson.

Rain scampered into his room, stripped, and threw his pajamas into the bottom drawer of his dresser. Next, he whipped his legs into a pair of jeans that had been wadded at the foot of his bed. A T-shirt, tucked in, and tennis shoes completed his fashion ensemble. Like a mini-tornado, he made his bed, the first chore. Reaching onto his tiny nightstand, he grabbed and strapped on the watch his father had given him for a Christmas present, a digital Casio that could chime several different songs. He checked the time. It was already 7:30. He had twenty minutes to feed the chickens, gather the eggs, and milk Tonia. Wayne's mother usually picked him up at 7:50 and seldom was late.

Rain raced back down the stairs, scooped up the milk pail in the back foyer, kicked open the screen door, and started across the backyard for the barn. Meanwhile, Mackel had grown bored with harassing squirrels and secretly waited, behind some bushes and out of sight, for his young master to emerge from the house. As Rain passed, with the swiftness and stealth of a cheetah, the frisky dog sprang into action. At the last possible second, Mackel leapt through the air and pushed his front paws into the young boy's back. The attack caught Rain completely unaware.

Suddenly face down on the ground, Rain struggled to turn over from his prone position, but Mackel's strong legs and wide paws wouldn't allow him. A sloppy tongue washing, directly behind the ears, ensued. Rain had failed to remember one of Mackel's favorite tricks because he was in a hurry. Rain arched his body as much as he could, kicking and shouting at the giant mass of fur-covered flesh above him to get off. Finally, Rain was able to roll out from under the playful pet and jump to his feet. Saliva thickly coated the back of his neck and thin blades of grass had smeared green streaks all over the front of his jeans and T-shirt.

Rain shook his finger at the grinning cheetah, which sat victoriously a few feet away wagging its tail from the excitement and thrill of a successful ambush. "Very funny, Mackel, you stupid dog! Now I've got grass stains all over my clothes and your spit all over me. And I've still got chores to finish." He threatened Mackel with a playful kick in the air. "Now go on, get outta here!"

Rain yanked up the milk pail and wiped the back of his neck. He rubbed the resultant sticky fingers on his pants before striking out again for the barn. This time, however, he frequently checked over his shoulder to keep an eye out for the rambunctious pet. Mackel stood in the same place, his tail swishing back and forth furiously. As Rain reached the barn, something must have caught the dog's attention because the cheetah sprang into action again. Probably saw a rabbit, Rain concluded, as Mackel bounded toward his grandmother's garden by the opposite side of the house.

Rain entered the barn and placed his milking stool next to Tonia, the dairy cow they purchased, about two years before, because the price of milk kept going up at the grocery store. One day, his father simply said, "Why are we buying milk at these outlandish prices? We have a farm and a barn; we'll just build a new stall and get a milk cow."

After the week it took to modify the barn, Jim Henry bought the cow the next day. Granny was immediately skeptical, saying she preferred the store-bought variety, but eventually even she agreed that her son made a wise economical choice. As far as Rain was concerned, he definitely preferred the store-bought milk because it meant one less chore.

Tonia gave about a half gallon a day, which the Henrys shared with the Williams family. Rain thought Tonia was a peculiar name for a cow, and once he had asked his father why he named her Tonia.

"Son, one day you will read one of the great literary books of all time, *Dr. Zhivago*, by Boris Pasternak. It's a story about a family that undergoes class upheaval during the time of the Russian revolution. Pasternak tells of a man who loved more than one woman and wound up losing both. He should have stuck with Tonia, because in my opinion, she provided his children's milk. But some would make an excuse for his behavior and argue he was a victim of circumstance. Everyone, however, is a victim of circumstance. People must continually take advantage of favorable circumstances or overcome poor circumstances. I expect you'll have the chance to read the story when you're older and can better understand."

Rain hoped his father was right. He envisioned the Tonia from the story to be half woman and half cow. How else could a man be in love with something that also produced milk children could drink? This image intrigued him for a long time.

With a precision that comes with practice, he made fast work of milking Tonia. He carried the heavy pail of fresh milk to the kitchen, then returned and cleaned her stall. Rain also provided Tonia fresh hay and water in her trough.

Feeding the chickens was easy enough – he simply took the bag of chicken feed down from the top shelf in the barn and scattered it on the ground inside the protected area outside the coop. The chickens, well accustomed to the ritual, emerged as soon as they heard the feed hit the ground. While they ate, Rain crept into the henhouse and collected all the eggs from their nests. These he placed into a thickly woven straw basket. Like the milk, he delivered the basket of eggs to the kitchen and placed them on the counter for his grandmother.

His chores completed, he quickly returned to the upstairs bathroom. Taking the black comb from the side of the sink and running it under the tap, he tried taming his wild hair. Rain had reached the age where his physical appearance was starting to become important. Who knew? Perhaps someone might "discover him" at the airport and ask him to train to be a pilot. If that happened, he wanted to look good. In the bathroom mirror, he contemplated the seriousness of the grass stains, but decided they were not bad enough to warrant a change of clothes.

With roughly three minutes to spare before Mrs. LeRoy's arrival, Rain grabbed his math and history books from his bedside table, hustled downstairs, and headed out the front door.

"Goodbye, Granny!" he shouted.

"Goodbye Rain! Don't get hit by any of those airplanes!"

"I won't!"

Mrs. LeRoy had almost brought the car to a complete stop and was already tapping her fingers impatiently on the steering wheel. She liked everything to be in perfect order and function with a high level of efficiency. Viewers of the old television show *Starsky and Hutch* would have noticed the resemblance of the LeRoy family's red Gran Torino, which sported a white L-shaped stripe down each side, to the car used in the TV series. As usual, Wayne rode in the back seat, while his older brother, Roy, sat in front next to his mother. Rain's watch read 7:50; he was right on time. Seeing his best friend approach, Wayne LeRoy jumped from the vehicle and held the door open. Rain scrambled into the back seat, Wayne followed, and Roy leaned the seat back and closed the door. Mrs. LeRoy punched the accelerator, and the car's tires crunched and spewed the tiny jagged rocks that lined the gravel driveway.

"Good morning, Rain," Mrs. LeRoy offered as she briefly

twisted to face her new passenger. She spoke with a soft feminine voice enhanced by a delicate southern accent. Her dark hair was combed straight back, but puffy on top. It looked as though someone had placed an upside down U-shaped balloon just under the hair's surface, right beyond the forehead.

"Good morning, Mrs. LeRoy. Good morning, Roy."

Three years older than Rain and Wayne, and already an 8th grader, Roy offered no response except a slight nod.

"Good morning, Rainy," Wayne said as he tried to mimic his mother's voice.

"Good morning, stupid," Rain responded with heavy emphasis on the last word of his sentence.

"Now Rain, you shouldn't call other people stupid. That ain't a polite thing to do, especially when you're tryin' to be a young southern gentleman." Mrs. LeRoy checked for eye contact in the rearview mirror to ensure she had been heard.

"Yes, ma'am," Rain gave her a quick glance.

"Yeah, Mom's right," Wayne added for good measure. "Besides, I'd rather be stupid than be ugly like you."

"Wayne LeRoy!" This time, Mrs. LeRoy's voice was stern.

"Yes, ma'am," came Wayne's weary reply. His tone indicated he repeated this phrase on a regular basis whenever his mother was around. The foursome rode on in silence for a few minutes after Wayne's rebuke.

A few miles later, Mrs. LeRoy turned into the school's driveway and Wayne punched Rain. Not too hard, but with the exact amount of measured intensity to make his ribs sting. Rain swiftly retaliated and the exchange of blows escalated until Mrs. LeRoy threatened to tell both their fathers about their behavior if they didn't cease immediately.

After the hitting subsided, Roy spoke up from his shotgun position. With more than a little exasperation, he exclaimed, "Why don't you two kids grow up? You act like brats. Can't you see how much stress this puts on mother?"

Wayne and Rain looked at each other and sinisterly

snickered. If Mrs. LeRoy had not been there, they would have yelled at Roy to shut his mouth and mind his own business. Neither of them held much respect for Roy LeRoy. Although he was older, he was gangly and unathletic. He insisted on a weekly, bowl-style haircut, which he allowed only his mother to perform. His eyes were narrow and beady, and his face had recently started the early skirmishes of what would not be merely a series of battles, but an all-out war with acne. Roy had never expressed any interest in sports, and he was slow-witted, barely passing his classes at school. Considered a loner, he had few friends. It seemed that no one cared what Roy thought about anything, so his questions and comments were almost always disregarded. Besides, it had become somewhat of a game to see how much roughhousing they could get away with before Mrs. LeRoy reprimanded them. Although the routine deviated slightly from day to day, this was generally how the ride to school unfolded for the two best friends.

With an audible sigh of relief, Mrs. LeRoy dropped off the trio at the administrative building of Jefferson Davis Academy, quickly U-turned the Gran Torino, and headed for home. Without a word, Roy sauntered toward the junior high building. Rain and Wayne were about to enter the elementary school building when Wayne shouted after his brother, "Hey, Faggo! Too bad you don't get to go on the field trip today; it's only for 'brats,' you know!"

Roy continued without so much as a glance over his shoulder. Rain knew that Roy LeRoy probably had become accustomed to ignoring insults or negative comments hurled his direction.

When the two boys entered the front doors of the elementary school, Rain shook his head, "Wayne, your brother sure is strange."

"Yeah, I've heard Daddy talking to Momma about him. He keeps finding weird things in his room, like books on flowers and plants he's checked out from the library. When Daddy asked him why he's readin' about pansies and ferns, Roy told him he wants to raise flowers when he grows up. He calls it being a 'horaculturist' or something like that. Daddy ain't too happy with his grades, neither. He keeps makin' D's and F's in most of his classes."

"Maybe you shouldn't pick on him so much, Wayne. That's what my dad says."

"Well, maybe I wouldn't pick on him if he quit actin' like a girl! He helped Momma can vegetables all weekend, then said he liked it!"

"Wow, maybe he is a girl!" The two laughed as they entered Mrs. Flanagan's homeroom class. The time was exactly eight o'clock.

Colleen Flanagan had taught at Jefferson Davis Academy for almost ten years.

The pay wasn't the best, but then no one got paid much in Mississippi, especially teachers at small private schools. Anyway, it wasn't as if her family truly needed the money. She taught because she loved working with kids. Her heart warmed and adrenaline still coursed through her bloodstream every time a student's face lit up whenever he or she "got" a difficult concept. When her husband, a naval aviator, had been assigned duty as a flight instructor at the Meridian Naval Air Station, she said goodbye to her friends in Norfolk and prepared, once again, to uproot the family as she had done countless times before. She chose this life when she married the hotshot pilot fresh out of the Naval Academy who undoubtedly loved her, but possessed a non-ebbing passion for flying the world's most advanced, first-strike military aircraft. Like her, he found instructing to be a rewarding career. So, wherever he went, so did the rest of the Flanagan family. It was her role to put the best possible spin on the all-too-frequent transitions to a new life in a new place. Now, both of their children had graduated from Jeff Davis and were away at college. And, as Commander Flanagan's retirement shimmered on the horizon just a few years away, she could see no more involuntary moves in their future. When she sat down at her desk and started to quiet the class, she realized again what she already knew: East Central Mississippi was a pretty good place to be now, and maybe a great place for them to stay the rest of their lives.

Rain took his assigned seat at the back of the far right row, next to the bank of windows, and Wayne sat at his desk, located two rows over and on the far left side of the classroom against the beige tiled wall. Rain liked Mrs. Flanagan, even though she separated the two best friends after the first day of class because of their antics. He considered her very pretty for an older woman and hoped that his future wife might be as attractive as Mrs. Flanagan when she reached the same age.

While the talking died down, Rain glanced around the room. He ignored Wayne who tried to attract his attention by making some sort of bizarre contortion with his face. The classroom consisted of students seated in three rows of desks. Each row had eight desks, which were attached to one another with curly, black iron-rod sides and bolted to the plank floor to make them immovable. The front of one desk supported the backrest of the one ahead of it, like a T lying on its side. A square wooden slab served as the main work area, and each writing surface had a long groove at the top, which was designed to keep a pencil from rolling onto the gritty floor. This groove proved necessary because all the desktops tilted downward toward the students' laps.

Rain's eyes focused on Stacey Cottrell, who sat in the very first desk at the beginning of the middle row. She took out her history book and began flipping through the pages. Her hair was long, brown and well kept. One of the taller girls in the class, she had a thin face and high cheekbones. Her green eyes glistened sharp and inquisitive. Rain admired her athleticism on the playground. Easily the fastest girl he knew, she could throw a rock as far and as hard as most boys. Last year, in fourth grade, Wayne made fun of her one day during recess for something (Rain couldn't recall about what), but Stacey was not amused. Rain watched in awe as she slowly and methodically reached down to the ground and picked up a rock about the size of an egg. It almost seemed as if she decided to give her tormentor a chance to run away, or perhaps she simply wanted to enjoy the sport involved. Realizing his precarious predicament, Wayne took off like a bullet fired from a .22-caliber rifle, but could not get away fast enough or far enough and caught a zinger square in the backside of his jeans. Rain fell to the ground and laughed so hard that he nearly peed in his pants. Wayne wheeled with a wild look on his face; however, his watery eyes couldn't mask what must have been excruciating pain. He tried to reduce the sharp discomfort by rubbing his wound, which made Rain laugh even harder. Wayne's temper flared. It was bad enough to be mowed down by a girl, but to have his best friend rolling on the grass laughing hysterically pushed him over the edge. His face turned beet red, his lips puckered with anger, and he began stomping back toward Rain and Stacey like an angry bull. But El Toro stopped in his tracks once Stacey calmly reached down to pick up another stone at her feet. After this development, Wayne backed up quickly with an apologetic look in his eyes. Her point made, Miss Cottrell slipped the rock into the pocket of her overalls for insurance, then confidently turned and headed back to the elementary school building. She would never have to earn Wayne LeRoy's respect again, or Rain Henry's, for that matter. There would be no more direct teasing of Stacey Cottrell, at least that she could hear, anyway.

Mrs. Flanagan rapped her red apple paperweight against the top of her desk. "Okay, class, let's calm down and get settled. I know everyone's excited about today's field trip, but there's still some history, English, and math to learn first. Let's open up our history books to chapter seven, which discusses..."

In Rain's mind, Mrs. Flanagan's voice trailed away like an oak leaf flowing down a lazy river. Looking out the window, he began daydreaming as the fields and the forests in the distance blurred. As far as he was concerned, he didn't need to pay attention anyway, because, as usual, he had read the entire chapter the night before, twice. He felt comfortable with every detail of chapter seven's contents and could answer any question that might be posed. School came easily for him. He enjoyed it, but sometimes found it to be tedious and boring. He made mostly A's with an occasional B without even trying or having to seriously study. History provided the one exception. He read history for pleasure, and thus did not consider studying history studying at all. Mostly, Rain used class time to either daydream or complete the homework assignment for the next period. At first, his teachers disapproved of his "attention deficit," as they called it, but since he consistently scored well on his tests, they accepted his behavior and focused on the rest of the class.

At eleven o'clock, when the third bell of the morning rang, the children shut their math books in unison and sprang from their chairs. The time had finally come to leave for the fieldtrip. Mrs. Flanagan stood and frantically waved her arms, but to no avail. Not even the apple pounding against her desk got the children's attention.

As a last resort, she shouted as loudly as she could. "Children! Children! Please calm down and line up single file at the doorway. The sooner we do this in an orderly fashion, the sooner we're on the bus and on our way to the airport." Partially listening to their frantic teacher, every fifth grader jockeyed for position at the classroom entrance like a tightly bunched group of thoroughbreds racing around the final turn at the Kentucky Derby. Though Rain and Wayne had both been originally seated at the back of the class, by some minor "physical persuading," they ended up first and second, respectively. Stacey Cottrell stood right behind them in third.

Rain, satisfied with his position, turned to his friend. "Hey, Wayne, if we use the buddy system, I'll probably get

Mrs. Flanagan, since I'm first, and you'll get Stacey. Just make sure she ain't got a rock in her pocket."

Before Wayne could answer, Stacey, who had overheard, shot back, "If I did have one, I'd probably use it on you Rain Henry, and I'd aim right for the middle of your eyes!"

Wayne's grin stretched from one ear to the other. "I guess she told you, Rain!"

Eventually, the kids morphed into a single-file line, and Mrs. Flanagan led the giddy fifth-graders out of the building and to the waiting bus that would take them to the Meridian Regional Airport, or Key Field as the locals called it. Rain felt like he had escaped from prison. The get-away vehicle was the same bus that also carried the sports teams and was not colored yellow like traditional school buses, but instead painted gray with red stripes that proclaimed in bold white letters "Jefferson Davis Academy – We are the Rebels." The school mascot, a giant red-and-white Confederate soldier, stood painted silhouette-style on both sides along the front portion of the bus. Johnny Reb, as the kids called him, appeared to be quite relaxed. His Civil War-era cavalry hat fit neatly on his head, his gray mustache was thick and curly, and the lower part of his legs crossed into a soft X as he leaned back on his cane.

Ms. Helen, the bus driver, waited for them at the curb, engine running. Rain climbed the steps, and Wayne followed closely behind. They picked the two back seats, Rain the right side and Wayne the left. Stacey Cottrell, not unexpectedly, chose the very first seat at the front of the bus.

After what seemed like and eternity to the young friends, the remainder of their classmates boarded, picked their seats, and settled in for the ride. Everyone quieted as Mrs. Flanagan stood at the front and addressed the entire fifth grade from Jefferson Davis Academy, all twenty-three of them. "I know everyone here is excited about the trip, but there are some rules we must follow. The first rule is that we will all behave like gentlemen and ladies. There will be no rambunctious behavior, and that goes double for those seated, we won't mention any names, in the back of the bus. The next rule is that the group sticks together. Once we arrive at the airport, do not go off on your own for any reason, unless it's to the bathroom and you better make sure you tell me first. Several students from two other schools will also participate in the field trip, and I don't want anyone to get separated or wind up on the wrong bus. If any of these rules are broken, the guilty party or parties will be severely punished. I want everyone to have a good time, but I also want everyone returned to school safely. Finally, we'll all pick a partner so it'll be a little easier for me to keep track of you. As we head for Meridian, I'll make my way back and write down the pairs on my clipboard. Since we have an odd number in the class, I'll partner with Stacey Cottrell. Any questions?"

There were no questions, so the bus departed the parking lot, turned north on Highway 19, and bumped toward Meridian and its airport.

A few miles into the trip, Rain found an old piece of hard candy on the floor and hit his friend in the back of the head as Wayne looked out of his window. "Looks like you lucked out, Waynie. I thought for sure you'd have to buddy-up with Stacey."

"Why don't you just shut up about Stacey? You're the lucky one, 'cause if she heard you she'd probably whip your ass."

"I don't think so, buddy. I'm just a little faster than you and can dodge better." Rain waited for Wayne's verbal counter punch, but it never came. Instead, Wayne unbuttoned his shirt, which revealed a small, draw-stringed bag hidden against his chest.

"Hey, what are you doin' over there, Wayne?" Rain leaned forward to get a better look. "You been hiding a purse under your shirt or something? Gonna put on some lipstick?"

"Shhhhh!! Not so loud, big mouth," Wayne implored. "Come over here, and I'll show ya."

Rain scooted across the aisle and plopped down next to his

best friend. As though he held a bird nest full of eggs, Wayne's hands gently removed a small model airplane from the felt-covered bag. It was a single prop World War II fighter, painted olive green. Shark mouth decals were located on each side of the fuselage next to the propeller. Wayne also produced a black, fine-tipped marker that had been clandestinely tucked into his pants.

"Wayne, what do you plan on doing with those?"

"I'm gonna have my plane autographed by a real pilot."

Rain started to laugh and then realized that Wayne was serious. Quickly, his laughter turned to concern. Sometimes he had to watch out for Wayne to keep him from doing something stupid. "Wayne, people don't get model planes autographed. They get things like pictures, balls, books, and gloves autographed, but not toy airplanes."

"Well, I brought it, and I'm gonna ask Commander Flanagan if he'll sign it. Do you ever think about what you wanna be when you grow up? If I can't play baseball, I might wanna become a pilot. If I have an autographed plane from a real pilot, it might help me get into flyin' school."

"Okay, you can try, but I doubt he'll do it. He'll probably think you're crazy like I do right now. And I certainly wouldn't let anyone else see you try, or they'll just laugh." Rain hopped back across the aisle to his seat, and Wayne carefully returned the plastic plane to its protective bag and placed it back inside his shirt. They were getting close to Meridian now, and after the two signed up as partners on Mrs. Flanagan's clipboard, Rain challenged Wayne to the "wave game" for fun. The game helped pass the time and soon the entire bus, save Ms. Helen, Mrs. Flanagan and Stacey Cottrell, played, which made keeping score and determining a winner nearly impossible.

When the bus turned by the small rectangular granite sign that announced they reached Meridian Regional Airport, a loud cheer exploded from the children like the finale of a Fourth of July fireworks show. At the bottom, the sign proclaimed the airport address as 2811 Highway 11 South. Ms.

Helen expertly pulled the bus into the loading zone directly behind two other buses. The standard-issue yellow bus represented Newton Academy, a school similar to Jefferson Davis, about twenty miles west of Meridian in Newton, Mississippi. The other bus shined brand-new and sported a magnificent blue raider galloping along each side. The raiders seemed to leap forward and hover in midair against the gold backdrop of the bus. Huge, bold letters announced to the world, or at least anybody stuck in surrounding traffic, that the bus represented Pamar Academy. Rain and Wayne knew Pamar to be the wealthy school where many of Meridian's rich and elite sent their children not merely for an education, but for "college preparation."

The two boys admired the Pamar bus on their way into the terminal. "Wow, Rain, that's a nice bus. I bet they even have a water fountain in the back of that thing."

"Yeah, I remember playing all-stars last year against some of the kids that go to that school. All of their moms and dads drive really nice cars. And, they always have new bats and practice with the whitest baseballs. My dad said all that doesn't matter, though. He said it's what's inside the person, and not the things they own that counts."

"Did you win the game?" Wayne asked.

"Nah, they killed us. But I didn't pitch. Got three hits, though."

Rain, Wayne, and the rest of the Jefferson Davis students filed through the airport and then exited through the double-glass doors onto the runway side of the building. They joined the kids from the other two schools who sat Indian-style on the grassy lawn. Off slightly to the left stood a brightly painted white brick tower that resembled the last remaining corner of a great medieval castle. An oversized glass bucket sat perched at the top of the structure, which was painted a glossy black at the top, bottom, and along the lines that separated each large, tinted window. A figure emerged from the small door at the base of the tower and started their direction. The figure soon became a short man in a dark blue suit. He was completely bald on top, and the long hair on the left side of his head, which had once covered his baldness, blew wildly in the breeze as he approached the podium that had been placed at the edge of the lawn. The sun glared down from a cloudless sky, and Rain had to squint when he focused his attention on the speaker.

"Good morning, everyone. My name is Nelson Barrow, and I am the airport manager here at Meridian Regional Airport, which sometimes is called Key Field. I'm very excited today, because I know we've got some really smart students here from Newton, Pamar, and Jefferson Davis Academies who are excited about learning more about our airport. Can anyone here tell my why some folks call this place Key Field?"

In less than a millisecond, a hand shot up almost directly in front of the podium. All the kids stretched their necks to gawk at the kid bold enough to raise her hand so quickly. Rain and Wayne could have guessed without even looking. Stacey had struck again. They both rolled their eyes and let out a collective groan.

A huge grin spread across Mr. Barrow's face. "Well, now, that's what I call eager. Please stand up and tell us your name, little lady."

"My name's Stacey Cottrell, and I'm in the fifth grade at Jefferson Davis Academy."

"Okay, that's great. Now tell us..."

Stacey cut him off. "Some people call this airport Key Field because of the Key Brothers, who hold the record for the longest flight without landing. They did this in 1935, and it was known throughout the world." Upon finishing, she abruptly sat down next to her field-trip partner, Mrs. Flanagan. With her head pitched high, Stacey acted as if she'd just won the county spelling bee.

Barrow, smiling, continued. "That's very good, Stacey, but that's only a small part of the story. I hope you all are excited about visiting our aviation museum inside to learn more about the Key Brothers and their historic flight. Since it's almost noon, we're going to bring out some box lunches for everyone. I'm going to my office for about an hour to finish some paperwork. Just before one o'clock, I'll be back and then we'll start the Jeff Davis group with a tour of the control tower, which y'all can see over here to your left. Pamar and Newton will tour the two other areas, and then we'll rotate until all groups have seen everything."

Almost on cue, the lunches arrived in the back of two pickup trucks, and shortly thereafter, the bus drivers and teachers passed out the white boxes to the clamoring children who acted as if they were merely minutes away from starvation. Each student also received a canned soda pulled from one of two ice-filled tubs. After making sure everyone received a boxed lunch, Nelson Barrow departed for the control tower.

Rain and Wayne sat down and examined the contents of their boxes: one turkey sandwich, one bag of plain potato chips, and an apple. Rain started in on the sandwich, and Wayne pulled open his bag of potato chips.

After crunching a few of the salty chips, Wayne popped the top on his soda and took a swig. "That Stacey Cottrell, she's a… a…"

"Know-it-all teacher's pet," Rain finished.

"Yeah, yeah. Take a look at her now. She's over talking to some girl from another school. Probably explaining how the sun works or something."

Rain took another bite from his sandwich and, while he chewed, glanced over to where Wayne pointed. He could see Stacey easily enough because she faced him. Her face was animated and her lips chattered nonstop. He couldn't see the girl to whom she spoke because the girl's back faced Rain. However, he immediately noticed her long blond hair and stopped mid-chew. Even from where he sat, it seemed as though she had hair made of golden silk. The way it glistened reminded him of the way a horse's coat shines after about a hundred brushings. The hair literally soaked up the light of the sun and then seem to cast it directly into Rain's eyes. He continued to stare, hoping that she might turn so he could see her face.

When Wayne had almost finished his chips, he tilted his head back and held the bag over his mouth to allow the last few crumbs to trickle onto his tongue.

Rain gently poked his friend. "Hey, Wayne, I want you to go over there and find out that girl's name. While you're at it, find out how she knows Stacey, too."

Wayne's attention shifted back to his box lunch. "What girl?" he asked.

"The one Stacey's pesterin', you idiot."

"Why should I? You just called me an idiot."

"'Cause I want to know and I'll give you my chips." Rain held out the reward to seal the deal.

"Done!" Wayne stood up, snatched the bait, and headed for the girls.

On his way over, Wayne tried to think of what he'd say first, but nothing in particular came to mind. Once there, his mind went completely blank, and he stood frozen behind them for what seemed like several agonizing minutes. Thoroughly embarrassed, he was about to turn and run away when Stacey stopped jabbering and noticed him.

"Wayne LeRoy, what do you want?"

The other girl twisted and looked up at Wayne. Her beauty sent his mind into a tailspin, which confused him even further. "Ummm, ummm, Rain wanted to know this girl's name and how you know her. He gave me these chips to come ask." He thrust forward the unopened bag as proof of the transaction.

The two girls covered their mouths and giggled.

"Rain Henry? Wants to know my cousin's name, does he?" Stacey asked through her fingers.

"That's what he said," Wayne shrugged.

Stacey lowered her hand. "You go back and tell Rain that if

he wants to meet Catherine, he should come over himself and not send a messenger because he's scared. You go back right now and tell him I said that."

Happy to leave the frying pan, Wayne started back, but before he could get away he heard a delicate, almost hypnotic voice. "Is Rain a friend of yours?" Catherine asked.

Wayne turned and answered with pride. "He's my *best* friend."

"Where is he? What does he look like?"

Wayne glanced at Rain, who got caught staring their direction and quickly tried to play it off by intently searching for something in his boxed lunch. "That's him over there digging in his box lunch. He's the one with the grass stains on his T-shirt and jeans."

"Oh, I see him. Thank you, Wayne. It was nice to meet you."

"It was nice to meet you, too. I'd better get goin'."

Wayne got away quickly this time but not far enough out of earshot to hear Stacey shout out, "Wayne, don't you forget to tell Rain what I said."

By 12:45, the lunches were in the trash and Mr. Barrow came to meet the refueled school kids as promised. The tour started with the Jefferson Davis group visiting the control tower, while the Newton group visited the airplane maintenance hangars, and the Pamar group examined the various planes parked out on the tarmac. After thirty minutes at each location, the groups rotated.

Time moved rapidly, and soon, the Jeff Davis group visited its final stop, the maintenance hangars. Everything seemed interesting, but Rain found it hard to focus after Wayne had come back and described Catherine's beautiful face and hypnotic voice.

Rain really couldn't have cared less about what Stacey Cottrell said-or thought. The fact that this girl was her cousin was not lost on him, but he would meet Catherine on his own terms. However, such an introduction proved to be challenging because the groups were separated. It seemed the only chance he might have had to intermingle would have been during lunch. He wasn't about to make a fool of himself, as Stacey suggested, by running right up to her in front of everybody. He would bide his time and wait until the moment was right. He hoped it would come. Wayne, meanwhile, became an intellectual sponge as he soaked up as much information as he could about vectoring traffic patterns, the difference between planes equipped with VFR and IFR, and repairing jet engines. Rain had never seen his friend so consumed by anything before; maybe he really was serious about becoming a pilot.

At 1:30, the groups reassembled on the lawn between the terminal and the tarmac. Mr. Barrow returned to the podium and checked his watch. He pointed north, toward Interstate 20 that ran along the edge of the runway and instructed everyone to listen closely. The sound started slowly, but a few seconds later, a distinct rumbling spread across the sky like steady thunder from an approaching storm. Rain had still been focused on trying to get a good look at this cousin of Stacey's, but the roar of the approaching jet unequivocally demanded his attention. In what felt like only a few seconds, the military aircraft went from a tiny dot to a discernable flying machine and proceeded to shriek down over the runway and past the crowd. The jet couldn't have been more than 500 feet above the ground. As it ripped over the airport, the plane dipped its wings to the left and to the right. Everyone gasped as the sound waves shooting from the jet engines tickled the tiny hairs on their arms and the backs of their necks. Rain was impressed; Wayne was mesmerized.

Once he passed the airport, Commander Thomas G. Flanagan banked hard to the left before looping back to the right for his landing approach. He touched down perfectly and then taxied one of the Navy's main air assault weapons, the Grumman A-6 Intruder, down the runway to the waiting crowd. As Commander Flanagan killed the engines and coasted to within a hundred feet of the spectators, he chortled under the cockpit's canopy. "The show" got the same results every time. The girls covered their ears and looked terrified, yet curious. The boys were wide-eyed, gaped-mouthed, and ready to stampede the jet as soon as it stopped. He had done this public relations bit for the Navy for several years now. It began as a request from his wife for her fifth graders and had spread to the other schools. Commander Flanagan truly enjoyed meeting with the kids and fielding their questions. Plus, it gave him a chance to play the role in life he loved: military jet-jockey.

Everyone ogled with reverence as the pilot slid the canopy open and gracefully descended from the cockpit to the runway. Commander Flanagan wore his olive green combat flight suit, which had straps and buckles in every conceivable place. When he pulled off his helmet, his aviator sunglasses acted like silver-coated mirrors that reflected the rays of the sun into the crowd like tiny searchlights. He appeared extremely fit for his age and the small amount of gray that could be detected from his high-and-tight haircut communicated a level of self-confidence only attainable through thousands of hours of experience. Flanagan embraced his wife and gave her a quick peck on the cheek. The girls swooned and the boys felt envious of this man, his life, his job, and mostly his toy. Mrs. Flanagan held her husband's helmet while the commander walked over and enthusiastically shook hands with Mr. Barrow. The children sat completely hushed, hanging on every move the aviator made. Suddenly, his back to the children, he snapped to attention and executed a perfect "about face." A second later, his body exploded into a rigid "parade rest." Commander Flanagan paused momentarily for effect, surveying the crowd. With a booming voice, he continued the PR mission. "Good afternoon, future pilots! What do you think of my aircraft?"

Loud shouts of approval attacked his ears from both genders. Flanagan held his hands out to signal silence as if he were a military dictator addressing his loyal followers. The children obeyed immediately, granting their leader his wish.

"My name is Commander Thomas Flanagan. I am a pilot for the United States Navy and am stationed at the Meridian Naval Air Station. I train people not much older than you how to fly these incredible machines. It's a great job, and I would encourage each and every one of you to seriously consider pursuing a career as a pilot. The Navy is always willing to train the best and the brightest to fly these multimillion-dollar jets. Does anyone have a question?"

Wayne jumped to his feet before anyone else could have possibly had a chance to think of a question. He didn't even give Commander Flanagan a chance to call on him before he blurted out, "Sir, how old do I need to be before I can train to be a pilot like you?"

Flanagan rubbed his chin. "That's a good question, young man. The military wants all of its aviators to take military classes called ROTC courses when they're in college. Then, the ones that score the best and want to become pilots get what are called pilot slots in the Navy, Air Force or Marines. So, to answer your question, you'd have to be old enough to finish college if you want to fly military aircraft, say twenty-one or twenty-two years old."

When Wayne sat back down, Rain looked at his friend incredulously. He couldn't believe Wayne LeRoy had exhibited the courage to ask the first question. With wide eyes, Rain leaned over and whispered in his ear, "Hey Wayne, why don't you just run on up there and have Commander Flanagan autograph that plane of yours right now?"

Wayne clutched his chest and began again to stand. Rain quickly pulled him back down on the grass, however, and convinced him that he was only kidding and Wayne should wait. Wayne sat back down and continued intently listening as Flanagan answered Stacey's question about which courses he recommend studying in high school and college to best prepare for flight school.

After five or six questions and about fifteen minutes after

Commander Flanagan started, Mr. Barrow broke in. "Kids, I'm sorry, but you all need to be back at school by 3:30, and Commander Flanagan has to fly back to the base. How about a round of applause for our favorite aviator?!"

Instantly, the kids enthusiastically clapped their appreciation, and Commander Flanagan felt like a superhero. Moments like this made him feel like a kid again, too. His body stiffened with pride and he looked at his wife. Colleen Flanagan returned his stare with love and admiration, just as she had done during their first dance at The Naval Academy.

Finally, the applause subsided, and Mr. Barrow continued. "The final part of the tour will take everyone through the aviation museum in the terminal. Ya'll will all be in there at once, so please be careful not to break anything, because it might be a little crowded. When you get through, simply exit the front of the building and board your respective school buses. Thanks for coming, and don't forget to remind your parents that they don't need to drive to Jackson when we've got a fine airport right here."

A general murmur began as the mass rose in unison and headed back for the rear entrance of the airport. Rain had noted where Catherine sat while Commander Flanagan fielded questions, but he lost visual contact when everyone clambered to their feet. He was still trying to relocate her when he felt a sharp kick to the shin.

"Dang you, Rain! I had my chance for the autograph, and you stopped me! Now I probably ain't gonna get it."

Rain bent down to rub his aching leg. "Wayne, I saved you about three bushels of embarrassment by not lettin' you run up there after you asked your question. Besides, it ain't over yet. I bet Commander Flanagan will come in with Mrs. Flanagan, and you'll get your chance then. Be patient! Now, where'd Stacey's cousin go? I want to see if she's as pretty as you say."

Wayne, though, felt both angry and frustrated with his friend. He didn't want to look for any stupid girl; he wanted to get his plane autographed. Ignoring Rain's question, and tired of Rain's crazy obsession over Stacey's cousin, Wayne ran ahead and into the museum.

So much for the "buddy system," Rain thought. He decided to let Wayne go. He knew by now that Wayne LeRoy was actually serious, if baseball didn't work out, about becoming a pilot. Rain also felt a little at a loss himself, because Wayne still hadn't gotten that darned plane autographed. He would have to think of something after he met Catherine. As his portion of the queue entered the museum, he still had yet to relocate her.

After ten minutes of fruitless searching, Rain decided a meeting wasn't meant to be. Many kids had already exited the museum and were undoubtedly on their way to the waiting buses. Wayne had also mysteriously disappeared, and thus could offer no assistance with Rain's last-ditch effort to find Catherine. Rain even broke down and asked Stacey if she knew of her cousin's whereabouts, but Stacey maliciously scoffed at his request and walked away. Completely dejected, Rain stood in front of a large brass plaque and read it for lack of anything better to do.

The Flying Key Brothers

On June 4, 1935, a silvery high-wing Curtis Robin monoplane named "Ole Miss" lurched heavily from the grassy flats of Meridian's municipal airport and fought to gain altitude. Some 100 nervous onlookers observed this otherwise unheralded event.

When, 27 days later, the "Ole Miss" touched down at Meridian, she was to be greeted by the roars of over 30,000 wildly cheering people from far and near who had gathered to witness first-hand the conclusion of a historic flight. Pilots Al and Fred Key had accomplished a stunning feat: a non-stop endurance flight that totaled 653 hours and 34 minutes! In moments, telegraph keys flashed the news to the world's newspapers and the "Flying Keys" were proclaimed America's newest heroes for an achievement that remains unbroken in the record books to this day.

For Al and Fred Key, the flight was the successful culmination of three years of patient and exhaustive trial and error development that included two earlier attempts that had to be aborted.

The Key brothers were pioneers in Mississippi aviation. Al earned his pilot license in 1926 and Fred in 1928. They began Meridian's first flying school in 1929, and the following year the two were hired by the city to manage the new municipal airport. Sometime during this period the germ of the idea about a record endurance flight began to germinate and when a friend, W.H. Ward, donated two Curtis Robins to the project, work began in earnest.

The inspiration and genius of another man, A.D. Hunter, was to prove invaluable. The three men developed a unique system that enabled the "Ole Miss" to be refueled in-flight from another airplane flying overhead. Hunter invented an automatic cut-off valve that made the system feasible.

They also designed a metal catwalk enabling one of the Key brothers to leave the cabin and climb forward and service the engine in flight, all the while being blasted by the prop wash. A two-way radio was installed, as was an extra 150-gallon fuel tank, and an oversize battery and generator. All the modifications increased the payload of the "Ole Miss" from a normal 925 pounds to a staggering 1,681 pounds.

James Keeton and W.H. Ward were to pilot the sister ship. They had flown many hours, perfecting techniques by which the refueling hose could be lowered through the slip stream and transfer gasoline to the "Ole Miss."

Nobody paid much attention to the flight during its first week. But by the tenth day, wire service reports began to get longer and more exciting and newspapers all over the country started carrying day-by-day accounts.

On the 27th of June, the "Ole Miss" reached and passed the existing endurance record set by the Hunter brothers of Chicago. The Meridian city council renamed the airport Key Field in honor of the occasion.

When the Key brothers landed "Ole Miss" at 6:06 pm, on July 1, 1935, they had far surpassed the distance record held by Dole Jackson. The Keys had flown 52,320 non-stop miles, all of it over eastern Mississippi and western Alabama.

The Wright engine, which had not skipped a beat the entire 27 days, had burned 6,000 gallons of gasoline, and used 300 gallons of oil. They had made 435 refueling contacts with the sister plane flown by Keeton and Ward.

In 1955, on the 20th anniversary of the epochal flight, Fred Key flew the "Ole Miss," which had been completely restored, to Washington, D.C., where she is now on permanent display at the Smithsonian.

Following the record flight, Al Key went on to serve two terms as mayor of Meridian, and Fred continued for many years as Meridian airport manager.

As soon as Rain finished the final sentence, he felt a light tap on his left shoulder. When he turned, his eyes fixed on the most beautiful girl he had ever seen. This girl, who must be Stacey's cousin, stood right next to him. Rain stared dizzily into her chilly blue eyes. Catherine smiled coyly and cocked her head slightly to the side. Rain's lips moved, but nothing came out. Mentally, his tongue had been twisted into a thousand knots.

"You're the only boy here with grass stains, so you must be

Rain Henry. I heard from your friend Wayne that you wanted to meet me."

Rain felt woozy and embarrassed. He should have taken the time to change his shirt and pants after all. Quickly, he gathered himself and tried to untie his tongue. "I.. ahh…ummm…my name is Rain Henry and I go to Jeff Davis Academy."

Catherine giggled. "Yes, I already know that. Tell me something about you I don't already know."

Rain slowly felt his senses returning and his tongue unwinding. Catherine had sought him out! He couldn't believe it. "Okay, let's see… Something you don't know about me. Ummm, I bet you don't know I'm the best baseball player in Mississippi, for my age, of course."

Catherine placed her hand over her chest and leaned backward as if his reply had caused her to lose her balance. "So, here I am with Rain Henry. The best baseball player in Mississippi, for his age, of course."

Rain, oblivious to her mockery, felt proud of coming up with something she obviously didn't know. "That's right, and one day I'll play in the major leagues and be an all-star. I'll be rich and famous, too, and probably have lots of girlfriends."

Catherine laughed out loud. "I guess you'll have lots of girlfriends then because you don't have any now?"

Rain silently cursed at his brain for this foul-up and tried to cover as best as he could. He certainly didn't want to come off as a loser without a girlfriend. "I don't have any now because I haven't found the right girl to be my girlfriend."

Rain thought Catherine was impressed by this response. She was about to say something else when the cozy, private world they created was suddenly invaded by a loud voice at the front entrance of the museum. The male teacher and chaperone from Pamar Academy said, "All right everyone, the field trip's over. Please exit and head for your buses."

Catherine held out her hand, and Rain shook it. "Don't worry, Rain. As cute as you are, there will be plenty of girlfriends, and I'm sure they'll come along before you make it to the major leagues. That was Mr. Butler – I'd better get going."

Rain couldn't believe she had called him cute. Her words were honey to his ears, and he wished he could have recorded them to play over and over again. So many thoughts came so quickly. He wanted to learn more about her. He wanted to see her again. He wanted to hear her voice say his name. "Catherine, would you give me your phone number, so I could call you sometime?"

"I'd love to, Rain, except my boyfriend might not like it. But who knows what'll happen in the future? If we do ever break up, I'll let Stacey know and she can give you my number then."

Then, as a hummingbird delights the eyes by hovering in one spot for a few seconds before darting away, Catherine walked through the door and was gone.

Rain stood like a statue as he watched her go. His heart ached, and he knew he had just met the girl with whom he would spend the rest of his life. Already, questions about this girl formed in his head and bounced inside his brain like peas in a drum. Who was her boyfriend? Did she really think Rain was cute? Where in Meridian did she live? Had she ever milked a cow or fed chickens? What was her favorite color or favorite flavor of ice cream? Did she even like baseball? He put both hands over his ears in an effort to stop the pinging, because he began feeling lightheaded.

Rain was still collecting himself when Wayne approached and solemnly stood next to him. Wayne's eyes looked moist and his head hung so low that his chin and chest nearly touched. Wayne's voice sounded as though he had been crying. He kept mumbling over and over, "All I wanted was an autograph..."

Rain's encounter with Catherine gave him an explosive rush of adrenaline. He spun and faced the exit that led to the runway. Mrs. Flanagan had just come through the door and was heading right for them. She shooed the few remaining children ahead of her like a sheepdog, repeating firmly, "C'mon children, it's time to go, it's time to go."

Rain grabbed Wayne and the two boys headed for their bus. Mrs. Flanagan caught up to them as the other buses, fully loaded, shut their doors. The Newton bus pulled away and the Pamar bus followed. "Wayne, I've got a plan. Stay close to me and follow along with what I say."

Wayne mouthed a reply, but whatever he had said was inaudible. As they hit the first step, Rain jumped in the air and spun 180 degrees. "Mrs. Flanagan, do you remember where the restrooms were? Wayne said he couldn't find them, and I think I need to go, too, before we ride all the way back to school."

After a deep sigh, Mrs. Flanagan started to respond when Wayne snapped out of his coma. He recalled something about Rain mentioning a plan and to play along. "Yes, ma'am, I really need to go, but I couldn't find 'em."

Mrs. Flanagan gave them a suspicious look before ordering them to wait a second. She entered the bus and at the top of the steps, she asked the rest of the class if anyone else needed to use the restroom before the ride back. No one raised a hand, so she descended the stairs.

"All right, you two. The restrooms are next to the double doors that lead to the runway area. You'd better hurry. I'll give you thirty seconds. And no monkey business!"

The boys took off running. Within ten seconds they were back inside the museum, with the door safely closed behind them. They both slowed to a fast walk, and Wayne wheezed, "I lied. I don't really have to go to the bathroom."

"Neither do I, Wayne, but you want that plane autographed, right?"

"Right!"

"Well, then c'mon; we've only got thirty seconds!"

Rain led the way as they pushed open the glass doors and stepped onto the concrete tarmac. Commander Flanagan already had his flight helmet buckled and was going through some final exterior checks on his A-6. While the two missiles streaked at their target, Rain madly flailed his arms while Wayne began unbuttoning his shirt. Flanagan removed his helmet and a sheepish grin spread across his face. Moments later, Wayne glowed as he thrust the plane at the Commander with one hand and the black marker with the other. "Sir, I'd like it very much if you'd autograph my plane," he said breathlessly.

The commander took the tiny aircraft and the marker, and while his head shook back and forth in amazement, he signed his name across the wings. "You boys are sure crazy, but I love it. The P-40 was a good aircraft and it looks like you've got a Flying Tiger right here, young man. When you get back to school, you should go to your library and ask to check out a book on the American Volunteer Group. They're the ones that flew these Flying Tigers on missions from China against the Japanese before World War II officially got started."

He handed the plane back to Wayne, bent down and looked them squarely in the eyes. "Now I suspect the both of you could get into some mighty big trouble for running out here alone like you did, so I'd recommend we all keep this a code blue military secret."

"Yes, sir!" came the enthusiastic reply from both boys, in unison.

As soon as the two had re-entered the terminal, they saw Stacey waiting for them like a prison guard. The look on her face was the same; she lacked only a nightstick and a prison-guard uniform. Wayne hadn't yet returned the plane to its hangar in his shirt and tried to hide his new prized possession behind his back.

"Well, well," the guard said. "I guess by now, even your tiny brains have figured out that Mrs. Flanagan sent me in to see what you troublemakers were really doing in here. So, let's hear it, bathroom boys. Looks like I was right when I guessed you were going back inside to try to steal something. Wayne's hiding whatever you took behind his back."

Rain spoke first. He had had enough of Stacey's know-everything attitude. "Stacey, in case you haven't figured it out, you're not our mother or our teacher or even our sister, which is lucky for you. Because if you were our sister, we'd probably both beat you up every day, thanks to your smart-alecky mouth. So, no, we're not going to tell you what we were doing. Let's all just go outside, get on the bus and head back to school."

"That's fine talk coming from such a gentleman as you, Rain Henry. And to think, you fell in love with my cousin today. You can forget about her ever loving you, because she's so far above you, you'll never get a chance. As for the sister thing, both of you might be able to beat me up, but it would be a good fight, and I'd get my share of licks in, too. You let me know whenever you're ready. And it's fine with me if we go out and get on the bus now. I know Mrs. Flanagan will get the truth out of you, and I'm sure to hear it because I'll be right there in the front seat."

Wayne, accustomed to bowing to Stacey's whims, gave up. "Rain, let's just tell her what happened; we're gonna get in trouble, anyway."

"No way, Wayne! I'd rather get in trouble!"

Rain's words came too late. Wayne had already extended his hand, showing Stacey his freshly autographed P-40. "Stacey, I wanted to get my model plane autographed. This was our last chance."

Amazingly, Stacey appeared genuinely taken aback and at a loss of words for a few moments. Wayne handed her the plane, and she gingerly turned it over in her hands. After reading Commander Flanagan's name across the wings, she gave it back to Wayne with a curious smile. "I've never heard of having a toy plane autographed before. That's a pretty cool idea, Wayne." Spinning on her heels she added, "C'mon, we'd better get back on the bus."

Ms. Helen and Mrs. Flanagan has grown impatient. The thirty-second bathroom break approached five minutes. As she was about to head inside herself, the three appeared from the terminal with the two boys trailing Stacey.

When they entered the bus, Mrs. Flanagan stopped them cold at the top step. “Stacy, what happened?”

“I’m not sure, ma’am. I saw them outside the bathroom and told them to hurry up and get back on the bus.”

“You know what? I don’t even want to know. We’re already running late; the three of you just hurry up and get in your seats so we can go.”

After Rain and Wayne retook their empty seats in the back, Rain decided that he had found a new level of respect for Stacey Cottrell. He stole a glance at Wayne, who softly stroked the protrusion in his shirt while staring out the window at the A-6 that began taxiing down the runway.

CHAPTER THREE
THE KNUCKLE CURVE

After the field trip, when Mrs. LeRoy stopped at the Henry farm, Rain invited Wayne to stick around and play baseball. However, Wayne was not interested in playing "spectacular catch" or "beat the Yankees." His plane now autographed, he planned on taking some fishing line and hanging it from the ceiling of his room as soon as he got home. Wayne LeRoy proclaimed that he would become a pilot when he grew up, whether baseball worked out or not. The way he figured it, the faster that plane dangled from his ceiling, the faster he could learn more about how it flew. Rain couldn't convince him to hold off, even for only a few hours, and finally gave up.

When Rain ascended the steps to the house, the distant, high-pitched whine of a chainsaw penetrated his ears and mingled with the soft crunching of the tires from the LeRoy family car as it headed home. His grandmother sat waiting for him in her rocking chair on the front porch.

Rain grimaced as her cheerful face suddenly warped into a scowl. "Rain Joseph Henry! I can't believe you slipped by me and went to school with grass stains all over your clothes."

"Yes, ma'am. Mackel knocked me down this morning, and

I figured I didn't have time to change 'em before Mrs. LeRoy picked me up. What's Dad doin'?"

Trying to change the subject half worked. "I think Mrs. LeRoy would wait a few minutes for you to change your pants and shirt the next time something like that happens. I don't want people to think we don't give you clean clothes to wear. As for your father, he and Mr. Williams are out by the south field cuttin' some more trees down to make fence posts. Shoot, he's probably got enough now to build a fence from here to Toomsuba, if he wanted to, but you know your father. He said he'd rather have too much of somethin' than not enough. I guess we'll use whatever's left over for firewood this winter." She paused briefly, and her sanguine disposition returned. "I'm sure you can hear the chainsaw, or did those airplanes ruin your ears today?"

Like a rabbit slipping from the snare, Rain skipped past her into the house and retorted, "Sorry, Granny, did you say something?"

Rain skidded into his bedroom and tossed his history book on the disorganized desk in the corner. He flopped facedown on his bed and reached over the far side into the small space that separated the wall from the mattress. There it was. Rain retrieved the leather baseball glove his father had given him for his birthday two years before. Back then, the glove swallowed his left hand to the point that he could barely bend it, much less catch anything. Now, after receiving thousands of throws and smacks of his fist, the pocket was broken in to perfection. Apparently, his hand had also physically grown, because together, they made a snug fit. He slipped the glove on, rolled over to the other side of the bed, and picked up a baseball that lay on the floor. Rolling back to the middle, he focused on the ceiling and flexed the glove with his left hand. With his right hand, he held the ball close to his chest. Applying precisely the right amount of pressure, he gripped the ball across the threaded seams with his index and middle fingers. Rain Henry, pitcher for the Atlanta

Braves, was ready to throw heat. He closed his eyes, and the distant radio announcer's voice roared to life like the sound of an oncoming freight train.

"Here we are, ladies and gentlemen. It's the top of the ninth, two outs, and the Yankees are down one. Pinella's the tying run on first as Graig Nettles comes to the plate. Nettles is two-for-three in the game and hitting .340 for the series. Rain Henry, the young right-hander from Mississippi, checks in for the sign. He's got it and goes into the stretch. Checks Pinella once, twice, and now goes to the plate. It's a heater on the outside corner and a called strike. Folks, this kid can bring it. Nettles steps back for a moment. Now he's collected himself and settles back into the box. Henry's back on the rubber. I wish you could see the expression on this kid's face. I don't think he could concentrate any harder if his life depended on it. Okay, Henry's got the sign and he's ready. Here's the pitch. Swing and a miss! That was Henry's change-up and what a beauty it was! One strike to go, and the Atlanta Braves are World Champions!! What a miraculous season this would be if Henry can get one more past this tough hitter. Henry's ready. Nettles is ready. Oh and two count. Looks like Benedict called a fastball, and I'd be disappointed if the kid threw anything but. Folks, here it is. Swing and a miss on a heater at the letters and, oh my goodness, the Atlanta Braves have done the impossible and won the World Series! It's pandemonium here at Fulton County Stadium!"

Rain opened his eyes and shot both arms at the ceiling in exultation. His hands still clutched the ball and glove. Victorious again! Still pumped from whiffing the Yankee's all-star third baseman, he sprang to the floor and headed downstairs. The ball and glove tagged along. As he passed the baseball cards of Lou Pinella and Graig Nettles on his dresser, he leaned down and whispered, "Nothing personal, guys; you faced a hall-of-fame pitcher tonight, that's all."

A minute later, Rain entered the kitchen where his grandmother stood preparing their supper. The meal was one of Rain's favorites: southern sausage with gravy and white rice, served with a mixture of slow-cooked spring tomatoes, squash, and onions with cornbread muffins on the side. From the corner of his eye, Rain watched her sprinkle a touch of Parmesan cheese onto the simmering vegetables. He passed through the kitchen to the screened-in porch at the back of the house, where he carefully placed the glove and baseball on the ground next to the door. They would remain there until he and his father played catch right after dinner. He checked the numbers on the digital watch. They read 5:30. His father would be back soon. Rain re-entered the kitchen, and the screen door made a sharp whack as the tight spring pulled it shut behind him. He leaned against the kitchen counter and inhaled deeply through his nose. The scents of his grandmother's cooking could excite his sense of smell like nothing else.

"How's supper coming along, Granny?"

"Oh, it's coming along very well. Your dad better hurry back, though. We'll be ready to eat in about thirty minutes, and I'm sure he'll need to get washed up." The family matriarch ceased stirring for a second and turned her attention to Rain. "Tell me about your field trip."

Rain didn't want to seem too eager, but he had been dying to share the details of the trip, especially those concerning Catherine, with his grandmother and father. He made a man-sized effort to remain calm and started off with the tone of a deliberate, well-rehearsed monologue.

"We left school and took the Ole Reb bus to Key Field. The ride in was pretty fun 'cause Wayne and I made up a game where you wave at people and see which ones wave back. The winner is the player who gets ten return waves first. By the time we got to Meridian, almost the whole bus was playing." Rain paused for a moment and shrugged. "I won the first few games, and then it got kinda boring with everyone doin' it, so I quit playing. Wayne said I cheated and should forfeit any games I won 'cause I made weird faces when I waved at people. He said I was funnier lookin' than he was and that made people wave back 'cause they felt sorry for me. I told him he was a sore loser. But that's not the coolest thing that happened."

Mildred Henry grinned. "Well, don't just stand there holding up that counter, tell me about the *coolest* thing that happened on the trip."

Rain could contain his excitement no longer. His insides wanted to burst open like a ripe watermelon falling off an over-stacked pickup truck. "Granny, I met the most beautiful girl I've ever seen today at Key Field. Her name is Catherine, and I'm going to marry her, just you wait and see. Her hair looks softer than anything ever. I didn't get to touch it, but if I could have, I know it would have been really soft. She has a really pretty face, too. Her eyes are bluer than the clearest sky, and they twinkle like stars when she talks to ya'. She's Stacey Cottrell's cousin. I think she lives in Meridian. I know she goes to Pamar Academy. She's..."

"Hold on a minute, Rain! Slow down so you can catch your breath and I can comprehend everything you're sayin'. How exactly did you meet this young lady?"

Rain explained how he had bribed Wayne to approach the two girls. Then, with wide eyes and upturned hands, he described how he had later searched for Catherine in the museum but couldn't find her, only to have her surprise him at the Key Brothers plaque.

After a momentary pause and a light stir of the simmering tomatoes, squash, and onions, the grandmother continued her questioning of the breathless boy. "Quite interesting, Rain. Did you happen to ask her if she had a boyfriend?"

For a brief second, this specific inquiry deflated Rain's memory of the event as he recalled that Catherine had said that she did. He glanced down at his shoelaces. Then, with a rising tone that expressed hope he answered, "Yes, ma'am, she does, but she said I was real cute and she never knew what might happen."

Mildred Henry let out a dry, suspicious laugh. "I wonder! Sounds as though she took a liking to you, Rain, but she's not ready to give up the fellow she's currently seeing." Her eyes squinted and she waved the wooden stir-spoon at her grandson. "You watch out; this is an old trick some women use quite frequently. Until they get married, a few girls like to have a backup in case something happens to the starter. Sort of the way it works in baseball, too, I reckon."

Rain had never been a backup in baseball or anything else, and he didn't plan to be, either. His lips wrinkled as he smashed them together, and his facial muscles tightened. "Granny, you wait and see. I'll marry that girl. I ain't ever gonna be a backup in baseball or nothin' else."

The screen door whacked again and Jim Henry strolled into the kitchen. His sweaty socks made moist footprints on the checkered linoleum floor as he shuffled to the refrigerator. As was his custom, and primarily to appease his mother, he left his work boots on the back porch steps whenever they were excessively dirty or caked in mud. Cleaning them would come later in the evening while he smoked a few cigarettes after Rain went to bed.

Rain focused first on his father's earth-streaked and deeply tanned face. The farm's dirt had drawn thick, irregular lines across his brow and cheeks, and the pungent aroma of the newly turned soil and fresh tree sap escaped freely from the fabric of his clothes. These fragrances, combined with that of his father's perspiration, slow-danced with the smell of his grandmother's spicy cooking to create a unique and saucy bouquet. Rain loved it.

Jim Henry opened the refrigerator and extracted the pitcher of cold milk. With haste caused by excessive thirst, he poured a tall glass of the bright-white liquid. Rain watched intently as his father tilted the glass to his lips. Like a tiny elevator, his throat constricted up and down as it transported the cool fluid to its final destination.

Jim Henry's thirst satisfied, he wiped his mouth on his

dusty shirtsleeve and inquired of the two onlookers, "So, what's all the excitement about? Rain, I could hear you all the way over by the shed."

Rain took a deep breath in preparation for repeating the tale of his romantic encounter, but his grandmother cut him off as soon as he opened his mouth. "Jim, today your son met the love of his life. He'll tell you all about it over dinner. Now, everything's almost ready, so hurry and get washed up. Then we can hear all about Rain's trip to Key Field and this Catherine, whose beauty could launch a thousand ships."

Rain's father flashed a surprised look at his son and then offered an enthusiastic "thumbs up." He finished the small amount of milk left in the glass and placed it in the sink. On his way to the shower, he squeezed Rain's shoulder. "I wondered when you would start chasing girls. There for a while, I thought you and Wayne would grow up to be bachelor buddies forever."

"Dad!" was all Rain could exclaim as he tried, unsuccessfully, to escape from his father's playful pinch.

After the arrival of the freshly scrubbed patriarch, the trio gathered for their supper on the screened-in back porch. While Jim Henry recited the prayer, Rain's hands moved back and forth along the underside of the magnificent table before him. His sense of touch drank in the thick laminate coating that protected both sides of their "outdoor" dining table. Like this evening, whenever the temperature felt comfortable, the Henry family ate on the screened-in back porch. They sat at an enormous slice of polished cypress that had once served as the executive room conference table at the headquarters of the First Chicago Bank. As Jim Henry finished the prayer, Rain remembered the story of how his grandfather had received the special table decades before as a gift from a Chicago businessman.

The story went that many years prior, the same businessman had requested a loan to purchase a small portion of waterfront property along the shores of Lake Michigan that many people considered rough and undesirable. On this land, he planned to build the area's first high-rise condominiums to have an unobstructed view of the lake. Every other bank in Chicago had rejected this man's proposal because they considered his project sheer lunacy. No sane person would ever reside in that part of town, or so every loan officer quickly concluded.

Frank Henry, a young branch manager at the time, researched the man's idea and his character and came to believe in both. When the officers of the First Chicago Bank discovered Henry granted a sizable loan to someone every other financial institution in town had refused, they strongly considered terminating him on the spot. His job was saved, barely, when Henry revealed his own research into the project and explained that he himself had invested personal funds.

The high-rise condos sold almost instantly, and the businessman went on to become one of Chicago's most celebrated real estate developers. Not only did Frank Henry make a tidy sum from his initial investment, he convinced First Chicago to become the businessman's exclusive financial partner. This arrangement tremendously benefited everyone involved, and before long, First Chicago's officers, the same ones that almost fired Frank Henry, were filthy rich because of his daring decision.

Thereafter, Rain's grandfather became a blur as he ascended the First Chicago corporate ladder faster than anyone ever had or probably ever would. Henry became vice president of real estate investments and a bank board member within two years of granting that initial "excessively risky" loan.

Mr. Sears never forgot the young branch manager who put his job on the line to help him get started. On the fifth anniversary of the original project's completion, he personally supervised the delivery of the cypress table and presented his financial business partner with a bottle of the finest champagne. Sears claimed the table had been cut from one of the largest cypress trees ever found in the swamps of central Florida and said it was worth in excess of $5,000, which was quite a sum in the late 1950's.

Rain could only imagine the meetings that must have taken place over the wondrous slice of polished wood before him. He wondered if the table felt happy with its current job of providing the necessary, albeit mundane, task of supporting their forks, knives, napkins, plates, and sweating glasses.

During supper, Rain enthusiastically retold the events of the day with a heavy emphasis on details surrounding Catherine and their meeting.

After swallowing his last bite of summer sausage, Jim Henry dabbed the corners of his mouth with a linen napkin. "Son, all I can say is that Catherine is one heck of a lucky girl to have Rain Henry in love with her. I mean, what other girl can say they're being pursued by this state's best baseball player?"

Although Rain knew his father's comments were meant in jest, hearing his father say them nonetheless made him feel like he could conquer the world. The words reinforced his fantasy that one day, he would indeed win Catherine's heart. He was envisioning their first kiss when his grandmother rudely interrupted his reverie.

"Jim, Rain already told you this girl has a boyfriend. Neither you nor I can force her to break up with him and fall in love with our little Casanova here. We've got to let things take their rightful course. Let's not get his head too big, either. You don't need to encourage his preposterous belief that he's the best baseball player in Mississippi. If that doesn't sound like we've raised an arrogant braggart, I don't know what does!"

"Yes, of course you're right, Mildred." He faced his son and pointed directly at Rain.

As Rain looked down his father's finger, it brought to mind images of a loaded gun barrel. He rarely pointed, and only did so when he wanted to stress the importance of what he was about to say.

"Rain, I hope you understand that when *you* claim to being the top baseball player, others will label you vain and conceited. You'll truly be the best when those who have witnessed your playing ability judge you to be so. It won't be necessary for you to say a thing."

Jim Henry pushed back from the table and added with a smirk, "Maybe, instead of addressing you as Rain, we'll start calling you 'Top Five.' Now, if you want to become 'Number One,' for the noble purpose of winning Catherine's heart, we'd better get outside for some practice before the sun goes down. I've got a new pitch I've wanted to teach you for a long time. Since you consider yourself so great a baseball player, Top Five, I think you may be ready to handle it."

The father and son laughed as they stood from the table and made for the door.

As Mildred cleared the table, all she could do was shake her head in amazement. The Henry boys never lacked self-confidence. That was an undeniable fact.

After father and son traversed the grassy backyard, they reached the small shed that housed various tools as well as the elongated leather bag full of baseball equipment. By the time Rain procured the bag and his cleats from the wooden floor of the shed, Mackel arrived to round out the group.

While Rain plopped down on the shed's steps and began loosening the laces of his left cleat, his father spoke. "Rain, I hope you realize that the last part of what I said at dinner was a show for your grandmother, but the first part about not bragging on yourself is very important for you to understand."

Rain, his left cleat tied on securely, began loosening the laces on his right one. "I know, Dad. I didn't mean to brag or anything. I didn't know you and Granny would make such a big deal out of what I said. Catherine caught me off guard by asking me to tell her something she didn't already know. My mind just sorta spit out the baseball thing."

The father leaned down and playfully spread his right

hand and fingers into a net. This he cast on top of his son's head. Rotating the net and it's captured prey, Jim Henry warmly gazed into his son's hazel eyes. At ten-years-old, he was well on his way to becoming a man. "That's okay, Son. You've got a lifetime of adventures ahead when it comes to communicating with women. You've also got a lifetime of baseball adventures ahead of you, too, if you really want them. That's how much I think of your playing ability."

"Thanks, Dad," Rain responded proudly.

Shoes on, equipment gathered, and ready to get started, the three jogged to the far edge of the soybean field. They stopped where, several years before, Jim Henry and Mr. Williams had built two pitching mounds, complete with nailed-down rubbers. The first hill stood precisely sixty feet, six inches away from home plate, which replicated the major league distance. The other mound lay adjacent to the first, but stood a little lower in stature and closer to home. This mound measured only forty-six feet to the dish, which represented the official Little League distance. Jim Henry believed that having Rain throw fastballs from the major league length would strengthen his arm considerably. From the mound of shorter distance, Rain would practice his off-speed pitches, along with spotting a few fastballs.

To help warm up, Rain removed a thin inner tube from the elongated bag. The rubbery hose, which had once supported a bicycle tire, had since been reborn as Rain's main stretching apparatus. He held one end of the tube with his left hand behind his back while he mildly simulated throwing the other end with his right arm. The resistance created by the elasticity of the giant rubber band gently stretched his pitching arm. While Rain stretched, his father led Mackel about twenty yards away to the edge of the pine trees and commanded him to lie down and stay. As customary, Mackel gave a few barks of protest and then obeyed by settling his head on top of his outstretched paws.

When his father returned, Rain flipped him the catcher's

mitt, which he slid onto his right hand. Now ready to start throwing, father and son stood about twenty feet apart. Rain lightly tossed the scuffed baseball, which his father caught at chest level. Although Rain could have easily started farther away and thrown harder, they always started with soft tosses from short distances. Rain's father didn't want to take a chance on hurting his son's young arm by throwing too far or too fast before proper warm-up. After catching Rain's first throw, in the blink of an eye, Jim Henry tucked the mitt under his left armpit, removed the ball, and sailed it back to Rain with his right hand. The way Jim Henry played catch amazed many people the first time they saw the process, but it was nothing special to Rain. Because of the car accident, Jim Henry had been forced to learn how to catch and throw using only one functional arm. Rain had never seen him do it any other way.

Gradually, the expanse between the two increased, and Rain began throwing harder and with less arc on the ball's trajectory. After a few minutes at this intensity, Rain's arm felt limber and loose. He signaled his readiness and Jim Henry squatted behind the plate. Rain scaled the major league mound and toed the rubber with both feet.

Rain's father set up in the middle of the strike zone and opened his mitt wide. "Okay, Top Five. Let's see what you've got. Give me some fastballs. Remember to focus on the mitt."

Rain craned his head forward and stared at the target as though he tried to melt it with X-ray vision. From now until the ball reached its destination, his eyes would remain transfixed on the pocket of the catcher's glove. Taking a deep breath, Rain clasped his hands together to make a leather and flesh cocoon located slightly above his beltline. Inside the cocoon, Rain's fingers lightly clutched the hidden baseball. Their tips gripped the edge of the red stitches while his thumb and pinky finger linked underneath. Locked in mentally, he began his windup by making a small step backwards with his left foot. Rain allowed his whole body to sway along for the ride. As he leaned back, he raised his arms and hands in concert until they formed the outline of a mountain over his head. At this point, Rain momentarily stopped, as if shifting gears from reverse to forward, and then changed momentum and direction. He now wanted to coil his body, which would give him as much power as possible. Rain rotated his right cleat and pointed his toes at third base, which positioned his foot parallel to the front of the rubber. This foot would become the pusher, providing his body the necessary thrust for maximum pitch velocity. At the same instant his right foot rotated, he lifted his left leg up along the side of his body, bending it at the knee. Simultaneously, he moved his hands to his waist and slightly bowed his back.

Rain pictured his body as a dangerously overloaded steel spring before he released the safety latch. His arms and legs unwound and furiously lashed toward the plate with great force, mustering every ounce of energy his uncoiling body could deliver. As he lunged forward, his coddled cocoon hatched a vicious, livid wasp ready to sting whatever lay in its path. Rain's left cleat thundered as it hit the front portion of the dirt mound, while his body and arm violently released the attacking wasp. After the venomous insect left his hand, Rain could hear its stitched wings slice through the air, creating a soothing buzz that sounded like "ffffffffssssst."

While his fastball rocketed for the mitt, Rain completed his delivery by allowing his momentum to bring the right side of his body even with his left. He was now in proper fielding position. While Rain watched the ball vector closer to the target, he imagined the wasp morphing into a lit firecracker, its fuse almost burned up. In less than an instant, the firecracker detonated. The resultant pop made from the ball impacting with the leather of the mitt delivered a satisfactory report that tickled his ears with pleasure.

Jim Henry already had the baseball in the air and headed back to his son. "Excellent, Top Five. Great mechanics!"

Rain threw about two dozen more fastballs from the major league mound. Each time his mind visualized the coil, the wasp, and the firecracker. After they both agreed it was time to practice Rain's off-speed pitches, the young hurler moved to the Little League hill. Here, Rain alternated between hitting the corners with his fastball and deceiving the hitter with his changeup. Many pitchers his age were starting to throw curveballs, but Jim Henry felt adamantly opposed to kids that young violently snapping their wrists, something necessary to produce the desired spin and resultant curve. For this reason, he had taught his son the changeup. Changeups look like fastballs to the hitter, but are slower. The batter typically swings before the baseball crosses the hitting zone. A pitcher with a good changeup never changes the motion of his pitch delivery or arm speed, which increases the pitch's guise as a fastball. Last summer, Jim Henry taught his son the three-fingered changeup, which uses the middle three fingers to grip the ball. Rain had tried the other type of changeup called the circle change because one grips it by making the "okay" sign, or circle, with the thumb and index finger, but Rain's fingers were too small to effectively control the pitch. Rain threw the three-fingered changeup with the same arm motion he used for his fastball, but at the end of the delivery, he pretended to pull down a window shade by choking back his wrist as the ball left his hand. The choking action reduced the speed but still produced a spin similar to a fastball.

Rain loved throwing the heat, but he equally relished tossing a changeup. Both pitches made statements to the opposing hitter. When a batter helplessly waved the bat at an overpowering fastball, it was as though his manhood had been insulted. Throwing smoke by a hitter changed him into a feeble little girl flailing at nothingness. Conversely, the changeup was a finesse pitch, one that required a skilled artist to paint it properly. Good changeups embarrassed the hitter's intellect, turning him into an uncoordinated oaf, his mind unable to control the actions of his own body, including his hapless swing. Whenever Rain threw a changeup, he imagined the wasp that hatched from the cocoon to be a cunning, masked robber, ready to stealthily sneak into the hitter's house. A good whiff that resulted from blowing a fastball by someone made Rain smirk, while baffling the batter with a changeup brought chuckles under his breath.

After Rain perfectly painted three consecutive changeups on the inside corner, his father rose from his squatting position and strode to the mound. "Okay, Top Five, it's time to learn that new pitch."

"Is it a knuckle ball?" Rain asked excitedly. He liked knuckle balls because of the way they literally danced to the plate because of a complete lack of spin.

"No, but you're close. It's a knuckle curve," his father answered.

"What does a knuckle curve do?"

"A knuckle curve is like a fastball, only with a twist. Instead of coming in hard and straight, a knuckle curve zooms in a tad bit slower than a regular fastball and then drops straight down at the last second."

"Wow, that sounds cool, Dad. How do you throw it?"

Jim Henry held the baseball against his right knee and positioned his fingers over the top. His index and middle fingers were doubled over at the main knuckles, and the knuckles closest to the tips of the fingers were wedged tightly against the rawhide. His ring finger and pinky wrapped around the right side of the ball, fully extended. After showing Rain the grip, he made a throwing motion with his arm.

"Rain, you throw the knuckle curve exactly like a fastball. You want to come straight over the top. The index and middle fingers keep the ball from spinning backwards, while your ring finger and pinky create a forward spin as it's released. That's how you get the downward break." He flipped the baseball to Rain and headed back behind the plate.

Once Jim Henry squatted again and faced the mound, he called out, "Okay, Rain, let's see your grip."

Rain showed him the grip, but his knuckles were a little too angled to the left.

"Straighten up your knuckles, Son. They should fit squarely on the ball and not off to one side."

Rain fixed his knuckles, but the grip still felt awkward.

"Okay, okay. That looks pretty good. Let's see you wind up and throw one."

Rain had no idea what to imagine for his vision with the knuckle curve, so he thought that an insane, dive-bombing wasp might do the trick. He wound up and threw the ball, precisely as his father had instructed. As funny as the grip felt, when he let go of the pitch, the release felt even funnier. The ball traveled about thirty feet, slightly more than halfway to the plate, then bit hard into the ground. Jim Henry tried to catch it on the bounce, but it sailed well over his head. Mackel, a casual spectator to this point, took off like a shot to retrieve the baseball. Rain's father stood and laughed.

Embarrassed and frustrated, Rain kicked the bare ground at the front of the mound.

Mackel brought the ball to Jim Henry's feet, dropped it, then returned to his warm spot in the grass to become a spectator again. Rain's father used his shirt to wipe the dog's saliva from the ball and tossed it back to his son.

"That's all right, that's all right. To be honest, that's better than I expected for your first knuckle curve. It's a great pitch, but it takes lots of practice to master. Throw me a fastball then we'll try it again."

Rain tried again and again, but he grew more and more irritated with the knuckle curve. If he tried to throw it too hard, it hit well in front of home plate, and his father bailed out as if he tried to dodge an oncoming car. If Rain attempted to compensate and throw the pitch higher, it sailed way over his catcher's head. Mentally, Rain felt close to a breaking point. Mackel had turned the ball into a soggy potato, and dusk settled hard upon them. Only dim remnants of the sun filtered through the distant forest. "Dad, are you gonna let me hit before it gets too dark?"

"Not tonight, Son. We can hit tomorrow. Listen, I know you're frustrated, but let's not give up yet. Throw me one more knuckle curve, and this time don't think about it too much, just relax your body and let everything flow freely."

Rain turned away from his father, stepped off the back of the mound, and collected himself. He looked around at the trees surrounding them in the distance. Rain could make out their leaves softly fluttering in the evening breeze, and he imagined they were thousands of fans that had come to watch him pitch. He couldn't let them down. Rain took a deep breath and exhaled. He returned to the rubber and shook out his right arm before plunging his hand into the cocoon. He made the knuckle curve grip on the ball and started his windup.

Mentally, Rain filled his body with a cool orange liquid, which he hoped would allow him to do as his father had suggested. This time, something mentally clicked when the ball left his hand. As Rain anxiously watched, the baseball zipped toward the mitt like a fastball. Then, as if it understood its mission, at the front edge of the plate, the pitch surged downward as if a divine hand had spanked it from above. Rain Henry had thrown a perfect knuckle curve.

Rain's catcher leapt to his feet. "Yes! Yes! That's what I'm talking about Rain! If you can throw pitches like that, you'll be Number One before you know it!"

Rain was even more ecstatic than his father. He danced and gyrated on the mound as though he hoped to conjure up a thunderstorm. "Dad, let me throw it again! Let me throw it again!"

Sensing something special had happened, Mackel raced to Rain and barked wildly as Jim Henry shook his head and began putting the baseball gear back in the bag.

"Rain, I think you've had enough of that knuckle curve today. Let's end things on a positive note. Help me gather up this equipment, and we'll go have some lemonade and a piece of your granny's pecan pie. There's still lots of time to practice before your first game. We've got over two weeks to get that pitch under control."

Rain pranced over to help his father pack up. They returned the gear to the shed and headed back to the house in the twilight. It was a beautiful evening. The stars winked from above and the temperature had pleasantly dropped into the middle 60's. A perfectly round and full green moon peered over the eastern stand of pines like a child peeking over the lip of a cardboard box of puppies. Rain nearly burst with happiness. In a single day he had met the girl he would marry and thrown his first real knuckle curve.

"Dad, do you think I'll have the knuckle curve ready by the first game?"

"We'll give it lots of practice. Remember, your changeup and fastball are pretty good pitches, too."

"I know, I know. I just *want* to throw that knuckle curve."

"Maybe you can get Wayne to stay over after school for some extra practice. He'll need to learn to catch it just as much as you'll need to learn to throw it. Better make sure he's wearing all of his catcher's gear, though."

"That's a great idea. I'll *make* him practice with me."

"That's fine, but I want you to be patient with Wayne. He hasn't played baseball as long as you have. He's got great potential as a catcher, but we don't want him to get discouraged and all banged up."

"Yeah, I'll be careful. Did you really like that last one, or were you only saying it was good because I'm your son?"

"That was one of the best knuckle curves I've ever seen."

Once the trio reached the house, Mackel left them and circled around to the front where he usually slept on the porch. Rain headed upstairs for his nightly bath. Jim Henry remained on the back porch, lit a cigarette, and began cleaning his work boots with an old rag. Mildred Henry had moved her rocking chair to the back porch and was enjoying some snuff, one of the few southern habits she embraced. A large Mason jar with a crumpled paper towel served as her spittoon.

"Mildred, your grandson has a gift for baseball. It'll be interesting to see how far he can go with it."

"He sure seemed excited about that knuckle curve you taught him. Did you ever throw it when you were a kid?"

"Sure did. Father O'Sullivan taught it to me when I was as old as Rain is now. Do you think he'll be able to make it down this summer? I'd like to see him; it's been a few years."

"Why don't you write and invite him?"

"That's a good idea. I think I will."

When Rain returned to the porch from his bath, he found an extra large slice of pecan pie and a cold glass of lemonade waiting. Like a man lost for days in the desert, Rain woofed his dessert and sucked down his lemonade in less than a minute. The ice cubes made a dull tingling sound when he set the empty glass back on the polished cypress table.

As Rain contentedly leaned back in his chair, Granny made a hook with her finger and pulled out the rest of the snuff that hid between her cheek and gums. This she flicked into the jar and onto the juicy brown towel. She rinsed her mouth with some lemonade, returned inside, and spit into the kitchen sink. Rain heard a gush of water from the tap wash the pinkish brown liquid into the drain.

Heading into the living room she called out, "Rain, Jim, come on inside. I've got a special treat for you."

When father and son reached the living room, they found Mildred Henry sitting at the piano, leafing through a tattered songbook.

Rain's dad spoke first. "Where in the world did you get that old thing?"

"Fanny from church gave it to me last Sunday. Said she planned on throwing it out, but heard somewhere I played piano. She claimed it had some good old southern folksongs, and since we're from Chicago, she thought we could use some exposure to real culture. While you boys threw the ball around, I flipped through it and found one that I thought would be appropriate for Rain, since he's now in love with this

Catherine. Ah, yes, here it is. The book says it has two names: 'The Riddle Song' or 'How Can There Be?'"

Rain and his father settled into the leather sofa. Granny had a marvelous voice and Rain always enjoyed her singing immensely, though he felt somewhat uncomfortable that the song would focus on his feelings for Catherine. At least only his family would hear it and not Wayne.

Like a songbird regaling a sunrise, Mildred Henry's voice filled the room with a bright spiritual light. The piano perfectly complemented the song that went like this:

I gave my love a cherry that had no stone,
I gave my love a chicken that had no bone,
I gave my love a ring that had no end,
I gave my love a baby that had no cryin',

How can there be a cherry without a stone?
How can there be a chicken without a bone?
How can there be a ring without an end?
How can there be a baby without no cryin'?

A cherry when its bloomin' has no stone,
A chicken when its peepin' has no bone,
A ring when its rollin' has no end,
A baby when its sleepin' has no cryin'.

CHAPTER FOUR
SUMMER SNOW

A Sunday dawn broke over the eastern edge of Meridian and somewhere a distant, high-powered deity slid an enormous dimmer switch, which blurred the edges of light that separate night from day. The resultant fuzzy, rose-colored rays permeated the hospital room and chased away Rain's Sleep Spirits. While his body stirred in the uncomfortable vinyl and steel chair, his tongue smacked the bitter stickiness at the roof of his mouth and his head rolled from one shoulder to the other. One set of fingers rubbed his eyes, and the other ran through his short hair, which had turned oily overnight. For a moment, he felt lost. Then, the objects of the room sharpened, and his mind relocated the memories of the previous few hours. The patient's yellowish face remained unchanged by the transition from dark to light. Unfortunately, this was no nightmare. Rain's father still lay directly ahead, silently dying.

The hands of the hospital room's wall clock, like skinny black legs searching for the floor, indicated the time to be 6:38. Rain endeavored to head to the bathroom, but the rectangular metal support bar at the front of the chair had pinched a nerve, leaving his left leg numb. Although he needed to urinate desperately, he decided against limping across the room on one leg. He could hold it until the feeling returned, and, hoping to speed the recovery, Rain caressed the underside of the prickling appendage.

He was still rubbing vigorously when an older nurse in a neatly pressed, white uniform entered the room. She nodded a business-like greeting Rain's direction and explained that she needed to check his father's vital signs. Taking mental note of the readouts from each machine, she compared Jim Henry's numbers with the normal ranges listed on her clipboard. After muttering a few "mmms" and "uh-huhs," she scribbled a few notes at the bottom of the page. Finished with the chart, the nurse placed the clipboard on the end of the bed and began checking the physical connections between the tubes and wires that connected the patient to the diagnostic machines. During the inspection, she addressed the palpable anxiety emanating from the far wall. Her voice lacked the syrupy southern accent Rain expected and instead sounded crisp and efficient.

"Everything here indicates your father's condition has stabilized, which is good. We'll still keep a close eye on him to see if anything changes. Dr. Littleton will stop by in a few hours." She continued checking the connections, but her tone became noticeably softer. "Looks like you had a long night. I'll bet you could use a hospital guest kit. Might get cleaned up a bit. I'll go get one for you after I finish." The connections passed her rigorous inspection and the nurse reclaimed the clipboard. "Do you have any other questions or need anything else?"

"Ma'am, do you think he can hear what we're saying? I've already told him I love him, but I'm not sure he can hear me."

The nurse's rigid posture, including the taut muscles that worked her expressionless face, relaxed. With a smile, she nodded. "I think so. Many folks believe that comatose patients have the ability to not only hear, but also sense the physical presence of others around them. If that's true, and I think it is, he knows you're here and how much you care for him. Now, I'll get that guest kit for you. Be right back."

The nurse opened the door and departed, but no sooner had she left than the door re-opened and she poked her head back in the room. "I apologize. I forgot to let you know you have a visitor waiting out here in the hall. Claims she's an old friend. It's before official visiting hours, but she works in hospital administration, so I'll allow the visit if it's all right with you."

Rain had anticipated this moment. He wished he could have had a chance to clean up first. His left leg almost cured, he rose from the chair. "Sure, let her in."

A beautiful and sophisticated woman cautiously appeared in the doorway. Their eyes momentarily connected before Rain looked away. As he gazed out the window past his dying father, his peripheral vision tracked the woman's hesitant approach. A few feet away, she stopped. Rain turned and they stood face to face. Just as the first time he had seen her, her golden blond hair, which today was pulled straight back, struck him. With perfect geometrical lines, it flowed precisely into a silk-like bun at the back of her head. She wore a dark navy business suit that ran nearly the entire length of her slender body. The smell of her perfume, which had trailed along like a shadow, caught up and passed her, enveloping Rain in a cloud of exhilaration. He tried to ignore the cloud, but could not. Silently, and with great hunger, he consumed Catherine's scent as though it represented the last thing his sense of smell would ever experience. Rain's mind struggled to recall anything more exquisite or more desirable than this woman before him. Rain gasped for air as he imagined himself drowning again in the coolness of her piercing blue eyes.

Catherine lunged forward and hugged him tightly. As she did, Rain felt each drop from the moisture of her breath settle and cling to the tiny hairs on the back of his neck. With her lips only millimeters from his left ear, she whispered, "My God, Rain. I'm so sorry. I'm so sorry."

Rain delicately pulled away from the embrace and forced a smile. "Thanks, Catherine. Thanks for coming."

"How is he?"

"I'm not sure. The doctor said he had a massive heart attack yesterday. He also said he's got advanced heart disease and cancer that's spread everywhere. It doesn't look good."

Like an angel, Catherine floated to the end of the bed. She placed her hand, ever so gently, on the two lumps under the sheet, which she correctly presumed to be Jim Henry's feet. She closed her eyes and silently prayed.

Rain stepped beside her. Sadness tried to overtake him, but unlike before, he was able to hold it back. He shrugged and broke the silence. "Dr. Littleton says there's no treatment for his condition. There's nothing anyone can do."

Catherine reached for Rain's hand and held it tightly. "Miracles can happen, Rain. Always remember that." Her eyes were compassionate and loving. "I guess we'll have to pray for one, and in the meantime, try to make him as comfortable as possible. How long can you stay?"

Rain latched his thumb over hers and stared blankly at the wall. "I'll stay as long as it takes."

They stood together for several minutes, hand in hand, Rain's dying father before them. Then, history repeated, and the private world they created was interrupted by the return of the business-like nurse. She cleared her throat to announce her arrival.

"Sorry to interrupt. Here's the kit. It's got a toothbrush, toothpaste, soap, shampoo, a comb and some deodorant. Don't forget to pull the chord if something happens or if you need anything else." Rain accepted the small black bag, and the nurse left to continue her rounds.

"Rain, the doctors don't start showing up to check on their patients until 8:30 or so. We've got time to eat, and then you can get back here to catch Dr. Littleton. Could I treat you to some breakfast in the cafeteria?"

Rain's stomach eagerly churned at the mention of breakfast. He remembered that he hadn't eaten anything since late the afternoon before. He squeezed her hand and then released it. "I'd like that very much. Would you come back and get me in about twenty minutes? I'd like to take a shower, and I'm afraid I'd get lost if I tried to find the cafeteria myself."

Catherine's mood lightened. "Somehow, I doubt you'd get lost, Rain Henry; the cafeteria is on the ground floor right next to the lobby, but I'll come get you anyway." Checking her watch, she added, "I'll see you again at 7:15 sharp."

Once Catherine left, Rain returned to his chair and began slowly removing his clothes. As they were the only ones he had with him, he carefully draped them on the back of his chair. He allowed himself several minutes to get undressed, all the while staring blankly at his father. Since Rain had arrived, Jim Henry had neither moved nor given the slightest twitch. The bags of exhaustion below his father's eyes seemed to darken with each passing second and there was still no discernable change to his sickly, yellowish coloring.

Now wearing only his boxers, Rain headed for the room's tiny bathroom. Before passing by, he stopped and gingerly massaged the exposed portion of his father's scarred left forearm. He was careful not to disturb the plastic tubes delivering the clear fluids to his veins. He hoped the nurse was right when she said people in comas could still hear and feel the love from those around them.

"Dad, I want you to understand how much I love you. I also want to thank you for everything you've ever done for me. I know you're ready to go see Mom in heaven, but hold on for just a little while longer, okay? Call me selfish, but I also want the chance to say goodbye first. Even Catherine stopped in to see how you were doing. Anyway, it's been a long night, and I need a shower."

Rain closed the bathroom door behind him and finally relieved himself. Staring hard into the mirror, he held his hand in front of his mouth and exhaled. Rain winced at the terrible odor. Next, he raised one arm and then the other, inhaling a sample from each armpit. Ouch. He could only shake his head in embarrassment. No wonder that nurse wanted to get him some toiletries as soon as possible. He unzipped the bag and dug for the toothbrush, toothpaste, and deodorant to make sure they were really in there. They were, thank goodness. He put them one by one on the sink and studied the haggard face looking back at him. "Stay strong," he commanded of the reflection.

The showerhead spit the water directly at Rain's chest. Such were the consequences of being extraordinarily tall. To wash his hair and face, he had to bend forward like a hunchback touching his toes. Despite this inconvenience, to which he had grown accustomed over the years, his aching muscles rejoiced in the rush of hot water. The warmth reminded him of Catherine's embrace, though it was a cheap imitation. Today was the first time he had seen her up close in more than ten years, and her metamorphosis amazed him. She had blossomed from a young girl, flush with the innocence and the promise of youth, into a sophisticated, mature woman at the height of her sensuality. As the water cascaded over his body, he mentally re-examined the obstacles that had kept Rain Henry and Catherine Landerson apart. The first had been the summer snowstorm.

Like a thin vinyl accordion, Rain shoved the shower curtain to the back of the tub and pulled the thick, yellow towel from the rack. Mrs. LeRoy had hung it for their overnight guest earlier in the day. He patted his face dry first, and then whipped the towel through his hair.

Wayne pounded on the bathroom door. "Come on, Rain! What's takin' so long?"

"Leave me alone! I'm almost done!" Rain shouted back.

Now dry, Rain pulled on his cotton briefs and quickly brushed his teeth. After rinsing, he returned the toothbrush to the black overnight bag his grandmother had given him for "spend-the-nights" at his friends' houses. Then, he slipped into his pajamas, which consisted of an old T-shirt and some cut-off jeans.

Wayne shouted again, this time from his bedroom. "C'mon slowpoke! Do you want to play or not?"

"Shut up, Wayne! I'll be there in a second."

Rain stepped into the short hallway that connected the bathroom and the two upstairs bedrooms of the LeRoy house. Roy's room was to the right, and Wayne's to the left. In front, stairs led down to the playroom and the rest of the house. The upstairs addition was brand new. Mr. LeRoy, along with the help of some relatives, had built it himself the previous summer. The enlarged house now had three bedrooms, allowing Wayne and Roy's original bedroom to become a playroom and more importantly, giving the two ever-fighting brothers their own private space. Although Rain spent many hours in Wayne's room, he had seen the inside of Roy's only once or twice. Roy zealously guarded his privacy and possessions. He remained locked behind his door most of the time.

When Rain entered his best friend's room, he found Wayne sitting at the edge of his bed playing the new Atari 2600 he had gotten for his birthday a few weeks before. A dark gray Pac-Man darted to and fro within a black-walled labyrinth. The objective was to eat all the dots lining the pathways before any of the four roaming ghosts ate you. The game had "power pills" located in each corner of the square board. Each time your Pac-Man ate a power pill, he had a few seconds to turn the tables on the ghosts and eat them for bonus points. Rain and Wayne would have preferred to play on a color TV, but had to settle for the nineteen-inch black and white Wayne had commandeered from the playroom. At least the sounds of the game were the same.

Rain sat down next to Wayne, whose eyes were glued to the TV. His hand and wrist jerked the joystick violently in every direction.

"Wayne, you sure you'll be able to throw the ball back to me tomorrow?"

"What are you talking about?" Wayne asked as his tongue stuck out from the side of his mouth from sheer determination.

"I'm talking about the way you're gonna wear out your wrist playing Pac-Man."

"If I can't, I'll just roll it back to you. Besides, you've been playin' too."

"Yeah, but I don't try to rip the joystick apart when I play."

The two took turns and after a few hours, Wayne's door swung open. Mr. LeRoy stood in the doorway. His body carried a permanent tan from years of working in the sun, and deep furrows crisscrossed the skin that covered his forehead and the back of his neck. Rain compared Mr. LeRoy's neck to the way a pond bottom looks after all the water's gone and the mud has baked in the sun for a few weeks. On the top of his head, Wayne's father still owned a little blond hair that wispily clung together like dingy, squash-colored yarn. Mr. LeRoy wasn't a large or tall man, but he did possess a deep voice that commanded respect, and his rock-hard body was the envy of many men. Royston Mitchell LeRoy, Sr., was as blue collar as blue collar could be. He left every Sunday afternoon for a week's worth of welding oil tanks along the Mississippi River in Louisiana before returning home every Friday afternoon. Maybe it was because of this time away that he seemed to hold a special place in his heart for his family, especially Wayne.

"It's ten o'clock, girls. That means bedtime for all eleven-year-olds at the LeRoy castle. Turn off all that mess and get some sleep. Mr. Henry and I want you two fresh for the game tomorrow."

Wayne continued to wrestle with the joystick. "Aw, c'mon, Daddy, I'm about to beat the high score."

"Boy, you can forget about any high score tonight. All that's gonna get beat is your butt if you don't shut that thing off right now."

Wayne released an exasperated moan, but at the same time reached up and clicked off the TV. Mr. LeRoy waited until the tiny white dot in the middle disappeared. "Now I know it'll be tempting for you girls to turn off the lights, turn down the sound and try to keep on playin' after I leave. So Wayne, just so you know, if I come up here later and catch ya, I'm gonna give you a *double whippin'* with the belt."

Wayne looked shocked and confused. "Daddy, wait. Why you gonna give me a double whippin'?"

"Because, boy, it ain't polite to whip a guest, so you've got to take Rain's whippin', too." Roy LeRoy, Sr., flashed a grin at the two boys that dared them to disobey. As he descended the carpeted stairs, he shouted back, "Lights off in five minutes. That goes for you too, Roy."

Rain settled under the light covers on the far side of the double bed. Wayne clicked the window air conditioning unit to low and increased the ceiling fan speed to high. Then, he picked up a large plastic bottle of baby powder from his nightstand and pulled a box containing his baseball cleats out from under the bed.

"Wayne, you're so weird for puttin' baby powder in your shoes."

Wayne began sprinkling the fine white powder into his cleats. "I've told you before. It keeps the smell down and my feet dry. Daddy does the same thing with his work boots."

Rain chuckled. "I know something funny we could do with that white powder."

"What?"

"We could pour it all out into a cup and throw it into Roy's ceiling fan when he's asleep. It'd fly everywhere and make his room look like it got hit by a blizzard!"

Wayne leaned back against the headboard for a moment and a sinister smile grew across his face. "Let's do it," he proclaimed.

Rain, realizing his mistake, quickly shook his head. "I was only kiddin'."

"No Rain, I think it's a great idea. I give you all the credit. We'll do it later tonight when he goes to sleep. That's usually about two or three in the mornin'."

"You're crazy. I'll be asleep by then."

"No you won't, 'cause we'll be playin' Pac-Man," Wayne replied matter-of-factly. "I turned off the TV, but not the game. It's right where we left it." Wayne flicked off the overhead light and returned to his gaming position at the foot of the bed. He tugged at the TV's round power knob and the black-and-white picture promptly returned. A large "PAUSED" flashed on the screen. "See, I told ya."

Rain pulled the covers over his head and then the pillow on top of that. The image of Wayne getting whipped twice by his father was not pretty. Rain rubbed his own fanny under the sheets to make sure it was still intact. He could almost feel the pain the leather belt would inflict. Rain mumbled a barely audible, muffled warning. "Go ahead, you nut, but don't blame me when you can't sit down tomorrow."

Wayne ate a power pill and attacked the ghosts. "Oh, you'll play in a few minutes. Either that, or you'll have to fall asleep knowing I own the high score."

Rain exploded from under the covers. "Liar! You'll never even get close to my high score."

Sure enough, Wayne spoke the truth. He was within a few hundred points of the high score Rain had set earlier, and to make matters worse, Wayne still had two extra men. Rain gave in to his competitive nature and resumed his spot next to Wayne in front of the TV. A challenge had been issued and accepted. Wayne's score soon became the high score, and as the scores escalated on the screen simultaneously, Rain decided it didn't matter if they got caught, anyway. Wayne would get the beating, not him. He might even enjoy it a little, particularly if Wayne held the high score at the time.

Wayne LeRoy and Rain Henry continued the fight for Pac-

Man supremacy of the universe for hours. As the night got later and later, the high score changed possessions at least six or seven times. Around 1:30, the toilet next door flushed and startled Rain. It almost caused him to lose a man.

"Relax, Rain. It's Roy taking a leak."

"Well, he messed up my pattern. If I get killed, I get to start over and play a whole new game."

"No way!" Wayne shouted. "You've gotta learn to concentrate better."

Rain was about to continue the argument when knuckles lightly rapped from outside Wayne's door. Wayne rolled his eyes, then reached over and hit the pause button on the console. Rain presumed it had to be Roy because Wayne's father would have burst in without the courtesy of knocking. The door cracked open, and Roy poked his narrow face with its beady eyes into his younger brother's room. The glow from the TV reflected a bluish white off of his pimpled cheeks and oily forehead.

Wayne jumped to his feet, his fists clenched. "Did I say you could come in my room, jerkoff?"

"Daddy said you'd better get to bed and that was hours ago. The light from your childish game is keeping me awake. If you don't cut it off this instant, I'm gonna go tell on both of you."

Wayne growled like a hungry dog and methodically moved in for the kill. "You're full of it, Roy. There's no way you can see the light in your room. Now get the hell out of here before I kick your sorry ass!"

Roy waited until Wayne got to within an arm's length and then pulled the door closed as hard as he could. It slammed shut in Wayne's face like a bomb, sending sound waves reverberating throughout the house.

"Eat me, Wayne!" Roy shrieked from the other side.

Wayne opened his door just in time to see his brother's door slam shut, which set off another bomb. Wayne lunged forward, but Roy clicked the lock before Wayne could grab the knob. "You're lucky I didn't catch you, Faggo," he whispered through the door. Momentarily defeated, he returned to his room, where Rain was getting closer to setting a new high score. Wayne snickered. "Sorry, Rain. Dumbass over there probably woke up Momma and Daddy slammin' the doors. We gotta shut everything off."

"No way! I'm too close."

Suddenly, Rain heard a small electrical pop and snowy static took over the TV.

Wayne stood next to the wall and twirled the Atari's power cord the way a lifeguard twirls a whistle.

"I said I was sorry." He dropped the cord and climbed into bed. "Do me a favor and cut off the TV, since you're already down there. Hurry up, too. Daddy's likely to be here any second, and we've gotta make like we've been asleep."

As predicted, Rain heard muffled footsteps ascend the carpeted stairs. Mr. LeRoy's voice boomed like a cannon, literally shaking the walls. "Boys, if I hear one more noise from this part of the house, I'm gonna come down so hard on your asses you'll think they were soaked in gas and lit on fire." He stomped back down the stairs.

Wayne shook his head in the cool moonlight that had overtaken the room. "Roy's done it this time. Daddy's pissed. He only talks about lightin' asses on fire when he's really mad."

"Okay. It's settled. Let's just go to bed, for cryin' out loud. The lights are already out. Let's just get some sleep. I'm really tired."

"Not just yet. I think someone needs to be cooled off, maybe from a freak summer snowstorm. Remember? It was your idea. Anyway, he cost you the high score."

"I told you I was kidding about that."

"Look, Roy needs to be taught a lesson. I don't want him thinkin' he can barge into my room anytime he wants and order us around. If you're too scared that Roy might hurt you, I'll do it myself." Wayne slid out of the bed. "All I need is to find a cup big enough to hold the entire bottle of baby powder. By the way, I've got some good news about Catherine, but I think you're too wimpy to ever date her, anyway."

Initially, Rain ignored the verbal jab. He silently watched Wayne continue the search under the bed, pushing aside toys like a sea turtle sweeping away sand to build its nest. It seemed like only yesterday that they had taken the trip to Key Field where Wayne got his plane autographed. The P-40 hung from the ceiling in the far corner of the room, its wings tipped downward to the left as if banking to strafe a target. Rain found it hard to believe the trip had taken place more than a year ago. Before the visit to the airport, Wayne was a timid introvert. Rain often had to stand up and protect him like a big brother. No longer. That field trip and subsequent autograph changed him; it gave him a new sense of self-confidence that bordered on cockiness. His life had a purpose, he told anyone who would listen. Wayne LeRoy would play baseball and become a pilot. If they both didn't work out, he knew one or the other would. Those were his aspirations, plain and simple. In fact, he mentally drew up the necessary plans to achieve his goals and openly discussed them with Rain. In school, he studied harder and his grades went from D's and C's to mostly B's with an occasional A. Wayne's new confidence had even won him a girlfriend.

Not everything was positive about the new Wayne LeRoy, though. He began to physically harass Roy, even though he was three years younger. Someone needed to take Wayne down a notch or two, Rain decided. While Wayne dug farther under the bed, Rain crawled from under the covers and stood waiting for him to emerge.

Triumphant in his search, Wayne scooted backwards on his stomach and produced a scratched plastic cup, remnants of an extra-large soda slurped weeks ago.

From behind, Rain reached down and tapped Wayne on the shoulder. Surprised, Wayne turned to see his best friend standing over him in a menacing pose, his fist cocked.

"Wayne, you may boss Roy around, but you'll never boss me. Suppose you tell me what you know about Catherine before I smash in your face. How's that for wimpy?"

Wayne scrambled to his feet. "Okay, I take it back, I take it back. Stacey's coming to the game tomorrow and since Catherine's spendin' the weekend with her, she's comin' too."

Rain didn't believe it. He thought of Catherine almost every day, but he hadn't seen or talked to her since their meeting at the Key Brothers' plaque. Stacey Cottrell and Wayne were boyfriend and girlfriend now, but Stacey didn't reveal much about her cousin. In fact, it irritated Rain the way Stacey completely avoided the subject whenever he brought up Catherine's name. Rain had stopped asking Stacey for information long before. About all Stacy told him was Catherine's last name: Landerson. His grandmother said that Catherine was most likely the daughter of Dr. and Mrs. Landerson and a direct descendent of Dr. Oliver Landerson, who had founded Landerson Hospital in the late 1800's.

"You're sayin' that Catherine Landerson, Stacey's cousin, is coming to the game tomorrow."

"Yep. Course it makes sense 'cause we'll be playin' her boyfriend's team."

Perplexed, Rain rubbed his chin. "I thought Stacey said her boyfriend doesn't play baseball."

"Her old one don't, but her new one does. His name's Trip Chanick or somethin'. His father owns two or three jewelry stores in Meridian. They've been goin' together since the spring."

Rain slumped on the bed. Whatever fight he had a few seconds before rushed away like air from a burst balloon. "How come Stacey didn't tell me she broke up with her boyfriend? Catherine said she'd tell her, if she ever did. Did you know about it?"

Wayne sat down beside his friend. "Yeah, I knew. But I didn't tell ya' 'cause I thought it'd really hurt your feelings.

Stacey was gonna tell you, but by the time she found out, Catherine was already goin' with this Trip kid. She said their parents kinda pushed 'em together."

"Wow, thanks for the good news. If it'd been any better, I might have jumped out the window."

Wayne smacked Rain's leg. "I ain't finished yet. So here's the plan for tomorrow. You whiff that Trip kid every time he comes up. We'll both hit two or three homers. We kick that team's ass, and you'll be the hero. Catherine will run from that loser like he's a mangy mutt with rotten teeth. Then, after the game, guess where Stacey's mom is droppin' them off."

"Where? The church, so Catherine and Trip can get married?"

"Wrong! Same place we'll be after we come home and get cleaned up: Haystack's Skatin' Palace. Momma's already agreed to take us. We'll come pick you up at your house, and then she'll bring us home when Haystack's closes. Stacey and I arranged the whole thing, just to get you and Catherine together. Catherine don't know about it yet, and I wanted to surprise you, but now you know."

"Wayne, that's about the coolest thing anyone's ever done for me. Thanks, man."

They slapped high fives and Wayne continued, "I figured I owed you one after you helped me get that plane signed. After that happened, I understood how important it was to go for things you really want." Wayne laughed. "And, if it hadn't been for us getting caught by Stacey on the way back to the bus, I might never have asked her to go with me."

Wayne held up the cup. "So, old buddy. You gonna help me teach my brother not to mess with us, or do I have to do it all by myself?"

Rain smiled. "I'll help you, old buddy."

"That's more like it. Why don't you start pourin' the powder into this cup while I sneak downstairs and get the master key that'll open Roy's door."

Rain emptied every speck of powder into the plastic cup. They had searched for another cup so Rain could share equally in the dastardly deed, but were unsuccessful, so they decided Rain would open Roy's door and switch on the fan. Wayne would then toss the powdery snow into the whirling blades.

Wayne returned with the key and Rain met him in the hallway. Wayne got down on all fours and put his ear next to the small space at the bottom of the door. "He's asleep," Wayne whispered.

Rain inserted the key into the tiny hole next to the knob. With a slight click, it unlocked and Rain opened it. His hand reached along the wall and found the switch. The sound of the humming motor filled the room as the fan got up to speed. His job finished, Rain moved to the side of the doorway. Wayne stepped in and, with a sudden underhand lurch, launched the powder. In the dim moonlight that filtered through Roy's window, everything moved in slow motion. The white powder hung together in a clump as it inched upward and into the ominous blades. When the clump reached its destination, the blades repeatedly struck the ball of powder, making a dull "ploof, ploof, ploof" sound. The fan seemed to come to life as it held the clump in place while each blade, like the arms of a maniacal boxer, hit it over and over until nothing remained. The scene turned out even better than Rain had originally imagined. Wayne whooped with joy. In only a few seconds, Roy's room filled with a fine white fog that settled over everything like fresh, powdery snow.

Mission accomplished, Wayne turned the knob before silently pulling Roy's door shut. He didn't want to set off another bomb to rouse his father. With great haste, the two boys rushed into Wayne's room and locked the door behind them. They hopped into bed and huddled under the sheet, giggling like schoolgirls. Both felt miles away from the coughing and wheezing coming from the bedroom at the other side of the hall.

Everything quieted down eventually, and Rain and Wayne were almost asleep when they heard a soft rapping at the door. They both froze and Rain felt too afraid to even twitch a muscle.

"Is that you, Frosty?" Wayne cautiously inquired.

The raspy, evil voice that penetrated the door from the other side sent chills down Rain's spine. "I wanted you to know, Wayne LeRoy, I just prayed to the devil. I asked him visit you tonight in your dreams and kill you."

CHAPTER FIVE
THE BIG GAME

June LeRoy rose early for weekend breakfasts. By nine o'clock, she had already peeled the potatoes that would become deep fried wedges lightly seasoned with paprika. By 9:30, lean slices of bacon jumped and popped inside Blackie, her giant iron skillet. Blackie was a major star of the LeRoy kitchen. When not in use, she hung on a thick steel nail hammered deep into the wall beside the refrigerator. She had a commanding presence, a huge black spot that stood out against the white walls and cleanliness of the rest of the kitchen. Blackie had been passed down by generations of women from Mrs. LeRoy's side of the family and would eventually be given to Roy's or Wayne's wife, whoever expressed the most interest in having her.

Once the bacon angrily crackled, Mrs. LeRoy plucked the sizzling strips from Blackie's mouth and placed them on a stack of paper towels to absorb some of the bacon grease. Next, with extended arms, Mrs. LeRoy dumped the raw potato wedges in the molten pool of bacon fat. Blackie immediately roared to life, spitting tiny drops of hot grease into the air like a volcano. Mrs. LeRoy quickly lowered the gas flame, and soon the searing grease tanned the wedges a golden brown. Mrs. LeRoy scooped these out and placed them on a separate stack of paper towels adjacent to the bacon.

Except for the fried eggs, which Blackie could cook in only a few seconds, breakfast was ready. Mrs. LeRoy reminded herself to make sure the boys were awake. She didn't like the notion of her boys being lazy and sleeping all morning, even if it was a summer Saturday. Besides, Wayne and Rain had a big game today, and she wanted to get them started with a good breakfast. Strolling to the base of the stairs, she hollered for Roy, Wayne and Rain to roll out of their beds.

Rain watched as Wayne literally pushed himself out of bed in order to wake up. Rain, who had been awake for some time, felt elated Satan hadn't killed his best friend overnight. Now that Wayne had lived, Rain's thoughts turned to seeing Catherine again at the game and then getting to couple skate with her later at Haystack's. He had to give credit to his friend who looked like a fish out of water as he flopped around on the bedroom floor. Wayne's plan held definite promise, and Rain decided to make sure it happened. Today, he would be unstoppable on the baseball field, become the hero, and consequently Catherine would have no choice but to drop that Trip kid and become his girlfriend.

"Where's your brother, Wayne?" Mrs. LeRoy asked after Wayne and Rain seated themselves at the small kitchen table.

Wayne lifted his head. He still acted half-asleep. "He hollered back at ya that he didn't feel good. Said he'd be down later. Probably just chillin' out in his room." His toe jabbed Rain under the table to make sure he got the joke. Rain gave him a kick back that indicated he did.

Mrs. LeRoy set plates in front of each boy. Both held two fried eggs, five pieces of bacon, and about a dozen breakfast fries. She also placed the salt and pepper on the table, along with bottles of ketchup and Worcestershire sauce, Rain's condiment of choice. To Wayne, the aroma of the hot greasy food acted like a smelling salt. He bolted upright, then lowered his mug a few inches from the plate. His fork blurred as it rapidly shoveled squares of slimy egg into his mouth.

Rain reached for the Worcestershire and doused his fries with the dark, tangy liquid. Next came a dash of salt. This was his favorite way to eat potato wedges, and the tasty concoction gave birth to a gushing spring directly under his anticipative tongue.

Mrs. LeRoy complemented the meal with large glasses of cold orange juice. "Rain, what time is your dad coming by to pick you boys up?"

Rain wiped his mouth with a folded paper towel that functioned as a napkin. "He said he'd pick us up about 11:30. We're gonna stop by Buddy's for some batting practice before lunch."

"The game starts at three, right?" Mrs. LeRoy asked.

"That's right, Momma," Wayne replied. "You got any more fried eggs over there?"

"Sorry, Wayne. I only made six. I'm savin' the other two for Roy."

Wayne moved his head around as if he looked for someone. "Where's Daddy?"

Mrs. LeRoy started wiping down the stove with a damp cloth. "He got up early this morning to go help your Uncle Fred do some weldin' on his trailer. He said he'd be finished with plenty of time to make the game. Uncle Fred's probably comin', too. Ya'll are playing them city-boy all-stars from Meridian, right?"

"Yes, ma'am," Wayne enthusiastically confirmed through the pieces of bacon in his mouth.

"Well, I sure hope ya'll win."

Wayne gave Rain a wink. "We will, Momma. Just don't forget about takin' us to Haystack's tonight. Me and Rain's got dates."

Jim Henry pulled his blue Chevy pickup into the LeRoy's driveway a few minutes early. The team bats, balls, and helmets were in the back, as well as all of Rain's individual gear. "East Lauderdale All-Stars" was written in yellow cursive across the front of Jim Henry's scarlet jersey and navy blue block letters proclaimed "Coach" across the shoulder area of the back. Underneath, he wore his long sleeve turtleneck even though the day's predicted temperature would exceed ninety degrees.

While he knocked on the front door, Jim Henry reminded himself not to get too excited about the game, but he wanted to win this one and win it badly. This year represented his third postseason as coach of the all-star team from East Lauderdale County, and his team had yet to beat the Meridian All-Stars. In previous years, Rain exhausted his pitching eligibility to get the team to the regional championship game. Today, however, Rain still had several innings remaining and would be the team's starter. In addition, Wayne LeRoy, on his first all-star team, had blossomed into a top-notch catcher. The stakes were high. The winner would go to the state playoffs in Jackson, and the winner of that tournament played in Atlanta for a birth at the Little League World Series in Williamsport, Pennsylvania. Coach Henry literally licked his lips. He felt confident of the day's outcome.

Mrs. LeRoy opened the door. "Good mornin', Jim."

"Mornin', June. How'd our two star players sleep last night?

"I'm afraid they stayed up most of the night. Roy senior made 'em go to bed for the *second* time around 1:30 or so. You should be thankful you've got only one son and not two. Seems all they do is fight one another."

Jim Henry laughed. "I do admire how you keep them from killing each other during the week while Roy's gone. Rain's told me some stories. Anyway, I expect Rain and Wayne will be fine. Boys their age don't need a whole lot of sleep, and I think they'll be pretty up for the big game today. Are they dressed and ready?"

"Sure are. Put on their uniforms right after breakfast. I think they're upstairs brushing their teeth and combing their hair." Mrs. LeRoy shook her head. "Jim, our boys have done gone and discovered girls. Gotta look all pretty, I reckon, even though they're about to go out and get dirty and dusty playin' baseball. Wayne's girlfriend's goin' to the game and she's bringin' her cousin who Wayne says Rain likes. Did you know Wayne set up a secret double date for all of 'em tonight over at Haystack's skatin' rink?"

Rain's father smiled. "No, I sure didn't, though I'm sure I'll soon hear about it. Would you mind letting them know I'm here? I'd like to get going so we'll have plenty of time for the batting cages."

Mrs. LeRoy retreated a few steps into the house and called over her shoulder, "Ya'll c'mon! Coach Henry's here and he's ready to go!"

Shortly thereafter, coach, catcher, and pitcher left the tiny community of Vimville and headed northwest on Highway 19 for Meridian. The pickup bounced along at a leisurely pace. The weather looked beautiful – only thin wisps of clouds appeared high on the horizon against the background of a deep blue sky.

"Son, I hear you were up late last night. You sure you're ready to pitch?"

"Yes, sir," Rain answered with confidence.

"How 'bout you, Wayne? You ready to block a knuckle curve if it bites the dirt?"

"Yes, sir, Coach Henry."

"Rain, what's this I hear about a date tonight?" Jim Henry asked.

Wayne spoke before Rain could answer. "Ah, Coach Henry, let me explain. I set it up as a surprise for Rain. He didn't know about it 'till last night. That's how come he didn't tell you ahead a time. I hope it's okay. Momma's gonna take us to Haystack's and then pick us up so it won't be no bother to you."

"That sounds fine with me as long as Rain has enough allowance saved to pay his admission."

Rain nodded vigorously, "I sure do, Dad. I've got almost thirty dollars put away."

A mile outside Meridan, they pulled into the gravel parking lot at Buddy's. Buddy Thompson was one of the few major league baseball players to come out of Meridian and then actually come back. For over a dozen years, he played third base for the Cincinnati Reds in the late 1950s and early 1960s before retiring to his hometown. Buddy owned Meridian's only "athletic emporium," as he called it. Buddy's consisted of four batting cages, a driving range for golfers and a miniature golf course. Buddy's also boasted a small snack bar, where the trio planned on eating a late lunch before heading over to the field.

As the three piled out of the pickup, Rain noticed several men already on the driving range, whacking tiny white golf balls far into the distance. They all wore pressed tan or navy slacks with tucked-in knit shirts.

Rain and Wayne opened the tailgate and pulled over the bat bag. Wayne grabbed his favorite bat, an aluminum Tennessee Thumper. Rain removed his Louisville Slugger, a polished, wooden bat. He turned the stick of lumber over in his hands and admired the grains in the blond wood. With his thumbs, he traced the outlines of the two lightning bolts located above the handle portion of the bat. They served as quotation marks around the word "POWERIZED" burned black into its side. Rain used a wooden bat because his father, a baseball purist at heart, believed that baseball shouldn't be played with metal objects. Of course, he couldn't force other parents to purchase expensive wooden bats for their sons, so he begrudgingly accepted the presence of aluminum bats as well.

Coach Henry handed each boy a thick, round, metal doughnut to slide onto his stick to help limber up. "All right, you two, get loose. I'll go get the key."

Rain slid the doughnut over the skinny handle and slammed the end of the barrel into the ground, wedging the doughnut in place. Wayne did the same and they began swinging the weighted bats, which soon loosened the muscles in their arms and shoulders. After a few dozen cuts and windmills with both arms, they headed to the cages.

"Hey, Wayne, you gonna start in Coach Pitch this time? Or, maybe you should hop in the Slow Pitch Softball cage."

The Coach Pitch cage simulated the skill level for Pony League, which was the level after tee-ball. In Pony League, coaches pitched underhanded to their hitters. As for the Slow Pitch Softball cage, the boys knew only girls and old men with fat bellies played softball. "That's real funny, Rain. How about I get started by whacking your head with my Thumper?"

Rain continued swinging, ignoring the threat. "I think you should start out with the fastest pitches at the Major League cage. That way, everything looks slower and is easier to hit when you move to the Little League cage."

"Rain, why don't you shut up? Your daddy even said the way I do things is fine. Besides, all I see you do when you start in Major League is whiff. Every now and then you get lucky and foul one off."

Jim Henry approached from behind. "Boys, boys. We've discussed this before. The main goal here is to work on the mechanics of your swing and your timing. What's important is being able to make solid contact. Wayne likes to start slow and build up, and Rain likes to start fast and ease down. There's nothing wrong with either way. Both of you hit well during the games and that's what counts."

The coach entered the Major League cage and inserted the key into the coin box. "Okay, Rain, since I'm sure you're the one who brought up the debate, let's have you hit first."

Rain pulled his helmet down snuggly over his head and entered the cage. A right-handed hitter, he stood about ten inches from the left side of the plate while his head faced the machine that would deliver the dimpled, yellow ball. Rain spread his feet a little farther apart than shoulder width and slightly rocked from the front left leg to the back right leg.

He held the bat straight out in front to make sure the oval Louisville Slugger trademark faced the sky, which helped keep the bat from cracking. After a few slow practice swings, he pulled the stick back and held it close to his right shoulder. His right elbow, positioned parallel to the ground, was rigidly cocked and ready. Rain's eyes drilled a hole at the spot where the mechanical arm would shoot out the first fastball.

"Ready, Rain?" his father asked.

"Yes, sir."

Coach Henry turned the key and pushed the start button. He then joined Wayne who clung to the outside of the cage's fence like a monkey at the zoo. Within a few seconds, the arm of the pitching machine came to life, heading slowly downward along its circular path. It had a scoop-like shovel at the end that picked up a waiting ball from a basket along the back portion of its arc. An instant later, the arm violently lurched forward, launching the pitch like a mechanical slingshot.

Hitting is the same as pitching in the sense that the player tries to build up energy and then create an explosion. The major difference is that the build up for pitching takes much longer and is more fluid and deliberate. With hitting, the explosion that creates the swing must happen instinctively and without hesitation. During the game, a hitter has only a few tenths of a second to decide if the pitch will be a ball or strike and thus if he should swing or not. To make the task of hitting the ball even more difficult, only an extremely small period of time exists during the actual swing when contact with the ball can be made. After that, the wrists roll over, the bat angle shifts, and the bat moves through and out of the hitting zone before finishing on the hitter's shoulder.

Rain's body started the explosion as he tracked the ball's approach. He began by lifting his left foot and rotating it ninety degrees while stepping toward the machine. He maintained the majority of his weight over his back foot. Next, his arms became the trigger, and he yanked them forward through the hitting zone while rotating his hips for smoothness and added power. Although he thought he had precisely matched his swing to the pitch trajectory, something went wrong. Rain missed. The ball whizzed by and crashed into bottom of the chain link fence behind him, right at his father's and Wayne's feet.

Wayne snickered. "Thanks for the breeze, Rain."

"You're late, Son. Focus on your timing," Coach Henry advised.

By the fifth pitch, Rain found his timing and began fouling off the pitches. His father reminded him to concentrate even harder. On the tenth and last pitch, he laced a line drive up the middle that bounced off the pitching machine with a resounding "clank."

"Very good, very good. Now let's watch Wayne hit."

The father and son watched as Wayne LeRoy, helmet already on, stepped up to the plate in the Little League cage. Both were proud of the tremendous progress Wayne had made. Unlike Rain, who learned to catch, throw, and hit at about the same time he learned to walk, Wayne never played baseball until Rain convinced him two years before that he should start. Today, Wayne was an all-star and one of the best Little League catchers in the whole county. Rain's father had said Wayne's physical build and temperament were perfect for a receiver.

Although they both hit from the right side, Wayne was shorter and stockier than Rain and his stance reflected this difference in physical stature. Rain used only a slight squat during his stance, which might be better described as a mild bending of the knees. Wayne, on the other hand, appeared as though he might sit down right next to home plate. When it came time to swing, however, Wayne used his squat as the starting point to release the enormous energy of his swing. This squat, combined with a slight upper cut in the angle of his stroke, gave him more homerun potential than Rain. Wayne hit seven homers during the regular season and one during the all-star tournament. But conversely, what he gained with power, he lost with timing. Rain rarely struck out, almost always hitting line drives or putting the ball in play, at a minimum. Wayne struck out more than he should, especially on off-speed pitches, though not as frequently as he did last year.

The balls in the Little League cage came much slower than the ones thrown to Rain, and Wayne immediately began crushing shots to what would be left center.

"Very good, Wayne. We'll need that power later today. Now, I want you to focus on hitting line drives to the right side." One of the things Wayne needed to practice was hitting the ball to the opposite field. Effective opposite field hitting allows the hitter a better chance to hit curveballs and other pitches that typically cross the outside portion of the plate. Coach Henry continually worked with him on acquiring this skill.

"Sure thing, Coach," Wayne responded. He moved back from the plate to simulate pitches over the outside corner. As the pitch came, instead of stepping with his left foot toward the machine, he pushed it at a slight angle toward the front of home plate. After a few pitches, he started hitting the ball hard in that direction.

Pleased with their progress, Jim Henry let the two go for a few more rounds before he pulled the plug. "All right boys, I think that's enough. We've got to save some for the game. Who's ready to eat?"

They finished lunch around 1:30, said goodbye to Buddy, and piled back in the pickup to head for the ballpark. They were still about twenty minutes away and anticipated arriving a few minutes before 2:00. The early arrival would give them slightly more than an hour to warm up before the game started.

The trio arrived on schedule at Highland Fields, located along the eastern edge of Meridian's Highland Park. Highland Park's history dated all the way back to 1909. It was built after the Meridian Fair and Livestock Exposition when John Kamper, a local lumberman and vice-president of the First National Bank, donated the land to the city of Meridian for a cultural gathering place. Soon thereafter, Highland Park became the favorite playground of Mississippi's then largest city. At the time, its concrete promenade stretched more than 500 feet and was lit by electric lights, when few other towns in the state had sidewalks, and only a handful of houses anywhere had electricity. During the Great Depression, the theme of the park changed from passive recreation to active sports. A swimming pool, tennis courts, and baseball fields were built during the transition in the 1930's.

The field looked fantastic. Its freshly cut, green grass appeared so well groomed, it reminded Rain of carpet. The purest white lime outlined the batters' boxes and drew foul lines down the third and first base sides of the field. These lines ended at the base of bright yellow foul poles. The dirt on the mound, along the base paths, in the infield, and around the home plate area looked like it had been raked more often than Rain combed his hair in a week. Sponsor billboards covered the outfield fence. One billboard represented the new Highway 11 McDonalds, and others reminded folks about the Meridian Coca-Cola bottling plant, Peavy's Sound Systems, Subway Sandwiches, Sonic Drive Inn, Chadwick's Jewelers, and Landerson Hospital. As Rain helped his dad and Wayne gather the gear from the back of the truck, Rain decided the field reminded him of a real major league ballpark, only built to a smaller scale.

After the three finished carrying the gear to the third base visitors' dugout, Jim Henry walked over to greet Richard Chadwick, the coach of the Meridian All-Stars. He and his son, Trip, had arrived early as well. Coach Chadwick sported a wide, almost mockingly broad grin on his face. The two met by the first base coach's box and shook hands.

"Jim Henry, is this a fine day for baseball or what?" Dick Chadwick asked as he motioned at the sky.

"Absolutely, Dick. The field looks wonderful, too. I sure wish we could get ours out in Vimville as nice as yours."

Dick chuckled and rubbed his chin thoughtfully with his thumb and index finger. He leaned forward and whispered, "Jim, I've told you before, and I'll say it again. Anytime you want to come coach with me and have Rain play for the Diamonds, simply pick up the phone. You know as well as I do that the competition's better here in town. I think it'd help Rain's development as a pitcher tremendously, and as a bonus, we'd all get to play on this first-class field."

Jim Henry pulled back a little from the man who had come too close for comfort. He felt flattered, of course, that Dick Chadwick still wanted Rain to play for him. He remembered hearing somewhere that Chadwick made it all the way to AAA ball before a leg injury ruined his career as an outfielder in the Dodgers organization. He was well known around Meridian not only for his knowledge of baseball, but also for his money and successful entrepreneurial endeavors. Chadwick had built a chain of jewelry stores from scratch, and was a local legend for converting an abandoned Kentucky Fried Chicken restaurant, right off Interstate 20, into his first store. Today, Chadwick Jewelry was the region's most popular place to buy "that special gift that lasts forever." However, wealth gave him power, and Chadwick often used this power to try to either buy or bully whomever he wanted.

Jim Henry politely shook his head. "I appreciate the offer, Dick. I really do. But you've got to remember that it's a long drive over here from where we live. Besides, Rain's made lots of friends out there in Vimville. In fact, his best friend, Wayne LeRoy, is his catcher. This is Wayne's first year to make the all-star team, and they're both pleased as punch to be playing together in this tournament."

"Well, shoot, Jim. Rain's catcher can play with us, too if that's what it'll take."

"Dick, I thought Jeremy Langford caught for your team."

"Oh, he does. He does. But we could let Rain have his own catcher whenever he pitched."

Coach Henry extended his hand before he headed back to the visitors dugout. "We'll think about it. How's that?"

Coach Chadwick snared the outstretched hand and shook it hard. "That's all I ask, Jim. That's all I ask."

While Jim Henry returned to his dugout through the infield diamond, he heard a final shout from Dick Chadwick. "Think about it, Jim! A team from Meridian playing for the South Region Championship in Atlanta and then going on to the Little League World Series. It'd be a helluva lotta fun!"

By 2:30, players from both teams warmed up in the outfield along the foul pole closest to their respective dugouts. A few boys stretched while most loosened their arms by playing catch. Rain sat alone on the long wooden slat that was his dugout's bench. His father stayed with the rest of the team, ensuring they warmed up properly. As customary, Coach Henry would take his son over to the bullpen about twenty-five minutes before game time. After roughly five minutes of father-son throwing, he'd trade out catching duties with Wayne to hit pre-game infield.

While he waited for his father to come get him, Rain felt proud to be a part of the East Lauderdale All-Stars. After each regular season, the coaches of the teams from the surrounding area met together to elect the all-star coach as well as select up to three players from each community team. This year represented the third in a row his father had been selected coach. Another thing Rain liked was the primary rule for selecting the players. It stated that each community must have at least one player on the all-star team, thus ensuring that Vimville, Whynot, Toomsuba, Lauderdale, Dalewood, and Marion would all be represented. Rain thought it was cool the way his team wore similar all-star jerseys but kept their regular season caps. For example, Kenny Man, who was their speedy centerfielder from Toomsuba, sported a light blue cap with an orange T and played catch with their first baseman, Todd Eldridge. Todd, from Whynot, wore a yellow hat with a black W. Rain's own cap was navy blue with a golden V across the front. Rain also thrilled in knowing that these players, respected competitors during the regular season, were now his all-star teammates.

Instinctively, Rain felt the time had nearly come to head down to the bullpen. He took the bicycle inner tube from his bag, stood, and began stretching his arm. As he pushed the physical limits of his arm's muscles and tendons, he peeked over his right shoulder into the stands. The metal bleachers were filling fast with parents, grandparents, brothers, sisters, aunts, uncles, and anyone else who took an interest in Little League baseball. Mr. Williams sat next to Rain's grandmother, who busily worked crocheting an afghan. They both sat on the home plate side of the first and lowest bleacher closest to the visitors' dugout. Mr. and Mrs. LeRoy, sans Roy, sat with Wayne's Uncle Fred about halfway up in the middle of the stands. Rain expected an overflow crowd. *The Meridian Star* had even touted the game on the second page of the sports section, saying it featured one of the best Little League pitching match-ups the city had ever seen. Rain's picture was in the article along with the Meridian pitcher, Steven Atkins. Rain wondered if Catherine had seen it. As he scanned the bleachers for her and Stacey, a poke in his left side startled him.

He turned to see Stacey and Catherine standing behind him, giggling. Stacey had jabbed him with one of those giant Pixie Stix.

"Catherine, I think he's nervous," Stacey quipped.

Rain ignored Wayne's girlfriend and allowed his senses to revel in the beauty of her cousin. Catherine's stark white shorts provided delicious contrast to her lengthy tan legs, which seemed to extend forever until they delicately connected the rest of her body with the ground. Her red tank top tightly covered two ripening mounds that looked as if they desperately wanted to burst from captivity.

Catherine's smile revealed teeth as straight and white as the foul lines. Her golden, pony-tailed hair glistened and Rain remembered how, when he had first seen her at Key Field, Catherine's hair had impressed him the most. But now, he decided, her gorgeous eyes were, by far, her best physical feature. They reminded him of the rare "sapphire frosts" that occurred once or twice a year on the Henry Farm. Instead of the normal white variety, sapphire frosts coat the ground with millions of tiny blue crystals that brilliantly sparkle until the mid-morning sun melts them away. Mr. Williams explained that sapphire frosts occur when a dramatic drop in temperature causes the nighttime ground fog to freeze in midair and fall gently to earth. Mr. Williams also said that if the temperature drops fast enough, the crystals created are so big a man can pick them right up from the ground just like real sapphires, though he had seen such a frost only once in his lifetime. At that moment, Rain determined that God must have gently gathered two of those blue-tinted crystals from a sapphire frost, like the one Mr. Williams had seen, and delicately inserted them as Catherine's eyes when she was still a baby inside her mother's womb.

"I saw your picture in the paper, Rain. Are you nervous?" Catherine's voice reminded Rain of a dandelion, her words the parachute-like seeds that softly disperse in the wind after a good blow.

Rain refocused on his stretching and tried to appear nonchalant. "A little, I guess. It's a big game. The winner goes to Jackson next weekend to play for the state title."

"Well, Rain, I'm excited about finally getting to watch the best baseball player in Mississippi."

Rain remembered how his comment at the airport had gotten him in trouble. "I was wrong when I said that last year. My dad says I'll be the best when others who've seen me play call me that."

Stacey, who miraculously had been silent for almost two

whole minutes, said, "Sounds like your dad is a smart man. Is that him?"

Rain turned to see his father enter the dugout and bend down to retrieve the catcher's mitt from the equipment bag. He walked up behind Rain and squeezed the back of his son's neck. "Rain, are you trying to convince these young ladies to cheer for us today? Perhaps you should introduce me."

"Sure, Dad. This is Stacey Cotrell – she's Wayne's girlfriend. And this is Catherine Landerson, Stacey's cousin."

"Very nice to meet you both." Jim Henry stuck two fingers from his right hand through the fence, and the girls giggled as they shook them.

Both girls replied with a combined voice, "Nice to meet you, too, Mr. Henry."

Jim Henry tightened his neck clamp and lightly pulled Rain away from the fence. "Ladies, I hope you'll excuse us. C'mon, Son, let's head down to the bullpen."

"Good luck, Rain Henry," Rain saw Catherine mouth over her shoulder as the two girls departed for the crowded bleachers.

Rain had loosened his arm earlier, so it took only a few pitches before the wasps stung the mitt with a vengeance. After the fastballs, he located some changeups and then threw some knuckle curves, which bit down harder than mistreated snapping turtles. Something deep within his soul told him he had waited his entire life for this game. It was almost as though Rain's consciousness gave way to his subconsciousness, and he, too, became a spectator of this magnificent pitching machine, merely observing with awe from behind the mound.

Rain had just thrown another perfect knuckle curve when Wayne waddled up wearing his full catching gear. He carried his own left-handed catcher's mitt.

"Coach Henry, the ump says if you want infield practice, the team needs to hit the field right now."

"Okay, Wayne, you take over. Work on spotting the

fastballs and the changeups on the corners. Make sure you practice dropping down to block the knuckle curves if they hit the dirt."

"Yes, sir!"

Coach Henry jogged back to the dugout and yelled for the boys to hit the field. Thirteen players from east Lauderdale County erupted from the visitors' dugout and sprinted to their positions. While their teammates began infield, Wayne and Rain met halfway between the bullpen mound and home plate. Wayne's eyes looked as big as the silver dollars Rain's grandmother kept in a jar at the top of her closet.

"Ready to kick some city-boy ass?" Wayne shouted.

"Hell, yeah! Let's do it!" Rain's normally calm tone gave way to something more animalistic.

"All right, that's what I want to hear! Now, give me three each, then let's head to the dugout and get ready to hit." Wayne shoved his mitt hard into Rain's chest.

Rain punched back with his glove, and the two unexpectedly growled at each other like tigers, then feverously laughed at their odd behavior. Wayne shuffled behind the plate and squatted while Rain ascended the mound. After Rain threw three fastballs, three changeups, and three knuckle curves, the two best friends returned to the dugout, sat down, and started focusing on making solid contact with their bats.

Since East Lauderdale was the visiting team, they would begin the game by hitting during the top half of the first inning. Wayne removed his catching gear. The lineup taped to the fence indicated Wayne would bat fourth, right after Rain, who hit in the third spot. Soon, the rest of their team finished infield practice, sprinted off the field, and entered the dugout. Cheers from their side of the stands washed like a tsunami over the East Lauderdale All-Stars. The wave of cheers fueled the kids' restlessness and excitement even further. Several teammates patted Rain on the shoulder, while others offered verbal encouragement. Rain acknowledged their support with smiles and high-fives.

As the Meridian All-Stars took the field for their infield practice, Coach Henry gathered his team around him. He bent down on one knee, and with a slow sweep, made eye contact with each player. The visitors' dugout grew as quiet as a church.

"Boys, I don't have to tell you what this game means today. There's much more at stake than a chance to call yourselves area champions. No, this game runs deeper than that. Today, you all have the opportunity to prove what your folks and I know already: that a boy growing up in the country has a much bigger heart and just as much, if not more, talent than these kids from the city. I want you all to look at them out there."

The boys craned their necks to see the players from the other team. Coach Henry continued. "Sure they've all got nice new white uniforms, and sure they're taking infield right now with brand-new baseballs, but that's the great thing about this game today. When Kenny Man steps into that batter's box and leads off for the East Lauderdale County All-Stars a few minutes from now, it won't matter how much money your daddy has or their momma has or who drives a showroom Cadillac and who drives a beat-up, old pickup. What will matter is which team has the heart and desire to win this game. Now, I know you're all excited, and so am I. But what I want you to do after we break is to take a seat on the bench and quietly think about how each and every one of you can make a contribution to help this team win today. If you're not a starter, think about how you can root for your teammates and still be prepared to go into the game at any time. At the plate, I also want you all to think about hitting the ball hard, either on a line or on the ground. And when you're in the field, I want you to analyze every situation and decide, before each and every pitch, what you'll do if the ball's hit your direction. Think about how much you're going to hustle and be mentally prepared every single moment you're here on this field today. Visualize yourself being successful, and you will be. Now, I wanna hear 'win' on three."

Coach Henry had gotten their attention. He thrust his right fist into the middle of the half circle, and fifteen other hands fell on top of his, creating a mountain of sweaty palms. "One, two, three!"

"WIN!" the kids shouted from the bottom of their lungs, and a new wave of cheers crashed down over them from their fans. Rain, Wayne, and the rest of their teammates sat down and quietly began mentally playing the game as their coach requested.

After a few minutes, the Meridian All-Stars finished their infield practice and Steven Atkins took the mound. While Coach Henry and Coach Chadwick shook hands with the umpires and exchanged lineups behind home plate, Rain made mental notes of Atkins's motion and his release point. Rain had never seen Atkins pitch before, and rumor had it that Coach Chadwick recruited him this past spring from Noxubee County to play for his regular season team, which, as usual, won the city's league championship. Whatever his history, Atkins appeared to possess only two pitches: a high velocity fastball and a slow, Frisbee-like curve.

Coach Henry returned from the umpires' meeting and called his players out of the dugout. "Okay, boys; let's line up along the third base line for the national anthem."

Once the visiting team assembled along its foul line, the announcer in the small wooden press box, well behind and high above home plate, clicked on his microphone. He spoke with a thick southern drawl and sounded as though someone overstuffed his mouth with cotton. From the shiny speakers sheltered by the roof's overhang, he sounded something like this: "Gud afernuun, ladies and genelmen an welcome to thuh Liddle League Field at Hilan Pahk. 'Day we got two fine teams gonna play some basebaw for us. One's from here in Meridyan and the other's come from commun-tees all ova Eas Lawdale Cownie. Now let's all stan for the singin' of our nashnal ancm."

Once everybody stood, the announcer played an

instrumental version of the "Star-Spangled Banner." Players from both teams removed their hats and held them over their hearts. As soon as the song finished, a roar arose from the stands unlike anything Rain had heard before. Everyone, on and off the field, was eager for the game to finally get started.

Kenny, Billy Joe, and Rain all stood near their on-deck circle, helmets on and bats swinging, while Steven Atkins threw his final warm up pitches. When Atkins nodded his readiness, the Meridian catcher, Jeremy Langford, threw down to second. Rain didn't know much about the pudgy Langford kid, but what he did know, he didn't like. Jeremy wore his uniform like a slob. His leggings were always bunched around his shoe tops and his shirttail hung untucked in the back. Though Rain couldn't prove he did it on purpose, two years ago during a similar all-star game, Jeremy spit dip on Rain's right cleat while he stood in the batter's box. When Rain backed out of the box and challenged him on it, he laughed and called it an accident.

The ball finished its trip around the infield and returned to Steven Atkins's glove. The umpire shouted "PLAY BALL!" and Kenny Man stepped in. On the second pitch, a fastball, he hit a hard ground ball up the middle, but Trip Chadwick, the shortstop, made a nice play and easily threw him out at first. Billy Joe Thompson went to the plate while Rain moved on deck and Wayne advanced into "the hole." On the third pitch, Billy Joe chased an outside curveball after falling behind in the count 0-2 and struck out. From the third-base coach's box, Rain's father shouted for Billy Joe to keep his head up as the crestfallen youngster dragged his bat through the dirt back to the dugout.

Rain strode to the plate, pausing for a few seconds before he entered the box. Out of his right ear, he heard Coach Chadwick shouting for his players to move over toward the left side of the field. Once they stopped, Rain surveyed their new positioning. They overplayed him to pull, which opened a big gap between first and second base. He checked his father at third. With an emphatic karate chop, Coach Henry urged Rain to hit the ball hard. Then, as had happened for the previous two hitters, the announcer introduced Rain to the crowd. "Now battin' third for Eas Lawdale Cownie, the pitchure, Rain Henry." In the very back of his mind, Rain confidently knew those rooting for his team applauded his introduction, but by now he had turned off his sense of hearing.

He settled into the rear portion of the batter's box, which would allow him a few more milliseconds to judge Atkins's fastball. Rain's eyes squinted as his mind elevated his sense of vision above all others. He studied the face of Steven Atkins. Rain knew from experience that if a pitcher is nervous or is having trouble with the strike zone, he will usually throw his best pitch. Many times a pitcher's best pitch is the fastball, which is more easily controlled. Sometimes, a pitcher will throw a fastball to get ahead in the count and set up his off-speed pitches. Or, a pitcher that can throw gas will zip in a fastball because he's confident he can smoke you. Atkins looked sure of himself on the mound, and he had started off Kenny and Billy Joe with fastballs. Based on those observations, Rain concluded Steven Atkins would want to intimidate him by demonstrating the strength of his arm. Rain concluded Atkins would try to blow a fastball by him with the first pitch to both send a message and try to get ahead in the count.

Atkins started his windup, and Rain focused on the area in space where the ball would be released. After the pitcher shoved forward with his delivery, his arm shot straight down from behind his head and Rain's eyes picked up a small, rapidly rotating sphere coming in fast and low. Fastball, Rain decided. The ball didn't look pure white, but instead gave a pinkish, off-white tint caused by the spinning stitches of the red seams. Almost instantly, Rain judged it to be too far inside and chose not to swing. A split second later, the ball crossed the inside portion of the plate at Rain's knees. As it did, Rain tracked its path all the way into the catcher's mitt. Atkins had thrown the one pitch that gave Rain trouble: a good, hard fastball over the inside corner at the knees. It was an excellent pitch, and the umpire called it a strike.

Rain stepped out of the batter's box and took a few practice cuts. Atkins had the ball again and stood poised on the rubber, waiting. Rain returned to the batter's box, but this time he positioned his feet farther from the plate and closer to his team's dugout. The heels of his cleats almost touched the back edges of the lines on the batter's box. This new stance would help him in two ways: he would have a better chance of extending his arms to handle another low, inside fastball and should Atkins throw an outside curve, which is what he expected next, he had more room to stride into the ball and hit it hard to the right side of the field.

Rain guessed correctly again. Atkins threw him an off-speed curveball. When the ball approached, it spun sideways which created a small red dot at the top. The pitch started for the middle of the plate, so Rain judged its break would carry it over the outside portion of the strike zone. He timed the pitch perfectly, and as Wayne had practiced at the batting cages, Rain stepped for the front edge of the plate and swung. He crushed a line drive between the first and second basemen for a base hit. Rain sprinted down the first base line, and upon reaching the bag, made a rounded turn for second. The entire time, he watched to see if the right fielder misplayed or juggled the ball enough for him to advance, but the outfielder played it cleanly and threw the ball hard into Trip Chadwick, who straddled second base. Safely at first, Rain allowed himself a quick glance into the stands. Catherine and Stacey stood and cheered with the rest of the East Lauderdale supporters. The smile on Catherine's face made him blush as he readjusted his helmet.

Little League rules do not allow players to lead off from the bases, so Rain positioned his left foot snugly against the edge of the bag as he checked his father's signs from across the infield. Wayne stood a few feet outside the batter's box and he, too, watched as Coach Henry gave the signs. Jim Henry touched his belt, knee, and then tapped the brim of his hat twice. The hat represented today's game indicator sign, which meant the next thing the coach touched would represent the play signal. Touching the hat twice meant he wanted Wayne to hit away. If Rain's dad had touched the hat and then his shirt, he would have wanted Rain to try to steal second base. Rain agreed with his father's decision not to have him steal at this point of the game. Jeremy Langford might be a jerk dressed like a slob, but Rain recalled he had an excellent arm. It would be touch and go if Rain tried to steal.

Rain clapped his hands for encouragement as his best friend dug in. Rain crossed his fingers and hoped Atkins would throw Wayne a fastball. Wayne was one of the best fastball hitters on the team, and if he connected, they could quickly be up 2-0 on the scoreboard. Atkins must have done his homework because he started Wayne with two curveballs that Wayne chased in the dirt. Atkins then made a mistake. Rain felt certain Atkins meant to throw the fastball outside of the strike zone to see if Wayne would chase it, but it instead sailed right over the middle of the plate. Wayne smashed a high fly ball deep to center. Because there were two outs, Rain took off at the crack of the bat. After rounding third, he checked over his inside shoulder and saw the centerfielder catch Wayne's fly ball up against the fence. If Wayne had hit the pitch anywhere but there, it would have been a two-run homer.

Coach Henry shouted out to the defense, "Be alert! Play smart!" as the East Lauderdale fielders ran from the dugout to their positions. He met Rain and Wayne at the dugout entrance, holding them up for some last-minute advice. Coach Chadwick offered quite the distraction; in the other dugout he had Steven Atkins by the jersey and screamed in his face to never groove fastballs to fastball hitters, especially on 0-2 counts.

Coach Henry lightly shook the battery mates to get their attention. "Hey! Ignore that stuff over there. Now, keep your heads up. We're gonna get to Atkins, especially if Chadwick helps rattle him for us. It's time to focus on getting these guys out. Rain, these kids have probably never seen the action from a knuckle curve. I want you to throw it and throw it often, particularly when you're ahead in the count. Wayne, you've got to block 'em if they hit the dirt, especially on third strikes and with runners on base." Both kids nodded and Jim Henry released Wayne to start putting on the catching gear.

Coach Henry pulled a folded paper lineup from his back pocket and opened it for Rain to see. "Rain, their big guns are the two, three, and four hitters. Chadwick, Langford, and the new kid Rosenblum. I want you to really bear down when these guys hit, okay?"

"Okay, Dad."

"Good, now you call your own pitches, but if you want a second opinion, shoot me a glance."

"Yes, sir."

The umpire called for them to speed things along, and soon Rain warmed up while his father caught. Rain heard the usual murmurs from the Meridian side of the stands as Jim Henry returned the ball to his son. The murmurs were similar to the sound a group of people make when the barker lifts the curtain on the bearded lady at the state fair. Although Rain had grown accustomed to this response from the other team's crowd, he always used the reaction to motivate himself even more. After Wayne waddled to the plate, squatted, and caught a fastball, a changeup and a knuckle curve, he zipped a throw down to their shortstop, Justin Sanders from Dalewood, who applied the tag on an imaginary runner trying to steal from first.

The ball passed from Sanders to Billy Joe at second and then to Buck Brown, their slick fielding third baseman from the town of Lauderdale. Buck trotted halfway to the mound and underhanded the ball to Rain. He gave Rain a determined nod and then added some final inspiration with a deep voice that had already reached puberty. "Aw right, Rain, show these boys howda pitch."

Rain returned Buck's nod with one of his own and sauntered up the back of the mound onto the rubber. The announcer introduced Meridian's leadoff hitter, but Rain didn't catch the kid's name, because he really didn't care. Rain brought the glove to his mouth and spoke to the ball. "All right, wasps, get ready for some stingin'."

The leadoff hitter, whatever his name was, didn't stand very tall. No doubt, he drew many walks because of his small strike zone. The kid's small stature might bother some pitchers, but not Rain Henry. After two heaters over the outside corner, shorty chased a knuckle curve, which he missed by a foot, and headed back to the dugout. In honor of the strikeout, Wayne fired the ball to Buck, who whipped it to Billy Joe, who flipped it to Justin, who returned it to Buck, who completed the cycle by tossing it back to Rain.

Trip Chadwick was announced next, and Rain stole a glance at Catherine to see her reaction. She didn't seem to smile, and only clapped softly once or twice. Maybe she had already decided to dump him after seeing Rain hit in the first inning. That, or she felt afraid to cheer for the enemy when everyone else seated next to her rooted for Rain and East Lauderdale. Rain tried to refocus on the game, but became distracted when Coach Chadwick yelled to Trip at the top of his lungs, "Move up in the box to hit that drop ball!" Trip didn't seem to want to obey; he moved up only about an inch, if that much.

Rain took a deep breath and nodded when Wayne called for the fastball on the inside part of the plate at the knees. If that leadoff hitter thought he saw heat, Chadwick was really in for a treat. For a second, Rain thought of nailing Chadwick with the pitch, but then decided to simply strike him out instead. Besides, Chadwick had never done anything to make Rain angry, and Rain had to admit that he admired Chadwick's taste in girls.

Rain unleashed his fastball, and it was a good one. He was surprised when Chadwick caught up with it, fouling the pitch to the backstop. Wayne got up and retrieved it, and after the umpire checked the ball for scuffing, he allowed Wayne to toss it back to Rain. Rain checked his father in the dugout. Jim Henry sat with his legs leisurely crossed as if he watched a Sunday night TV movie. With his right index finger, Jim Henry tapped his forehead. He wasn't calling a specific pitch, only reminding Rain to keep the hitter off balance.

Rain looked back at Wayne, who called a changeup. Rain agreed again and soon the cautious bandit wasp stealthily headed for the mitt.

The speed of the pitch fooled Chadwick. Way ahead with his swing, he barely put the ball in play down the third baseline. While the swinging bunt trickled toward third, Rain sprang from the mound and Buck Brown charged hard. Rain got to the ball an instant ahead of Buck and threw Chadwick out at first by half a step. Rain had made a tough play and the East Lauderdale fans roared their approval.

Jeremy Langford batted next, but three knuckle curves later, all he had made contact with were molecules of air. The third knuckle curve bounced in the dirt, but Wayne did an excellent job of keeping the ball in front of him and easily threw out Langford, who jogged down to first as if he had all the time in the world.

A standing ovation from the East Lauderdale fans greeted Rain as he walked from the mound to the dugout. He caught his grandmother's eye, and she gave him a wink. Mr. Williams stood tall and clapped loudly with his big, rough hands. Catherine and Stacey bounced up and down while they cheered from the top of the bleachers. Rain couldn't wait to see how everyone reacted after East Lauderdale actually won the game.

The pitching dominated, and neither team got a base runner aboard until the fifth inning, when Meridian's left fielder hit a blooper to right field. Rain struck out the next hitter with a fastball to end the threat. In the fourth, Rain lined out to Atkins and Wayne grounded out to Chadwick at short. The tension mounted as both teams started the top of the seventh and final inning locked in a 0-0 tie. Coach Chadwick paced the Meridian team's dugout like a caged animal, and Rain decided he could never play for anyone who berated his players for the slightest mistake, the way Coach Chadwick did. The more uncertain the outcome, the more volatile Chadwick became.

As he did before the start of the game, Coach Henry gathered the team around him once again. "Men, it's time we stopped playing around and won this thing. We've got the meat of the order coming up, so let's get some runs!" He singled out Billy Joe. "We need you to get on base. One run could very well win this game."

"Yes, sir, I'll get on," Billy Joe replied confidently.

Steven Atkins's fastball had come down a notch in velocity, but his curve still broke sharply. He maintained outstanding command of both and did an excellent job of mixing his pitches to keep the East Lauderdale's hitters off balance at the plate. After Atkins completed his warm ups, he and Billy Joe Thompson faced one another. Atkins delivered his first pitch, which, from the on-deck circle, Rain determined to be a curveball. At the last possible second, Billy Joe squared and pushed a perfect bunt up the first baseline. The bunt surprised everyone, including Atkins and Meridian's first baseman. Neither could make the play. As Billy Joe hustled by, Atkins scooped the ball with his glove and attempted a diving tag. He missed. Coach Chadwick threw his cap to the dugout floor and stomped on it. Rain could see the blood vessels in his neck pulsate as he screamed at the first baseman, accusing him of loafing. Chadwick called time and angrily strode to the mound.

Usually, when a coach visits the mound, he wants to talk to his pitcher, but Chadwick apparently had other ideas. He continued verbally undressing the first baseman in front of his teammates and everyone else. It appeared as though the poor kid, who Rain believed had tried his best, would start crying any second. If anyone deserved blame, it was Coach Chadwick for playing the kid too far behind the bag. Even the East Lauderdale contingent of fans, initially delirious with joy at Billy Joe's trickery, grew silent as Coach Chadwick's belligerence continued. Finally, even the umpire had heard and seen enough and sternly instructed Coach Chadwick to return to the dugout. Kicking the dirt as he left the mound, Coach Chadwick shouted for the third baseman to play in. "You, too, idiot," he seethed at the first baseman.

Finally, both sides were ready to continue. Rain checked his father at third, and once again, he flashed a series of signs. He touched his hat, then his belt, which put on the sacrifice bunt. But right after he tapped the belt, he gave Rain the karate chop. Coach Henry had put on a special play that teams use maybe once or twice during an entire season. Rain would square to bunt, just as he knew Coach Chadwick anticipated, putting the infielders in motion. The first and third basemen would charge, the shortstop would cover second, and the second baseman would race to the bag at first. However, instead of bunting, as the pitch arrived, Rain would pull back his bat and try to slap the ball past the moving infielders for a hit. The key was to maintain the element of surprise by fooling the fielders on the first pitch. If the scheme couldn't be executed with the first pitch, the other team would be better prepared for the trick play if they tried it again.

Rain stepped into the box. By now he considered Atkins a good pitcher, and every good pitcher knows to throw a high fastball strike in a sacrifice situation to try to get the bunter to pop the ball up. As he had done in the first inning, Rain moved as far away from the plate as he could. Rain knew exactly what he wanted to do.

Atkins wound, and as Rain hoped, a high fastball came directly over the plate. He squared to bunt, and while the infielders charged and shifted to cover their bases, at the last possible second, he pulled the bat back and slapped the ball hard on the ground past the charging first baseman, who dove out of the way to protect himself. The second baseman, who had been moving to first base anyway, dove to his left and knocked the ball down. Quick as a cat, he barehanded the ball, spun his body, and threw from his stomach to Trip Chadwick covering second. The throw barely beat Billy Joe, who slid in hard. It was one of the best plays in baseball Rain had seen at any level. The fans of the Meridian All-Stars went wild, jumping up and down on the metal stands until they shook on the verge of collapse. Yet the second baseman, Reece Rosenblum, seemed completely unaffected by what he had just done. He simply got up, dusted off the front of his uniform with a few strokes of his hand, and got ready to field again. In fact, none of the Meridian players showed any emotion whatsoever over the marvelous play they had witnessed. Coach Chadwick, who should have been elated at the fine defensive play, instead promptly benched the first baseman and started yelling at him again, this time for "costing him a double play by trying to protect his sorry candy-ass." Coach Chadwick had created a collective bunch of emotionless robots, and it frightened Rain to think that Chadwick dreamed of doing the same thing to him.

The new "go ahead run," Rain stood at first with one out. As Wayne calmly strolled to the plate from the on-deck circle, he planted a big kiss on the barrel of his Tennessee Thumper. Rain could only shake his head in astonishment. Here they were in the area championship game, and Wayne's giving his dusty bat a lucky smooch in front of all of these people! Rain wondered what Stacey thought of that stunt. Her face partially covered with her hands, she seemed to grimace. She and Catherine both stood with the rest of the fans, anxiously awaiting what would happen next.

Coach Henry gave Wayne the sign to hit away and implored him to stroke any curveballs to the opposite field.

Rain couldn't tell if Wayne listened or not. A strange look of concentration settled over his face as he stared down Steven Atkins. Wayne fouled back a fastball that represented another mistake pitch from Atkins. He took two curves for balls and fouled off a third. With the count at 2-2, Atkins tried to sneak a fastball by on the inside part of the plate, but Wayne crushed it. The sound of the metal bat meeting the ball must have echoed clear to the other side of Highland Park. Wayne launched a towering moon shot down the left field line, and Rain watched its flight from his position near second base. The baseball seemed to keep going and going, and as it went high over the foul pole, Rain decided it could be either fair or foul, depending on the spectator's angle. From where Rain stood, it looked fair.

The East Lauderdale fans erupted with jubilation, and so did Wayne who cruised to first, his arms raised high from emotion produced by pure ecstasy.

Quickly, everyone anxiously glared at the home plate umpire. "FOUL BALL!" he cried.

Rain cringed and headed back to first. When he approached the bag, he saw Coach Chadwick sincerely smile for the first time since the game started.

"Great call, Ump!" Chadwick offered from the dugout.

Rain doubted the umpire heard Coach Chadwick, however. Boos rained down from the East Lauderdale fans like angry storm clouds firing ice pellets. Even Rain felt sorry for him, and no one feels sorry for the umpires in baseball. Visibly drained by the quick ride on the emotional roller coaster, Wayne stopped on his way back to home and picked up his Tennessee Thumper.

Seeing the look on Wayne's face, Coach Henry called time out. The two met halfway between the third base coaching box and home plate. Jim Henry bent down and wrapped his arm tightly around the neck of his son's best friend.

"My goodness, you hit that one a long way."

"I thought it was fair, Coach Henry."

"Well, whatever it was, the ump called it foul, so we've got to put it behind us. You've still got to think about and visualize hitting the ball hard again. Can you do that, Wayne?"

"Yes, sir."

"Good. Now, I've watched this pitcher all day, and I think he's gonna throw you a curve on the next pitch. Like we practiced at Buddy's today, I want you to knock the cover off the ball and hit it to right field, okay?"

"Yes, sir."

"All right!" Jim Henry turned Wayne toward home and gave him a swat on the rump. "Get up there and get us a hit."

The pep talk seemed to help enormously, and Rain got ready at first as Wayne positioned himself for the next pitch. Atkins delivered, and Rain knew it was a curve from the arch and slower speed. As Rain hoped he would, Wayne stayed with the pitch and crushed a line shot over the leaping Reece Rosenblum. If Rosenblum had made that play, Rain would have stopped dead in his tracks and shaken his hand. Instead, Rain rounded second and visually picked up his father, who frantically waived him around third for home. The ball must have gone all the way to the fence, Rain decided, and he ran harder than he had ever run in his life. About three-fourths of the way to the plate, an alarm in Rain's internal baseball clock went off and told him it was going to be close. Buck Brown, who hit after Wayne, knelt in Rain's line of sight behind home and motioned with all of his strength for Rain to slide, slide! Buck looked like he tried to extinguish a brush fire with both of his palms as he slapped them hard against the ground. Jeremy Langford threw away his facemask and stood poised for the throw at the front of the plate. With his left leg and shin guard, Langford effectively blocked Rain's most direct path to paydirt. Rain's mind told him the only chance he had was a headfirst slide that aimed for the back corner. At the same time he heard the ball hit Langford's mitt, Rain slid. He felt the tag on his hip, but not before his left hand skidded over the beautiful, white smoothness that represented the last three inches of the plate where it narrowed into a point. He was safe and the umpire agreed. The East Lauderdale All-Stars took the lead over the Meridian All-Stars one to nothing.

Pandemonium erupted in the stands behind the visitors' dugout. Rain jumped two or three times in the air as the approaching wave of his teammates mobbed him. After a few seconds, Rain fought his way into the clear and solemnly pointed at his best friend, who stood calmly atop second base with his hands on his hips as though he had just conquered the world. Maybe he had. Wayne beamed back.

For a minute, the kids forgot they had a game to finish. Finally, the combined efforts of the umpire and Coach Henry calmed everyone down enough so play could resume. After collecting his breath, Rain checked the home dugout expecting another explosion from Coach Chadwick, but instead, he sat at the far end of the bench and blankly stared at something beyond the left field fence. His dusty cap sat in his lap, and he stroked it delicately with both hands.

Back in the dugout, Billy Joe told Rain the reason why he was safe: the new first baseman relayed Rosenblum's throw from the outfield grass, instead of letting it go all the way to the catcher. Rain thought he saw a look of redemption on the face of the former first baseman who sat, surreptitiously grinning, at the opposite end of the bench from Coach Chadwick.

The rest of the top of the seventh proved anti-climatic, comparatively speaking. Buck Brown flied out to left field, and Justin Sanders grounded out to Rosenblum at second. But no one who rooted for East Lauderdale seemed to care that their team didn't score any more runs. Today's game was in the bag. They were headed to Jackson.

After Rain finished his warm-ups, Buck Brown flipped him his customary underhand toss, and everyone stood on their feet. Fans from both sides cheered for their respective teams, and Coach Chadwick ordered his own players to get off the bench. After receiving their programmed instructions, the robots all lined the fence of the dugout and loudly shouted words of encouragement to their hitters. The noise on the field became almost deafening, and Rain found he had to concentrate even harder than normal to block everything out.

Rain and his team needed three outs, but he would have the challenge of facing the top of Meridian's batting order. Outwardly confident, the short leadoff hitter stepped in. He tried to duplicate Billy Joe's surprise bunt, but the ball spun and died two feet in front of the plate. Like a hungry panther on an injured rabbit, Wayne sprung from behind home plate, smothered the ball, and easily threw the copycat out at first.

"One down, two to go," Rain reminded himself. Trip Chadwick hit next, and Rain peered deeply into his eyes. Rain saw that Chadwick's spirit had vanished; he had already given up. His body language said he wanted to head home and sip lemonade by the pool in his backyard. Rain didn't know if Chadwick actually had a pool or not, but the thought of sending the rich kid back to his pool, imaginary or real, delighted him. Rain threw two fastballs that Trip Chadwick watched go by for strikes.

Obviously not impressed by his son's rigor mortis, Coach Chadwick's normal game persona came thundering back. From the third-base coach's box, he threatened Trip that he'd make him walk home if he watched another strike go by.

Rain decided to end Trip Chadwick's suffering with a knuckle curve and Chadwick swung like an old lady flailing her cane at a stray dog. He missed the pitch by a mile, but a funny thing happened. The knuckle curve bit into the dirt a mere inch in front of Wayne's glove, and, as he was supposed to do, Wayne collapsed his body to block the wild pitch. But this time, the ball refused to be tamed. It kicked off the heel of Wayne's mitt and ricocheted all the way to the edge of East Lauderdale's dugout.

Wayne leapt to his feet and discarded his facemask. Many voices screamed at once. Wayne screamed, asking where the ball went. Rain screamed it was over by the dugout. People screamed from the stands. But the most important scream came from Coach Chadwick. He screamed for Trip to run, and run he did. By the time Wayne retrieved the ball, Trip stood safely at first, representing the tying run.

His first wild pitch of the day stunned Rain and Coach Henry instructed his catcher to go calm his pitcher. Wayne asked for time, and the umpire granted his request. Wayne retrieved his facemask and shuffled to the mound.

"That was my fault, Rain. I should have blocked it."

"No, no. I should have blown another fastball by him."

"Hey, it's like your daddy told me when I hit that foul ball. It's over, now. Let's get these two more outs, so we can be the heroes, and then we'll get ready to meet the girls for some skatin'. It'll still be just like we planned. Now, if you can't whiff these next two hitters like you've been doing all day, I'm gonna have to kick your tall, skinny ass."

Rain laughed at his friend's bravado. "Yeah, I'd like to see you try. But you're right, it's time to end this thing."

"That's what I'm talkin' about, Rainman! Let's do it!" As he did in the bullpen, Wayne hit Rain hard in the chest with his mitt, then returned behind the plate.

Rain took a stroll behind the mound. He examined the distant oaks beyond the outfield fence and found they settled his nerves. Calmly, he climbed the mound and faced the hitter. He was ready to dominate his next victim. Jeremy Langford didn't stand a chance. He waved feebly at a changeup, swung over a knuckle curve, and watched a fastball whiz by for a called third strike on the outside corner. The East Lauderdale fans went crazy. Meridian was down to its last hitter. Only this kid named Reece Rosenblum stood between Rain and his teammates playing in the state championship tournament.

Again from the back slope of the mound, Rain collected

his thoughts and analyzed the situation. Rosenblum had hit most of Rain's pitches well all day. He had lined a changeup to Justin Sanders at short and rocketed a fastball down the third baseline that Buck Brown had to backhand before throwing him out at first. The only pitch Rosenblum hadn't hit hard was Rain's knuckle curve. All day, Rosenblum stayed disciplined enough to lay off the pitch that crossed the plate as a ball more often than not. For only the second time that day, Rain glanced at his father in the dugout. Coach Henry held his right hand over his knee, recommending his son throw the knuckle curve.

Rain stepped onto the rubber and after Wayne cycled through the signs for the fastball and changeup to the knuckle curve, Rain nodded. The pitch was a good one, but only ankle high after it broke over the front of the plate. Rosenblum watched it without swinging, and the umpire called it a ball. Should he throw it again? Rain checked his coach. Jim Henry recommended the same pitch.

"Bring it up just a touch, Son," his father shouted from the dugout. He also called out to the umpire, "Hey, Ump, remember it's where the pitch crosses the plate, not where it's caught."

Rain Henry threw another knuckle curve, a beauty. It broke precisely over the front of the plate, again, but this time finished at the knees. Wayne framed the pitch for several seconds, so the umpire could get a good look, but he still called it a ball. The fans from East Lauderdale booed and hissed. The 2-0 count was in Rosenblum's favor. He could look for his pitch, and most likely, he wanted a fastball. Rain didn't want to give in and throw him a fastball, but he also didn't want to take the chance to go 3-0, either. He didn't look at his father, because he decided on his own to fool Rosenblum with a changeup. Wayne agreed, and like an expert tightrope walker, the pitch clung to the fine black strip that represented the outside edge of the plate. Completely fooled, Rosenblum began his stride way to early. However, he checked his swing and the umpire again called the borderline pitch a ball. The count moved to 3-0, and the boos and catcalls rose several octaves as the East Lauderdale fans continued their verbal assault.

Wayne tossed the ball to his pitcher with a reassuring nod and Rain descended the rear of the mound again. He didn't want to take the chance of walking the tying run into scoring position and putting the potential winning run at first. He felt confident Rosenblum would get the take sign from Coach Chadwick. He'd be nuts to have Rosenblum swing away on a 3-0 count in this situation. For the heck of it, Rain checked his dugout, and the hand on the thigh told him his father agreed with the choice to go with the fastball.

Rain returned to the rubber, and as Wayne dropped his right index finger between his legs, Rain nodded and mentally challenged the wasp in his glove to sting the mitt right down the heart of the plate.

When Rain Henry let go of the pitch, everything moved in slow motion. Rosenblum's normally calm and cool demeanor changed. Rain noticed a wild look in Rosenblum's eyes that told him this kid didn't like to do what others expected. Rosenblum represented the rare type of individual that held a certain unpredictability no one could ever comprehend or understand. For the first time all day, Rain's baseball instincts were wrong. Dead wrong. Rosenblum swung on 3-0 and swung mightily. The ball seemed to cry from the inflicted pain of the bat as it was crushed high and deep. Seconds later, when the blast landed out of sight and into the ditch well beyond the center field fence, something changed deep within Rain Henry. For the first time in his life, baseball had not just beaten him, it had failed him. One pitch and one swing destroyed his innocent relationship with the game he loved.

While Rosenblum stoically circled the bases, Rain simply sat down on the soft manicured dirt at the top of the mound. He couldn't believe what had happened. He couldn't believe the game was over. Most of all, he couldn't believe he had finally gotten to pitch against the great all-star team from Meridian and had given up the game-winning homer.

Most of Rain's teammates couldn't believe what had transpired, either. Some, like Rain, sat on the field while others stumbled for the dugout. As Rosenblum crossed the plate and was mugged by the cheering androids, Rain peered into the crowd of East Lauderdale fans. Their mouths hung open, but no sounds escaped. They had become an inanimate flesh-colored wall of faces pocked by dark caves that led to an emptiness Rain felt as well. On the other side, the Meridian fans clamored from the stands and raced onto the field twirling and dancing as if they themselves had hit the home run.

Like a field medic, Coach Henry started the task of pulling the shell-shocked players to their feet and directing them off the field. Wayne met Rain at the mound and helped up his best friend. Without a word, Wayne guided them both to the entrance of the visitors' dugout.

As one might expect with a group of eleven and twelve-year-old boys, tears streamed down several cheeks. Each East Lauderdale player sat on the bench and stared at his shoelaces as if they possessed the power to reverse time and change the outcome of the game. Jim Henry, coach, father, and former baseball player himself, knelt in front of the team.

"Boys, you all played your hearts out, and I'm proud of you." He gestured at the stands where the wall of faces began to crumble as people gradually regained their senses and climbed from the bleachers. "All those folks who watched you play today are proud of you, too. You have nothing to be ashamed of, and I want you to keep your heads held high. Today, you learned a few important lessons I hope you remember for the rest of your lives. Don't assume anything's over until it really is, and never give up, because you've always got a chance. I tip my hat to their second baseman, because he never gave up."

Jim Henry checked over his left shoulder and saw that Coach Chadwick had quieted his team and had lined them up to shake hands. Coach Henry stood and asked for his players' attention. "Everyone, look at me. C'mon, now – look up here." Slowly, fifteen pairs of eyes met their coach's gaze. "I want all of you to wipe your faces on your sleeves and then go shake hands with those boys from the other team. Believe it or not, they wanted to win as badly as you did, and we should all wish them good luck in Jackson. After you shake hands, you're free to go. It's been a great summer of baseball, and you all have been a pleasure to coach. For you eleven-year-olds, Rain, Wayne and I look forward to playing you again in the regular season next year. For you twelve-year-olds, I wish you the best of luck when you start the Mustang League. Now let's go on over there and shake some hands."

As commanded, but without much enthusiasm, the East Lauderdale players marched single file across the infield and wished their counterparts the best of luck. Rain, still in a state of shock, walked at the end of the line. A few of the kids complimented Rain on his pitching performance and halfway through the Meridian players, Coach Chadwick shook his hand so hard Rain thought his arm would be ripped from its socket at the shoulder. The last three Meridian players were Jeremy Langford, Trip Chadwick, and Reece Rosenblum. Langford arrogantly sneered as he briefly touched Rain's hand. He said nothing after Rain wished him good luck in Jackson. Chadwick seemed neither happy nor sad, but carried a blank expression as he limply brushed Rain's outstretched palm. He, too, said nothing. When Rain met Rosenblum, the two kids paused momentarily.

Rain spoke first. "Good luck next weekend."

"Thank you. You pitched a great game. I got lucky."

Then, as athletes who carry a newfound respect for each other do, the two boys simply nodded at one another before they both spun back toward their respective sides of the field. Most of the East Lauderdale players were already headed for the parking lot with their parents. Many mothers held their sons tightly as they walked, their little boy's sides heaving from the sadness of watching a victory slip away so quickly.

Wayne and Coach Henry had packed away most of the equipment by the time Rain reached the dugout. Rain picked up the last two baseballs on the floor and tossed them into the elongated bag. His father zipped it closed.

"Tough luck, Son. I thought about throwing Roseblum another knuckle curve, but I sure didn't expect him to swing on 3-0."

"Me either."

Wayne picked up the bag containing the catcher's gear. "Coach, Rain made a good pitch; that kid just hit it hard."

"I know he did, Wayne. Don't worry, though, boys. I'm sure you'll have your chance at these characters again in the future." He motioned behind them. "I hope you're not too sad, because here come your dates for the evening."

Stacey and Catherine cautiously approached with melancholy faces. Catherine spoke ahead of her cousin. "Rain and Wayne, I thought you both played very well. The other team got lucky, that's all. Especially the kid who hit the home run."

"We're still meeting ya'll at the skating rink, right Wayne?" Stacey asked softly.

"I don't care. It's up to Rain," Wayne coolly answered.

Jim Henry left the dugout and began chatting with Wayne's father behind the bleachers. Rain swung his bag over his shoulder and started to leave. He wasn't going to say anything unless they forced him to. He wanted to walk away and be by himself.

"Rain, don't you want to meet us at the skating rink?" Catherine asked him directly.

Rain stopped but didn't turn. He spoke in the general direction of the left field foul pole. "I don't know."

Catherine looked at her cousin. Stacey shrugged. Catherine motioned for Stacey to stay where she was and then walked over to Rain. Rain refused to look at Catherine Landerson. If she tried to walk to his left, he spun to his right. When she cautiously approached from the right, he twisted back to his left. Rain didn't want her to see the tears that stained his face.

Finally, Catherine spoke to the back of his head. "Okay, Rain. Fine. Stacey and I are going skating tonight, and I hope you and Wayne come. If you don't, I'll find someone else to couple skate with, and so will Stacey. I'm sorry you lost, but it's only a game."

Catherine Landerson returned to Stacey and the two strutted, noses pointed at the sky, for Mrs. Cottrell, who waited for them in the parking lot by the family station wagon.

Wayne left the dugout and stood next to his friend. Rain had stopped crying, but was in no mood for chatter.

"Dang, Rain, can't you tell that Catherine wants you to go skatin'? She likes you, man. I overheard what she said and she's right, you know."

"About what?"

"About the fact it's only a game. A game we lost and can't do nothin' about, now. Heck, let's go skatin' with 'em. It'll cheer us both up."

"That's easy for you to say, Wayne. I didn't see that Rosenblum kid jackin' one off you. You can go skatin' by yourself."

Wayne rolled his eyes. "Fine, I will."

Jim Henry and Royston LeRoy approached the boys. "Ain't ya'll ready to go yet? What the heck are you girls talkin' about over here, anyway?" Mr. LeRoy asked.

"Skatin', Daddy. Rain's bein' a baby. Says he don't want to go skatin' cause we lost the game."

"Skatin'!" Mr. LeRoy laughed. "Boy, you ain't goin' skatin!"

Wayne stared back with disbelief at his grinning father. "What are you talkin' 'bout, Daddy? Momma done said she's gonna take us and pick us up tonight. Me and Rain got dates with Stacey and Catherine. I planned it weeks ago."

Mr. LeRoy laughed again. "Well, I guess you might could go. How much money you got saved up?"

"I dunno, Daddy. Maybe twenty dollars."

Mr. LeRoy whistled through his teeth. "Son, I'm afraid that ain't enough. Roy Junior's stereo cost eighty bucks, and since you ruined it with that baby powder stunt last night, it's only fair that you buy him a new one. I wanted to whip you and be done with it, but your momma felt sorry for you. She said you outta just be grounded until you've saved enough money for a new stereo."

Jim Henry acted as surprised as the two boys. "Rain, did you have any part in this?"

"Yes, sir." Rain answered timidly. He wondered how much worse the day could get.

Jim Henry took his wallet from his back pocket and handed Mr. LeRoy two twenty-dollar bills. "Roy, I think Rain should pay for half of that stereo." He turned to his son. "Rain, you're also on restriction until you pay me back. I think you said you had thirty dollars in allowance saved up, so you can work off the extra ten by helping Mr. Williams and me clear some trees next weekend."

Mr. LeRoy took the money and shoved it in the front pocket of his jeans. "Thank you, Jim. That sounds like a good idea. I've been wantin' to re-sod the back yard, and I think I'll have Wayne help me with that."

After parting handshakes, the fathers and sons headed for their vehicles. Rain faintly heard Wayne vehemently begging his daddy to just whip him and not take all his money. Mr. LeRoy continued to laugh as he declined Wayne's offer. Rain and his father were the last two to leave, except for Coach Chadwick and a few players who raked the infield's dirt. One of Meridian's players ran laps counterclockwise along the fence. Rain figured Chadwick had decided to further punish the first baseman. As the player ran past the left field fence and turned to face their old dugout, Rain recognized the punishment's recipient. It was Reece Rosenblum.

"Look, Dad! Coach Chadwick's got Rosenblum running laps."

"Looks like you're right, Son. I wonder why."

"Let's go ask him."

Jim Henry hunched his shoulders and raised his eyebrows. "Why not? I gotta admit I'm a little curious myself."

Rain's father pulled the pickup behind the home plate fence, precisely between the two sets of bleachers. He leaned out the window as Rosenblum stoically jogged past. "Hey Dick, why is the game's MVP running laps."

Coach Chadwick leaned forward from where he sat on his dugout's bench. "Son-of-a-bitch ignored my take sign on a 3-0 count."

CHAPTER SIX
THE RAILROAD COMES TO VIMVILLE

His shower completed, Rain left the cramped hospital bathroom and returned to the uncomfortable vinyl and steel chair across from his dying father. He slid on his dress shirt without its customary T-shirt underneath and the fabric felt foreign to his bare chest. Although he talked himself into reusing the dress socks, Rain drew the line at wearing his boxers for a second straight day. He wadded the pair worn last night into the corner of his overnight bag, next to the dirty undershirt. Rain hoped either to buy some new clothes that afternoon, or at a minimum, have some brought to him from New Orleans. The hands on the wall clock read 7:14. Catherine would arrive shortly.

Rain slipped on his dress shoes and headed for the door. On the way, he checked over his father and the connections of the tubes that ran in and out of his body like thick electrical wires. As Rain decided everything seemed fine to his untrained eye, he heard a soft knocking.

Rain leaned down and whispered to his father, "I'm going to get some breakfast, Dad. I'll be back soon. Can I bring you back anything?"

Jim Henry's expression never changed. His eyes remained closed, his lips silent.

"I'll take your lack of a response at my invitation as a no." Rain tried to force a smile but could not. He again stroked his father's left arm. "Only kidding, Dad. I'll be back in a second. You just lie there and get some rest. Love you."

After Rain met Catherine in the hall, they headed for the elevator, the same one Rain had ridden earlier that morning with Dr. Littleton.

"Rain, I imagine you're running short on clothes. You can take my car if you want to go buy some."

"No, I'd rather..."

Catherine cut him off with a smile and the wave of her hand. "Don't worry about being away from the hospital. I got this pager for you in case anything happens. Maybe you can go later this morning after Dr. Littleton checks on your father." She dug in her suit pocket and handed Rain a small, rectangular pager.

Rain hooked it over his belt. "Thanks, Catherine."

"No problem. We're treating you the same way we do all of the out-of-town relatives of our ICU patients. Pagers are standard issue, but the car's a special offer."

A few minutes later, they reached the cafeteria, entered the food line, and picked up their trays. Despite Rain's earlier stomach rumblings, he found his appetite lacking. He settled on a miniature box of raisin bran, two half-pints of milk, and a banana. Catherine's tray held a small bowl of mixed fruit and a bottle of orange juice. When they reached the register at the end of the line, Catherine picked up the tab. The two settled at a small table in the corner. The cafeteria was still relatively empty.

Catherine unscrewed the top to her juice while Rain dumped his cereal into a small plastic bowl. Catherine took a long swig and leaned forward.

"Rain, seeing your father like that reminds me of how quickly time can get away from us. I'm still having trouble believing that today is the first time we've seen each other in over ten years. Do you remember the first time I ever saw you pitch? We were all supposed to go skating after the game, but you and Wayne never showed."

Rain swallowed his mouthful of raisin bran. "I guess I wasn't in the best of moods after Reece hit that homerun to win the game." He then took a chug of milk. "You regret we didn't go?"

"Maybe," Catherine answered playfully.

"I'm sure Stacey told you we got in trouble for a prank we pulled on Wayne's brother the night before. We couldn't have gone, even if we'd wanted to. So, on one hand, you could say Reece did us a favor by beating us. I think the whole experience changed Wayne and me forever. It taught us both the close association between disappointment and depression. Anyway, you ever see him around town?"

Catherine's posture straightened. She had hoped to relive what might have been if they had met that night at the skating rink. What she had never told anyone, including Stacey, was that she had broken up with Trip Chadwick the night before that all-star game in anticipation of becoming Rain's girlfriend. Now, Rain steered the conversation in another direction. Catherine sighed. "Who? Reece Rosenblum?"

Rain nodded. "Yeah."

"We see him every now and then at fund-raising events and balls. You know, he kind of distanced himself from the people at Pamar after he left."

For the first time in a long time, Rain's cheek muscles pulled back, creating a wide smile. "He sure did, didn't he?" It was more of statement than a question.

The March morning began like any other school day. Rain was a fifteen-year-old ninth grader and already possessed his unrestricted driver's license. Instead of Mrs. LeRoy picking him up for school, Rain drove Wayne to Jeff Davis in his father's former work truck. Jim Henry didn't need the services of "Old Blue" anymore, because Rain's grandmother bought her son a new pickup for Christmas. The faded blue Chevy got handed down to Rain like a ragged, old sweater, but he felt delighted to get it. It was also the same truck his father had used during his former coaching days, which abruptly ended after both Rain and Wayne made the varsity baseball team at Jefferson Davis Academy. Rain never got the chance to pitch against the Meridian All-Stars again, and Coach Henry's East Lauderdale All-Star teams never advanced past the area championship game. Now, the big games for Rain and Wayne would pit the baseball, football, and basketball teams of Jeff Davis against their archrivals from Pamar Academy.

The ninth grade student body had lost one student since the fifth grade and now consisted of twenty-two teenagers. The freshman class had also graduated from the wooden junior high building the previous year and subsequently moved two hundred yards over to the sandstone-colored brick high school.

Freshman study hall, which was held every Monday, Wednesday, and Friday morning at 11:00, had reached its midpoint. Instead of the rows of connected desks from junior high and elementary school, Rain found himself seated at an individual tabletop desk on the left side of the classroom. He busily worked on completing his French homework, which was due later that afternoon. Wayne and Stacey sat next to each other in the middle of the class. This seating arrangement represented their compromise. Wayne had always sat in the back and Stacey in the front before they became boyfriend and girlfriend in the sixth grade. When Rain thought about it, he still found it hard to believe they were together. They had been "in love" for more than three years.

Rain took a break from conjugating irregular verbs and stole a glance at the two lovebirds. Stacey's face wrinkled and she slapped her hand over her forehead in frustration. Must be trying to help Wayne study for their history test tomorrow, Rain concluded.

At about 11:30, a loud knock at the classroom door interrupted their studies. The door cracked open and Ted Stark, the baseball coach and high school's science teacher, stuck in his head. He grinned wider than a first-time father.

Coach Stark made eye contact with the elderly study hall monitor, who sat at the large desk at the head of the class. "Sorry to interrupt, Mrs. Crum. We've got a new student and I wanted him to meet his classmates as soon as possible."

He opened the door the rest of the way like a game show host revealing the prize behind curtain number one. Rain immediately understood his coach's giddiness. The prize was Reece Rosenblum. He simply stood in the doorframe, motionless and emotionless. His face looked as blank and empty as the cover of the new spiral notebook he held in his left hand. Over the years, Reece hadn't grown much taller, but had become thick, like the trunk of an old oak tree. He was solid muscle.

Rain always wondered what passion, if any, lived deep within Reece Rosenblum. Surely something existed beyond the external stoic mask of ambivalence he wore so well on the baseball field. Perhaps, Rain concluded, he would now have the opportunity to find out.

Coach Stark's lips started moving again. "Mrs. Crum, class, this is Reece Rosenblum. He's decided to join us here at Jefferson Davis Academy. Some of you may already know Reece from playing against him in summer league baseball."

Coach Stark patted Reece on the shoulder and nudged him a tad forward. The class remained silent as Reece fed this newly generated kinetic energy with a few steps of his own. Then, he hesitated. Rain decided, empathetically, that if twenty-two pairs of eyes attempted to dissect his soul, he'd hesitate, too.

On cue, Mrs. Crum stood from her chair. "Glad to have you, Reece. We're about halfway through study hall, so please find an open seat and sit down. Do you have anything to study?"

Reece shook his head, so Mrs. Crum pulled open one of the drawers of her desk. "Here, you can read this." She handed Reece a dusty copy of an old science magazine as he passed by.

Rain and Wayne exchanged glances. Rain's eyes danced with delight and so did Wayne's. Both boys knew that Reece might carry enough weight to tilt the athletic scales in their favor. Each tried to make eye contact with Reece. Rain wanted to silently extend a welcome, but Reece seemed content to stare at the center of the magazine spread open before him. His head hovered only a few inches above the pages. Reece Rosenblum became a spider trying to spin an invisible web that might shield him from the probing visual jabs shot from every direction.

Thirty minutes later, the bell ended study hall and signaled the beginning of lunch period. Reece was the last one to leave the classroom. The hallways had already filled with students by the time Reece entered the throng of teenagers moving in all directions. Most wanted to drop their books off at their lockers before heading to the cafeteria.

Jeff Davis had a small student body, the kind where everyone knew everyone else, and as Rain observed Reece slink down the hall, whispers from the inquisitive other students swirled around the new student like bees swarming a hive. Reece's eyes never left the floor, and Rain felt sorry for his former all-star adversary.

Rain and Wayne's lockers were located side by side. Here, they waited as Reece slowly plodded in their direction. As Rain hoped, Reece stopped at the vacant locker on the other side of Wayne's.

Reece had to look up when he got to his locker to spin the numbers on the combination lock, and as his eyes moved from the floor up to the locker, Rain thrust his head to within a foot of the new student's face and mirrored his movements. Reece had no choice. Finally, he made eye contact with someone.

Rain stuck out his hand and sarcastically grinned. "Rain Henry, nice to meet you."

Wayne did the same. "Wayne LeRoy, welcome to JD."

Reece's face indicated he didn't pick up on the sarcasm right away. Then, after a few awkward seconds, he cracked a thin smile. "I know who ya'll are," he said coyly and shook their hands.

"Jeez, Reece, we didn't know, with the way you were actin' and all," Wayne commented with raised eyebrows. "I thought maybe your dog died this mornin' or somethin'. This ain't Pamar, but we did ditch the outhouses for indoor plummin' last year."

The three boys laughed together at Wayne's joke. "It's not that, Wayne. I just got into some trouble at home, that's all."

"Trouble, what sort of trouble? What'd you do, get kicked out of Pamar?" Rain conjectured.

"Sort of. I got suspended, but I'm not going back there."

"Suspended for cheatin'?" Wayne asked.

"No, I got in a fight with a tenth grader."

"How come?" Rain inquired. By now, he was willing to skip lunch, if necessary, to hear the rest of this story. It was getting good, and Reece's mask seemed to be thawing.

"Kept calling me names."

"Like what?" Wayne and Rain asked together.

Reece squirmed. "C'mon guys. It's been a rough couple of days. I don't really feel like going through the whole story for the hundredth time."

"Okay, then. Just give us the highlights," Rain offered.

Reece deposited his green notebook, closed the door of his locker, and gave the combination knob a spin. "If I do, will you leave me alone long enough to eat lunch? I'm really hungry."

"Sure," Wayne responded for them both.

"Thank you. There's really not much to tell, anyway. This guy and I used to be pretty good friends, but over the last few months he started hanging out with a weird crowd at Pamar."

"What do you mean by 'weird crowd?'" Rain inquired.

"There were three or four kids that started talking and meeting secretly about white supremacy and the KKK. You know, calling black people niggers, saying the South was a better place when white people had slaves. That sort of stuff."

Wayne interrupted. "So, you got pissed because some white boys called some black folks niggers? I don't want to shock you, Reece, but people out here call 'em niggers, too. That or darkies, or colored people when they feel like bein' nice."

Rain stood silent. His father and grandmother raised him to respect people of all races and colors, but if he reprimanded everyone he ran across that used the word "nigger" he would go hoarse.

Reece continued. "That doesn't make it right, Wayne. What if people called you a redneck or a cracker?"

"I wouldn't care. I probably am a redneck *and* a cracker."

"See there's the difference," Reece replied. "Black people *do* care. They don't like being called those names."

Rain stepped in. "Reece's right, Wayne. End of the debate about what everyone calls black people. I'm starting to get hungry, too. Go on with the story, Reece."

"Anyway, I understand that I live in Mississippi and I've got to deal with ignorant people. And even though I never approved of it, it really didn't bother me a whole lot that these kids were running around saying the word 'nigger.'" The look he gave Wayne indicated his interruption had done nothing but waste their time. "What bothered me was when these kids starting drawing swastikas on the backs of their hands and studying Hitler."

"What the hell is a swastika?" Wayne asked.

Rain released a long, condescending sigh. Wayne's question served as yet another reminder of how history was not his strong suit. "Wayne, that was your last question until Reece gets finished. A swastika was the symbol of Nazi

Germany before and during World War II. It looks kinda like two flat S's crossing in the middle. If you'd have paid attention in history class last year instead of drooling over Stacey's legs the whole time, you'd remember." He turned to Reece. "Reece, don't stop again. If Wayne says something, just ignore him and keep talking."

An irritated look crossed Wayne's face, but he remained silent.

Reece picked up the story again. "The swastikas bothered me. Why? I'll tell you. That bastard Hitler exterminated millions of us. Yes, I'm Jewish." He paused for a few seconds. "I guess this group of kids learned I was Jewish, and someone told me one of the members, the tenth grader, began referring to me as the 'Reece's Peanut Butter Jew' behind my back. I tracked him down in the hall and asked if what I had heard was true. Some of the other members of this group happened to be with him, so I guess he felt emboldened. He got in my face and called me that name."

Rain noticed that Wayne twitched with anticipation. Rain knew his best friend loved a good fight, and this story had all the makings of a rumble to remember. Rain anxiously guessed at what happened next. "So you fought this kid after school and the teachers found out about it?"

"Nope. I punched the kid right there on the spot. Hit him as hard as I could and square in the nose. He crumpled to the ground and blood gushed everywhere. His buddies jumped on me, but by that time several teachers had arrived. They separated us before I could teach the rest of his racist friends a lesson, too. Heard later the kid's nose was broken in three places, but I didn't care. He deserved it. When I wouldn't apologize to him and his father at a suspension hearing for 'overreacting' at what the kid referred to as 'making a joke,' Pamar suspended me. I guess since his dad's on the school board, they said I could only come back when I apologized, so my mom and I decided it was time to go to another school. That's the story, and here I am."

Wayne looked thoroughly impressed. "Damn, Reece. I want you to promise right now that you'll let me know if I ever do anything to piss you off. That way I can get a running start and avoid catching the power punch to the nose. Was this kid anybody we knew?"

"Probably, you two have played against him in all-stars. His name's Trip Chadwick."

Rain's mouth dropped open. He wondered if Catherine knew what a jerk her boyfriend had become. "Trip Chadwick! Were there any other Meridian all-stars in that group?"

"Yes. Jeremy Langford, the catcher."

Like a long-lost brother, Rain Henry and Wayne LeRoy openly extended their bond of friendship to Reece Rosenblum. Within his first few weeks at Jefferson Davis Academy, brick by brick, Reece dismantled the wall it had taken years to build around his personality. With Rain and Wayne by his side, Reece's entire demeanor transformed from that of a walking hermit into one of a confident, gregarious young man. Reece became not only one of the most popular boys in the ninth grade, but a favorite of the entire high school. He was smart, responsible, and respectful, so the teachers loved him. In athletics, he combined a hard-nosed, hustling attitude with strength and natural ability, so the coaches loved him. In fact, Reece's only shortfall, ironically, was his physical height. Although thick and muscular, he was the shortest person in the entire building, so the girls liked him, but refused to love him. But, the new Reece accepted this in stride. For the first time in his life, he had not one, but two best friends and an entirely fresh outlook on the world spread before him.

Rain and Wayne also made it their personal mission to indoctrinate Reece to the ways of a country boy. They made him listen to Hank Williams, Jr., until he knew the words of each song by heart. In fact, Reece spent the night with either Rain or Wayne at least one night every weekend. During the days, the trio would explore the hundreds of acres of fields, forests, streams and rivers that comprised the Henry

Farm. They became inseparable, and many times Rain and Reece would tag along on Wayne's dates with Stacey for she, too, wholeheartedly welcomed Reece into their circle of friendship.

Okatibbee Creek looked more like a river by the time it reached the Henry Farm and meandered lazily through the back portion of the property. At the southwestern edge of the farm, the creek passed under an old railroad trestle. The Southern Line, which had connected Mobile to Meridian for more than 100 years, ran parallel to that edge of the Henry property. Twice a day, freight trains going each direction wailed their passing as they crossed the creaky wooden bridge.

The three boys came to love that trestle. The biggest catfish in the creek could be caught with chicken livers at the base of its thick supports. During the summer after the ninth grade, Reece hooked and landed a channel cat as long as Rain's leg.

The accumulation of fine brown sand that had collected over hundreds of years along the adjacent eastern bank provided the perfect spot for building a bonfire, cooking the day's catch, and toasting marshmallows. The hard ground atop the high bank on the western edge of the creek supported the stakes that held the boys' tent when they camped overnight.

But best of all was the trestle itself, for it served as a diving platform some twenty-five feet or so above the surface of the creek. The currents carved a deep channel immediately beyond where the water re-emerged from its passage under the bridge. Into this channel Rain, Wayne, and Reece entered the water with dives, flips, or twisties. If they pointed their feet at the water and fixed their bodies straight and rigid like a telephone pole, they could shoot all the way down to the creek bottom, where the soft cool mud squished soothingly between their toes. Other times the boys molded their bodies into cannon balls, can openers, preacher seats, or some other form of human bomb, which exploded with huge splashes upon impact with the water. Rain and Wayne were astonished to learn that Reece had never before swum in a creek or a river until they introduced him to the trestle that first summer after he came to school in Vimville.

One cool Saturday morning in March, the three boys struck out for their favorite railroad bridge. Almost exactly a year had flown by since Reece first walked through the door into study hall at Jeff Davis. The three tenth graders carried Rain's .22-caliber rifle and a basket of fresh fried chicken Rain's grandmother had cooked for their lunch. They planned to have a picnic between the trestle's two parallel steel ribbons that seemed to run forever, or at least until they disappeared around the distant bend. If they happened to see any river turtles or snakes while they ate, the reptiles would be fair game for target practice.

Reece especially enjoyed target practice. He had never shot a rifle of any kind until the previous summer, again thanks to Rain and Wayne's efforts to expose their new friend to essential "country living" skills. Reece fell in love with shooting guns. At first, his aim was worse than atrocious, but that changed after he begged his mother to buy him his own rifle for his birthday. It was the only gift he wanted and the only one he said he'd accept. Finally, his mother relented and purchased Reece a top-of-the-line semi-automatic .22, complete with scope. Day after day, if he wasn't with Rain and Wayne, Reece Rosenblum practiced with his .22 at the Meridian Shooting Gallery. Within six months following his birthday, Reece could shoot George Washington's eyes out of a quarter from a hundred yards away. Rain and Wayne knew this because that was the bet they had lost with him about a month ago. But today, Reece seemed a little out of sorts. The way he acted reminded Rain of when he first came to Jeff Davis. It was as though he had searched his attic at home and found the box that stored his protective mask.

The three sat on tracks in the middle of the trestle and

started in on the fried chicken. The aluminum foil had kept the pieces nice and warm, and the salty, greasy, golden batter tasted delicious. The boys wiped their mouths on the sleeves of their windbreakers and their hands on their jeans. They didn't see any turtles in the cold, murky, water, and Rain decided it was most likely because they were still buried deep in the mud. The snakes probably still hibernated, too.

Rain thought about trying to uncover the reason for Reece's sullenness when Wayne beat him to it. "Reece, what's eatin' you?" he asked between chews of fried chicken. "You ain't said a word the whole way out here."

Reece took the first bite of his buttermilk biscuit. "It's my dad. He's being a jackass again. A few months ago, I got this idea that it might be cool to go up and hang out with him for a few weeks this summer. He's got this forty-five foot sailboat docked on the Hudson River that Mom says he never uses. I decided to do all this research and plot a course for us to sail down to the Bahamas and back. Even Mom thought it would be a good idea and said I could go."

Rain swallowed a mouthful of fried chicken. He realized how lucky he and Wayne were to have the kind of father-son relationships they had. He tried to empathize with his friend and proceeded as gently as possible. "So I guess your dad said no."

"Hell yes, he did. Turned it down in less than a second. He wouldn't listen even when I tried to tell him I'd do all the work with the sails and the whole boat, for that matter, if he'd only show me how. Then Mom got on the phone, and they got into a big fight. Dad hung up on her." Reece stared into the distance. "My dad's acted like a complete jerk ever since I was ten years old, right after Mom decided to move us from Newark to Meridian to live with her sister. He was really pissed when we left. Claimed we abandoned him. I guess he's still not over it."

Today represented the first time Reece even remotely confided anything regarding his family to Rain and Wayne.

In the past, Reece made it quite clear that his religion and his family were off-limits, and should never be discussed under any circumstances. Sometimes Rain tried to imagine Reece's home life. It was difficult to do, because while Reece had stayed over with Rain and Wayne dozens of times, almost becoming another member of their respective families, Rain and Wayne had spent the night at his house only once. That was after his birthday party last November.

"Did he tell your mom that was why he didn't want see you?" Rain inquired.

Reece flipped the last bite of his biscuit into Okatibbee Creek. The small blob slightly expanded as it soaked up the muddy water and then gradually sank beneath the surface. "I don't think so. He just said he was too busy. Claims running his company takes all of his time. You know, I'm sixteen now, and I've probably seen him twice over the last six years."

Wayne shook his head back and forth. "That sucks, man." Sometimes Wayne's succinct way of putting things spoke volumes.

"Yeah, that sucks," Rain agreed. He tried to think of something to say that would make Reece feel better. "At least now you've got two extra weeks this summer to hang out with us."

"Thanks for trying to help, Rain. No offense, but I'd rather sail down to the Bahamas."

"I guess I'd rather sail to the Bahamas than hang out with us, too," Wayne agreed.

Lunch finished, the three boys sat together silently, their legs dangling over the edge of the trestle. Each allowed their specific thoughts to carry them away. Wayne wondered if Stacey would miss him if he left for two weeks to go sailing and then decided he'd probably take her with him. Rain remembered the Bahamas' historical ties to Great Britain and pondered whether or not cars in the Bahamas drove on the right or the left hand side of the road as a result. Reece imagined an old and wealthy man in a hospital bed, bitterly dying alone because his beloved money couldn't afford the type of friends who cared if he lived or died.

Rain broke the silence. "Know what we could all do this summer?" he asked breathlessly.

"What?" Wayne and Reece said together.

"We could build a raft or get a canoe and float down the Okatibbee! It wouldn't be sailing to the Bahamas, but have you ever looked at a map? This creek links up with the Chunky River around Enterprise, then joins the Chickasawhay River. Farther down it becomes the Pascagoula River and flows into the Gulf of Mexico. We'd camp all the way down and hunt and fish for whatever we needed to eat. I bet we could get my dad to come get us when we finished the trip!"

Wayne bought in to the idea immediately, but Reece seemed less than even remotely interested. "We could just as easily jump in a train and go wherever we wanted, and we'd get there a lot faster," Reece said.

Rain caught a strange twinkle in Reece's eyes. It was the exact same look Rain had seen before Reece hit that infamous home run years ago.

"Reece, what the hell are you talkin' 'bout? I think Rain's got a good idea. It sounds fun. Besides, I ain't interested in hoppin' no train like a hobo," Wayne declared.

Before the debate could begin in earnest, they were interrupted by the powerful sound of a diesel engine horn approaching from around the bend to the southwest. Rain determined the train to be about a half-mile away, but he knew it approached quickly. As recently as the previous summer, the trains would slow to a crawl as they traversed the rickety wooden bridge. Now, after the railroad company reinforced the trestle about six months ago, the freight trains rounded the corner at full speed and crossed the bridge going between fifty and sixty miles an hour.

"C'mon, we've gotta get off this bridge," Rain ordered as he gathered the basket and the plastic jug of water.

Wayne, who had been holding Rain's .22, was already

headed to safety at a brisk clip. He didn't run, but hurriedly walked like a bank robber trying to leave the scene of the crime as fast as possible without drawing suspicion. Wayne LeRoy was too cool a customer to appear to panic. Rain jogged to catch up with him, which he did with a few hundred feet to go before they reached the end of the bridge. Reece followed right behind him, or so he thought. When they climbed off the tracks and onto solid ground, Wayne wheeled to continue the river versus rail debate with Reece, but Reece wasn't there.

Rain and Wayne gasped at the same time. There, where they had just finished their picnic in the middle of the trestle, stood Reece Rosenblum. He stood atop one of the steel rails and waved at them the way a child waves goodbye to his parents. It was the type of exaggerated gesture that says, "If I never see you again, I hope you'll remember this goofy image of me waving goodbye."

Wayne muttered, "Jesus," then screamed with his hands cupped around the sides of his mouth. "Run, Reece, you dumb ass! Get off that bridge!"

But Reece gleefully continued to wave. His lips, which earlier created a straight line across his face, were now upturned at the corners in a dastardly smirk.

Like laying in the final piece of a puzzle, everything clicked in Rain's mind. It all made sense. "Wayne, I think he wants to kill himself. That's what he meant when he said 'jump in a train,'" Rain mumbled.

"Ain't gonna happen! I'm gonna go drag his sorry ass off that bridge. That way he'll owe me for the rest of his life." With grim determination, Wayne started scrambling back up the embankment to the tracks.

Rain tackled him. "Wayne, you can't! There isn't time! Look!" He pointed to the line of trees that shrouded the edge of the bend. Like the head of a metal-jointed snake, the engines of the freight train emerged. It raced along on the tracks faster than Rain ever remembered, and its ear-shattering horn ripped through the spring air. Angry black plumes of soot shot from the tops of the engines like dark, ominous smoke signals. Reece seemed completely oblivious to his impending doom. In fact, Reece appeared to be bent over, laughing hysterically, and Rain squinted to make sure his eyes weren't deceiving him. Rain failed to find the humor in this macabre scene and grew angry that Reece wanted to permanently scar his friends by having them witness his own selfish and masochistic destruction.

At any time, Rain expected the train's conductor to slam on the brakes, but Rain knew it wouldn't make any difference. It would be impossible for the train to stop now until it had already crossed the bridge. He braced for the shrill screams of the locked wheels as they skidding along the tracks, but the dreaded sound never came. The conductor must have been reading something or simply not been paying attention, because the train hit the trestle at full speed. It never slowed.

When the train reached the start of the bridge, Wayne covered his eyes and sobbed. Rain thought his reaction would have been similar, but instead he couldn't avert his gaze from the sight before him. His mind forced him to watch the death of Reece Rosenblum.

When the train came within twenty yards of splattering their friend like a juicy bug, Rain watched as Reece raised his arms to the heavens, took two steps backward and executed a perfect back flip off the edge of the bridge. His red windbreaker flapped in the breeze as he fell, and just before he entered the water, he thrust his left leg straight out and pulled his right knee into his chest. Reece performed a magnificent can-opener. The top of the giant splash doused the bottom of the trestle as the train wheels clickety-clacked past.

The train departed almost as quickly as it came. Cautiously, Wayne uncovered his eyes. He didn't look at the water or the bridge, but at Rain, who chuckled softly and shook his head.

"Jesus, Rain. What's so funny? Did the train get him? Is he dead?"

"No, just wet."

"Wet? What the hell are you talkin' about?"

Rain pointed to the water a few dozen yards from shore. "Look."

Like a hyena on a casual swim, Reece continued to laugh as he paddled directly for them. He looked awkward swimming in his sweatshirt, jacket, jeans, and tennis shoes.

At first, Wayne felt angry at being tricked, but then he, too, burst out laughing. "I hope your pecker's shrunk for good in that cold water, you crazy bastard!" he shouted.

Rain slapped Wayne hard on the back. "C'mon Wayne, let's go pull 'Railroad' out of the creek."

CHAPTER SEVEN
TASTE OF FIRE

From the moment Rain and Wayne pulled their fully-clothed, soggy friend from Okatibbee Creek, in their minds, he was no longer named Reece Rosenblum. He became simply known as Railroad and to Rain, the nickname fit perfectly. Each time he or Wayne said it, the nickname served as a tangible reminder of Reece's unpredictable personality and his driven determination to succeed against the odds. In everything he did, Railroad was the "little engine that could." Even the initials of his real name, RR, corresponded to the abbreviation for the word itself.

At first, Railroad didn't like his nickname. He had been known as Reece his entire life, and to be called something else now seemed inappropriate and unnecessary. Besides, he had only wanted a thrill from watching his friend's reactions as the train approached; coming away with a silly nickname was not part of his plan. Unfortunately for him, his initial resistance encouraged Rain and Wayne to address him as Railroad even more, and eventually, Railroad begrudgingly relented and stopped complaining.

By the Christmas holidays during their senior year

at Jefferson Davis, Rain Henry, Wayne LeRoy and Reece Rosenblum held the tree of life by the throat and shook loose anything that wasn't nailed to its branches. Accolades and recognition of their athletic accomplishments fell upon them like the yellow-gold leaves that drift to the ground from sweet gum trees on a windy, autumn day. At the beginning of the school year, the weekly-circulated *Vimville Times* splashed a full-page, front-cover picture of the triumvirate menacingly posing in full-pad football uniforms with their JD helmets smartly tucked at their sides. The feature story referred to them as the "Triumphant Trio" and proclaimed that with their talent, Jeff Davis had a legitimate shot of winning state championships in all three of the school's major sports: football, basketball, and baseball.

As Rain and Wayne originally hoped, Reece more than tipped the athletic scales in their favor. Railroad became the key that unlocked the door to sports successes the likes of which had never been seen at Jefferson Davis Academy and probably never will be seen again. Before Reece arrived, Rain and Wayne combined to make a strong two-threaded rope that weaved mediocre teams into good ones. Post Reece, with his added third thread, the rope transformed into a steel cable that not only pulled the best possible effort from each player, but also administered harsh punishment for teammates who were lazy, lacked discipline, or caused distractions to the team's collective goals. All great teams have perhaps one or maybe even two great leaders who serve as on-the-field coaches and commanders. Jeff Davis had three that year and it showed.

On the football field, with their nostrils aflame from the passion of competition, the trio transformed themselves into fire-breathing dragons. Their message to their teammates was simple: treat every single down as though it might be the last in which you ever got to play. Rain, Wayne, and Railroad led by example, and the team responded. Every Friday night, from the latter part of August through the end of the regular season, the Jeff Davis Rebels mercilessly punished the competition. By the middle of October, they carried an undefeated record.

Finally, the game arrived that Rain, Wayne, Railroad, and the rest of the Rebels had looked forward to all year. The time had come to avenge the home field loss from their junior year when Pamar's quarterback, senior Trip Chadwick, launched a last-second Hail Mary that was tipped and caught in the end zone for a game-winning touchdown. Like a boiler with a plugged valve, the Jeff Davis Rebels were ready to release the passionate fury born of the emotion that comes from being regarded as inferior by others. On October 18, Rain, Wayne, Railroad, and every other player on the roster envisioned physically and emotionally brutalizing the cocky Pamar Raiders on their home turf.

The Jeff Davis football team reached its apex on that special Friday night. Led by a tall, lanky defensive end/tight end, a stout, hard-hitting linebacker/right tackle and train-like nose guard/fullback, the Jeff Davis Rebels steamrolled the Pamar Raiders 43-0. It was worse than a beating; it was a humiliating annihilation that went down on record as the worst loss in Pamar history. Finally, the poor country hicks had exacted revenge on the rich snobs from the city.

Defensively, Rain had three quarterback sacks and intercepted a screen pass, returning it for a touchdown. From his spot at linebacker, Wayne amassed twelve tackles, including five that resulted in a loss of yardage on the play. Though double-teamed the entire night, Railroad was constantly in the backfield causing problems from his nose guard position. In the second quarter, he knocked Pamar's starting tailback out of the game with a helmet-to-helmet lick that left the kid lying unconscious for over five minutes.

Ultimately, however, Railroad did most of his damage offensively. He ran over and through the Pamar defenders as easily as an electric knife carves a juicy turkey at Thanksgiving. By the end of the night, Reece Rosenblum totaled 216 yards running the football and scored three touchdowns. The team appropriately chose Railroad as the game's most valuable player.

But for Rain, the moment tasted bittersweet. By that time, he had long since come to the realization that his innocent and childhood dream of dating and then marrying Catherine Landerson was nothing more than a boyhood fantasy. Shortly after Wayne and Rain failed to show at Haystack's Skating Palace that fateful day years ago, Stacey and Catherine's families feuded over an inheritance. This feud halted the frequent weekend spend-the-night visits and phone calls between the two girls. As a direct result, neither Stacey nor Wayne had the power to arrange any "second-chance" surprise double dates for Rain and Catherine. What had once been a flourishing friendship between the cousins turned gray and lifeless, like kudzu in the winter.

A few days after the no-show at Haystack's, Stacey had given Catherine's unlisted phone number to Wayne to pass along to Rain. But many years passed before he dialed it and for a long time, he believed he never would. That belief momentarily changed the Saturday night after their 14-10 loss to Pamar their junior year, the same one that featured Chadwick's Hail Mary. Rain and Reece had cruised 8th Street while Wayne and Stacey caught a movie by themselves. At about 10:00, the two cruisers ran into an old acquaintance of Reece's from Pamar, who informed them that Catherine had broken up with Trip Chadwick on the previous Thursday. One of Catherine's friends had caught Trip making out with a Meridian High School cheerleader at a late night party the weekend before. Right up until that moment, Rain almost admired Trip Chadwick despite his racist views. Trip had athletic talent, he had good looks, he had luck, he had money, and most of all, he had Catherine. But now he had cheated on the girl who, in Rain's eyes, sat high on a pedestal like a goddess. Chadwick defiled Catherine's sacred image openly and thoughtlessly, and Rain decided that Trip deserved her no longer. At last, he knew his big break with Catherine had presented itself, and his tongue tasted the succulent fire of opportunity. He felt sure she'd at least go out with him on one date.

While every hair on his body stood nervously on end, he had called her that Sunday evening. Catherine answered, and though her voice couldn't hide the fact she'd been crying, she spoke calmly and clearly when she politely declined Rain's invitation. She went on to explain that she and Trip were going to work things out and she didn't want to take a chance on throwing everything away at this point in their relationship. Rain couldn't believe his ears. When he blatantly challenged her on her rationale for sticking by a cheating boyfriend, he could sense that on the other end of the telephone, his question scared the delicate and sensitive turtle into its protective shell. During the long period of silence that followed, he jammed the receiver portion of the phone into his ear waiting for her to say something. Rain thought she had hung up on him. Finally, a barely audible voice crawled through the line. Catherine timidly replied that Trip had gotten drunk that night and didn't understand what he was doing, so he couldn't be held responsible for his actions. Rain would remember that conversation and that excuse for the rest of his life. As he hung up the phone, the fire on his tongue that had been opportunity the previous night became the acidic taste of rejection. The acid washed over and thoroughly cauterized the lining of his mouth before he choked it down with a hard swallow. He had felt devastated.

And so, in the wake of the 43-0 slaughter, one goal was finally accomplished, but another was not. Catherine Landerson remained Trip Chadwick's girlfriend, even though Chadwick, now a freshman scholarship baseball player at Ole Miss, probably cheated on her every night he could. And yet, as Rain's teammates continued to celebrate the victory by raising their maroon helmets to the starry sky and dancing on the painted logo of the Raider at mid-field, Rain gave one final glance to the Pamar sidelines. He searched for the captain of the Pamar cheerleaders, but couldn't find her. She was long gone.

That team finished second in the state in football, losing the championship game 9-7 to Heidelburg Academy after Heidelburg's all-world field goal kicker split the uprights three times, the last kick being a fifty-six-yarder as time expired. For their efforts during the season, Rain and Wayne were named all-conference. Railroad, quite deservedly, was named to the all-state team.

Now they were in the thick of basketball season, and Rain garnished the majority of the spotlight. *The Meridian Star* listed Rain as a pre-season all-state selection in basketball and he averaged twenty-one points and twelve rebounds as a center and forward for a team that stood 9-0 and was ranked third in the state. Reece, who started at point guard, was steady and reliable, if not flashy. Basketball was admittedly not Wayne's sport, and he sat the bench for most of the time as a reserve forward. When Wayne did enter a game, he maintained his linebacker mindset, focusing on quickness, aggressiveness, and punishment. Coach often inserted Wayne to guard the other team's hot shooter. After a few solid fouls, ones hard enough to bring purple bruises to the kid's arms, the hot shooter's ability to accurately stroke the net mysteriously disappeared. Although Rain knew it wasn't the noblest way to slow down an opponent, he couldn't argue with the results his coach's strategy produced.

Jeff Davis had beaten Winston Academy 67-61 the previous night, and after the long bus ride back to school, the trio decided to spend the night at Rain's house. Outside, the December Saturday began frosty and frigid, but inside, thanks to the Henry's oversized stone fireplace with its roaring fire, the air felt dry and toasty warm. Mildred Henry loved playing grandmother to all three boys, and they happily played along, overtly returned her affections as if she actually were. For breakfast this morning, she prepared each of her grandsons an enormous bowl of piping-hot, apple-cinnamon oatmeal. As she placed the bowls on the table, the fragrant columns of steam momentarily curled toward the ceiling before the thirsty air absorbed them like magic.

Granny sat down and took a sip of her black coffee. "What do you boys have planned today? Squirrel hunting with Mackel, I'll bet."

Rain's eyes met his grandmother's. "Not this morning, Granny. We've all got other stuff to do."

"Like what?"

Wayne downed a mushy bite and rolled his eyes. "Stacey's been on me to go Christmas shoppin' at the mall, so I promised I'd take her today. You'd think we's already married or somethin' the way she nags me."

Rain and Railroad exchanged glances. Wayne LeRoy and Stacey Cottrell already were married. They lacked only the rings and marriage certificate.

"What about you, Reece?" Mildred Henry asked.

Always the proper gentleman, Railroad swallowed the oatmeal in his mouth, put his spoon down, and folded his hands in his lap before he replied. "Well, Mrs. Henry, I've got to work on some admissions applications today."

Over the years, Mildred came to realize that Reece was as intelligent if not more intelligent than her own grandson. Everyone knew, often because she reminded them, Stacey Cottrell held a lock on the valedictorian position for the senior class, but a close battle raged between Rain and Reece for the slot of salutatorian. Rain's grandmother enjoyed the competition, and because Reece Rosenblum was such a nice young man, she almost found herself rooting for the enemy. "That sounds nice, Reece. Rain's told me that Mississippi State wants you to come and play both football and baseball. Is that one of the applications you're working on?"

"Yes, ma'am. And also Princeton."

"Princeton?" Rain and his grandmother blurted at the same time. Wayne looked up, but didn't stop eating.

This represented the first time Rain had heard about Railroad's interest in Princeton. "You mean Ivy League Princeton?" he asked.

"Yep, same one, Rain. My father's an alumnus of the undergraduate school. Even though I hadn't spoken to him since he turned me down for the sailing trip a few years ago, he called out of the blue last week and said he's sending me an application. Says he'll pay my tuition if I want to go."

"I think that's wonderful, Reece." Mildred beamed at the thought of one of her adopted grandsons attending such a prestigious school. "I wish I could get Rain to apply with you."

This time Rain and Wayne exchanged glances before Rain spoke. "Granny, you know Wayne and I have already applied to the Naval Academy. Commander Flanagan even wrote letters to the Office of the Superintendent on our behalf. We've been over the plan with you several times. If we get selected in the June amateur baseball draft, we're going pro. You know we want to play baseball first, and then go to school down the road. Dad's okay with it, and I thought you were, too. It's easy to get back into college, but it's not so easy to get back into baseball, right Wayne?"

"Right," Wayne agreed between shovels of oatmeal.

Mildred Henry stood from the table, her coffee cup empty. The tone of her voice reflected her frustration. "Yes, I know the plan, Rain. But it doesn't mean I have to like it. All three of you have some marvelous talent on the athletic fields, but I don't think it should unrealistically swell your heads. An education will last you a lifetime, and once you've got it, no one can ever take it away from you. That's what your grandfather used to say, and he was right. What if you don't get drafted and don't get accepted to the Academy? What then? By the end of spring, there should be several acceptance letters sitting on your desk so you have some options."

Wayne and Rain had tried to get Railroad to apply to the Academy with them, but he made it clear that he was not interested in a military education, period. Reece claimed that he couldn't tolerate being made to do things against his will by somebody who was only one or two years older than him. And if anyone ever tried, he'd probably beat him to a pulp. Ironically, when Rain and Wayne had told him of their plan regarding the draft, Railroad gave them the exact same speech Rain's grandmother just delivered. Now, Reece leaned back in his chair directly across the table from Rain. His bowl sat empty, and while his eyes sparkled, his mouth displayed the slightest hint of a smirk.

Deep down, Rain knew his grandmother and Railroad were right about the need to send out multiple applications. In his room, blank admission forms from Ole Miss, Tulane, and Vanderbilt, his grandmother's favorite, all lay on his dresser. Each school requested that he submit lengthy and time-consuming essays, and simply put, laziness kept him from taking the time to complete the applications and send them in. Besides, Rain felt confident he would matriculate at Annapolis next fall if he didn't get drafted.

Wayne finished his oatmeal, and his spoon clinked as he dropped it into the bottom of his empty bowl. "I got a letter yesterday from Coach Porter over at Mississippi Military College. He wants me to apply. Said he might be able to get me a full baseball scholarship."

Rain's grandmother beamed. "Why, that's great, Wayne! MMC's a fine school with an excellent southern tradition, and Natchez is an absolutely beautiful town. Do you think you'll apply?"

Wayne wiped his mouth on the sleeve of his flannel shirt. "Yes, ma'am. I know the military's the best way to get into pilot training. The way I see things, if my first choices don't work out, I could go there, and still move on to military flight school after graduation."

Mildred Henry looked visibly impressed. "Now that's what I call logical thinking, Wayne." She looked at her grandson. "Why don't you apply there, too, Rain?"

"I'm not so sure, Granny. Last year, Jeremy Langford accepted a scholarship to MMC and even though I know Wayne would beat him out at catcher after the first practice, the thought of being on the same team with that kid bothers me."

Wayne put his hands on the table and faced his friend. "Aw, don't worry about Langford, Rain. If he gives us any trouble, we'll fold him into an empty burlap sack and float him down the Mississippi River. Coach Porter did mention your name in the letter. Said he'd like both of us to come visit the campus and watch a game one Saturday next spring."

Like a streetlamp at dusk, Rain saw his grandmother's eyes light up. "That's a wonderful idea, Wayne! While you and Rain tour the campus, Jim and I can shop for some antiques. We'll make it a weekend. Reece, you must come along, too. What do you think, Rain?"

"Okay, Granny! Okay. If it'll make you that happy, we'll all go visit MMC next spring, and I promise I'll also send out the rest of the applications over the holiday break, including the one for Vanderbilt. Will that keep you off my back for a while?"

"It might, if you behave yourself in the meantime." She laughed, and Wayne and Railroad laughed along with her. "Now, all you boys bring your empty bowls over to the sink so I can wash 'em."

While Rain, Wayne, and Reece did as they were told, Rain heard his father's pickup screech to halt in front of the house. Seconds later, Jim Henry flew through the front door. Rain immediately could tell something was terribly wrong.

Jim Henry tried to force a smile, but failed. "Morning, boys. How was breakfast?"

The three blankly nodded, and Jim Henry spoke again. "Glad to hear it. Ah, Mildred, could I see you outside for a second, in private?"

Rain's grandmother dropped the soapy sponge, and together, she and her son hurriedly exited the house through the back porch.

Mildred and Jim Henry didn't want to unnecessarily alarm the boys, whom they knew watched from the kitchen window, but an important decision had to be made. Should or shouldn't they risk bringing in outside help? There needed to be agreement.

"I think we have to call them. We're going to need their help; it's worth the risk. Do you think you can get them here tonight, Mildred?"

"I don't think so, Jim. By the time I get through, it'll be too late."

"What about tomorrow? Can they come tomorrow and maybe throw some weight around?"

"I think so."

"Okay, then, I think you should get on the phone right away, don't you?"

"Yes, we'd better try to nip this before it gets out of hand."

"Mildred, it's already out of hand. I just hope nobody gets killed."

"Damn, Rain. What's goin' on?" Wayne demanded.

"Beats me," Rain said as he peered out the kitchen window and saw his father as upset as he'd ever seen him. He and Rain's grandmother stood all the way over by the storage shed. While Jim Henry spoke to his mother, he pounded one fist into the other and his lips formed hushed exclamations. His grandmother alternated between shaking her head and nodding it. For the most part, the conversation appeared to be one-sided. Finally, the two began walking back to the house. Rain ducked out of view from the window. "Looks like we might find out here in a second. Here they come."

The three boys leaned against the counter and pretended to discuss last night's game when Jim and Mildred Henry returned to the kitchen. Rain's grandmother offered a nervous smile before swiftly retreating down the hallway to her room.

Jim Henry sighed deeply. "Boys, we have a problem, and I

might need your help." He motioned for them to follow him to the living room where the three friends sat down on the sofa. Immediately, the heat from the oversized stone fireplace enveloped them. Jim Henry paced back and forth directly in front of the fire.

"What is it, Dad?" Rain inquired.

"Son, it's something that's been coming to a head for a little while now. I hoped the situation might work itself out and blow over, but I guess I was wrong. It seems little Cynthia Williams has been getting into trouble at school."

When all three boys squinted their eyes and looked away in thought, their faces reflected their confusion. Cynthia, Mr. Williams' daughter, was in the eighth grade at Southeast Vimville Junior High School. By now, Wayne and Reece knew her almost as well as Rain, and none of them could picture Cynthia getting into trouble at school. She was a well-behaved kid and a straight A student.

"What are you talkin' about, Dad. That doesn't make any sense."

"I know it doesn't, and that's why it's so frustrating. It's racial trouble."

Reece leaned forward. "Racial trouble, sir?"

"I'm afraid so, Reece. It seems Cynthia Williams, academically, does a little too well in school, and some parents don't like it."

Now Wayne leaned forward. "But I don't get it, Coach Henry. How would other kids' parents know unless they saw her report card?"

"It's not just about the grades, Wayne. Cynthia keeps winning all of the extra-curricular events, the ones the other kids' parents see or hear about from other parents. Last year, after she won the math challenge, the father of the runner-up 'ran into' Mr. Williams at the co-op store and warned him that his daughter was too smart for the color of her skin. Well, all you boys know how much he worships his little girl, and he came to me extremely upset. When he told me what happened, I felt sure this guy just wanted to blow off some steam. I convinced Mr. Williams not to worry about it."

Rain joined his two best friends at the front edge of the couch. Something clicked in his mind. "Dad, didn't Cynthia win first place in the science fair last week? Did something happen this morning because of that?"

"Yes and yes, Son. When Mr. Williams went down to the co-op first thing this morning to pick up some tools I'd ordered, he saw the same fellow from last year. Seems, once again, this guy's daughter came in second to Cynthia, and he was none too happy about it. Mr. Williams ignored the insults while he paid for the tools, but this fellow wouldn't let it go. He followed Mr. Williams out to the parking lot, and as Mr. Williams put the tools in the back of his truck, this guy told Mr. Williams to expect some visitors tonight. This man said the visitors would be wearing white sheets and planned on delivering a 'special gift' for their front yard."

Reece solved the riddle a millisecond before Rain and Wayne. He threw his body against the back of the sofa. His eyes opened wide. "The Ku Klux Klan!"

"That's the same thing I thought when Mr. Williams came by this morning and told me the story, Reece. As you might imagine, he was quite shaken by what had happened. So, I decided to drive down to the co-op, try to find this guy, and talk some sense into his head. I also wanted to see if I could determine whether or not he was serious or simply trying to scare Mr. Williams."

"Did you find him?" the three boys feverishly asked at once.

"Yes. He was still there. I talked with him for almost an hour, but he flat out lied to me. Said he never said anything to anyone and claimed he hadn't even heard of Cynthia or Chester Williams. I told him that was fine, but if anyone came on our property looking to cause trouble, I had the right to stop them with whatever means might be necessary."

Rain, Wayne, and Reece all nodded. "What'd he say to that?"

"Nothing, he just stood there and grinned."

"Have you called the police, Coach Henry?" Wayne asked.

"That's why I might need you three to help me out tonight, Wayne. I don't think we can expect much from the local law authorities. The guy causing the trouble is a deputy sheriff. His name's Jack Langford."

Railroad sprang to his feet. "Langford! Why I bet he's related to Jeremy Langford! Jeremy used to brag that he could always get out of trouble, because he had a cousin or uncle or somebody who was a cop."

Dealing with the mental image of Jeremy Langford twice in one morning caused Rain's blood to boil. Rain's memory recalled another episode that had further enhanced his disdain for the kid. By the time they reached high school, Langford became even more of a dirty player at Pamar. Like Trip Chadwick, he was one grade ahead of Rain, Wayne, and Reece. Last spring, while they played on Pamar's home field, Langford "accidentally" let the bat slip out of his hand after a hard swing. The projectile nearly decapitated Rain on the mound. After Rain struck him out with a knuckle curve on the next pitch, he watched Langford return to the dugout where Trip Chadwick gave him a high-five. The next time Langford batted, Rain located his best and hardest pitch of the day, an "accidental" ninety-plus mile-per-hour fastball right under Jeremy's chin. Langford hit the deck, then jumped to his feet and charged Rain. Wayne gave chase, but his gear slowed the catcher-turned-pursuing-linebacker. Rain didn't care if Wayne caught him or not. Coiled like a cobra about to strike from the top of his mountain, Rain stood ready for the attack. But the cobra never got its chance. A blur from the right side of Rain's peripheral vision crushed Jeremy Langford the way a freight train bows a stranded car stuck on the tracks. In less than an instant, Railroad, from his shortstop position, turned Langford's body into one of those "less than" signs in an algebraic equation. When Jeremy's ribs cracked, it reminded

Rain of the sound a thick limb makes when you break it in half before tossing it onto a bonfire.

As Railroad drove Langford into the ground, both benches cleared. However, everyone was so awed by the power of Railroad's devastating hit, they simply stood by their respective foul lines, mouths dropped to their shoelaces. While Railroad slowly peeled himself from the limp body beneath his own, the umpires and coaches regained control. Rain and Railroad were promptly ejected, Jeremy Langford was carried off the field by stretcher to an ambulance, and two innings later, Pamar rallied for three runs in the bottom of the ninth to win 3-2.

Rain never really knew whether Railroad obliterated Langford that day to protect his friend or to settle an old score with a kid who once bragged about admiring Adolf Hitler. Railroad claimed he acted to protect the team's star pitcher and one of his two best friends. Whatever the reason, as Reece sat next to him on the sofa, Rain thought he detected drool at the corner of his friend's mouth.

"Tell us what needs to be done and we'll do it, sir," Reece offered coldly.

"I'm in, too," Wayne concurred.

Rain made the decision unanimous. "You know you can count on us, Dad."

"Thanks, boys. In case this Jack Langford's serious, I'd like you three to back me up tonight at the Williams's house. Here's the basic plan: right before sunset, you'll take your rifles and settle into the woods along the side of their house. We'll need to make sure you're hidden well and dressed warmly. It'll be a cold and, most likely, a long night."

The fact that his father asked them to bring their guns shocked Rain. "Wow, Dad, do you really think we'll need the rifles?"

"Better to have them and not need them, Rain. I think whomever comes on their side will be armed. God forbid, if I can't convince them to back down, we may have to neutralize their firepower with some of our own."

Railroad's gentlemanly exterior gave way to something more dark and vengeful as he spoke. "Don't worry, Rain. I've done some studying of the law. If those racist bastards have guns and threaten us with their use, we have a right to self-defense, especially on your property." He turned to Rain's father, and Rain caught that wild look in his eyes he had seen only twice before. "Sir, I'll shoot every single one of them if necessary."

Jim Henry shook his head forcefully and put out both hands, palms facing the boys. "Now, hold on a minute. If we use the rifles, it'll be to scare them and nothing else. Maybe shoot out a headlight on their truck or something. I know you all are excellent shots, so I'd better not see one of them get hit, unless it's absolutely unavoidable. Is that clear?"

"Yes, sir," they answered.

"Good. Mr. Williams and I'll be inside the house unless someone does come, in which case we'll be on the porch while I try to talk them out of whatever it is they're about to do. In order not to appear openly hostile, I won't have a gun. Rain, you'll be in charge in the woods. Use your best judgment. You let Wayne and Reece know what to do and when to do it. Is that okay with everyone?"

"Yes, sir," they responded again.

"Boys, I really appreciate your help, especially yours, Wayne and Reece. I want you to go on and do what you had planned today, but be back here by three this afternoon, so we've got plenty of time to select the best place to put you in the woods. Wayne, Reece, this is really our battle. If you change your minds and decide you don't want to be a part of it, I'll understand."

"Coach Henry, you couldn't keep me away if you tried," Wayne proudly declared.

"I'll be here," Reece concurred without emotion. He acted as if he accepted clandestine sniper assignments every day.

Soon, the afternoon came and before too long, the winter sun reached its apex along the southern part of the sky and drifted toward the horizon. Earlier, Rain had worked on one of the essays for the Vanderbilt application, but his mind held captive the creative juices he needed to properly explain why he'd make a dynamic student at their university.

At 2:30, Wayne and Reece returned to the Henry farm and patiently waited in the yard by the front porch. Each wore thick brown coats and carried their scope-mounted .22 rifles. Their coat pockets were crammed with extra .22 cartridges, which rested beneath the wool gloves and the wrapped sandwiches that would become their dinner.

Similarly dressed and equipped, Rain descended the porch steps and joined them. Together with Rain's father and Mackel, the group began the half-mile walk across the fields and through one of the farm's pine forests to the Williams house. The frozen ground ominously crackled and crunched under their boots as they went.

By 4:30, the fading sun sat low on the horizon, barely winking through the naked lower branches of the pecan trees that grew in the southwest portion of the Williams's yard. In the woods that ran along the gravel driveway, almost all the way to the east side of the house, they selected Rain, Wayne, and Railroad's hiding place. A briar thicket grew up and over a sapling creating a prickly, but well-camouflaged dome. It provided perfect cover.

Rain had never heard Mr. Williams's voice tremble the way it did when he met them upon their arrival. It dripped with gratitude, but couldn't mask the nervousness that comes from anxiety. With firm handshakes and moist eyes, Mr. Williams profusely thanked each member of the group for coming, including Mackel.

At 5:00, the boys sat at the tiny dining table inside the bungalow and enjoyed the last sips of their hot chocolate, courtesy of Mrs. Williams. Rain's father, sucking hard on a cigarette, sat next to Mr. Williams on the adjacent living room's tattered couch. Mrs. Williams kept busy in the kitchen by beginning preparations for dinner. She pulled out a large pot, filled it with water, and set it on the gas stove. At the back of the house, down the hall and in the general direction of Cynthia's room, the boys heard faint, muffled sobs.

Rain's father mashed the butt of his cigarette into a glass bowl that served as an ashtray, then stood from the couch. "Boys, I think it's time you settled into that thicket. Make sure you keep each other awake. If nothing happens by three or four in the morning, I'll come get you and we'll head home."

Rain, Wayne, and Railroad got up and headed for the door. But before they could navigate the small space that separated the dining area from the living room, Mrs. Williams stopped them by holding out her arm like a crossing guard.

"Three or fo in the mornin', an all them boys gots is coats? Theys frost onna groun' by then. Them boys gonna freeze to death."

Jim Henry grinned at her motherly concern. "It's okay, Velma. They have on several layers under the coats and some thick gloves and hats in their pockets. They'll be fine."

"Doan care, Mr. Henry. These boys needs a warm blanket, if they's goan be out there so late." Without waiting for a response, she darted down the hall for one of the home's two bedrooms and returned with a bulky, black winter bedspread, which she forcefully thrust into Rain's arms. "Goan, now. Take it. Take it, I said!"

Rain looked at his father, and Jim Henry nodded his approval. "Thank you, Mrs. Williams," the three boys echoed one another.

They were about to head for the door again when Mr. Williams's voice filled the momentary void. "They's one mo' thing fo ya'll leave the house. Velma, go get L'il Cent. She needs to thank these boys for they help."

Mrs. Williams's expression said she didn't agree with her husband, but dutifully, she obeyed and again headed down the hall, this time to Cynthia's bedroom.

Rain's father shook his head. "Chet, there's no need for that. We all know she's not feeling well. Let her stay back there."

"Nawsuh, she's gonna tell 'em 'thank you.'"

A minute later, Cynthia Williams walked up the hall, her mother gently pushing her at the shoulders. Her eyes looked puffy and red, but her creamy, brown face carried a distinctive innocence and an emerging beauty. Even in despair, Cynthia lit up the room when she entered.

She had grown almost as tall as Wayne and stood a full three inches taller than Reece. When she looked at the three boys wrapped in their coats and holding her parents' bedspread, her chin quivered and her chest shuddered. She barely got out what she wanted to say. "Rain, Wayne, Reece, I want to thank you for helping us tonight. I'm really sorry about everything. It's all my fault for winning that stupid science fair."

Rain was about to tell her she shouldn't feel sorry when Reece, who had been third in the line of boys, shoved his way past Wayne and Rain to the front. He had to look up to catch the gaze of the slender girl who had tears streaming down both of her soft cheeks. Reece Rosenblum spoke with a warmth and compassion only attainable by someone who'd been there. "Cynthia, promise yourself right now you'll never apologize again for who you are or for excelling in something you desire to do."

Though she couldn't verbally reply, Reece's words found their target, and Cynthia Williams slowly nodded.

Railroad gave Cynthia one of his patented smiles. Then, he turned to Rain and Wayne, who beamed back with commendation and admiration for what their best friend had just done. "C'mon boys, let's hit the woods."

Once the sun settled below the horizon, the air turned bitterly cold. The trio huddled close together for warmth, but it didn't help. Neither did Mr. and Mrs. Williams's bedspread, which they wrapped around them all the way up to the bottom of their lips. Without muscle activity, the body quickly loses its ability to generate heat and by ten o'clock all three had a firm grasp of that concept. Mackel, even with his thick winter coat of fur, occasionally left his perch at the top of the Williams' porch and roamed around the yard to generate warmth, something the boys could not do.

They felt beyond miserable a few minutes before midnight when Rain, who sat between Wayne and Reece, nudged his buddies and unfurled his portion of the spread. He pointed at the porch where Mackel stood on the bottom step, a low growl emanating from deep inside his throat. Straining their ears, they heard the sound of a vehicle slowly and cautiously approaching. The rubber tires barely disturbed the gravel as it inched up the winding drive. As the vehicle came closer, the sound of its engine, running slightly above idle, told the friends that their wait for some action would soon be over.

Wayne and Railroad lowered their portion of the bedspread, and all three boys pulled their .22's from between their groins. They had kept the guns between their legs to keep the chambers from freezing. Next, all three rolled from their sitting positions onto their bellies and unlatched the safeties on their rifles. Adrenaline chased away any lingering cold from their bodies, and each of the boys' spines felt a different sort of chill.

"The moon's pretty bright. Think we'll be able to see good enough to shoot if we have to?" Wayne whispered.

"You mean 'well enough' and yes, so keep quiet," Rain admonished.

From where the gravel driveway bent into the trees to their left, an off-white 1950's style pickup materialized. In the bright moonlight, Rain could make out two people riding in the cab and three in the bed of the truck. All five wore cone-shaped hoods with large eyeholes. While the pickup advanced closer and closer to their position and the Williams's house, Rain noticed that the three men in back held a huge wooden cross that jutted at an angle out of the truck bed. Mackel sounded the alarm by barking with as much force as his twelve-year-old lungs could muster. The porch light came on, the door opened, and Rain's father and Mr. Williams emerged and stood waiting.

About fifty yards from the house and thirty yards directly in front of Rain, Wayne, and Reece's hidden position, the truck stopped. Its headlights, set to the high beams, flashed on and bathed the front of the house and the two men standing on its porch with blinding light. Mr. Williams shielded his eyes with his hands, and Jim Henry held Mackel firm by the collar, preventing the growling dog from charging forward and attacking the intruders.

After the driver cut the engine, he and his passenger exited the truck's cab and slammed their creaky doors shut. The three in the back jumped to the ground. One carried what looked to be a twelve-gauge pump shotgun, one carried a shovel and the other grasped a post-hole digger. All wore color-coordinated outfits that looked like flowing white silk pajamas with matching pointy hats. Standing side by side, the five Klansmen formed a straight line in front of the truck. The headlights cast their gigantic shadows on top of and over the house. The tallest of the five Klansman raised a bullhorn to the general area of his face where the white fabric hid his mouth, and a magnified, electronically enhanced voice shattered the stillness of the cold night air.

"Happy holidays from the White Knights of the Ku Klux Klan!" Rain watched and listened as each Klansman chuckled at their leader's sick wordplay.

Seconds later, the megaphone blared again, and the group's true feelings of hate spewed forth. "Congratulations, family of niggers! You have been selected to receive a sign of your race's inferiority and future damnation. Prepare yourselves, as all niggers should, for the fires of hell, which will soon scorch your black skin. Tonight we're gonna give you a taste of what's to come." The leader paused and glanced around the side of the bullhorn, taking a closer look at the two men on the porch. "I see we also have a nigger and Jew lover with us tonight. May he be a witness! Those who love the niggers and the Jews shall perish with the niggers and the Jews!"

Rain thought he would need to restrain Railroad when the word Jew burst from the end of the bullhorn, but when he turned to check on his friend, Reece's expression remained unchanged. Reece Rosenblum's face displayed pure determination, nothing more.

The Klansman who drove the truck made a sweeping movement with his arm, and the three men who had originally ridden up in the back of the truck ambled about ten yards forward. The one with the shotgun took a sentinel position on the left, while the other two began digging a hole.

Rain's father continued using every ounce of strength he had to restrain Mackel. Suddenly, he shouted as loud as he could at the blinding headlights. "I really wish you boys wouldn't do this. You're setting yourselves up for some major trouble. It would be best for everyone if you got back in your truck and left. As long as you never come back or harass my friend, we'll forget this whole thing ever happened." He paused for a moment, but only silence replied. "Besides, we've already got a well out back; you don't need to dig us a new one in the front."

Rain's father's joke must have had some effect on the two diggers because they stopped digging and looked at the Klansman with the bullhorn. Angrily, he pointed at the fresh opening in the ground and motioned for them to continue. If the leader had a response to Rain's father's attempt at humor, he didn't say it out loud.

The Klansmen had been given their chance, but obviously didn't plan to stop what they intended to do. Rain decided the time for action had come. He nudged Wayne with his left elbow and drew a circle in the air with his left index finger. On his signal, he wanted Wayne to shoot out the headlight to their left. Wayne nodded. Rain nudged Railroad with his right elbow and made a motion of pulling a trigger with his right hand. Reece was the trio's undisputed best marksman, and Rain wanted him to shoot the gun out of the sentry's hand. Railroad grinned and nodded. Rain would shoot out the remaining headlight, which he hoped would be enough to cause the Klansmen to turn tail and run. If his plan didn't work, Rain shuddered to imagine what might happen next.

Rain was about to give the signal to fire, when his father shouted from the porch. "This is your last chance, boys! You all are really setting yourselves up for some major trouble down the road. As for right now, I can't hold this dog much longer, and he's got some mighty big teeth!"

Again, the bull-horned Klansman said nothing in reply, but instead turned to the two diggers and the sentry. He addressed them with a loud whisper. "Hurry up with that hole! I coulda hired me a single nigger to dig faster than the two of you." He pointed at the sentry. "And you. You shoot the dog."

"What'd you say?" the sentry whispered back loudly.

The Klansman in charge leaned closer to the Klansman holding the gun. "I said shoot the dog!"

"But this is a shotgun. If I shoot the dog, I'm gonna hit the man, too. I thought you said we wasn't gonna shoot nobody."

"Listen, boy. Don't make me come take that gun from you and do it myself. You ain't gonna get in no trouble for puttin' a few pellets in the legs of a man who loves both niggers *and* Jews! Now pull the trigger!"

As the sentry reluctantly raised the gun to his shoulder, Rain, with a cool and dispassionate voice, simply said, "Now." The sound of three shots danced across the air and into the night. The two headlights on the pickup instantly disintegrated, sending tiny shards of glass flying every direction. Suddenly, only the dim rays from the distant porch light lit the scene, and Rain watched in slow motion as the Klansman sentry doubled over, clasping one hand on top of the other, just above his crotch. His twelve-gauge shotgun fell harmlessly to the frozen ground, landing with a solid thud as it hit.

For a few seconds, the wire filaments from the shattered headlights glowed a dull-orange before dying like the embers of a neglected campfire. Thoroughly confused, the Klansmen froze in their tracks. For Rain, the action returned to normal speed when the shrill screams of the sentry reverberated through the night.

"Aaaaaahhhhh! Aaaaaahhhhh! I've been shot! They shot my hand off!"

Then, a new voice erupted. It came from the driver Klansman. "Jesus Christ! Everybody in the truck! They've got snipers in the woods! Everybody get in the damn truck! We've gotta get outta here!"

While the Klansmen scrambled into the old truck, mixing obscenities among their unintelligible sentences, the scene of their distressed departure reminded Rain of a Three Stooges episode times ten on the nuttiness scale. Once aboard, the five men jumped and yelled simultaneously, causing the rickety pickup to gyrate up and down and side to side. The physical and verbal commotion had to make finding the correct key and starting the engine even more difficult. After a few seconds that must have been an eternity to the Klansmen, the ignition caught, and the driver slammed the transmission into reverse. But, his eyes must still not have adjusted to the lack of light because he backed up too far and at an awkward angle. The back of the truck plowed into a sturdy pine tree that merely laughed as it shivered with delight. With his one bad hand, the sentry couldn't hold on well enough to keep from flying headfirst from the bed of the pickup and onto the frozen earth that was as hard as concrete. As he lay motionless on the ground, apparently unconscious from the impact, Rain saw that dark red blood now streaked the front of his white pajamas. The sentry's two digger friends leapt from the back and threw his limp body up and over the side of the truck bed like a giant sack of potatoes.

The two shouted that they had reclaimed their comrade, and the truck zoomed forward, successfully negotiating the bend around which it had first appeared. Rain thought how hard it must have been to hastily try to navigate without headlights. As he, Wayne, and Railroad emerged from the thicket, Rain measured the progress of the Klansmen's getaway by the distant sounds of crashing branches that gradually faded away to silence.

Rain's father finally released Mackel, and he bounded from the porch toward the boys. In dog years, he had lived to be almost eighty, but tonight's action seemed to have restored his youth. As if everything had been one big game, he barked playfully while jumping in circles and twirling in midair. Jim Henry and Mr. Williams followed close behind. The five men studied the spoils of war that had been hastily left behind by the retreating army: one shovel, one post-digger, one twelve-gauge shotgun, a bullhorn and a giant wooden cross that lay next to the bruised pine tree and smelled like kerosene.

Rain's father reached down and picked up the red and white bullhorn. "Which one of you boys shot the guy in the hand?"

"I did, sir." Reece professed.

Rain stepped forward. "He had to, Dad, he was about to take a shot at Mackel on the porch that would have hit you, too. He was using a shotgun." He slapped his friend on the back. "Railroad's the only one of us that could have made that shot, anyway."

Jim Henry smiled. "Oh, I'm not angry, boys. You did what you had to do and we scared them off without anyone getting killed, I think. Though I have to admit, Rain, you were starting to worry me a little."

"Why's that, Dad?"

"I wasn't lying when I shouted out that I couldn't hold Mackel back much longer. For a while, I thought maybe you were all so cold that you wanted them to light that cross for warmth."

The humorous reflection helped ease the tension. Rain's father reached over and gave Railroad a congratulatory squeeze on his shoulder. "Excellent shot, Reece, but I hope you didn't injure his hand too badly. If anyone knows what it's like to be crippled, I sure do."

"I can't speak for the cracked skull he might have gotten after he flew from the truck, but he'll recover from my bullet."

Jim Henry squinted his eyes. "How can you be so sure?"

"Because, sir, I hit him right there." Railroad put his hand in the air, spread his thumb apart from his other fingers and pointed at the web-like fold of skin that connected his thumb and index finger.

Rain's father shook his head in amazement. "Like I said, excellent shot, Reece." He looked around again at the items left on the ground. "All right then, let's gather up this stuff for evidence. We'll put it under Mr. Williams's porch for now, then Rain and I will come pick it up later this morning. Let's get a move on; we've still got a long walk back home."

At first, Mr. Williams insisted on giving them a ride, but Rain's father convinced him to stay with his family, just in case. It was always better to be safe than sorry, though Jim Henry doubted the Klansmen would return anytime soon, especially with one of them wounded. He felt at ease now. What had occurred would buy them the time they needed to ensure the Klan would never come calling on their property again. While they headed for the Williams's front porch, the bullhorn swung by Jim Henry's side. Wayne carried the shovel, Railroad the post-hole digger, and Rain the expensive shotgun.

When they got a little closer to the porch, the light improved, and Jim Henry examined the bullhorn more closely. "Well, I'll be," he said as he stopped.

The other four stopped with him. "What is it, Dad?" Rain asked.

"There's an identification tag on the underside of this bullhorn, and guess what it says."

"What?" they all wanted to know.

"Property of East Lauderdale County Sheriff's Department."

The next afternoon, two men wearing black suits parked

their dark sedan in front of the Henry farmhouse. They met with Mildred and Jim Henry for approximately one hour. Rain never saw them; he and Railroad were watching pro football playoff games on the big-screen TV at Wayne's house. But Rain did see the news of the big FBI drug bust when it hit *The Meridian Star* and *Vimville Times* two weeks later. In the wake of the scandal, the East Lauderdale County Sheriff resigned after one of his top deputies was convicted of cocaine possession with intent to distribute. The judge sentenced Jack Langford to twenty-five years at the federal pen in Parchman, Mississippi.

CHAPTER EIGHT DECEPTION, DISSEMINATION, AND DIVINE INTERVENTION

"And don't forget to dust off the back of your pants when you get out," Catherine advised.

"I'm sorry, what did you say?" Rain asked.

Catherine laughed and wedged the empty bottle of orange juice into the Styrofoam bowl that had previously held her mixed fruit. "I reminded you that when you borrow my car to go buy some clothes, you'll need to remember to dust off the cookie crumbs when you get out."

"Oh, yeah. Cookie crumbs in the mini-van seats." He smiled at her. "Sorry, Catherine. I guess I'm still reeling a little after what's happened. How are your kids?"

"They're doing great, thanks for asking. Blake plays on the 125-pound class Meridian Wildcat football team and Blair's one of the cheerleaders."

"Following right along in mom and dad's footsteps, aren't they?" Rain said with a grin.

Catherine rose from her seat, tray in hand. "I guess so. Sometimes I think we, as parents, push our children too much. It keeps them busy, though." She nodded at her watch.

"We'd better get going. It's after eight, and I know you don't want to miss Dr. Littleton."

Rain followed her to the rectangular opening in the back wall of the cafeteria. Here, they placed their trays on a slow-moving conveyor belt that transported their trash, dishes, and silverware into the kitchen for sorting and cleaning. Catherine then guided Rain back through the main lobby and to the elevators that would take him to the third floor ICU.

When they reached the elevators, Rain hit the up button. "Thanks for breakfast, Catherine. I think I can find my way from here."

Catherine gave him a strong hug and a feeling stirred within Rain Henry that he hadn't felt for a long time. Unlike earlier that morning, in his father's room, Rain returned her embrace and as he did, he ran his hands up and down the long, fluid muscles that stretched the length of her back. Catherine hastily untangled herself. Embarrassed, she sheepishly acknowledged his gratitude. "You're welcome, Rain Henry." Then she paused as if she needed to remember what she was supposed to say next. "Oh, yes. Administration's located on the other side of the lobby and down past the cafeteria. We're in the rear portion of the hospital. Any employee can tell you how to get there. You can have the car whenever you want, for as long as you want."

By 8:15, Rain waited impatiently in his father's room while sitting, once again, in the uncomfortable vinyl chair that rested against the far wall. By now, his eyes had grown accustomed to his father's sallow appearance, so he was not shocked by the yellowish, blank expression that remained bonded to the face on the other side of the room. It was an expression of emptiness and lifelessness, and Rain decided he should scale back his hopes for his father's recovery. Instead of wishing his father would regain consciousness, perhaps he should simply wish for some natural color to return to his skin. Rain had been at the hospital for slightly more than six hours, and already the walls wanted to close in around him. He reminded himself to stay focused on the task at hand.

A knock at the door startled Rain, and before he could respond, Dr. Littleton, flanked by a nurse on each side, charged into the room. Acknowledging Rain with a quick wave, the doctor swiftly moved to his patient and probed the upper area of Jim Henry's neck, just below the jaw line. "Morning, Rain. How'd you sleep in that chair?"

"Not too well."

Dr. Littleton chuckled as he lifted his patient's eyelids and shined the light from his mini-flashlight into each pupil. "Nobody ever does. It's almost like a hospital initiation. They make some poor friend or relative sleep in that chair the first night and then send them home or off to a local hotel with a pager the next day. Did you get your pager yet?"

"Yes, sir," Rain replied as he fingered the device that hung over his belt.

"Good." Dr. Littleton let Jim Henry's eyelids close and addressed Rain. "There's been no change in your father's condition since we stabilized him last night. There's no swelling in his lymph nodes, and his pupils still respond well to light stimulation. He hasn't improved, but he hasn't gotten any worse, either."

Rain got up from the chair and joined the doctor by his father's side. The two nurses continued to hang behind Dr. Littleton, merely observing. Rain remembered his new plan. "Why is his skin so yellow?"

The doctor leaned over his patient. With his left hand, he rotated Rain's father's face carefully from one side to the other, to avoid disturbing the connections with the tubes. Littleton straightened back to his full, albeit short, height. "Rain, whenever the body goes through some sort of trauma, such as a heart attack, the organs react accordingly. The skin is an organ and without getting too technical, it's giving us an outward sign that something's wrong with your father. This is perfectly normal based on what happened yesterday."

Half satisfied with the doctor's response, Rain asked his next question. "When do you think it'll be safe to bring him out of the coma?"

Dr. Littleton reached up high to put his hand on Rain's shoulder. "Rain, his heart still needs rest and needs it very badly. If I woke him up anytime soon, I'm afraid it might give out like that." He snapped his fingers to illustrate how quickly another heart attack might occur. "Then, you'd never have another chance to talk with him because he'd be gone forever. I think we should continue to wait."

Defeated by the doctor's logic, Rain sighed deeply. "Okay, but how long do you think that'll be?"

Dr. Littleton removed his hand from Rain's shoulder and thrust it behind him for a clipboard held by one of his nurses. She fed it into his groping fingers, and he brought it forward. At the bottom of the form, his left hand scribbled a typical doctor's signature, unintelligible and illegible even to the doctor himself. "Tell you what, Rain. You go and check into a hotel. Get some rest this afternoon, and then have a nice dinner. I'll check his signs again around six and give you a page sometime thereafter. If anything's improved, we'll re-examine the situation. Is that all right with you?"

Rain consented. It had been a long day, and an afternoon nap in a comfortable bed would be more than welcome. Here, he was useless for the time being, and he knew it. Besides, the fabric of his slacks rubbing against his bare skin was starting to chafe him in areas he didn't like to be chafed. He needed to buy some clean underwear as soon as possible.

Rain whispered to his father once again that he loved him and he'd be back later. He caught Dr. Littleton's entourage as it exited into the hall, but when the doctor and his nurses turned to the left to continue third-floor rounds, Rain headed to the right for the familiar elevator that would lead him to the lobby and eventually, the administration department. While he had waited for Dr. Littleton, he had rummaged through his overnight bag and found his cell phone. As he stepped onto the elevator, it hung clipped to his belt and next to the hospital pager.

Based on Catherine's directions, Rain easily found administration. Like the entrance to a king's treasure room, two heavy mahogany doors protected the department from the outside. A security camera watched from the upper corner where the walls intersected with the top left portion of the doorframe. Rain rang a small wall buzzer and one of the doors unlocked with a sharp click.

Upon entering, Rain stood face to face with a Mrs. Florence Jenkins, according to the nameplate on her desk. Mrs. Jenkins was an older woman with graying hair that hinted it had once been the color of pure copper. Her eyes were large, but seemed well proportioned to the rest of her oversized, but not fat, body. Her nose was thick and hawkish and lived slightly north of a thin, black caterpillar on her upper lip that looked like something a sketch artist had drawn with a fine-tipped, charcoal pencil. Overall, she reminded Rain of a wide-eyed bulldog, except that bulldogs looked generally more attractive. But whatever she lacked in beauty, she compensated with a lofty level of physical confidence that she projected quite effectively. Rain guessed immediately that Mrs. Jenkins would have been successful on a women's pro wrestling circuit, had she not chosen receptionist as her career path. Rain hoped he knew the correct password, if only to avoid the prospect of receiving a body slam.

The caterpillar shimmied at the top of her mouth. "May I help you?" she asked in a low, husky voice.

"Yes, ma'am. I'm here to see Catherine Landerson."

"I'm sorry. We don't have anyone by that name who works in this department." Mrs. Jenkins squinted and eyed him even more suspiciously. The muscles in her arms tightened and the skin on her forehead wrinkled. "Unless you're referring to Catherine Chadwick, Dr. Chadwick's wife."

"Oh, yes, ma'am, that's her. Sorry about that. I had forgotten. It's been a long time since I've seen her. We've known each other since we were kids." Rain cringed. He had given the wrong password, and the ugly bulldog stared at him as if he were a trespasser about to become a snack.

"What did you say your name was?" Mrs. Jenkins held the phone receiver in one hand and appeared to reach under the desk with the other. Probably for a gun or a whip, Rain conjectured.

"Rain Henry."

"Very well, Mr. Henry. Please wait outside the doors and in the hallway. I'll let Mrs. Chadwick know you're here."

The bulldog didn't need to tell him twice. With a controlled sprint, Rain dashed back through the mahogany doors and waited. He expected a dozen security officers to show up with their pistols drawn.

A few seconds later, Rain breathed a sigh of relief as Catherine Chadwick flowed effortlessly through the heavy doors and quickly apologized for Mrs. Jenkins' distrustful behavior. "Sorry about the guard dog, Rain. Anyway, tell me about your father. What did Dr. Littleton say?" She handed Rain the car keys and the swipe card that would allow him to exit and then re-enter the employee parking deck.

"Same. No change. Dr. Littleton told me to get some rest, and he'd page me sometime after six with an update."

"That's about what I expected. You look like you could use some sleep. There's a nice LaQuinta Inn over by the new mall. They'll give you a ten percent discount if you mention the hospital. By the way, the mall opens at ten, a little over an hour from now. I should know, right?" She gave him a wink. "That'd be the best place for you to get some clothes."

"Thanks, Catherine. I really appreciate everything. What time do I need to have the car back?"

"Doesn't matter. I want you to keep it. Mom's got one of those new Jaguars, but she never drives it. She and my father always ride around together in his Mercedes, now that he's retired. She's offered before to let me try it out to see if I like it. I'll call her and tell her the van's in the shop and I need to borrow her car for a few days."

"You still have to lie to your mother after all these years? Why can't you tell her the truth?"

"Because, Rain, in certain situations, lying is still the best way to cope with my mother. The trick is masking the lie well enough so she believes it without following up. We learned that lesson the hard way, remember?"

"But that all happened so long ago."

Catherine sighed and looked up at the ceiling. "You're right. It was a long time ago. But I still live in Meridian. I have this job because of my father. I've never been able to be as independent as you, though I've tried. The way I live my life now is by the path of least resistance. That's what works for me." She narrowed her eyes and drilled a hole through Rain Henry. "I wouldn't expect you to understand, though I did try to explain it once, but you chose not to listen. Now, do you want to use the car or not?"

Rain fingered the keys as he held them in the palm of right hand. She was right about one thing. He never would understand the way she let her parents, especially her mother, and now probably Trip Chadwick, control her life and mold her principles. And, yes, he had chosen not to listen to her explanation back then, and he certainly didn't want to have Catherine's lying relationship with her mother explained to him now. He tried not to, but the smile he gave her was condescending. "I'll use it, but I'll have it back by lunchtime. I'll have Wayne or somebody take me to get Dad's truck this afternoon. I wouldn't want you to lie to your parents or anyone else because of me. I never asked you to then, and I don't want to be a part of a lie now."

Rain's words cut Catherine, but she effectively hid her feelings. It was a handy skill she had mastered many years before and sharpened often. Rain Henry had once been the cause of tremendous emotional pain, and she wasn't about to be pricked with a needle from him again. "Fine, Rain. Fine. Have it back by lunch, then." She turned and whisked through the mahogany doors, back to the protection of the citadel, its entrance guarded by the best that money could buy.

Catherine retreated before Rain got the chance to ask her where she had parked the mini-van. He didn't even know what color it was. He considered sliding the keys under the door and running for the lobby before the bulldog gave chase. He could take a taxi, but finding a taxi in Meridian was a short step beyond impossible. He'd have to call one out of the phone book and then wait for thirty minutes to an hour before the cab arrived. No, he decided. Catherine had offered her car, and he'd accepted. He'd use it to check into the hotel, buy some clothes at the mall, grab an early bite of lunch, and have it back by noon, as promised.

Rain exited the hospital's side entrance and entered the ground level of the adjacent seven-level parking garage. He caught the attention of a security guard riding past on a golf cart and asked him about employee parking. After Rain explained that a friend had loaned him her car and he showed the guard the keys and the pass-card as proof, the rent-a-cop dropped his veil of skepticism and informed Rain that employees were allowed to park only on the top two floors. Rain rode the elevator to the sixth floor. He could tell from the remote on the key chain that it was a Chrysler product. Rain decided the best way to find the vehicle would be to hit the panic button, which he did.

A pulsating horn blared on and off from above, so he hustled up to the next level and discovered the forest green Dodge Caravan. Rain hit the unlock button, which silenced the alarm, then climbed into the driver's seat. He remembered Catherine's warning about the cookie crumbs, but there were none to be found. He realized that she had probably mentioned them to see if he was paying attention, which of course he hadn't been. Besides, her twins were at least twelve or thirteen years old by now. It would be unlikely that kids their age would spill cookie crumbs all over the car.

As the engine warmed, Rain turned on his cell phone to see how many messages waited in his voice mailbox. The phone beeped as the display showed that he had fourteen messages. Rain was about to check them, when the phone rang. He recognized the number and answered. "How's the meeting? You catchin' some rays out by the pool?"

"Hell, I wish, old buddy," Railroad wearily responded. "You know these legal conventions, all work and no play, unless you happen to be working on analyzing the briefs of fellow lawyer with long legs and shapely buttocks."

They both laughed. Considered one of Meridian's most eligible bachelors, Reece's professional success had more than compensated for his lack of height. But while he openly flirted and often dated Meridian's most eligible bachelorettes, Reece lacked interest in any serious, long-term relationships with members of the opposite sex. Like many highly successful men, Reece married his career. No one in Meridian knew more about criminal law or could work a jury like Railroad. During a trial, whenever a criminal claimed to have been "railroaded" by the prosecution, the phrase took on a whole new meaning.

Rain felt proud of what his friend had accomplished. When Reece left for his freshman year of college, he had been a lump of pure coal: valuable in its current state, but capable of becoming much more if properly challenged by the pressures of high-quality academia. Nature requires eons to accomplish the same task, but it took Princeton University and Harvard Law School only seven years to transform Reece into a spectacular diamond. And like a diamond, Reece possessed a special ability with the light of the law. It filtered through him and he bent it as needed, splashing vibrant colors against the courtroom wall that judged all citizens equally, regardless of race or religion. He maintained an unshakeable reputation for researching a case until he found the angle that would tip the law and the jury's opinion to his favor. Reece Rosenblum had recently been elected District Attorney for Lauderdale County. Many thought he'd run for governor of Mississippi within ten years and few doubted his chances if he did. He simply had a way with people.

Railroad continued, "Speaking of buttocks, I watched the game last night with this shapely trial lawyer from Atlanta. Great game, though I would've thrown Ludski the change. That guy pounds your fastball like I used to."

"Thanks for the advice on Ludski," Rain mumbled into the phone. "And thanks for bringing up that delightful memory, old buddy," he said sarcastically.

Railroad chuckled on the other end. "I'm only kidding, so take it easy. Anyway, I didn't call to give you a hard time. I'm sure you're tired and hung over from celebrating all night. I called because I picked up a voicemail from Wayne saying he needed to get in touch with me ASAP. I tried to call his house, but the line's been busy." He paused. "I thought there might be an slight chance Wayne had left you a more detailed message and you knew what all this was about."

"We spoke last night."

"You spoke to Wayne last night? When? After the game? What's going on? He's not in any trouble, is he?"

"No, he was trying to get in touch with you on my behalf. My dad suffered a heart attack yesterday evening, and he probably wanted to see if you knew the best way to contact me."

Railroad's voice became sympathetic and lost the edge of a prosecutor cross-examining a defendant's witness. "Damn, Rain. I'm really sorry. Your dad's tough, though. I'll bet he'll be up an out of that hospital in no time."

"Afraid not. He's got brain cancer, too."

"Brain cancer?"

"Yes, brain cancer to go along with a diseased heart. They've got him in a medically induced coma right now, but they may try to wake him up tonight if he stabilizes a little bit more."

"Rain, I'm so sorry. Look, the convention finishes at noon, and I'm scheduled to be back in Meridian by 4:30. As soon as I land, I'll rush right over to the hospital to be with him. I bet Wayne's there right now."

"You lose the bet, counselor. Wayne's not there, and I'd rather have you meet me for an early dinner at Weidmann's. I could use a decent meal and some good company before I head back to the hospital tonight. "

"Rain, where the heck are you?"

"Meridian."

"How in the world did you get home already? How long are staying?"

"Corporate jet and as long as it takes."

"You planning on spending the night at the farm? You're welcome to stay at my place if you want – you know it's closer to the hospital."

"Thanks, Railroad, but I'm gonna get a hotel only a few minutes away." Rain's cell phone's call-waiting beeped in his ear. "Listen, I've got another call. Meet me at Wiedmann's around six. I'll make the reservations."

"See you then," Reece replied and hung up.

The other caller was Wayne asking for an update. Rain filled him in on the situation and invited him to round out the trio for dinner at Wiedmann's. He accepted. Wayne also agreed to meet Rain at one o'clock in front of the main lobby to take him to get his father's pickup. After he hung up with Wayne, Rain decided he'd also better call Mr. and Mrs. Williams to make sure they weren't about to make an unnecessary trip into town to visit his father.

As Rain exited the parking garage and headed for the hotel, he dialed the Williams's house. Mrs. Williams answered and said, as a matter-of-fact, they were preparing to walk out the door to head for the hospital. She put Mr. Williams on the line.

He sounded choked up. "Rain, suh, I shore am sorry 'bout your dad. I found him on the flo' when I come over to watch tha game, so I called the amlance an they come get 'im. Then I done thought I'd better call you, but I diden know how. So, mizus Williams, she's the one recommed I call Wayne, so I did."

"You did the right thing, Mr. Williams. I called to let you know that there's no point for you and Mrs. Williams to come to the hospital right now; they've got Dad on medicine to make him sleep, so his body can rest. The doctors might let him wake up later this evening. You could come visit him then. I know he'd appreciate your company."

"Yessuh, pleez give us a call. We'll be right here awaitin' to hear from you."

Rain hit the end button on his phone. Mr. Williams was his father's best friend and vice versa. A visit from him would help for sure. Although Mr. Williams was ten years older than his father, Rain knew the two still enjoyed working the land together from dawn to dusk. "The lan always gives a body sompen' to do," Mr. Williams liked to say. The black man served as a living memory bank of words of wisdom, parables, and folklore that had been passed down from generation to generation by southern African-Americans.

When Rain drove the mini-van under Interstate 20 and noted the puffy white clouds against the blue morning sky, he remembered the day, decades ago, that Mr. Williams explained the origin of clouds.

"See up there, Rain, suh. Them white clouds done come from Texas; dat's why they blow from Wes' to Eas'. Jus' like us, in Texas, they's got cotton fields, too. 'Cept Texas fields is so big all you see is white on the groun' for miles and miles. Looks like snow, they's so much cotton. Well, in the sprang, them tornadas come suck the cotton right up into the heavens. Then Gawd plays wit the cotton and makes all kines of shapes wit it."

Rain laughed at the boyhood memory of Mr. Williams twirling his arms over his head to simulate a tornado sucking cotton into the sky and then pretending to be God, molding cotton into a cloud with his big strong hands.

Rain slowed after he saw the LaQuinta located up ahead. A few hundred yards beyond the hotel, Rain could see Meridian's newest indoor shopping mall. Bonita Lakes Mall had replaced the old Village Fair Mall he knew as a kid. It opened a year ago, but he had yet to visit. That would change in a few minutes.

Rain checked in and negotiated a "king plus" room for $39, which included the hospital discount. He had plenty of money and could have paid any amount, but he still liked dickering a bargain.

Upon reaching his room, Rain collapsed onto the king-sized bed. The orange digital numbers on the nightstand alarm clock read 10:05. He stared at the ceiling for a moment before he decided he'd check voicemail. He dialed his own cellular phone number, and when prompted, tapped in his password. As he expected, most messages were from people expressing sympathy with a few more important ones he'd take care of later.

October in Mississippi often brings warm days and cool, chilly nights. The maid had left on the heater to counteract the early morning chill and now, as Rain lay on the bed with the cell phone close to his chest, the room started to become uncomfortable. He reminded himself that he needed to get rolling, especially if he wanted to have the car back by lunch. He grabbed the keys from the nightstand and headed for the door. Rain didn't want the room to be an oven when he returned that afternoon, so on his way out, he clicked the knob on the heater to the off position. Rain took a second to glance through the huge glass window directly in front of him. A few floors below, he noticed Catherine's green mini-van in the parking lot. It was a clean, practical vehicle that must have been handy for transporting the kids and their gear to and from football and cheerleading practices, but he'd always remember her driving that red Corvette convertible. Rain wondered if she remembered the sports car as fondly as he did. He closed his eyes and the memory returned.

On a late Friday afternoon, Rain, Wayne, and Stacey lounged atop the shiny red hood of Wayne's graduation present, a brand new Ford 150 pickup truck. Rain hated the taste of beer, but there he sat, drinking one out of a brown paper sack. The three were supposed to be celebrating. They had all graduated from Jefferson Davis Academy the previous weekend. Wayne had his arms around Stacey and held her tight. He had presented her with a diamond engagement ring the night before, and she had accepted his proposal. Rain watched from the corner of his eye as Stacey snuggled with her fiancé, lightly kissing him on the neck. Normally, Railroad would have been hanging out with them, but his dad had insisted he fly up to Princeton for the weekend to search for an off-campus apartment.

Rain turned up the bottom of the brown bag and winced as another bitter gulp slid down his throat. He checked his watch. It read six o'clock, and the early June sun still had about another hour to go before it would slide behind the western horizon. At Wayne's insistence, they had gotten to the College Park Shopping Center well over an hour before anyone else would even begin parking or cruising 8th Street. Wayne claimed he wanted to make sure they got one of the prime parking spaces for the evening. So there they were, drinking beer in front of the College Park's movie theater that had been designed by an architect who must have had a thing for giant sombreros.

Against his better judgment, which wanted to pour it onto the asphalt, Rain swallowed the last of the flat beer and crunched the aluminum can by squeezing it as hard as he could. He felt especially foul, mainly because he had not only given in about coming into town so early, but he also had to watch the two lovebirds coo over one another as if they were on a first date. Without looking, Rain flipped the crumpled can with its brown sack over his shoulder toward the bed of the pickup, then lay flat on his back against the warm hood and closed his eyes. The crushed can made a muffled plinking sound as it came to rest against the tailgate.

"Hey, Rain, this is a new truck. I don't want beer spilled all over it," Wayne admonished.

"I'll wash it for you tomorrow."

"You want another one?" Stacey offered.

"No, thanks."

"At least it's good to see your arm's gettin' better. A month ago you wouldn't have been able to throw anything that far," Wayne playfully added.

Rain failed to find humor in his friend's lighthearted observation. Everything had gone sour in a hurry after the Christmas holidays, and Rain still struggled against tears whenever someone reminded him of his misfortune.

In a January basketball game against Kemper Academy, Rain severely sprained his left ankle when he came down on the side of another kid's shoe after tipping in an offensive rebound. Those two points proved costly. Although he tried to play the remainder of the season through the pain of the sprain, he was never the same dominating player after the injury. The heavy tape, which lived on his ankle like a permanent, sticky fungus, limited almost every facet of his game. He could barely run the floor, he couldn't jump high for rebounds, and his ability to cut to the basket or post up defenders disappeared. The monster in the middle became the gnome in the dome. He no longer could block the shots of quick guards that penetrated the lane, which cut down his own team's defensive aggressiveness. Looking back, he shouldn't have played on the bad ankle. He should have let it heal properly before baseball season started, but his competitive nature wouldn't let him. At the beginning of March, with its star center at fifty percent strength, the Jeff Davis basketball team lost in the regional playoffs to a school they had beaten by twenty points at the beginning of the season.

Baseball turned out even worse. At the end of March, Rain still hobbled as he jogged with Wayne and Railroad from the locker room to the baseball diamond for their first day of practice. All three seniors knew baseball held their best chance to bring home a long-overdue state championship to Jefferson Davis Academy. Also at the forefront of their minds was the fact that baseball would give them the opportunity to play in front of several pro scouts. Rain, Wayne, and Reece all entertained dreams of earning a living as professional baseball players.

But the ecosystem of a baseball team and its season can be extremely delicate. Any change or variation of a single element can result in catastrophic consequences. An excellent example or comparison is the well-known parable that emphasizes the importance of the little things. “For the want of a nail, the shoe was lost; for the want of a shoe, the horse was lost; for the want of a horse, the rider was lost; for a want of a rider, the message was lost; for the want of a message, the battle was lost; for a want of a victory, the morale was lost; and for the want of morale, the war was lost.”

Rain’s nail, that spring, was a healthy ankle. At the end of his pitching delivery, every time he landed on the weakened joint, a sharp pain shot up through his entire leg as if he had stepped into a puddle of electricity. Although his father recognized what had begun happening and warned him, Rain continued compensating for his bad ankle by altering his delivery. He shortened his stride to relieve the impact on the ankle, and as a result, began overthrowing. His right arm never fully adjusted to the new mechanics. Although he had never experienced arm pain before, by his third start, his right elbow ached with soreness. By the fifth start, at the end of April, the pain had become unbearable. Between innings, he caked on a thick combination of analgesic balms in hopes of relieving the searing pain, if only for a few minutes.

Professional baseball scouts know baseball. Their sole job is to watch a young prospect and make a determination on whether or not the kid possesses the talent for a realistic chance to play in the major leagues. Before the season started, scouts drooled at Rain Henry’s potential based on his performance as a high school junior. He had a well-deserved reputation as a tough, cool competitor with a dynamite arm. Scouts held mild interest in Wayne LeRoy and Reece Rosenblum, as well, but great pitchers can dominate games and directly control whether a team wins or loses. These types of pitchers, true dominators, are worth their weight in platinum. When the scouts came to watch Rain pitch his senior year, they shook their heads. The radar guns indicated Rain Henry's fastball had lost almost ten miles an hour from the previous year. And when they craned their necks and saw Rain vigorously rubbing ointments on his pitching elbow in the dugout, many made similar notes at the bottom of their scouting reports: "Rain Henry, good competitor, but arm questionable. Ten percent or less." Others crumpled their scouting reports into a ball before throwing them away in a steel trash barrel on the way to their car; they'd never recommend that their organizations draft an eighteen-year-old kid with arm trouble. By the time the doctor completely stopped Rain from pitching in mid-May, it didn't really matter. The scouts had disappeared from the stands weeks before.

Wayne and Railroad carried the team to the playoffs, but without Rain in the lineup as a pitcher or a position player, they couldn't carry it much further. Because Rain had been diagnosed with severe tendonitis, the doctor advised him against even picking up a baseball for eight to ten weeks. When Reece stranded the tying and go-ahead runs on second and third by grounding out to the pitcher to end the season, Rain covered his face on the bench and cried. Injuries had relegated the team captain to the status of chief bench cheerleader, and Rain knew high school bench cheerleaders didn't get drafted.

After the loss, even the ever-sanguine Wayne LeRoy couldn't console his best friends. He invited Rain and Railroad to come join Stacey and him for some pinball at his parents' newly built house on Dalewood Lake, but neither accepted. Rain wanted to do nothing more than go home and spend time alone. Reece offered no excuse. Without a word, he made a bee-line to his Z-28 Camaro, jumped in, and sped off into the night.

Rain had ridden to the game with his father and grandmother, and now they climbed back into his father's truck to head for home. Mildred Henry sat between her son and grandson.

"Dad, Granny, don't they always say in church that God has a plan for everyone?"

"Yes, Rain. And I believe he does," Mildred Henry replied as she patted her grandson on the leg.

"What's his plan for me? I just knew I was supposed to play baseball."

They turned south onto two-lane Hwy 19, and Jim Henry switched his lights from the high to the low beams as cars approached from the opposite direction. "Rain, no one knows what God has planned for them until after it happens. Sure, you had some injuries that kept you down over the last few months, but it's not the end of the world. Maybe God wants you to know what it's like to feel disappointment before he allows you a taste of success. Maybe he wants you to attend the Naval Academy, graduate, and become an admiral. Maybe he doesn't. You know, just because Wayne didn't get accepted doesn't mean you shouldn't consider going without him. You and Wayne and Reece are always going to be close friends, but there will come a time when life will force you three to be more independent. Even if all three of you had great years in baseball and Jeff Davis had won the state championship, the odds of one team drafting all of you together is virtually zero."

Rain shifted his position as he leaned against the door. "Dad, do you think I'll get drafted?"

Jim Henry smiled as he turned on the blinker, indicating to the cars behind a right turn onto Braygen Road. "It's tough to say, Son. Scouts are probably afraid of your arm holding out over the long-term. When you altered your delivery at the beginning of the season, you changed your mechanics and lost some velocity as well. There may be a few organizations willing to take a chance based on what you did last year. I guess we'll find out in a few days, won't we?"

"Yes, sir," Rain answered. The draft began next week. Rain rubbed the sore tendons that ran in and around his right elbow with his left fingers as though it might bring some pre-draft luck. It certainly made his arm feel better.

They were about a mile from the farmhouse when something in the woods caught Rain's grandmother's attention. She pointed down one of the farm's old logging trails. "Did you boys see that?"

Jim Henry stopped the truck, backed up, and then turned onto the old road. About thirty yards ahead they saw the back of Reece's Z-28.

Rain opened the door and stepped out. "It's Railroad, Granny. He's probably sulking over at the trestle. I bet he tried to hide his car so we wouldn't know he was here. I'll go check and meet ya'll back at the house."

"You need a flashlight, Son?"

"No thanks; the moon's pretty bright."

"Jim, I don't like Rain going off into the woods by himself. You go with him."

"I'm sure he'll be okay, Mildred. Remember, he's grown up in these woods. Rain, do you want me to come with you?"

"No thanks, Dad. I'll be fine, Granny. I know the trail through here like the back of my hand."

Jim Henry shifted the transmission into reverse. "Okay, Rain. You've got an hour. If you're not back at the house by then, Mackel and I'll come look for you."

"Fair enough, Dad. See you both soon." Rain closed the door and headed down the trail past Railroad's car.

Sure enough, after a ten-minute walk, Rain made out a dark blob with two stubby legs dangling from the opposite side of the railroad trestle that crossed Okatibbee Creek. Rain scrambled up the gravel incline that supported the tracks and stepped onto the bridge. "You'll be here a few hours, if you want to throw yourself into the train. The next one comes tomorrow morning around seven."

Reece never turned his head, and his legs continued to scissor back and forth over the edge. "How'd you know I was down here?"

"Granny saw the reflection of your license plate. If you were trying to hide your car, you didn't park it far enough around the bend in the trail."

"Thanks for the tip."

"No problem. So you gonna show me a moonlit back flip now, or what?"

"Not tonight," Reece answered while the short scissors continued cutting the air.

"Well then, what are you doing?"

"Thinking."

"'Bout what?"

"Things."

Rain sat down next to his friend. "Like what?"

"Like how happy Wayne is with Stacey, and I can't even get a date, because I'm three hairs taller than a midget. Like how your dad loves you and has always been a huge part of your life, and mine vanished for eight years, only to resurface and throw guilt money my direction. Like how I can't even get a hit when our team needs it the most, and I'll never get drafted."

"Damn, Railroad. Are you gonna jump now, or do I need to give you a shove?"

"Thanks for your sympathy."

"If you're looking for pity, you'd better head home to momma, Reece Rosenblum, 'cause you ain't getting it from me. You don't have a date because the girls around here are too stupid to understand now what a success you'll be in a few years. I'll bet you'll be fightin' them off, then. As for your dad, you should be glad he ever came back into your life at all. And for cryin' out loud, he's offering to pay for you to get an Ivy League education. Take the money and then tell him to go screw himself, if you still don't like him after four years of free tuition, room, and board. As for getting drafted, no, you probably won't be. And neither will Wayne, and neither will I. Why? Because we play for a teeny tiny, all-white private academy in the middle of country-ass Mississippi. If anyone had a chance to get drafted it was me, because I was a pitcher with a good, live fastball, and now I can't even roll a baseball to home plate because it feels like my arm might fall off. So here we are, wallowing in our sorrow while the rest of the world moves on, just like the water flowing down there." He pointed.

Finally, Railroad cracked a smile. "Rain, your life does suck worse than mine. I think I'll end it for you." Quick as a lynx, he sprang behind Rain and tried to push him off the bridge.

For the first time in his life, Rain accurately anticipated what Railroad was about to do. He deftly moved to his left as Reece tried to shove him forward and gave Railroad enough of a pull so he lost his balance. Reece clawed madly at the air as he tried to reverse the momentum that would send him over the edge and into the creek, but he could not. Rain would remember the look on his friend's face for the rest of his life. It was a look of sinister congratulations, one that said, "Well, old boy, you finally got me this time." He landed in the cannonball position, which created a huge splash that sent silvery droplets of water high into the moonlight.

After Rain helped pull him to shore, Reece stripped all the way to his underwear. While they walked back to the Z-28, Rain helped him wring out his clothes. The car was in sight when Reece asked a peculiar question. "Rain, seriously, have you ever thought the pressure was too much and you couldn't handle it?"

"I think everybody feels that way at one time or another."

They reached the car and Reece stopped. "Let's say I wanted to start over with a completely new identity. I know you love to study maps. Where do you think the best place to do that would be, Florida?"

"Sure, if you wanted to stand around in a mouse costume and have your picture taken with bunches of kids. Heck, I don't know, Railroad. The Northwest, I guess. That's where I'd go. You could join a logging crew or a fishing boat and probably make some decent money without people asking lots of questions about your background."

"Thanks, Rain. I wanted your opinion, you know, in case the pressure gets to be too much at Princeton."

"So you've made up your mind, then."

"Yeah, I'm pretty sure. My best friend recommended I suck some of my dad's money for a few years."

"Sounds like your friend's a smart guy."

"He thinks so, anyway."

CHAPTER NINE
A NIGHT TO NEVER FORGET

Rain thought he might become ill. Wayne and Stacey cooed, giggled, and whispered in each other's ears over and over again. He had finished the rest of the flat beer fifteen minutes ago and his back now began to sweat against the warm metal of the truck's hood. He didn't care. Rain closed his eyes and his eyelids functioned as television screens that repeatedly played the disastrous events of the last six months with a distinct and cruel clarity.

Rain's eyes remained closed when his ears picked up the powerful rumblings from another car engine as it parked close by. At first, the gurgling sound served as a momentary distraction and without checking, Rain deduced that some redneck in a jacked-up, supercharged El Camino had decided to take his hick girlfriend to a Friday night flick inside the giant sombrero.

Maybe the couple had a good idea. Keeping his eyes closed, Rain considered following the new arrivals into the theater. He could watch the movie, eat some popcorn and a candy bar for dinner, and still be back outside before any serious cruising action got started. Anywhere would be an improvement over his current position. Being a third wheel for the millionth time was bad enough, but having to repeatedly listen to the newly engaged lovebirds profess rediscovered love for one another constituted cruel and unusual punishment.

Perhaps he knew the redneck couple. If he did, Rain felt sure they'd let him tag along. When he finally opened his eyes and rolled his head toward the sound of the shutting car door, what Rain saw took his breath away. Only one person got out instead of two, and the car was not an El Camino but instead a brand new, fire-engine-red Corvette convertible with its top down. The sleek and beautiful machine shimmered in the late afternoon sun like a brash colt ready to run.

Rain had heard the story of the graduation present, but he had seen neither the gift nor the recipient until now. The setting sun's rays cast a brilliant aura that outlined Catherine Landerson as she walked their direction. Rain's eyes caressed her from top to bottom. A gray Ole Miss baseball cap hid most of her golden hair, but a few silk strands managed to escape confinement on both sides. They softly blew around her face like hushed children's whispers. Catherine wore a white Delta Gamma sorority T-shirt and tight, faded blue jeans. Like a model strutting down the runway, her hips sashayed and her pearly smile widened the closer she came to her audience.

"Surprise!" Wayne and Stacey shouted together at Rain. After all these years, their chance to play Cupid had finally presented itself again, and they seemed to be enjoying the moment tremendously.

With the grace of a feline, Catherine sprang over the truck's front grill and rotated in midair before landing between Stacey and Rain. The hood momentarily crumpled from the impact before regaining its original shape with a metallic groan. "Nice truck, Wayne. Wanna trade?"

Wayne frowned. "It was until you put a huge dent in it." He stared at the Corvette for a few seconds, apparently mulling her proposition. "Nah, it'd be tough to haul things in the back of that," Wayne answered as he leaned over and gave her a shove Rain's direction.

Instantly, Rain avoided contact by sliding to the pavement. He was neither impressed nor in any kind of mood to be toyed with. Who the hell did they think they were, to pull a stunt like this on him? "Catherine, what are you doing here?" he seethed.

Catherine pouted. "It's good to see you, too, Rain." She began to slide slowly for the front of the hood. "Maybe I should leave."

"Maybe you should. I'd hate for you to be seen hanging out with me, which might, you know, potentially throw everything away you've built over the years with your frequently inebriated, cheater of a boyfriend." Though he didn't let it show, on the inside Rain relished the rush of moral superiority. He had waited a painfully long time to say those words. They had been well rehearsed for such a moment, and he delivered them flawlessly and with the flair of an Oscar-winning actor.

Stacey's words came fast and sharp, like daggers to his ears. "Rain, why don't you shut up! You're actin' like a jerk, or worse. You don't know all the facts."

Wayne stopped Catherine with his foot. "Hold on there, Catherine." Once she had been corralled, he turned his attention to his scowling friend. "Everybody take a deep breath. Rain, give us a chance to explain. It was my idea. I thought a double date with Catherine might cheer you up."

Draft week had come and gone, and every single major league team passed on Jefferson Davis's former pitcher, shortstop, and catcher. They had not expected to be selected, but all three still felt a stinging disappointment nonetheless. Rain held out hope that maybe he'd be chosen in one of the final rounds, but the phone never rang. And like the pro scouts, every major school went from hot to cold on Rain Henry and his troubled right arm. Only Mississippi Military College and coach Chain Porter maintained what

Rain considered to be sincere interest throughout the entire season.

When he, Wayne, Reece, Mildred, and Jim Henry visited MMC at the end of April, Rain found the campus and location acceptable, rather than spectacular. Certainly, it couldn't compare to the Naval Academy, which he had visited as a "PSC," or probable selection candidate, in March. The Academy's campus thoroughly impressed him. It boasted its own docks, complete with sailboats, and was situated on a sturdy peninsula that thrust majestically forward into Chesapeake Bay like the bow of a mighty aircraft carrier. But since Wayne hadn't been accepted to Annapolis, Wayne convinced Rain that MMC was the next best thing. Rain's father and grandmother were delighted with the decision, and Rain and Wayne had mailed their signed scholarship papers to Coach Porter yesterday. They would report to campus for freshmen indoctrination in August. Coach Porter even promised that he would make the necessary arrangements for the two best friends to room with one another. At least he and Wayne would have four more years of playing baseball together, despite the upcoming tribulations he expected from having Jeremy Langford as a teammate. Wayne, of course, was jubilant. He had taken an enormous step toward the light at the end of the tunnel: his goal of becoming a pilot. In fact, Wayne had already purchased his leathers at Meridian's Queen City Army Surplus Store and, in one week, rubbed on enough polish so that each shoe appeared to have been made of black glass.

Rain folded his arms, and his nostrils flared as he rotated his glare from Wayne to Stacey and back to Catherine. "Let's hear an explanation. And it better be a good one."

Catherine crawled like a crab back up the hood and leaned against the windshield. Her voice sounded soft and conciliatory. "I broke up with Trip last week, right before he left to spend the summer in Europe, because I wanted a second chance to go out with you. Aren't you still interested in having a date with me?"

Rain stood speechless. Somehow, Catherine's words dissipated his anger the same way a tranquilizer soothes a wild animal.

Stacey smiled and drew Wayne close again. "Rain, are you gonna say anything? I think Catherine just asked you for a date."

A warmth spread through Rain unlike anything he had ever felt before. His entire body tingled as if each and every cell excitedly jumped up and down to generate the heat that comes from pure joy. He grinned wryly. "Okay, Catherine, I'll go out with you on one condition."

Catherine returned his smile. "What's that, Rain Henry?"

"You've got to give me a ride in that new car of yours."

Catherine laughed. "I'll do better than that. I'll give it to you."

"Give it to me?"

"Yes, give it to you. It'd be the least I could do to show my appreciation for a date with the best baseball player in Mississippi." She took the keys from her pocket and flipped them to Rain. "But you've got to give it back to me later tonight. I might need it tomorrow."

Wayne leaned around Stacey and exclaimed, "Catherine, you don't need to fool around with this guy! He's too moody! I'll go on a date with you if give me the car for the night!"

Stacey punched her fiancé in the arm and bit him playfully on the neck. "Think again, Mr. LeRoy!"

Catherine motioned at the waiting Corvette. "Go ahead, Rain. Why don't you come pick me up? We'll make it an official date."

"Sounds good to me," Rain said as he turned. Tightly between his thumb and index finger, he held the thick black key that displayed the checkered flag and Chevrolet insignia.

"Hold on a minute," Wayne commanded. "I thought we were all going to a movie. Sorry, you two, but we ain't got time for ya'll to go on a joy ride."

Catherine patted Wayne's knee. "Wayne, I don't think

we'll be back in time for the movie." A dainty flick of her wrist reminded Rain to go get the car.

Rain eased back the Corvette's white leather seat and, surprisingly, found ample legroom for his long legs. He examined the cluster of instruments arranged before him. The speedometer went all the way to 160, and Rain wondered if the car could really go that fast. He slid the key into the ignition and rotated if forward with a slight twist. Like a volcano, the 350 cubic inch, 5.7 liter V-8 erupted with diabolical fury. Maybe it could go faster than 160, Rain thought as he tightly gripped the leather steering wheel.

Because he had grown up on a farm, Rain knew how to ride horses, but he had never broken one in. Now, he decided, the emotions that ran through his body as he sat in the Corvette's cockpit must be similar to those a cowboy experiences the first time he eases onto the back of a wild stallion. Rain hoped he could hold on to the magnificent beast he was about to spur.

Wayne, Stacey, and Catherine slid from the hood to the asphalt parking lot and waited in front of the pickup. Rain turned the steering wheel to the left and lightly pushed the accelerator, just enough to rev the engine one notch above idle. Slowly, the sports car moved forward a few feet at a time. A few seconds later, Rain stopped perpendicular to Wayne's truck.

"Watch out everybody, Rain Henry's trying to set a new speed record," Wayne said sarcastically. "You sure know how to make that thing *move*."

Rain smiled as he climbed out of the car, its engine still gurgling. "Sorry to disappoint you, Wayne." He took Catherine's velvet-like hand, led her to the passenger side, and opened her door. "But it's hard to make the car *move* when you have to stop in twenty yards, even if you're in a Corvette." Rain returned to his position behind the wheel and fastened his seatbelt. He checked to make sure Catherine fastened hers as well. Then, he gave a final look over his left shoulder at the two grinning matchmakers. "We'd invite you two along, but sorry, no back seat."

Wayne started to say something in reply, but nobody, including Stacey who stood right next to him, could have heard anything but the screaming rear tires as Rain's foot slammed the gas pedal to the floorboard. All 300+ horses rampaged at once, which pinned Rain to the back of his seat as though someone stuck a giant thumbtack through his chest. He had done similar peel-outs with his pickup, Old Blue, but never with a machine like the Corvette, and he almost fishtailed into a parked van before he regained control. Luckily, Catherine covered her eyes as soon as he hit the gas. Otherwise, she probably would have booted him from the driver's seat for coming so close to wrecking her graduation gift. In the rearview mirror, he saw the lovebirds coughing and waving as they tried to clear the pale blue haze generated by the Corvette's smoking tires.

Rain stopped about fifty yards from where they had been milliseconds before. He and Catherine looked over their shoulders at the same time. Rain shouted at the top of his lungs, "How's that, Wayne, you smart-ass?"

Wayne replied with the only sign language he knew, then steered his fiancée toward the sombrero.

Catherine and Rain burst out laughing.

From the College Park Shopping Center, they turned right onto Highway 19 North, which eventually led to Philadelphia, Mississippi. Rain kept the speed down as they passed the Highway Patrol office immediately to the left. After a few miles, they passed the Knights of Columbus lodge right next to Haystack's only competition for Meridian's roller skating dollar, Carousel Skate Center. The Dixie gas station on the right marked the northwestern boundary of Meridian's city limits, and here Highway 19 straightened into a long, two-lane drag strip. The road taunted Rain and the Corvette.

In twenty minutes, Rain had completely leapt from one end of the boredom spectrum to the other, with no stop in between. He contemplated punching the accelerator again, but resisted the temptation. Still, with no cars in front, he brought their speed up to seventy, fifteen miles over the posted limit, and settled back into the comfortable leather seat. As he watched the road zip under the giant, oversized hood, the wind whipped his hair and blew short, sporadic bursts of air into his ears. He didn't know where they might be going and he decided it really didn't matter, because this was heaven.

Although the study of art had never been Rain's favorite subject in school, the scene surrounding him reminded him of a fabulous painting, and suddenly, he realized why rich people paid thousands and sometimes millions of dollars for strokes of paint that simply hung on the wall. A beautiful painting expresses pure, uncensored emotion. The emotion comes from not only the subject of the work, but from the artist himself who conveys his feelings through the various colors arranged on the canvas. Rain had painted only when forced by the art teacher, and now he desperately wished he had put more effort into the assignments.

He would have given any amount of money for an artist to paint his current scene and paint it with the emotion it so richly deserved. His first date with Catherine Landerson, surrounded by a cloudless, late afternoon sky, and cruising down the highway in a brand-spanking-new red Corvette convertible with the top down deserved to be properly recorded somehow, some way.

Rain would paint the scene himself, damn his lack of experience. He decided to create a mental masterpiece, colorful and vibrant. A work filled with enough emotion to last in his mind forever.

Rain looked to his right at the beautiful young woman he had desired even before he knew or understood the true meaning of-the word. She removed her baseball cap, and her silken hair flew wildly in the backwash of the hurricane-force winds blowing only a few feet beyond the convertible's protective shell. Rain couldn't see Catherine's icy blue eyes behind her dark sunglasses, but he imagined the sapphires twinkling brilliantly, and he mentally painted them that way. His heart raced and his face flushed when Catherine placed her hand against his cheek and held it there. On his left, the dying sun burned from bright orange to orange-red as it made a final, mad dash for the western horizon. And yet, as a final present to Rain, it gave a glowing, natural light to his painting which served as a lacquer coating that would seal and safeguard his masterpiece for all of eternity.

Catherine's hand moved from his cheek to his hair and she gently messaged his scalp with her fingers. Soon, they came upon a slow-traveling station wagon that brought the Corvette back to the legal speed limit. The reduction in speed dramatically reduced the noise level.

"So, Rain Henry, do you like it?"

"I love it. It's got to be one of the coolest things I've ever done." His painting completed, he hung it on the wall of the room that also housed his soul.

"I'm glad. Have you guessed where we're going?"

"You're treating me to dinner at the finest McDonald's in Philadelphia, Mississippi."

Catherine giggled and pulled her hand from his hair to her lap. "Always the kidder, aren't you? Stacey told me to expect that. Anyway, that sounds like a wonderful idea, but I'd hoped for something a bit more romantic."

"Such as?"

"Such as get ready to turn up here to the right."

As quickly as she said it, Rain caught on. "Excellent idea, Catherine! I should have known. We're headed to the dam. You know I've been there once or twice, myself," he said with a devilish grin. Rain made the sharp turn from Highway 19 onto the road that led to the dam, and the Corvette's wide tires felt like they were riding on rails. "Let me guess. You've got some fishing poles and a bucket of chicken livers in the trunk. We'll catch some catfish and roast them over an open fire."

"Rain, did you study vocabulary words at Jeff Davis?"

"Every once in a while."

"Perhaps I need to define 'romantic' for you?"

They drove on the secondary road for about a mile, only traveling about thirty miles an hour. At that speed, virtually no wind swirled inside the Corvette. Catherine unbuckled her seatbelt and leaned against the passenger door as she waited for his reply. Something compelled Rain to reach over. His fingers brushed against the hair on the side of her face, and she leaned her head into the cradle of his hand. He remembered imagining how her golden hair might feel that day as a ten-year-old kid at Key Field. It didn't disappoint. Catherine's hair felt silky smooth and as soft as the fur on a kitten. "Sorry, Catherine. I'm giving you a hard time. In case you couldn't tell, I'm a little nervous. I've been on our first date a thousand times in my mind, but now that it's actually happening, it's rather surreal."

Catherine put her hand over his. "So you use humor and sarcasm as some sort of a protective defense mechanism to hide your nervousness?"

Rain shifted in his seat, but held his hand under hers and gently stroked her cheek. "I guess so. It probably comes from hanging out with the likes of Wayne LeRoy and Reece Rosenblum. I'll try to do better."

"Well, tonight you're hanging out with me, and me only." Catherine closed her eyes and guided Rain's hand to her forehead. Slowly, she moved his fingers down over her thin eyebrows and the outline of her nose before stopping at her lips. Here she paused, slightly opened her mouth, and ran her warm, moist tongue over the tips of his fingers.

For the second time on the trip, Rain nearly lost control of the vehicle. Luckily, Catherine's eyes were closed again and they were driving slowly. The sudden swerve to avoid running off the road ended the sensual moment. Rain claimed he had jerked the car to avoid a rabbit hell bent on suicide.

A minute later, Rain and Catherine passed below the half-mile Okatibbee Lake dam that rose to their left like the crest of an enormous, earthen wave about to crash over them. They reached the end of the grass-covered wave, and Rain guided the Corvette up a narrow road that snaked back and forth until it ended at a small parking lot even with the top of the dam. A tiny wooden sign announced that they had reached East Bank Park.

Rain turned off the ignition and handed Catherine the keys. Straight ahead, the dam held back a massive amount of water. On its surface, the reservoir waves were millions of tiny liquid ballerinas dancing blue, black, gray, and every hue in between beneath the teal sky. At the very far edge of the horizon, a dark green sliver that represented a distant forest separated the fiery red sun from the cool blue lake. "Catherine, this is beautiful. Do you come up here often?"

Catherine got out and headed for rear of the car. "It is beautiful, isn't it." She popped the trunk and pulled out an oversized straw picnic basket and red-checkered blanket. "Come, on, slowpoke! Help me carry something! I want to be set up before the sun completely disappears."

Rain grabbed the handle of the picnic basket with one hand and took Catherine's hand with the other. Together, they ran like schoolchildren at recess toward a small piece of land shaped like a shark's tooth that jutted about twenty yards onto the stage of the waving ballerinas. Against a lone tree, Catherine spread the blanket.

Rain, propped against the trunk, sat facing the vanishing sun. Placing the basket beside him, he looked up to see Catherine blocking his view. She clasped her hands together and then moved them apart with a look of anticipation. Rain understood and spread his legs. Catherine settled between them, her back leaning gently into his chest, and they fit together like two pieces of a jigsaw puzzle. Rain placed his chin delicately on her shoulder, and her hair tickled the side of his face. She smelled wonderful.

Around them, nature's symphony conducted its evening

concert and Rain listened intently. Birds and cicadas sang and chirped in the stand of trees behind them, and the minute waves made a lapping sound as they licked the shoreline and the rocks of the adjacent dam. The leaves in their supportive tree rustled with the breeze, and every so often, a fish jumped from the water, momentarily escaping its wet world before returning to reality with a "kerplunk." Although he really had to strain, Rain could also hear the humming from dragonfly wings as dozens flitted to and fro in an oversized game of aerial tag.

The sun became a giant circular saw, the type employed by a lumber mill, as it sliced into the horizon of timber on the other side of the lake. Across the water and directly in front of Rain and Catherine, the reddish ball produced a thick line of golden dancers that performed on the water solely for them.

Rain held his date tight. His folded arms enveloped Catherine just below her breasts, and he could feel the slow, rhythmic beating of her heart.

"To answer your earlier question, Rain, I come here whenever something significant happens in my life, whether good or bad. This place holds so much beauty, especially at this time of the day, it relaxes me if I get too high and lifts me up if I'm feeling low."

"What's it doing for you now?"

Catherine leaned forward enough to allow her flexible body to rotate, and she stared with dilated pupils into Rain's eyes. Like a magnet, her lips moved for his. Less than an inch before they connected, she whispered, "Relaxing me, definitely."

Before tonight, Rain had given up trying to imagine what a first kiss with Catherine might be like. Now, those adolescent memories and fantasies came flooding back to him as if the dam before them had suddenly burst. Back then, he debated whether the first time would be an innocent brush of the lips or a full-blown French kiss like the ones in the movies he, Wayne, and Railroad used to sneak in and see.

He had always hoped for the French kiss and had worn out a pillowcase practicing his technique. But as the years passed, Rain resigned himself to the fact that he'd be lucky to even get a simple peck; most likely he'd never get to kiss her at all.

But now, as he returned Catherine's kiss, meshing his lips with hers, Rain learned another lesson: fantasies seldom measure up to the real thing. After a few seconds, Rain lowered his jaw, and his tongue made a cautious overture, like a foreign dignitary meeting the representative of another country for the first time. Catherine's representative welcomed Rain's ambassador with genuine enthusiasm and affection. After a half-minute of undulating introductions, their tongues investigated each other's mouths as though they explored one another's souls.

Their first kiss came and went as the sun slipped below the horizon leaving a rose-colored sky in its silent wake. With his newfound artistic ability, he painted a second picture and hung it next to the one of them riding in the Corvette.

Catherine smiled as she hovered a few inches from his face. "That was worth the wait, wouldn't you agree?"

"Definitely. Let's not wait so long for the next one."

"We won't, I promise." Catherine winked as she stood. "Are you hungry? I'm famished."

"Sure, I could eat," Rain said, though he felt hungrier than he admitted. The nervousness he experienced earlier in the evening had consumed its fair share of calories. "Whatcha got in that basket, a six-pack of beer and some Kentucky Fried Chicken?"

Catherine frowned. "Rain, there you go again."

"Sorry. Seriously, what do you have?"

"I have what every picnic needs: a bottle of white wine, some cheese and crackers, and two chicken salad sandwiches from the delicatessen."

Rain slapped his hand on his forehead and laughed heartily. "Boy, if Wayne and the rest of those country boys at Jeff Davis could see me now! Here I am on a sunset picnic with a beautiful, city-girl debutante, about to chow down on some first-class grub."

Catherine thrust both hands to her hips. "Rain, are you making fun of me?"

"Were you a debutante?"

"Of course."

Like a drill from football practice, Rain scrambled to his feet. Catherine tried to dodge his lunge, but he had learned proper tackling technique from countless hours on the gridiron. Catherine's sexy waist gave her fake away, and he had her legs pinned together and the rest of her body bent over his shoulder in an instant. Catherine playfully hit him hard on his backside before he gently laid her down in the prickly grass. He spread his body over hers like a comforter. The brilliance of her sapphire eyes astounded him. "Then no, I wasn't making fun of you, but I am proud to say you represent my first debutante sack." Rain kissed her again.

Much to his surprise, Rain enjoyed the taste of the crisp wine and bitter cheese. They went well together. The sandwiches tasted delicious. Or perhaps the company enhanced the flavor of the food, Rain mused as Catherine slept, semi-nude, on top of him under the picnic blanket in the Corvette's passenger seat. Her head, turned to the side, lay nuzzled under his chin. The underside of her bare breasts brushed the tops of his cradling arms every time she drew a breath, and although the night had grown late, the car's top remained down while love songs played softly on the radio. Surrounded by darkness, Rain counted the shimmering stars above. He pondered if his two best friends had enjoyed their evenings as much as he had.

Rain might have guessed that Railroad ate a cordial dinner at a five-star restaurant with his father in Trenton, but Rain could never have anticipated what fate had planned for Wayne LeRoy that very same evening. Surely, Rain would have attempted to surpass the 160 on the Corvette's speedometer if he had.

After the movie, Wayne and Stacey picked up two milkshakes before cruising 8th Street. Traffic was light and though they saw and said "hello" to a few former Jeff Davis classmates, they decided to head home early. Wayne watched TV at Stacey's house until the local news came on at 10:00. Now that they were engaged, Wayne felt Stacey should have let him stay later, especially since her parents were out of town, but she led him to the front door instead of her bedroom. He desperately wanted to spend the night to further prove his love for her, but had been sent home frustrated instead. Stacey said she still wanted to wait until they were married, which put Wayne in an especially foul mood considering the circumstances.

Wayne's parents were not home either, and that increased his anguish, because he could have easily gotten away with spending the night at Stacey's. Every Friday night, his mother played bingo with her sister, after which she spent the night at her sister's house. Two weeks ago, his father had accepted a new, high-paying job in Arkansas that required Roy LeRoy, Sr., to remain gone for the next several months.

While he drove, Wayne remembered that Roy, Jr. would be home, and Wayne turned his frustration with his girlfriend into anger for his brother. Wayne began to think of Roy as a leech, sucking off his parents, with no ambition to move forward with his life or even move out of the house, for that matter. The fistfights of the past had given way to an occasional verbal spar because Roy presented no physical challenge for Wayne. For the most part, the two brothers avoided contact, but every so often, a major confrontation erupted.

When he walked in the door and found Roy sleeping on the living room sofa in front of the TV, Wayne kicked Roy hard. "Wake up, Cinderella! I wanna watch some TV, and you're takin' up all the whole sofa. Get up to your room and go to bed."

Roy sat up and blinked a few times. "This is my house, too. I can watch TV down here if I want to."

"Not if I say you can't. Besides, you were asleep, anyhow. Now get out of here before I whip your ass. I feel like being alone, and I don't want you down here hanging around and botherin' me."

"But, Wayne I..."

Wayne never let him finished. He reached down with both hands and yanked his skinny older brother to his feet, holding him at arm's length and about an inch off the ground. "Listen, you mooching son-of-a-bitch, it's time you got a life and moved the hell out of this house. You're twenty-one for Christ's sake! I'll give you the rest of the summer to get things straightened out, but if you still live here when I get home at Christmas break, I'm gonna give you a beatin' you'll remember the rest of your life." Wayne shoved him in the direction of the hallway that led to Roy's room.

Roy regained his balance at the hallway's entrance and glared at his brother. His eyes squinted as they filled with venomous tears.

Yawning, Wayne sat down and dug between the sofa cushions for the missing remote control. He found it a few seconds later and flipped through the channels as his defeated brother continued to glare at him from the hallway's protective darkness. Finally, Roy turned and silently slithered to his room.

Roy slammed his door and sat on the edge of his bed. He hadn't told anyone, but he'd been saving money from his department store job. Lots of money. Over a thousand dollars lay hidden away in a duffle bag at the bottom of his closet. He hated to leave without saying goodbye to his mother, but that was the way it would have to be. His father and Wayne could go to hell, for all he cared. He thought of killing Wayne and stealing his mother's car, but then his mind thought of something even more sinister. So Wayne wanted to play college baseball, did he? So Wayne wanted to become a pilot, did he? So Wayne wanted to marry his prissy girlfriend and live happily ever after, did he? Roy licked the cracks between his dry lips. He'd put an end to his selfish brother's plans. Roy would do what needed to be done and still take his mother's car. He doubted his family would care enough to pursue him because they'd be all weepy over Wayne, the family's favorite son. His only regret was that he wouldn't be around long enough to watch his younger brother suffer.

The local station had signed off the air hours before and Wayne slept soundly on the sofa. The sound of the static masked his brother's stealthy approach, but the fuzzy light from the TV cast Roy's ominous and exaggerated shadow on the wall directly behind Wayne. With both hands, like a medieval executioner, Roy lifted Blackie, the huge iron skillet, high over his head and pulled it down hard.

Wayne dreamt he was about to graduate from advanced jet pilot training and finally earn his pilot's wings from the Navy. On this, his last day in Pensacola, Wayne decided to take an A-6 for a final flight over the azure waters of the Gulf of Mexico. As he climbed high over the sparkling blue diamonds below, he reflected on his wonderful life. He had graduated with honors from MMC and after two years of flight school, he and Stacey would finally be married in Meridian the following weekend. After the honeymoon, he and his bride would be stationed in Washington. Wayne could hardly wait to join his new squadron at Whidbey Island Naval Air Station in Oak Harbor.

But when Wayne began to level off, something on the floor of the cockpit caught his attention. The object looked like a hand grenade. That was strange, Wyane thought, as he reached down. Suddenly, the miniature bomb exploded, and fire engulfed Wayne's knees and legs. Wayne tried to ignore the excruciating pain and maintain control of the aircraft, but his efforts proved futile. Frantically, Wayne realized he must escape. He searched for the ejection lever, but could not find it. While the A-6 pitched forward into a steep, spiraling dive, Wayne LeRoy screamed in agony at the top of his lungs.

PART II

CHAPTER TEN
REPORTING

The new boxer shorts and undershirt felt better against Rain's skin and private parts as soon as he put them on in the store's dressing room. On his way out, with a single phone call, Rain made arrangements for some additional clean clothes from his New Orleans' apartment to arrive later that evening. At the mall's food court, he ordered two chicken sandwiches and a large lemonade. While waiting for his food, Rain browsed the Sunday edition of *The Meridian Star.* The paper neither mentioned Rain's return to Meridian, nor his father's condition. At least he had the rest of today before the story would officially break in tomorrow's paper. Rain didn't forget his promise of returning the car to Catherine before noon, so he ate the chicken sandwiches and drank the lemonade on the drive back to the hospital.

Rain retraced his route back to the medical center garage and parked in the same spot from which he had originally departed. He readjusted the seat, to the best of his recollection, to its previous position before he altered it to accommodate his large frame. While he climbed from the mini-van, the same security guard that assisted him earlier puttered by in his golf cart. They exchanged cordial waves.

A few minutes later, after a quick facial scan, the medical center's "vault" granted Rain access to the administration department. Catherine was unavailable because of a meeting, so he dropped off the keys with the bulldog. This time, however, Mrs. Jenkins treated him with kindness and actually smiled as she invited him to come back any time.

Rain headed for his father's room, and as he passed the third-floor nursing station, the younger nurses shot him the biggest flirtatious smiles he had ever seen. Rain wondered if they knew who he was. If they did, maybe that explained Mrs. Jenkins's behavior as well. Was the news already out? If so, his grace period of anonymity was about to expire; his plate held enough already.

Rain opened the door to his father's room and a fresh, sweet-smelling aroma from dozens of colorful flowers hit him full-force. The bouquets rested in vases of all shapes and sizes against the far wall of the room, transforming the bareness into a magnificent 3-D floral landscape. In slightly over two hours, Jim Henry's room had become an exotic garden bursting with enough variations of color to make a rainbow jealous. The flowers cheered up Rain tremendously and he wondered if they subconsciously lifted his father's spirits. Rain's "favorite" chair was shoved into the far corner to make space for the new decor, but it didn't seem to mind.

Rain checked his father and found that the yellowness in his skin had dissipated. Perhaps the flowers were responsible. Rain felt much better. He ventured into the garden and checked the cards to see whom he should thank for sending his father get well wishes. The extra-large arrangement of orchids came from the team. The LeRoys, the Williamses, and Railroad were all represented along with a few other individuals, including a single pink rose from Catherine. Rain opened the last card and sighed. It read:

"To Jim Henry, father of Meridian's own hometown hero. Best wishes for a full and speedy recovery. – The Meridian Star Sportswriters."

So much for privacy from the media, Rain thought as he returned the card to its envelope and reattached it between the prongs of the clear plastic fork jutting from the stems of the yellow daisies.

Rain returned to his father's side. "Well, Dad, looks like one or two people out there care about you. I know you can't see them, but maybe you can smell all the flowers they've sent." He put his hand on his father's forehead. "I think you're getting some color back in your face. I was beginning to worry that you were turning into a banana."

The son thought he saw movement in his father's lips, but if they had twitched, Rain didn't see them move again. He removed his hand from his father's forehead and planted a kiss on the warm spot where it had been. Rain pulled the blanket closer to his father's chin. "Okay, then. I've got to get down to the lobby to meet Wayne. He's taking me to get your truck. Don't forget how much I love you."

Before he left, Rain tightly gripped the fingers of his father's left hand. The digits were useless now, in this life, but soon they would be operational once again. Rain muttered a quick prayer and asked God to grant him one more opportunity to say goodbye to his father.

Wayne had already pulled into the loading zone and waited, engine running, as Rain emerged from the lobby. His fingers tapped impatiently along the top arch of the steering wheel, just as his mother's once did so many years ago. Rain climbed in and buckled his seatbelt.

"Any change?" Wayne asked.

"Some color's finally coming back to his skin."

"That's good."

Rain and Wayne soon passed Rain's hotel as they headed south on Highway 19.

"Make it to church this morning?" Rain asked.

"Yep, every Sunday morning, unless I'm out on the road. But if I am, Stacey and Jack still go."

After the first operation on his shattered kneecaps, Wayne

spent almost six months confined to his bed. At one point during the recovery, Wayne's lower appendages developed dangerous blood clots and doctors considered amputating both legs slightly above the knees. Luckily, a new and more potent blood thinner received approval by the FDA, and Wayne's circulatory condition improved before the doctors had to take such drastic measures. Over the two years that followed, Wayne endured four additional operations, none of which improved the functionality of his knees and legs. The perpetrator of the heinous act was never held legally accountable for his actions. The LeRoy family, exactly as Roy, Jr., anticipated, allowed him to vanish without a trace or a chase. He hadn't been heard from since.

A few miles later, the two friends escaped the city limits. They cruised along at sixty miles an hour when Wayne did a double take in the rearview mirror. "Hold on Rain – this guy's about to blow our doors off!"

Rain looked over his left shoulder and saw a silver Porsche flashing its lights as it approached them at what Rain guessed to be the speed of sound. A blind curve in the two-lane highway loomed ahead, and the road warned against passing with its double-yellow lines. Impending danger didn't seem to concern the driver of the Porsche. He never slowed as he changed lanes, whooshed past on the left, and whipped back to the right side of the road. Three seconds later, the silver blur disappeared around the corner.

Wayne shook his head and clucked his tongue. "I guess when you're goin' that fast, passin' on curves ain't a problem. You see the decal?"

Despite the car's excessive speed, the decal of the driver's alma mater couldn't have been missed or ignored; it covered almost the entire rear window. It consisted of an enormous Mississippi state flag, which flew side by side with a gigantic flag of the United States. Both were perched atop a white, castle-like military-style building called a battalion. At the bottom, bold and scarlet letters screamed the acronym "MMC."

"Yeah, I saw it." Rain acknowledged.

Both men recognized the decal, and Wayne grinned while Rain frowned. "Those guys own this state," Wayne said with an air of respect and admiration. He turned to face his passenger. "Rain, after all these years, can you honestly tell me you never regret your decision?"

Wayne posed the same question Rain had struggled to truthfully answer for more years than he cared to remember. "Honestly? I regret what happened that forced me to make the decision, but I don't regret the decision itself. I wouldn't be who I am today if I hadn't made the choice I did."

In mid-August of his eighteenth year, Rain Henry reported to the sweltering campus of Mississippi Military College in Natchez, Mississippi. His father and grandmother dropped him off the Sunday before "the fun" would begin the following day. One of the guards on duty at the front of the battalion led Jim Henry and the incoming freshman to his assigned sleeping quarters, a room on the third floor of Bravo Company in First Battalion.

Once the father and son finished moving in Rain's meager belongings, the time came to say goodbye. Rain and his father embraced tightly. With moist eyes and a big smile, Jim Henry released Rain from his one-armed bear hug and offered some final encouragement and words of advice. "Rain, your grandmother and I are very proud of you. We know you can do this. Just remember that every day gets a little easier. Also, remember that most of what happens is nothing more than a mental game; don't take things personally. If you think you're getting picked on, most likely there's another freshman getting it much worse."

Before Jim Henry walked out the rickety screen door, Rain asked a favor. "Dad, will you check on Wayne and write to me about how he's doing?"

"You can count on it, Son," Jim Henry replied with a final, firm handshake.

Rain watched the door slam shut after his father departed.

For the first time in his life, he realized that he stood truly on his own. That thought made a profound impact, and Rain made a mental note of the date and time.

He sat down on the lower bunk's thin plastic mattress and visually inventoried his new surroundings. Although he had never visited a prison cell, the room reminded Rain of one. It was roughly ten feet wide by twenty feet long, with walls covered by cheap wood paneling. Each wall ended on a wooden floor that appeared to have last been polished sometime before the outbreak of World War II. At the far end of the room, thick parallel bars ran the length of the large, square window that overlooked the school's field house. At the other end, a porcelain sink stood guard by the screen-door entrance. Directly across from where he lay, two metal sets of drawers, side by side, stood about five feet tall. These sets of drawers were, in turn, positioned between two mammoth, rectangular-shaped, bins that nearly reached the water-stained ceiling tiles. The open-ended bins functioned as clothes closets, Rain decided, because they had a round bar that connected each side about three-fourths of the way up from the bottom. On the window side of the room, to his left, two metal desks and their metal chairs sat opposite one another, each against a wall. The cell and its steel furnishings, originally painted battleship gray, must have been conceptualized by an interior designer who had a relative that owned a local scrap yard. Rain wondered if the school kept a blacksmith on retainer, simply so he could periodically hammer out the furniture's dents and dings. If it did, he certainly needed to stop by for some repair work.

Temperature-wise, the room felt incredibly hot and stuffy, and the heat soon began suffocating its new resident. Rain had read that MMC took pride in the fact that it remained one of the last colleges in the United States without dormitory air conditioning. To combat the heat, Rain opened the window, which unfolded in the center like a hardcover book. Thankfully, the iron mesh, which was obviously designed to keep him in, failed to keep a breeze out. The invisible, but welcome, visitor entered from outside the battalion and meandered through the room like a leisurely strolling ghost before departing through the screen door at the opposite side of the room.

Next, Rain plugged in his oscillating fan and placed it on the top of one of the metal chest of drawers. The fan had been at the forefront of a list of required freshman necessities the school mailed him two weeks after Chain Porter received Rain's scholarship papers. Thankfully, the fresh outside air, circulated by the fan, cooled his perspiring skin. Satisfied he could do nothing else to lower the room temperature, Rain flopped in the middle of the lower-bunk mattress and stared at the steel springs that supported the bed above him.

As he lay there, Rain felt crushed by the thought of Wayne stuck in a different room, one more familiar, but still similar to a prison. Immediately after the attack, Wayne displayed a resolute and brave exterior, but both Rain and Railroad knew he felt devastated on the inside. A month after the initial operation, when it became clear that Wayne would be lucky to walk again, much less march around with a rifle at MMC or play baseball, Rain briefly considered following Catherine to Ole Miss. He knew he could make the baseball team as a walk-on, especially since Ole Miss's coach promised Rain special consideration if he tried out. But Wayne pleaded with Rain to go on to MMC without him. "Do it for me," Wayne demanded with fierce, earnest eyes.

Rain reported to MMC, albeit only partially because of his friend's unrelenting pleas. Rain genuinely liked and respected Coach Porter. Porter had been at MMC for more than twenty years and acquired a legendary reputation for his knowledge of pitching. Porter himself had once been a minor league pitcher with a wicked overhand curveball and an above-average fastball. Throughout Rain's and Wayne's recruiting visit earlier that year, Porter displayed inexhaustible wit, charm, and a level of baseball intelligence that thoroughly impressed everyone, including Railroad. Over dinner, on the final evening of the visit, Chain Porter even remarked about how his first name rhymed with the names of his two most important recruits. After the meal concluded, everyone thanked MMC's coach for being such a wonderful host, and Porter put his arm around Rain as they all left the restaurant. He whispered that he believed Rain possessed the talent to be the best player ever to come out of Mississippi, and he personally wanted to help Rain reach his potential. Rain had nodded and smiled his thanks at the compliment. Rain truly looked forward to beginning his apprenticeship under Coach Chain Porter, even if it meant having to team up with Jeremy Langford.

Although the baseball scholarship and Wayne's entreating pleas held weight, Rain lay sweating on that plastic mattress primarily because of Catherine Landerson. Between kisses during that magical sunset picnic at Okatibbee Reservoir, Catherine told him how much she admired and respected his decision to become a cadet. She bragged at how handsome her new boyfriend would look in his military uniforms and how she could hardly wait to drive down the picturesque Natchez Trace to visit him.

Rain remembered how, at the end of the picnic, Catherine produced an enormous scrapbook that had been hidden in the Corvette's trunk. Rain's heart had nearly melted when she opened it. The very first page contained the article from *The Meridian Star*, the same article published the day Rain, as an eleven-year-old, almost pitched the East Lauderdale All-Stars into the state tournament. Catherine chronicled Rain's entire athletic career, all the way up to and including his senior year. The most recent newspaper clippings documented Jeff Davis's 43-0 football victory over Pamar, followed by articles on Rain's injury-marred basketball and baseball seasons. On the final page of the scrapbook, a small blurb cut from the back of the sports section mentioned Rain and Wayne signing baseball scholarships to attend MMC.

And though the revelation didn't occur until the end of July, Catherine's parents finally seemed to understand that their daughter loved this boy, a farmer's son, and grew more tolerant of Rain's presence in their lives. Rain still got chills from Mrs. Landerson's cold shoulder, but Dr. Landerson seemed to take a genuine interest in his daughter's new boyfriend. Three Sundays before Rain reported to MMC, Dr. Anderson invited him to play a round of golf at Meridian's exclusive Magnolia Country Club. Rain had never played golf before, so he rented a set of clubs from Buddy Thompson the day before the outing. That same Saturday, Buddy was nice enough to give Rain a free lesson, and Rain spent more than five hours hitting hundreds of balls on Buddy's driving range. The practice proved pointless. All he received for his trouble were three huge blisters on each hand and the knowledge that his swing, ninety percent of the time, produced drives that sliced horrendously to the right. If he didn't slice the ball, he usually topped it, resulting in a hard grounder, which probably killed dozens of ants as it bounced along. As he feared he would, Rain played horribly the next day in front of his girlfriend's father and two of his physician colleagues. Rain felt embarrassed by his poor performance, but Dr. Landerson laughed off his astronomical score and said Rain only needed some good lessons combined with clubs long enough and properly adjusted for his height. They had even shared an ice-cold, draft beer together in the clubhouse after the final hole and for the first time in his life, Rain actually enjoyed the beer's bitter taste.

Still lying in the bottom bunk staring at the bed above him, Rain delved deep within his mind and visited the art gallery he began that day Catherine allowed him to drive her Corvette. The wall held several paintings now, and he lingered at the one he completed last weekend.

One night, Rain's grandmother suggested that Catherine and her horse come and spend a day riding the trails around the farm. Catherine loved the idea and asked her father to loan Rain his horse so they could each have their own mounts. That Saturday morning, a driver from the Magnolia Stables, where the Landersons boarded their horses, arrived at the Henry Farm with Catherine's chestnut filly named Mollie and Dr. Landerson's charcoal stallion named Midnight. Catherine squealed with delight as the stable hand backed the horses out of the double trailer and prepared to put on their saddles. She hugged Rain tightly as the work progressed. Rain felt excited, too. He couldn't wait to lead her to the railroad trestle and tell her about everything that had occurred over the years on and around that bridge.

Catherine and Rain, thanks to their spirited four-legged companions, explored virtually every inch of the farm. They rode hard and fast in the hot August sun, racing each other across clearings and laughing until it felt like their sides would split open. They shared a picnic lunch on the bank of Okatibbee Creek, then swam naked beneath the railroad trestle, splashing each other with the balmy, brownish-red water. Then, after laughing with the exhilaration that comes from sheer happiness, they brought their bodies together as one. With only their tilted heads jutting above the creek surface, Rain and Catherine's lips met, and they kissed as passionately as though they might never have such an opportunity again.

Gently, Rain closed the door to his mental art gallery and rolled out of his plastic bed. When he and his father had moved in Rain's things, another cadet guard wearing a white uniform with red shoulder boards stopped by the room and informed Rain that there would be an optional freshmen dinner from 6:00 to 6:30 in the mess hall. Rain stretched and checked the time. If he hurried, he'd still have a few hours to further explore downtown Natchez before returning to campus to eat.

Outside his room, Rain stood on the red ceramic tiles that covered the floor of the open-air hallway. He advanced a few steps and peered over the third-floor balcony railing. Down below and spread before him was a large, cement quadrangle painted into white and red squares. It reminded Rain of a giant checkerboard. Tall, four-story bulwarks, composed of similar cadet rooms and red-tiled galleries, surrounded the checkerboard on each side. Each corner was anchored by its own massive concrete tower that enclosed a circular staircase. These four staircases accessed the four levels of the battalion. A few feet above the ground level of the checkerboard, each tower was painted with either an A, B, C, or D in bold red. Rain knew from the *Guidon*, a book of information MMC had sent him about the school's history, that the red letters stood for Alpha, Bravo, Charlie, and Delta Companies, respectively. Rain headed left for the Bravo Company stairs that would lead him down to the main entrance. The battalion claimed four entrances, but only the main one between Bravo Company and Alpha Company stood open. Thick iron gates, complete with oversized locks, sealed the three other smaller entrances.

Rain nodded as he walked past the four guards that stood in the entrance corridor. Each flashed a broad grin as Rain hustled out of the battalion, the kind of grin worn by someone purposely holding back an important piece of secretive information, information that could change the person's life and potentially make or break him forever.

Rain turned right onto Sargent Avenue, which ran the entire length of campus. According to his *Guidon*, the avenue was named after Winthrop Sargent, who moved to Natchez in 1798 at the request of U.S. President John Adams. Adams appointed Sargent as the first governor of the Mississippi Territory after Spain ceded the area to the United States in October of 1795. Sargent proved to be an unpopular choice with the locals, one of whom called him too "frigid and sour" to govern free people effectively. However, despite this unpopularity, Sargent remained in Natchez as a cotton planter after President Thomas Jefferson removed him from office in 1801.

Sargent never forgot his military experience as a major in the Continental Army during the Revolutionary War and, in 1818, one year after Mississippi joined the Union as a new state, the wealthy planter purchased a mile of land at the western edge of Natchez that ran along a steep bluff overlooking the Mississippi River. Here he established Mississippi Military College and became its first president. When Sargent died in 1820, his widow donated more than $500,000 to the college before she moved north to Philadelphia, Pennsylvania. This money lured the best and brightest academic and military professors to MMC and instantly turned the young college into one of the most elite institutions of higher learning in the entire nation.

Rain followed Sargent Avenue until it passed the MMC's only other battalion, Second Battalion. Second Battalion housed Echo, Foxtrot, Golf, and Hotel Companies. Total enrollment at MMC was roughly a thousand with each company consisting of about 125 cadets.

While he timidly ambled along, Rain noticed a few other boys wandering about campus who wore regular clothes. He presumed these to be fellow freshmen. Others donned pressed, wrinkle-free gray uniforms with black caps and white gloves. Rain guessed that these were the members of the cadre, upperclassmen responsible for freshmen indoctrination. Every time Rain saw a member of cadre, the cadet never made eye contact and seemed to head for his destination as fast as his legs could carry him.

Rain opted to report a day earlier than the mandatory deadline of noon on Monday. By reporting on Sunday, Rain would have the opportunity to explore both the campus and downtown Natchez before the cadet training started.

First, Rain decided to buy a postcard for Catherine from one of the shops that lined Canal Street, which ran parallel to MMC's campus. Rain also wanted another look at Rosalie, the spectacular antebellum home at the southern end of campus he had toured yesterday with his father and grandmother.

Natchez, a quaint little city, was famous throughout the South for its magnificent mansions that dated back to the glory years of "King Cotton." On previous visits, the Henry family had already toured three of these mansions, including Gloucester, Sargent's former residence, as well as Stanton Hall and Rosalie.

Rain picked Rosalie as his favorite, not simply because it served as the home of General Grimmer, MMC's president, but because it possessed a colorful history that culminated when Rain's college accepted a controversial proposition. According to the tour guide, the grand, southern home dated back to 1823, when Peter Little, a Maryland-born lumber mill owner and cotton planter, built it near the original, historic site of Fort Rosalie. Andrew Wilson, a millionaire cotton broker, bought the stately house at a public auction in 1857, and six years later, during the Civil War, Wilson saved Rosalie's valuables from the advancing Union army by cushioning them with some of his own cotton and burying them in a hidden location. Andrew Wilson became the acorn that grew into an enormous oak of a family tree. By 1956, ten of Wilson's direct descendents were living alumni of Mississippi Military College. During Christmas of that same year, they made their alma mater an intriguing proposal. They would sell Rosalie to MMC for a single dime in exchange for the promise that their own sons, grandsons, great-grandsons, and so on could attend the college free of charge until the class of 2022 graduated, which would commemorate the school's 200th anniversary. MMC accepted the proposal, and the tour guide said that the debate still raged today over which party, financially, received the better end of the deal.

Rain continued down Sargent Avenue and passed Turner Mess Hall where he would eat later. The *Guidon* claimed it was named after Judge Edward Turner, the mayor of Natchez from 1815 to 1819. Judge Turner loved to eat and insisted that his financial donation to the school go directly to building the finest college dining facility in the South. The *Guidon* also said that Turner, once a week until his death, ate dinner with the cadets to ensure it met his high standards.

Rain approached the only campus exit and entrance, Ellicott Gate. According to The *Guidon*, Ellicott Gate was named after Major Andrew Ellicott who was a famous surveyor and cartographer in the late eighteenth century. Rain's guidebook went on to explain that Ellicott raised the territory's first American flag on a hill a few hundred feet north of Canal Street. This act took place on February 27, 1797, and asserted United States sovereignty over the Natchez District. The act also signified the end of Spanish rule. Afterwards, Major Ellicott taught briefly at West Point before returning to Natchez and MMC to become its first department chair of mathematics.

When Rain drew even with the Ellicott Gate's guardhouse, another cadet guard wearing a white uniform with red shoulder boards stepped out to block his path. Rain also noticed that the guard wore a maroon sash and a long, golden sheath complete with sword. "Hold on there! Where do you think you're going?"

Rain hesitated. "Umm, I thought it was okay to leave campus and look around."

The guard chuckled through a baleful smile. "You 'thought,' did you. That was your first mistake, Rat!" His eyes got big and he craned his neck as he stood on his toes to get as close to Rain's face as possible. He came so close, in fact, that Rain instinctively blinked when he whispered, "Rats don't think; they simply do what they're told. Here's another tip: you'll start addressing upperclassmen with a 'sir sandwich,' if you know what's good for you."

The guard started to say something else, when an approaching voice from behind Rain interrupted him. "Hey, Dave, whatcha doin'?"

The guard flattened his feet and leaned to his left to see around Rain.

Although Rain had the urge to either turn around and

see who was coming or attempt a dash past the guard, he did neither. He did, however, curse under his breath. Freshmen training had yet to begin, and he had already made an enemy with one of the upperclassmen, the cadet guard for Ellicott Gate to boot.

The guard recognized his inquisitor. "Hey, Brad, I'm just rackin' this rat a little bit."

From the corner of his eye, Rain noticed that the person named Brad had pulled even with him and smiled coyly. Like Rain, he was dressed in jeans and a T-shirt, but he possessed none of Rain's fear. "Come on, Dave. You know it's against the rules to pick on freshmen until tomorrow. I'd hate for Mike to find out that one of his cadet officers is standing out here at Ellicott Gate violating one of MMC's sacred *Red Book* policies."

The guard laughed nervously and took a few steps back. He looked all around before saying, "Hey, ease up, Brad. I was only having a little fun. It gets boring out here waiving through cars all day."

Then, in case someone else secretly watched, the guard stepped back into the doorway of the guardhouse, which stood in the road's median. He gave Rain and Brad a chest-level, rigid-handed salute indicating he wanted them to move through the gate. His voice boomed loudly in case anyone might be listening. "You boys go on through! Don't forget there's an optional meal at Turner Mess Hall that starts sharply at eighteen hundred hours!"

Rain and Brad were almost off campus when they heard a "psssst." Turning, both boys saw the guard leaning their direction. His hands formed a cave around his mouth as he tried to ensure only they heard what he was about to say. "Brad, I know we're from the same hometown and all, but you should start calling me Cadet Lieutenant Adams, especially since you're fixin' to be a rat."

Mockingly, Brad snapped to attention and saluted the guard. "Sir, yes, sir, Cadet Lieutenant Adams, sir!"

At this, the guard scowled and yelled for them to "get the hell out of there," which they promptly did. When the two incoming freshmen crossed the invisible line that represented the geographic edge of the MMC campus, Rain exhaled a deep sigh of relief. He had been safely paroled, if only for a few hours.

Brad extended his hand, and Rain shook it. "My name's Brad O'Johnovich. I'm from Madison, right outside of Jackson. How 'bout you?"

"Rain Henry from Vimville, just outside of Meridian. I've never heard of O'Johnovich. Where's your family come from?"

"Serbia, three generations ago. What company are you in?"

"Bravo."

A look of excitement spread across Brad's face. "Hey! Me, too. How's that for a coincidence?"

"Pretty coincidental, I guess." Brad seemed okay, but Rain had just met him. Already, the guy acted kind of hyper, and if he turned out to be a weirdo, Rain didn't want him clinging like a piece of duct tape that would prove difficult to peel off later. Rain changed the subject. "So, I take it you knew that guard back there?"

"That's David Adams. He's from Madison, too. We went to the same high school and our families have known one other for years. They live in our neighborhood, about five houses down. My older sister used to baby-sit Dave when he was a kid." Brad winked at Rain as they turned left onto State Street and prepared to cross South Broadway. "I also know Mike Manning, the regimental commander. His dad and my dad practice in the same physicians group."

"Sounds like you've got it made, with all of your connections."

"Ha! I wish! Unfortunately, there's tremendous pressure on me to be a model cadet. Did I tell you my father is also a retired colonel from the Army, MMC class of '63? He's on MMC's Board of Visitors."

"What's the Board of Visitors?"

"A group of seven alumni-elected MMC graduates who, combined, are as powerful as General Grimmer, MMC's president. They meet each semester to vote on any proposals the administration recommends. They also review faculty evaluations and corps policies."

"Seems like all that would make you untouchable," Rain concluded.

"In a way, you're right. Unless I get booted for bad grades or an honor violation, it'd be difficult for them to run me out." Brad slapped Rain on the back and laughed. "But I'm sure the cadre knows all this. I'm betting they plan on making my life twice as hellish as a regular rat's. It'll be their big chance to harass the son of one of MMC's big muckety mucks."

A break in the traffic materialized, and the two jogged across Broadway. "So, Rain, I know you hear this question all the time, but I gotta ask. How tall are you? Seven feet? Are you here on a basketball scholarship, or what?"

Now it was Rain's turn to laugh, and he did. The kid was definitely hyper, but well-connected. Rain decided it would be in his best interest to befriend Brad O'Johnovich, and he went into one of the more pleasant programmed responses to the same questions he had been asked a million times. "You know, Brad, if I got a quarter every time someone asked me about my height, I wouldn't need to go to college. But you're close, anyway. I'm six feet, seven inches and here on a baseball scholarship."

Brad appeared to be shocked and stopped dead in his tracks. "Baseball? Let me guess. You're a pitcher."

"Yep. But I also hope to play first base or somewhere in the outfield, too."

"Did Chain Porter tell you you'd play other positions besides pitch?"

"He said he'd give me a shot."

"Don't count on it."

Rain cocked his head to one side and squinted. "Why

would Coach Porter lie to me and how come you know so much about him?"

"Of course, I could be wrong, but I said what I did because of something that happened a few years ago. My father and I are big baseball fans. I grew up playing baseball, but I'm nowhere near good enough to play college, and I can accept that," Brad declared as though he had not truly accepted it. "Anyway, there were two kids about five years ago that Coach Porter recruited from Madison. These guys were studs. My father used to take me to watch them play when I was in junior high. Together, they led the school to the state championship their senior year with an undefeated record. One pitched and played shortstop. The other was a pitcher and a centerfielder. Porter promised them the same thing he promised you – that they'd also get a chance to play shortstop and centerfield."

Rain interrupted. "How do you know that?"

"We knew their families and they told us."

"Does every family in Madison know each other?"

"Pretty much. Isn't it the same way in Vimville?"

"Yeah, I guess you're right. So what happened to these guys?" Rain wasn't sure he wanted to hear the rest of the story, but he had let Brad ramble on this far.

"Porter never gave either a real chance to play anywhere but pitch. Said they'd be better off as pitchers only. The one who played shortstop transferred to Delta State after his freshman year, where he became an all-conference infielder."

"And the other?"

"He left the team the spring of his junior year, but stayed on at MMC and graduated. Porter explained to my father and the rest of the Board of Visitors he wasn't disappointed when he quit, because it would free up scholarship money for the next year. Porter claimed he had tried everything, but the guy never became the pitcher everyone thought he'd be."

"And why not, Brad O'Johnovich, baseball expert?"

"The guy claimed he lost 'it.'"

"Lost what? What the hell is 'it?'"

Brad shrugged. "Only he knew for sure, but if I had to guess, I'd say it was his passion for baseball. It probably didn't help when Porter tried to make him a sidearm pitcher and he blew his arm out."

CHAPTER ELEVEN
THE LONGEST DAY

The memories of that first Monday, the day Rat Year officially began, seared Rain's memory as if one of the cadre members cut open his skull and branded the surface of his brain with a white-hot iron. The day started when Rain awoke to the sound of barked commands coming from dozens of yelling cadre members on the quadrangle. Rain decided he should report to someone, somewhere. He had just finished dressing when a cadre sergeant burst into his room like a S.W.A.T. team member – there are no locks on the doors at MMC – and screamed for Rain to get his "rat ass" downstairs. "Rat ass" would be the nicest thing from the upperclassman's lips as obscenities spewed forth from his mouth the way excrement gushes from a broken sewage pipe. As fast as his long legs could carry him, Rain sprinted down the stairs while the cadre sergeant's vile commentary chased him all the way to the bottom. Once he arrived at ground level, three other Bravo Company cadre members grabbed him and physically "instructed" him to join a line of four other freshmen. Rain did, and together, the anxious teenagers formed a short, rigid line. Their toes almost touched the edge of the quad, and Rain noticed other freshmen being lined up in a similar fashion directly across from them in Alpha Company. From the corner of his eye, Rain took a quick peek and immediately wondered if he looked as petrified as his new classmates. Each appeared to be in a state of shock.

Rain, the newest member of the squad, tried to stand at attention, but he wasn't sure if his stance was correct. A short, skinny corporal with a black cap and white gloves "politely" corrected it.

"Jesus Christ, you rat bastard! You call that standing at attention?" The corporal, whose nametag over his left shirt pocket spelled Zandon, stepped forward and kicked Rain hard in the shin. "Legs together! Heels touching, and feet spread at a thirty-degree angle!"

Rain looked at his shoes and slid them apart at what he guessed was about thirty degrees. He checked the corporal's face for approval.

Zandon's mouth dropped open as if Rain had insulted his mother. Rain could see the veins bulging under the tight skin that covered his scrawny neck.

"Don't you ever look at me, you scum! I'll rip out your eyeballs and fornicate your rat brain through the sockets. Rats stare straight ahead at all times. What's your name?"

"Rain."

Corporal Zandon kicked Rain in the other shin. "Dammit, boy, you'd better give me a 'sir sandwich' when you speak! Now is that your first name or your last name?"

Rain resisted the urge to lean over and rub the two bruises he felt sure were forming above his ankles. Yesterday, Brad had explained "sir sandwiches" and how to use them, but Rain had forgotten due to the stress of his current situation.

"Sir, first name, sir."

Zandon reached up, grabbed Rain's shirt collar, then pulled Rain's face down even with his, about five feet, nine inches above the ground. Rain stared straight ahead as the spittle splattered all over his neck and chin. "Good God almighty, boy. You must take me for a fool. Do you think this is some sort of a joke? We don't want to know your first name, because nobody around here gives a damn. You may be on the basketball team, but I'm still gonna run your pansy ass outta my school." Zandon released the collar and shoved Rain back to a standing position. "Now, let's try it again, Rat! What's your name?"

Rain took a deep breath that swelled his chest. He yelled as loud as he could. "Sir, Henry, sir!"

Zandon took a few steps back on the quad and shook his head. "You mean Cadet Recruit Henry, right Rat?"

"Sir, yes, sir!"

"Then say it, dirtbag!"

"Sir, Cadet Recruit Henry, sir!"

After a few minutes, another rat joined the squad and received essentially the same treatment: two kicks to the shin and a facial coating of spittle. Then, the corporal took his squad of six rats onto the quad and began teaching them how to march as soldiers. They learned how to forward march from a standing position, halt on the appropriate foot and make column movements to the left and right. Rain's squad also learned all of the facing movements, including left and right face, about-face, parade rest, and the appropriate way to stand at attention. Soon, the quadrangle filled with other squads from the various companies learning the same basic military commands. Each squad became a geometric snake, complete with a head and tail, marching in straight lines across the checkerboard. The snakes only changed directions by turning at right angles. Occasionally, one snake would run into another, and both snakes would momentarily disintegrate from the resultant confusion. Nothing seemed to incite the corporals more, and Rain wondered if they arranged the collisions on purpose, just for an excuse to exercise their vocal cords.

After almost two hours of training the snake, Corporal Zandon halted his squad. "Rats, it's my pleasure to introduce you to your worst nightmare, Cadet Sergeant Sawnay." He turned to the grinning sergeant. "They're all yours, Mr. Sawnay."

Rain recognized Sawnay. He was the same person who had nearly broken down his door a few hours earlier. The large man's muscles rippled beneath his uniform. Though not quite as tall as Rain, his presence still towered above the freshmen. For a brief moment, Sawnay glared at the lumps of clay he would mold into cadets. Then, after executing a crisp left face, the cadre sergeant moved to the end of the squad. Starting with Rain and working down the line of freshmen, Sawnay ran his white-gloved hands through each rat's hair. During a quick, secretive glance, Rain noticed a disturbing, erotic grin spread over Sawnay's face.

When Sawnay reached the last lump of clay, he released an orgasmic moan. "Awwww, yeah! Rats, look down here at your classmate!"

Rain turned to his left, as did the four freshmen next to him. Sawnay ran both hands back and forth through the freshman's thick, long hair the way a salon stylist massages a client's scalp. "I bet you rats didn't know you had a rock star as a classmate, did you?" Nobody answered, so Sawnay commanded the squad back to attention.

"What's your name, shaggy?"

"Sir, Cadet Recruit Tice, sir!"

"Where you from, you faggot loving hippie?"

"Sir, Indiana, sir!"

"That's great. We got ourselves a longhaired, hippie-ass Yankee on our hands. Corporal Zandon, please come down here and ask this scumbag which floor he lives on. I'm tired of smelling his turd-eatin' breath."

Rain recognized the name Tice. While Rain and Brad visited Natchez and Rosalie the afternoon before, Rain's roommate had moved his belongings into the room. Rain had hoped he would return to the room after dinner, so they could get to know one another, but soon it became clear that his new roommate chose to spend his last night of freedom away from the barracks. Before going to bed, Rain sneaked a peek into one of his suitcases and found some boxing gloves with the name "Tice" written across their cuffs. Now, Rain decided having the benefit of a boxer sharing his room was counterbalanced by the fact that he looked like a hippie.

Corporal Zandon stepped in front of the new cadet recruit from Indiana. "What floor's your room on, scum?"

"Sir, third floor, sir!"

The corporal looked at Sawney with raised eyebrows. "Looks like he'll end up in our squad, Mr. Sawnay."

With a look of disgust, Sawnay winced and threw back his head. He spread his arms wide, and a mock prayer rose to the sky. "Dear Lord, please keep me from killing this shaggy, fudge-packin' hippie! But if it's your will that I should claim his life, please help me think of a way to accomplish the task in a creative and especially gory manner."

An hour later, everyone, including Zandon and Sawnay, forgot about Tice's long hair, because every rat received a buzz haircut at MMC's barbershop. Rain decided the haircut looked and felt more like a close shave. Less than a tenth of an inch of stubby hair remained on his head.

Post shearing, Rain and the rest of his squad marched from the campus barber shop to the cadet store, where other cadre members, assigned for duty from various companies, threw them giant laundry bags. The bags were subsequently stuffed with uniform trousers and shirts, workout clothes, and everything else a freshman might need. The burgeoning bags grew so heavy that Rain and the rest of his squad members could barely carry them back to their rooms.

After they dragged their new belongings up the stairs and into their prison cell, Rain and Philip Tice met over a brief handshake. Quickly, because Corporal Zandon gave everyone only thirty seconds, they changed from civilian clothes into their new PT, or physical training, outfits. The outfits consisted of scarlet running shorts and a white T-shirt with Mississippi Military College emblazoned across the front. Sergeant Sawnay had instructed them, however, not to complete the ensemble with their running shoes. Instead, he ordered them to wear patent leathers with their black dress socks pulled high.

When Rain and Philip returned to the quadrangle, the cadre segregated the rats into four squads, determined by the floor level of their rooms. Rain joined the third squad, and he thought he saw Brad O'Johnovich second from the front in first squad. The Bravo cadre assembled the squads into a platoon and marched it onto the wide field in front of the battalions, directly on the other side of Sargent Avenue. Here they drilled for another hour under intense rays of heat that shot down like flaming arrows from the sultry, round archer in the sky.

Rain guessed the time to be shortly before noon when his platoon formed up with the freshmen platoons from MMC's other companies. Soaked with perspiration, Rain's white shirt clung to his torso. Beads of sweat tickled his face and neck as they trickled down over his forehead and behind his ears.

Rain believed that finally, he and the rest of the freshmen were headed to lunch. But instead, the freshmen platoons marched past Turner Mess Hall and right through Ellicott Gate. The Alpha platoon led the procession and when it turned left onto State Street, the Bravo freshmen followed, as did the rest of the platoons. The Natchez police department had blocked the side streets and thousands of people lined the route. As Rain and his classmates marched into the masses, a human cacophony greeted them that insulted whatever dignity remained. Little boys and girls giggled as they pointed at the cadet recruits' shoes, socks and lack of hair. Women shook their heads and clucked with sympathetic laughter. The men that lined the street chanted, "kill the rats, kill the rats, kill the rats!" Several chanters thrust their fists at the freshmen as they passed, and with his peripheral vision, Rain saw they wore thick, gold MMC class rings that magically glinted in the bright sunlight.

After five blocks of deafening verbal harassment and mockery, the platoons turned left onto Union Street. Again, police barricades protected the route. But this time, the freshmen encountered a dramatically different crowd. Instead of thousands of people, only a few hundred or so middle-aged, somber couples lined the street. While some smiled with tears in their eyes, others acted as though they had come to witness a funeral. Eerily silent, the parents of the incoming freshman class waved as their stone-faced sons marched past. Occasionally, Rain heard a father shout words of encouragement such as "Hang in there!" or "Give 'em hell, Boy!" The mothers seemed more emotional. Their voices quivered as they yelled, "We love you, Son" and "We're proud of you." Several slumped in their husband's arms.

After five blocks on Union Street, the platoons marched up a slight hill and turned left onto High Street. Here, dozens of upperclassmen waited to ambush the new rats. The upperclassmen had returned to Natchez a week early to participate in the Freshmen March of Tradition, followed by six days and nights of drunken partying. Most of these non-cadre cadets, still considered civilians for another week, dressed smartly in either creased jeans or khakis. When the freshmen arrived, the upperclassmen walked along beside them, hurling insults and lobbing water balloons into the platoons. Rain welcomed the cool drops of water that splashed all over his body until a balloon hit him square in the side of his head like a brick. The blow staggered Rain and he nearly fell sideways into the heart of the platoon. Luckily, a classmate caught and steadied him. In a flash, Sergeant Sawnay grabbed Rain and pulled the dizzy freshman from the ranks. Rain sank to his knees while tiny black dots danced before his eyes.

"You okay, Rat?"

"Sir, I think so, sir," Rain replied as he struggled to his feet.

"Can you still march?"

"Sir, yes, sir," Rain replied.

"Good. Get back in formation," Sawnay ordered as he released Rain and peeled back to deal with the perpetrator. Tossing balloons as the rats was an accepted part of the ritual, but intentionally trying to take a rat's head off from three feet away crossed the line. Luckily, Sawnay had seen everything from his position at the rear and knew exactly who had thrown the water-filled, latex missile.

Sawnay seethed as he approached Jeremy Langford. "That was outta line, Langford. If I catch you pulling a stunt like that on a rat again, I'll have you humping tours on the quad until Christmas."

Langford grinned sarcastically. "It slipped."

Already pissed, Langford's nonchalant attitude pushed Sawnay over the edge. He got hard into the arrogant sophomore's face. "Listen, you squatty sophomore freak. I could care less that you're the baseball team's starting catcher. I hate baseball. Just remember, if I see you go overboard on a rat again, you'll pay. By the way, find a razor and tuck in your shirt. You're an embarrassment to my school."

Sawnay paused for a moment to see if Langford made any other sarcastic comments. Langford replied with only a blank expression, so after a few seconds, Sawnay wheeled and jogged back to his position at the rear of the Bravo platoon.

The march ended when Alpha Company turned left onto Broadway and sprinted the quarter of a mile back to Ellicott Gate. Rain and the rest of the Bravo Company freshmen turned next and also broke into a sprint back to campus. They were successively followed at precise intervals by the rest of the freshmen platoons and their cadre. No spectators lined the route. If they had, the freshmen would have been moving too fast for the onlookers to see anything anyway. When Rain's platoon finally pulled up at the steps that led to Turner Mess Hall, he thought he would collapse from a combination of thirst, hunger, exhaustion, and the slight pinging sensation that still floated in his head.

For lunch, Sergeant Sawnay, Rain's mess carver, allowed his rats to eat one French fry and two bites of their corndog. Their brownies went untouched because rats were not allowed the pleasures of dessert, or so Rain surmised. However, Sawnay, along with the other cadre members, highly encouraged the freshmen to drink as much tea as their stomachs could hold. Rain hated tea, so Sawnay's recommendation served as a mixed blessing. Rain felt thankful for the fluids, but almost gagged on the tinny, stale taste. While Rain hurriedly finished his third glass, he presumed he had made it through the first half of the day. He was wrong.

After lunch, Rain and his classmates picked up their M-14 rifles from the campus armory and drilled until sunset. The freshmen learned the rifle commands on top of the marching and facing commands they had learned earlier. The heat, physically and mentally, became overwhelming. Rain strongly considered throwing his rifle to the ground and simply walking out of Ellicott Gate. Finally, their platoon leader, Cadet Lieutenant Nichols, ordered the staff sergeant to march the Bravo freshmen back to the battalion for rat showers before dinner mess.

Once in their room, Rain and Philip managed a few sips of water from the sink faucet. The water tasted warm and the room felt like an oven.

Rain heard someone stop outside the door. "Hurry up, Rats! Get your asses out here! You'd better be wearin' your rat shower uniforms," Zandon shouted.

The two roommates stripped naked before sliding on their red-striped bathrobes and flip-flops. As previously instructed, in their left hands, they carried a bar of soap, and in their right they grasped a plain white bath towel. Rain and Philip also donned their red baseball caps, which sported the black outline of a rat on the front. The screen door closed with a whack as the two roommates joined the line that had already formed on the red tiles outside their room.

Rain happened to stand right next to Brad O'Johnovich,

and like a ventriloquist, he whispered to Rain without moving his lips, "Your head okay?"

"Yeah, thanks. How you doin'?" Rain answered using the same technique.

Brad probably meant to say "piece of cake," but it came out "tiece of cake" through his clenched teeth.

Cadet Lieutenant Nichols emerged from the bathroom and addressed the freshmen. The senior's accent sounded distinctly southern, yet smooth, as though he came from a long line of Mississippi aristocracy. "Now listen heah, because I'm only gonna say this one time. When you walk into the bathroom, put your cap, towel, and robe, in that ordah, on the wall peg. Cadre will direct you from theah. Any questions?"

The line of freshmen shouted a chorus of "Sir, no, sir."

Their platoon leader frowned. "Now, how do ya'll expect me to heah a question with all that shoutin'? Any questions?"

This time, the freshmen understood and remained silent.

"That's better." Nichols pointed at a freshman standing directly in front of him. "You, theah. Come here and turn around." The freshman took three steps forward and executed an awkward about-face in his flip-flops. Nichols shouted from behind. "What's the ordah for the wall peg, Rat?"

"Sir, cap, towel, robe, sir!" Rain's classmate shouted.

"Excellent, genius. Now ya'll all start repeatin' that with your classmate on my command."

Nichols kicked the rat's ass and Rain's classmate began shouting, "cap, towel, robe," over and over again.

Rain, Brad, Philip, and the rest of the Bravo freshmen quickly joined in, and "cap, towel, robe" echoed throughout the battalion.

Rain still repeated "cap, towel, robe" when he entered the bathroom waiting area and placed his gear onto the peg in that order. Naked except for his flip-flops, Rain stood at the right side of the shower entrance as Corporal Zandon held him by his right arm. Inside the tiled room, Rain saw six showerheads spitting water full-blast at the dusty, greasy bodies below them. Another cadet corporal, one Rain did not recognize, stood at the left of the entrance and counted down, "Five, four, three, two, one, switch!" As soon as he said, "switch," the freshman at the far left showerhead turned and exited. At the same time, Corporal Zandon shoved Rain toward the far right showerhead. The bathers that remained moved down one showerhead to their left.

The cold water caused Rain's body to flinch. He held his new bar of soap with both hands against his chest and bent his head forward in an attempt to deflect the chill with the back of his neck. Rain had just gotten used to the temperature when he heard "switch" over his shoulder. He moved one spot to his left and jumped back. This shower's water felt scalding hot, or maybe it seemed that way because his body had grown accustomed to the cold water from the first showerhead. The third shower felt cold again, and Rain understood the game. Better prepared for the last fifteen seconds of his shower, he was thus able to lather and rinse his face and crotch before vacating.

After Rain and his Bravo classmates completed their first rat shower, they put on their duty uniforms and reassembled on the quadrangle for the march to Turner Mess Hall for dinner. During this meal, Rain's mess carver acted much more generous. Sergeant Sawnay allowed each of the rats at his mess three bites of their chicken fried steak and two bites of green beans. Rain contemplated asking permission to drink water instead of tea, but decided against it, because he remembered Brad's advice: never let an upperclassman know you don't like something.

Upon completing the evening meal, the freshmen returned to their rooms where they practiced making their beds, or "racks" as the cadre called them, tight enough to bounce a quarter six inches above the bedspread. Rain thought this concept was simply a military expression for having a wrinkle-free bedspread, but Sawnay returned with a quarter and actually tested it. The quarter failed to bounce six inches, and as a consequence, Sawnay seemed to take great pleasure in ripping off Rain's and Philip's sheets and bedspreads before slamming their plastic-covered mattresses to the floor. The cycle repeated three or four times over the course of the next few hours. Finally, after one final mattress-slam, Sawnay instructed them to forget about their beds for the moment and concentrate on a copy of "his list," which he handed to Rain.

"Rats, I'm not allowed to tell you to stay up past lights out at 22:30. And I'm not telling you to hang a blanket over your windows in case General Grimmer drives by at 0200 to make sure all of his rats are getting their proper rest. What I am telling you is that if you don't have everything on my list completed by 0600 and morning PT formation, you'll regret it. Do I make myself clear?"

"Sir, yes, sir!" Rain and Philip answered together.

Rain and Philip studied the list. It looked like this:

Sergeant Sawnay's List for All Third Division Rats
(To be completed by morning PT formation)

1. *Remake bed to Sawnay and MMC (S&M) standards – remember the quarter bounce test.*
2. *Shine all brass to S&M standards including: MMC garrison cap insignias (both black and white garrison caps) and corresponding buttons, all uniform buttons, belt buckle (sand off the letters on back first), and belt tip.*
3. *Shine leathers to S&M standards, complete with fresh coatings of heel and sole.*
4. *Arrange and fold clothes in half-press drawers to S&M standards (see page 19 of the* Red Book*).*
5. *Arrange hanging uniforms in full-press from left to right starting with the longest hanging uniform to the shortest uniform (see page 20 in* Red Book*).*
6. *Arrange hats and shoes in the full-press as described in* Red Book *(find the page yourself).*

7. *Clean and polish wood floors to S&M standards for inspection to take place after morning PT run.*
8. *Clean and polish sink, cabinet, and wall mirror to S&M standards for said inspection.*
9. *Clean all room windows.*
10. *Have two duty uniforms properly prepared with nametags and insignias (don't forget the cardboard backings).*
11. ***MOST IMPORTANT ITEM: DON'T PISS ME OFF BY NOT HAVING EVERY SINGLE ITEM ON THIS LIST COMPLETED BY TOMORROW MORNING!***

Rain and Philip recognized immediately that the list would be impossible to complete, but they did their best. When the bugle sounded at 5:30, indicating it was time for morning PT formation, they had finished everything but the windows. Sawnay gave them each an earful of vulgarities and ten demerits for that infraction, but receiving demerits became the least of Rain's worries as his freshman year continued.

CHAPTER TWELVE
SINK OR SWIM

By Halloween of Rain's freshman year, living the life of a rat remained scary, but it wasn't nearly as challenging as it had been prior to the end of the cadre period, which culminated with the freshmen rite of passage known as the "Louisiana Letter Swim."

Since the middle of the nineteenth century, cadre training concluded on the last Thursday of each September with The Swim, as the event was affectionately nicknamed on campus. Over the previous six weeks, the cadre's primary responsibility had been to physically and mentally prepare the freshmen to officially join the cadet corps. Those who completed The Swim graduated from cadet recruit to cadet. Those who failed were asked to resign and cordially invited to reapply for admission again the next year, if they so desired. The Swim represented the cadre-training period's ultimate Darwinian challenge: the stronger rats survived, while the weaker ones perished. Like cheese at the end of a maze, The Swim rewarded the successful rats with a delicious morsel for their efforts – their respective company's letter. Only the MMC class ring, which could not be earned until senior year, was considered more valuable than the inch-long, company-letter insignia. Rain could hardly wait until he wore his B, for Bravo Company, proudly pinned on the shirt collar of his duty uniform, where it would remain displayed for the rest of his cadet career.

At the beginning of September, each freshman received his own three-foot log cut from a cedar tree about as thick as a man's leg. The cadre strongly encouraged each rat to sand the cedar and carve the log into a personal totem pole, which the cadre called a "rat stick." On one side of his log, Rain attempted carving a portrait of Catherine. The result looked nothing like his girlfriend, but the crude etching reminded him of her, nonetheless. On the other side, he carved a large "56," which represented Wayne based on the number he once wore on the back of his high school football and baseball jerseys.

But Philip, Rain's roommate, basically ignored the cadre's advice. He sanded his log a little the first week he got it, but chose not to carve anything on it. When Rain asked him why, Philip always evaded the question. The Bravo cadre, especially Sergeant Sawnay, made his life miserable because of his lack of participation, but Philip still refused to carve his log. For the last three weeks, Philip's log simply collected dust in the corner of the room.

Rain, along with the rest of his classmates, started hearing more and more rumors about The Swim shortly after they received their rat sticks. The most popular rumor, and one backed by Brad O'Johnovich, said that the totem poles would be used as flotation devices to counteract the deadly currents that hid in the deep waters of the Mississippi River. Whether the rumor held any truth or not, the cadre refused to say.

After dinner one unusually cool evening, Lieutenant Nichols instructed Rain and his classmates to return to their rooms, strip-"bayah-ass naked," and reassemble in platoon formation on the Bravo section of the battalion quadrangle. Corporal Zandon had collected third squad's rat sticks the day before, so Rain and his classmates anticipated that the time had arrived for The Swim.

Rain's pulse raced as he and Philip left the safe confines of their room and joined the rest of his classmates on the quad. The other naked freshmen from Alpha, Charlie, and Delta companies did the same, and the non-cadre upperclassmen whooped and hollered at the naked boys standing at attention before them. Draped over the railings of every floor, First-Battalion sophomores, juniors, and seniors acted like drunken spectators at a bootlegger-sponsored dogfight. Rain could overhear them placing survival wagers on individual freshmen in between the jeers and catcalls that tumbled down from above, stinging their exposed skin and fragile psyches like droplets of acid. Rain clenched his teeth so hard, it felt like his mouth might implode from the pressure. He hoped several of the bastards placed bets against him because they would all lose. He didn't know if The Swim worked like a race, but if it did, he wasn't merely going to survive, Rain Henry planned on winning the damn thing. Despite his confidence, Rain still nervously shivered as his nude platoon marched from the battalion out into the unknown.

Five minutes later, MMC's naked freshmen gathered on a small, grassy strip of land that stretched across the back portion of campus. The strip overlooked the narrow bank along the eastern shore of the Mississippi River, which flowed lazily by at the bottom after a sheer, 100-foot drop. If Rain or one of his classmates had wanted to end it, right then and there, all he would need to do is scale the small iron fence at the edge of the cliff and jump. Rain decided he and his classmates had become nothing more than hairless lemmings, which had reached the end of their existence and were all about to instinctively follow orders into the purgatory that beckoned beyond the cliff's edge.

Rain surveyed the scene around him and winced. During high school, he had read several history books on World War II that contained pictures of the naked, malnourished masses the Allied soldiers liberated from Nazi concentration camps. The images delivered stark and disturbing examples of how a small group of men could systematically starve, humiliate, and brutalize their fellow man. The MMC fourth-class system served as another example, he decided, while he looked around at his stripped, emaciated classmates. It had taken only six weeks of extreme physical exertion and mental exhaustion combined with a drastic reduction of food and sleep to transform vivacious teenage boys into human scarecrows. All a photographer needed was some black and white film – what remained of the MMC freshman class would surely have passed for liberated Jews at the end of the war.

The temperature dropped in conjunction with the fleeting sun as it slipped faster and faster beyond the cotton fields on the flat, low-lying, and far away Louisiana side of the river. The freshmen were neither allowed to move nor fend for themselves against the late summer mosquitoes that feasted on the buffet of naked flesh. Rain hoped the cooling temperatures would slow down the carnivorous insects, but the merciless onslaught continued unabated. Even the cadre members, who covered themselves with a musky smelling repellant, complained about the ferocity of the attack. When Rain glanced down, he noticed his penis had recoiled to the size of a thimble and seemed to want to crawl inside his body. He closed his eyes and tried focusing on anything except the sharp pains that came with each new bite and the almost irresistible urge to scratch the forming lumps. Mostly, he imagined what he would be doing exactly four weeks and one day in the future: dancing close with his Catherine at the Rat Dance.

Finally, after what seemed like days, but was only an hour and a half, Rain heard a jeep pull behind them and stop. The faceless voice that pulsated through the bullhorn belonged to Cadet Colonel Mike Manning, the regimental commander.

"Congratulations, Rats! You've made it to the Louisiana Letter Swim and your final cadre mission. Tonight, the last night of cadre, is when we separate the boy rats from the girl rats. Those of you mentally and physically strong enough to complete the The Swim, in the allowable time of less than three hours, will continue the journey to manhood at our fine institution of higher learning. Those who do not will be removed from campus by noon tomorrow and sent home to mommy and daddy on a Greyhound bus. Before we begin, please indulge me by listening to some statistics regarding the test of courage and endurance you are about to attempt. Your class is the 133rd class to undertake The Swim's 1.2-mile roundtrip length. Over the years, fourteen rats have drowned attempting The Swim, but none since 1928, when motorboats were first used for water rescues instead of canoes. The Swim eliminates an average of thirty-eight rats each year, and the current 'over-under' number in the battalions for your class is forty."

Manning motioned for the cadre to disperse the water rescue devices to the freshmen, and soon Rain and his classmates held what were essentially nothing more than glowsticks that could be bought at any state fair for a dollar. Once each freshman held his rescue device above his head as commanded, Cadet Colonel Manning continued.

"Rats, you now have official MMC water rescue devices. You are to carry these with you for the entire swim. If you begin to drown, bend the device, and a glass capsule will break on the inside, creating a chemical mixture that glows bright yellow. Hold the device above the water, and you will be rescued shortly thereafter. Remember, if you are rescued or assisted by any means from someone in a boat, you fail The Swim and will be headed home tomorrow. Since you have no pockets, I recommend you hold the device between your teeth or the cheeks of your ass." Manning lowered the bullhorn momentarily as he and the rest of the cadre enjoyed the joke. The laughter died, and Manning pressed the bullhorn to his lips once again. "Either way, the choice is yours, but DO NOT LOSE YOUR GLOWSTICKS! Are there any questions?"

Rain and his classmates remained silent.

"Are there any freshmen who want to resign before the mission begins? Remember, if you leave now, your parents will be refunded one half of this semester's tuition." Manning lowered the bullhorn and surveyed the shaved heads, skinny backs, and bony asses in front of him. Another traditional bet among the upperclassmen involved whether or not a rat would quit before The Swim even started. Manning himself had bet in the affirmative.

Slowly, from the corner of his right eye, Rain saw a rat raise his hand from the Charlie Company platoon. A chorus of cheers erupted among the cadre. Rain would later learn that cadre tradition dictated the freshmen trainers always bet at least one rat would "bail on the bluff."

Instantly, one of Charlie Company's cadre members swooped in like a hawk and removed Rain's former classmate, who began sobbing uncontrollably. They headed back toward First Battalion, Rain presumed, to start packing the kid's belongings. Rain wondered if he counted against the total for the over-under bet.

Cadet Colonel Manning, now $20 richer, went on to explain The Swim's rules. "Remember, rats, you have only three hours to complete your mission. There will be a staggered start, beginning with Alpha Company, to ensure each platoon of rats has its fair share of time. First, you must hop the iron fence and descend to the shore below using the four rope ladders that dangle over the edge of the bluff. Then, you must swim across the Mississippi River to the beautiful beaches of Louisiana's Catahoula Parish. A bonfire will help guide the direction of your swim. Around that bonfire, you'll find your rat sticks, which are arranged by company. Use your rat stick as a flotation aid to help you paddle back here. When you reach the sacred soil of Mississippi, leave your rat stick at the base of the cliff. Then, scale the rope ladders, and you're finished. Now, doesn't that sound easy?"

"Sir, yes, sir!" Rain and his classmates exploded with a collective roar that could be heard all the way to Louisiana.

A starting gun fired and the freshmen from Alpha Company charged forward, yelling "AAAAAAAHHHHHHHHH!!!" as if they assaulted a nest of machine gunners. They quickly scaled the iron fence and disappeared from sight four at a time. Rain's battalion classmates became irregular shaped, flesh-covered marbles, momentarily pausing at the end of a table before falling off the edge.

The gun fired again, sending Rain and Bravo Company scampering into action with a loud shout of "BRAVO ROCKS!" just as they had been instructed to say. Rain jumped the fence and was one of the first four on the rope ladders. At certain intervals, the ladders were secured to the cliff to keep them from swinging out of control, so it took Rain less than thirty seconds to reach the shoreline. When his feet hit the crusted, brown sand the color of feces, he looked to his right and saw Brad O'Johnovich reach the ground at the same time. They both smiled. Suddenly, Brad pulled his glowstick from his teeth and hurled it far downstream.

Brad's action shocked Rain, and as they plunged into the murky water, Rain removed his glowstick from his mouth but clenched it in his left hand instead of throwing it away. "Why'd you do that?" Rain asked as they began swimming at a hurried pace for the speck of light on the other side of the river.

"It's easier to swim without it, plus I eliminated the temptation to use it. I'd rather drown than have to face my father if I got sent home from failing The Swim. Are you a good swimmer?"

"Pretty good."

"Think you can beat me?" Brad asked.

"No doubt about it."

"Then you should ditch yours, too."

"No thanks, I think I'll save mine. That way I can sell it to you later, when the cramps hit and you change your mind about drowning."

Rain meant what he said as a joke, but Brad either didn't

hear it, or found it lacking in humor. Without a reply, Brad lowered his head and churned water faster than a fuel-injected paddleboat. Not long afterwards, the distance between Brad and Rain increased, and Rain's goal of being the first Bravo freshman to finish The Swim appeared to be in jeopardy. Brad O'Johnovich was a strong swimmer whose lead grew larger by the second.

Rain had swum over a hundred yards into the river when he reluctantly released his grip on the glowstick and picked up the pace. Brad was right – the lack of a rescue device made an enormous difference in his speed. Soon, he caught and passed some of the weaker swimmers from Alpha Company. A short time later, Rain thought he could see Brad about fifty yards ahead.

Much to his surprise, Rain's emaciated body felt magnificent. He had reported at a skinny six feet, seven inches and 205 pounds, but felt sure he had lost at least twenty pounds over the six weeks of cadre training. Only sinewy muscles remained on his frame, and they propelled him forward like a sleek torpedo vectoring full-bore at its designated target. While Rain continued to pass his classmates from Alpha Company, he wondered how his roommate was faring. Philip had politely declined Rain's invitation to race.

Because a majority of the other freshmen started behind him, on the way to Louisiana, Rain saw only one classmate, an Alpha Company rat, break his glowstick and hold it high out of the water. The former classmate gave up almost exactly halfway across the river. When the boat swooped in to rescue the despondent freshman, it nearly swamped Rain. He dove deep under the water to avoid the fiberglass bow and the rotating propeller. When he surfaced, Rain took the opportunity to briefly glance over his shoulder. The rest of the freshman class swam straight at him like a continuous school of threshing baitfish. Their flailing arms functioned as fins that created faint splashes of silver in the moonlight, which were silhouetted against the blackened walls of the cliffs supporting his school campus and the city of Natchez beyond that. Rain turned back for Louisiana and saw the Alpha rat hauled, coughing and wheezing, into the boat. The boat sped from his path, and Rain resumed the mission. Soon, Rain was three-fourths of the way to the bonfire and only three classmates remained ahead of him.

Rain caught the trio as they exited the water. The bonfire burned bright and raged hot and felt oh, so inviting. Rain seriously contemplated taking a few minutes to warm his dripping, naked body. But as it had done so many times before, his competitive spirit took over. Rain, Brad, and the two Alpha freshmen grabbed their rat sticks and hit the water together. Rain kissed Catherine's wooden lips and touched Wayne's "56" for luck.

Brad noticed the lack of Rain's water rescue device as they paddled for home. "Took my advice about the glowstick, did you?"

"Nope. Sold it to an Alpha rat who claimed he collected them."

"Rain, I should have told you something before I encouraged you to let it go."

"What?" Rain asked as the distraction from their conversation allowed the two Alpha competitors to open up a slight lead.

"Even though they don't explicitly tell you before The Swim starts, there's a time penalty assessed if you don't make it up the cliff with your glowstick."

Rain stopped paddling and reached over in an effort to grab Brad O'Johnovich. Unfortunately, there was nothing to grab, and Brad easily escaped as Rain's fingers slid down his slippery back. "Damn you, Brad! How much of time penalty?"

Brad laughed at the desperate look on his new friend's face. "Relax, Rain. It's only an hour. They add it to your official time. We've got plenty to spare, anyway. We're at under an hour-and-a-half pace."

Brad began pumping his legs, and Rain paddled harder as well. "How can you be so sure of our pace?" Rain inquired.

"Because I practiced swimming this same stretch of river six times over the summer."

Rain shook his head and kept scissor-kicking the water. Brad O'Johnovich was insane. What a way to spend the summer! "So you swam this river six times for practice? You're crazy."

"Not crazy," Brad corrected him, "simply trying to win a bet with my father."

"A bet?"

"Yeah. My dad finished The Swim his rat year in one hour and twenty minutes, back before they required rats to use glowsticks. It's one of the fastest times ever recorded. He bet me ten dollars I couldn't beat it and gave me a hundred to one odds."

"So you'll get a thousand if you do. And to think, my motivation was simply to win."

"Tell you what, Rain. If you push me, we make up some time and I clock in under one-twenty, I'll give you a hundred bucks of my prize money."

Rain readily accepted Brad's offer. He didn't know of anyone who couldn't use an extra $100. "Well then, hell, get a move on, you sorry-ass rat!" he screamed in Brad's ear.

After roughly two hundred yards, Rain and Brad began separating themselves from the two Alpha freshmen about the same time the majority of their Bravo classmates passed them going in the opposite direction. Rain looked for Philip, but he was not among the group. Rain could only hope that he had somehow passed by unseen.

Before long, Rain could easily predict which of the freshmen swimming for Louisiana were in trouble. Their forward progress stopped and they frantically slapped at the water's surface as if holding down hidden demons bent on escaping from the muddy underworld below. Rain could only imagine the final thoughts that raced through their minds as they debated whether or not to give up and break the glowstick or continue the fight against exhaustion and the searing pain of cramped muscles. Often, a classmate swimming up from behind would offer assistance only to be rebuffed by the last ounce of pride the struggling freshman could muster. A few collected themselves, discovered new strength, and continued. Most took the easy way out and broke the stick. Those who did were pulled from the river with an invisible demon clinging to their backs, one that would serve as a constant reminder of the night they had failed themselves and their families.

Rain was thinking how failing The Swim could scar a young man forever when Brad pointed ahead to a spot where a rat had stopped swimming and begun to flail in desperation. "Look at that one up there, Rain. You think he'll break the stick before we pass him."

Rain gauged they would pass the hapless freshmen in about fifteen seconds. "I don't know, but I sure hope he holds on. An earlier rescue nearly killed *me*."

Rain and Brad strained their muscles even harder to make it safely past before the freshman succumbed. Like a vulture, a motorboat pulled beside the doomed rat and patiently waited for the yellow light that would signify the carcass was ready for consumption. As the pair moved closer, the dying rat struggled less and less, and one of the men on the boat leaned down, ready to pluck the cadet recruit from the river and relieve him of the mission that had beaten him. In one final struggle, the freshmen turned his ashen face toward the pair of strong swimmers approaching from Louisiana. Rain gasped in horror. It was Philip Tice.

Rain pushed his totem pole to Brad and thrashed for his roommate. Philip's eyes were almost closed and Rain began screaming his name over and over. When Rain closed the gap to five feet, a masked boatman reached for the pale, soggy mass of flesh that barely remained floating. Part of the job of a rescuer was to act like a referee during a boxing match. If a participant had been beaten, the rescuer had the responsibility to stop the fight, regardless of whether or not the freshman broke the glowstick. This freshman looked as beaten as beaten could get.

Rain seized Philip's arm and jerked him away from the boat and the rescuer's outstretched hands. "Don't you touch him!" Rain shouted with wild eyes.

The boat motor gurgled as the driver erased the short distance between them that Rain had created. A silky-smooth voice from the taller of the two masked rescuers drifted to Rain. "It's okay, son. Your classmate's finished. We need to get him out of the river." His words sounded sympathetic, but Rain knew his actions could ruin Philip's life forever. He couldn't let that happen.

"He doesn't need any help from you! I'll pull him the rest of the way if I have to!"

Both men straightened up on the boat, and the same one who had spoken before sounded offended. "That's up to you. But I seriously doubt either of you will finish The Swim in under three hours if you try to do that." He checked his watch. "In a third of the allowable time, this rat's covered only a fourth of the distance."

By now, Brad had joined them. "Rain, I know he's your roommate, but he's almost unconscious. He's done. We still have a chance to win the bet if we hurry."

"Then go on with your bet, Brad. You and I are lucky we're strong swimmers, but Philip isn't so lucky. All he wants to do is finish in under three hours and stay in school."

Brad started to paddle away, but apparently changed his mind. "Ah, hell. It'd crush my old man if I beat his time, anyway. Rain, see if you can wake him up."

On cue, Philip squirmed underneath Rain's bent left arm that kept his head above water and allowed him to breathe. "I think he's coming around!" Rain shouted. Brad slapped Rain's roommate hard across his pale cheeks.

Philip opened his eyelids, revealing two glassy marbles. "Rain? Is that you?" he muttered.

"Yeah, it's me! Can you swim?"

"I don't think so," Philip replied groggily as he rolled his head back and forth. "Both of my legs are cramped up."

"How about your arms?"

"They're okay."

Rain laughed delightedly. "That's perfect, Philip! I'm gonna teach you how to float on your back and swim using only your arms. That'll give your legs a chance to rest before you paddle back across. Brad, show him what I'm talking about!"

"Brad's here, too?"

"Yep, Brad's here, too. Can't you see him?"

"Everything's kinda fuzzy. Is he that blob waving at me?"

"Yes. Now try to focus. We don't have much time. I want you to watch him closely. He's gonna show you how to swim the easy way."

Brad pushed the totem poles to Rain, took a deep breath and floated on his back. He held his two feet above the surface and kept his legs motionless to prove Rain's point about not using his legs. Simultaneously, Brad pulled his body through the water using long, fluid backstrokes from his arms. After about ten yards, Brad turned around and glided past them again. "Philip, remember to try to keep your lungs as full of air as possible – use a shallow breathing technique," Brad instructed.

Apparently, the brief rest helped. "Okay, let me try," Philip said confidently.

Rain released his grip and Philip took a deep breath, settled on his back, and swam as he had been taught. Only one problem remained; Philip headed in the wrong direction. Rain grabbed him again and pointed him at a spot on the Louisiana shore significantly upstream from the bonfire. "Philip, you've got to check every now and then over your shoulder to make sure you're going the right direction. Aim for a few hundred yards to the right of the bonfire to compensate for the current."

"I'll try to remember that, Rain. Thank you both for your help. Even if I don't make it, I'll always remember what you did for me tonight." Philip placed his glowstick back in his teeth and smiled as he swished by them using his newly learned stroke.

"We'd better get going, Rain," Brad remarked. "We've drifted with the current for the last several minutes. Philip's got his second chance. Now, we'll be the ones cutting things close if we don't start for the other side. Don't forget about that time penalty."

Rain noticed that well over half of the other freshmen and their totem poles had passed their position as they steamed for the eastern shore. "Brad, would I get kicked out if not finishing with the glowstick pushes my time over three hours?"

"I don't know, Rain. I never thought about it, because I knew it'd never take me longer than two hours to finish."

The masked men on the boat had rocked alongside silently as they watched the swim lesson. The talkative one bent down and answered Rain's question. "I'm afraid so, young man. Not very many rats intentionally discard their rescue devices. Those that do usually are trying to break speed records or the times their fathers set before glowsticks were used. When you boys were in the lead, you probably had a shot at one of the best times ever, but if you don't get moving right now, you'll have to push it to finish under two hours, especially since you'll have to fight through traffic the rest of the way."

Rain checked his roommate's progress and saw that Philip's stroke was strong, but he had started swimming in the wrong direction again. "Brad, you go on without me. If I don't guide Philip, he'll never make it."

Brad squinted. "Are you sure? If you help him now, *you'll* never make it."

"Hell, I wanted to go to Ole Miss anyway."

Brad shook his head, wished him luck, and then paddled back toward the rest of the freshmen. He fully expected it would be the last time he would see Rain Henry, the would-be MMC baseball star who washed out because of his ridiculously futile attempt to keep a fellow classmate from failing The Swim.

Rain sped to Philip's side and corrected his course. Soon, they headed along an unwavering vector straight at the bonfire, which grew more and more dim as it crumbled from age and a lack of fresh fuel. The men in the boat followed closely behind Rain and Philip, who were, by now, the last two rats still swimming for Louisiana. At about thirty yards to shore, the non-talkative boat driver stood from his seat behind the wheel and spoke up. His voice vibrated deep and guttural, like that of a troll. Rain thought he recognized it, but couldn't place where he'd heard it before.

"Boy, how'd you lose your glowstick?" he asked Rain.

Rain yelled at Philip to keep going, then turned and hollered back his answer. "I let it go in the water, sir. It slowed me down, and I wanted to win the race. I didn't know anything about the time penalty. If I did, I would have kept it."

The troll-voiced man seemed to consider Rain's answer for a few moments, then reached down and picked up something from the bottom of the boat. In the moonlight, Rain saw the man holding a clear plastic cylinder, similar to the one his hand had released earlier. With an underhanded flip, the man sent the container and its encapsulated chemicals tumbling through the air. After it landed in the water with a "plop" only a few feet away, Rain reached forward and retrieved the unused glowstick.

"We fished this one out of the river earlier tonight. Maybe it was yours to begin with." Once the glowstick left his hand, the man understood that technically, one might argue that his act disqualified this valiant cadet. But hell, he thought, if anyone could skirt a rule every now and then, he could. Besides, this boy was willing to sacrifice his own cadet career to aid his fellow soldier. If The Swim were a real battle, this unselfish soldier would be decorated with the Medal of

Honor for demonstrating such self-sacrifice. How could he, as the leader of the finest military college in the country, allow something as insignificant as a plastic tube end this young man's promising career? He'd simply have to make sure that nobody found out. Momentarily breaking eye contact with the incredulous freshman, he removed his mask.

The exposed face sparked Rain's memory. His benefactor was none other than General Grimmer, MMC's president.

Grimmer laughed at Rain's astonishment and motioned at the surrounding water. "It's amazing how the current can shift in the favor of those soldiers who sacrifice themselves to help others. Looks like your water rescue device has just floated upriver. It's lucky you saw it."

Rain's voice deserted him for a few seconds while his mind comprehended the significance of the general's gift. It meant he still had a realistic chance to earn his company letter and avoid a shameful bus ride back to Meridian. "Thank you, sir!" Rain finally managed to say.

"No need to thank me. You and your classmate have only one hour to finish The Swim. I simply provided you with a personal incentive to get back across this river as fast as you can. I'd hate to lose a cadet with your integrity and loyalty to a watered-down institution like The University of Mississippi. Let's just keep what happened tonight to ourselves, agreed?"

"Sir, yes, sir!" Rain agreed. He was still spellbound by the general's benevolence.

Grimmer pointed his finger at Rain the same way Rain's father did. "There's one more thing. We're gonna tail both of you the rest of the way back to Mississippi. If your friend falters again, he'll be in the boat, but I want you to keep swimming. Understood?"

"Sir, yes, sir!"

Rain's roommate did not falter on the journey home. Thanks to determined paddling, fueled by an implacable desire to remain a cadet, Philip Tice completed his personal race against the river. Tired beyond exhaustion, Philip collapsed on the grass as soon as he scaled the rope ladder and reached the finish line at the top of the bluff. He never heard Mr. Manning announce his time of two hours, fifty-eight minutes and thirty-seven seconds, but Rain and Philip's other classmates did. The entire MMC freshmen class celebrated Philip's triumph as if his success represented a collective and final victory over the brutal cadre-training period.

Three days later, while recuperating in the infirmary, Philip revealed his shocking secret: he didn't know how to swim. He had dog paddled the entire way until Rain and Brad taught him how to swim on his back. He explained that after Brad said they wouldn't be able to use the logs as flotation devices until the trip *back* from Louisiana, Philip decided he had no realistic chance of successfully finishing the cadre's final exam. He believed he'd need to be rescued during the initial crossing and decided it would be pointless to carve something that represented a personal future failure.

But after completing The Swim, Philip's uncarved rat stick became a tangible symbol of the night he overcame odds he previously considered insurmountable. Philip also acknowledged Rain's substantial role by asking him to autograph his prized piece of cedar. Rain happily signed Philip Tice's smooth-sided totem pole. It never collected dust again.

Rain maintained secrecy, as General Grimmer requested. When Brad inquired how Rain happened to find another glowstick, Rain told him the truth – he had happened upon it floating close to the Louisiana shore.

CHAPTER THIRTEEN
LETTERS

Thanks to the events of that night in September, Rain Henry became an instant celebrity, while Philip Tice became a legend. Not only did Cadet Private Tice possess the courage to attempt The Swim without knowing how to swim, he recovered from the brink of dismissal and still finished in less than three hours. Sure, Philip received help, but Rain and Brad enhanced their friend's feat by accurately stating they merely taught him to swim on his back, nothing more. Neither had physically pushed or pulled Philip across the finish line.

The next day, several upperclassmen – cadre was officially dissolved after The Swim – also weighed in with their opinions of Rain's primary role in saving his rat classmate. Thirty-nine freshmen resigned after failing The Swim, one less than the "over-under" number of forty. Upperclassmen who bet the "under" cashed in and joyously slapped Rain on the back while complimenting him on his gallant deed. Those who bet the "over" kicked and cursed him for jeopardizing the strength of the corps by helping a weaker rat survive. However, those who punctuated their harsh comments with the tips of their shoes didn't bother Rain Henry. He had earned his company letter and so much more. In a single night, Rain established a unique bond with two friends he knew would endure for the rest of his life.

After finishing his last afternoon class, Rain visited Philip in the infirmary, and then returned to his room to get ready for his first official Friday parade. He was shining his breastplate when Sergeant Sawnay, using his customary SWAT team technique, burst through the door.

"Rat Henry, report to my room, shirtless, in five minutes!"

"Sir, yes, sir!" Rain blurted.

Five minutes and five seconds later, Rain hung like a chimpanzee from the metal clothes bar in Sawnay's full-press. Because Rain's legs were too long to dangle freely, Sawnay forced Rain to flex them at the knees as far as he could until both heels nearly reached his buttocks. Sawnay tied each leg to itself with bungee cords knotted at the ankles and thighs.

"Henry, you cost me fifty bucks by saving Tice's ass. How do you think I feel about that?" Sawnay asked with a painful look on his face.

"Sir, no excuse, sir," Rain answered, which was the rat way of saying, "I don't know." By training freshmen to say "no excuse," MMC taught cadets the lesson of accepting responsibility for either not knowing the answer to a question or using poor judgment instead of espousing excuses.

"It makes me feel like beating the hell out of you," Sawnay responded matter-of-factly as he opened a small cardboard box on the top of his half-press and pulled out a gleaming brass B about twice the size of Rain's thumbnail. At the top and bottom of the B's underside, Rain saw two nail-like tips. Using one of the tips, Sawnay teasingly spun the letter in front of Rain's face for a few seconds, then moved it an eighth of an inch from Rain's lips and held it there. Rain guessed Sawnay wanted him to kiss it, so he did.

Like a striking snake, Sawnay's coiled right fist bit into

Rain's stomach. The blow felt as if he had been shot in the gut by a cannonball. While Rain struggled to maintain his grip on the pole and avoid vomiting, his former cadre sergeant mashed the brass insignia's two tips into the flesh over Rain's heart. Rain winced at the intense pain as the tiny nails plunged into his skin. A few seconds later, Sawnay withdrew his thumb, stepped back and admired his bloody operation. He deemed the implant successful and untied Rain's legs.

"Looks like you're the lucky one, Henry. That's the first time I've been able to get the letter to stick on the first try. It took me four attempts to pin one of your squad mates earlier this afternoon. I guess practice makes perfect."

Rain's feet felt numb as they reconnected with the floor of the full-press. He released the metal bar, stepped out of Sawnay's metal closet, and stood at attention with his arms clamped by his side. "Sir, will that be all, sir?" he expectantly asked.

"Yeah, that'll be all. Now go get dressed for parade, you rat bastard, before I change my mind about your worthiness to wear our company's sacred symbol!"

Once Rain returned to his room, he delicately extracted the B from his chest and rinsed away the blood in the room's sink. The letter glittered in his eyes the way a newfound nugget of gold winks at a destitute prospector and Rain dried his treasure with soft caresses from a cotton undershirt. With great pride, he took a duty shirt from his full-press and poked the letter's nails through the left portion of the shirt's collar, fastening the B into place with two brass tip covers. He could hardly wait to show it to Catherine when she came to visit in exactly twenty-eight days and two hours. While he wiped away the light trickle of blood from his chest, Rain vowed to make time over the weekend to write everyone he knew about the events of the previous twenty-four hours.

Rain would have preferred to call them, but freshmen weren't allowed to have telephones in their rooms until second semester. Thus, Rain relied on the old-fashioned method of communicating with pen and paper to keep in touch with his friends and family. While speaking over the phone produced spontaneous interaction and instantaneous feedback, Rain discovered that conversations spoken via letters were special in their own unique way. Letters transformed his eyes into ears and Rain listened intently as the letter's author articulated his or her thoughts and feelings by using unique collections of words and sentences. He kept every letter he received in shoeboxes hidden above his room's cardboard-like ceiling tiles. Each letter served as a window to the world outside Ellicott Gate and the shoeboxes were Rain's personal time capsules. Whenever Rain opened his cadet mailbox and found a letter waiting inside, his heart sang.

While Rain had written Wayne frequently, Wayne wrote back only once. The letter thanked Rain for his correspondences, but explained that Wayne had difficulty writing, primarily because of the constant pain. Wayne closed the letter by asking that Rain not hold it against him.

Rain and Railroad wrote one another often, and Rain enjoyed listening to Reece's perspective on attending a somewhat "normal" college. Reece said he found Princeton's classes challenging, but felt confident he could handle the work. And, as Rain suspected Railroad would, he had already made numerous new friends.

Rain's grandmother possessed a marvelous flair for writing that Rain never knew existed until she began sending him weekly letters that usually arrived every Saturday. Her words and sentences eloquently kept him informed on local events around Vimville and Meridian as well as the latest news regarding the farm or her garden. Often she cut out articles or a cartoon that made her think of her grandson and included them with her letters.

About every other week, Rain's father sent a short note that updated him on Wayne's rehabilitation progress and included a check for $20 to $30. Rain saved the money in anticipation of taking Catherine to a nice dinner and paying for her hotel room when she came down for the Corps Day Rat Dance at the end of October.

Rain enjoyed reading letters from everyone, but those scented with Catherine's perfume and stamped with an Oxford postmark were the ones he cherished most of all. He read her daily letters as soon as he slid them from his mailbox. They were like a glass of ice water to a man journeying on foot across the Sahara Desert. Her words of love and encouragement gave his mind and body the strength it needed to continue the hellish trek until he reached the next day's oasis.

But shortly after The Swim, Rain started to worry. Catherine sent him a letter that mentioned she was about to begin the process of following in her mother's footsteps by pledging the Delta Gamma Sorority. The letter went on to explain that during the rush period, Catherine wouldn't be able to write as frequently, but promised to try at least once a week. Rain understood, yet still felt disappointed.

After almost three weeks without water, the man crossing the desert panicked that he may never drink again. Nearly every day, Rain heard about a fellow rat who received a "Dear John" letter from his girlfriend back home or away at a regular college. Why hadn't she written as she promised she would? Had something bad happened, like a car accident? Had she met someone else or gotten back together with Trip Chadwick? Was Rain next in line for a Dear John? Rain lost his mind. With her previously planned visit to attend the Rat Dance a mere two weekends away, Rain decided to take drastic action.

A single pay phone in the small sallyport located on the ground level between Bravo and Charlie Company might provide the answers. Originally, the phone had been placed there years before with the idea that first semester freshmen could use it a few hours to call home each Sunday. However, once it had been installed, the cadet battalion commander at the time decided pay phone access represented too nice a rat privilege and suspended its use. Apparently, the suspension remained in effect, because the cadre made it clear that if a rat ever got caught using the pay phone, he would be "pulled," or punished, for gross poor judgment, one of the most severe offenses listed in the *Red Book.* To try using the phone would be a pointless risk, anyway, the cadre explained. They claimed a deranged rat, distraught over a romantic breakup, broke the phone in the 1970s, and many expressed doubts that it had ever been repaired.

Rain decided to take the risk that the pay phone worked and he wouldn't get caught using it. Rain needed to hear Catherine say, with her own sweet voice, that she loved him and still planned to drive down for the Rat Dance. A large calendar, which also served as a desk blotter, constantly reminded Rain of the upcoming date every time he studied. Rain had circled the special Friday a thousand times, and the mere thought that she might not come crushed him. Catherine's visit would be the first time he would have the opportunity to stroke her golden hair, touch her beautiful face, kiss her moist lips, and gaze lovingly into her sapphire-blue eyes since he left Meridian to report to MMC.

Rain waited until he knew the battalion, including Philip, slept soundly. The digital clock on his half press read 1:45 when Rain rolled from his rack and dressed again into his duty uniform. He slipped from the room, turned left on the red tiles, and after reaching the stairwell, tiptoed down the stairs. The battalion sounded eerily quiet as Rain headed for the sallyport that housed the pay phone. To his left, the quadrangle was tinged yellow by warm, hazy light directed by the four giant floodlights perched atop each concrete tower in the corners of the battalion.

Rain reached the phone that glowed reddish-black across from the well-lit soda machine. After a final check to see if anyone watched, Rain picked up the receiver. Thankfully, he heard a dial tone. So much for the cadres' tall tale, Rain thought as he hit zero. An operator answered, and with his hand cupped around the mouthpiece, Rain asked to place a collect call. Catherine answered on the sixth ring and accepted the charges from Rain Henry.

Her voice sounded sleepy as it crackled through the line. "Rain, how are you calling me? I didn't think you had access to a phone until next semester."

"I'm calling you from the battalion's pay phone."

Catherine paused for a few seconds. "Didn't you say in a letter that it was off-limits to freshmen?"

"Yes, but I had to talk with you. Did you break your hand or what? Why haven't you written me?"

"Rain, I'm really sorry. I've been unbelievably busy with sorority stuff. My mom even moved up here about three weeks ago to help me get through everything."

This was bad news. Rain believed Mrs. Landerson had never approved of their relationship and he imagined that if she had a chance to break them up, she would. Rain heard a distant knocking through the phone. "What was that?" he asked.

"It's Mom. Hold on a second." Rain heard Catherine turn from the phone and tell her mother everything was all right and return to bed. "Okay, I'm back."

"Catherine, I need to know you love me."

"Rain Henry, I'll *always* love you," Catherine cooed.

The fear of the unknown had built a knot in his heart the size of a walnut, but as soon as Rain heard those words, the knot melted away like an ice cube on summer asphalt. "Then you're still coming down next Friday for the dance?"

"Of course, silly! I'm meeting you in front of First Battalion one hour after the parade, just like you said."

"And your mom is okay with everything?"

"Rain, my mom is heading back to Meridian after she helps me move into the Delta Gamma house this weekend. I got accepted! Isn't that wonderful!"

Catherine had dodged the question, so Rain felt less than enthusiastic as he extended his congratulations. "Way to go,

Catherine. That's great. I'm really proud of you. Now, please tell me your mom knows you're coming to Natchez to spend the weekend with me."

"I've told her I'm going to visit you that Friday afternoon."

Rain could sense something was amiss. "Why are you being so evasive? We planned for you to spend the whole weekend down here. Can't you give me a straight answer? Does your mom know you'll be here for the entire weekend, or doesn't she?"

"Please don't yell at me, Rain," Catherine pleaded. "My relationship with you has erected a wall between my mother and me that I'm gradually trying to tear down. I want her to accept you as my boyfriend as much, if not more, than you do. I think we've made some real progress over these last three weeks. When I first told her about coming to see you for the dance, she didn't want me to make the trip at all. Finally, she relented on the condition that I return to Oxford and not spend Friday night in Natchez."

Rain calmed himself. Upsetting his girlfriend certainly wouldn't help, but maybe logic would. "Does your mother understand the dance ends at ten and it'll take you about four hours to drive back to Ole Miss?"

"I promised Mom I'd be back by midnight."

Rain quickly calculated the math, and he didn't like the result. At best, they'd have only two measly hours together. Parade finished around 4:30. It would take Philip and him another hour to prepare the room for weekend inspection at 5:30. By the time inspections finished and he finally escaped the battalion for general leave, it would be almost 6:00. The dance started at 7:00. Rain and Catherine would have to rush through dinner and then have maybe an hour at the dance before Catherine needed to hit the road by 8:00 to make it to Oxford by midnight. "Then maybe you shouldn't come, " Rain muttered.

A long silence ensued. "Rain, is that what you really want? You want us not to see each other at all?"

"No, of course not."

"Then what do you want me to do?"

"I want you to tell your mother the truth. I want you to tell her that we've had this weekend planned since we've known it existed. Will you tell her the truth?"

"Yes, if that's what you really want," Catherine detachedly answered.

"It is. Catherine, I'm serious. Do you promise you'll tell her?"

"I promise."

"Thank you. I'm sorry, but I get greedy when it comes to spending every possible second I can with you. Two hours isn't enough." From behind, the distant sound of slippers shuffling his direction caught Rain's attention. Only a few seconds remained to hide before he would be discovered. "Listen, Catherine, someone's coming. I've got to go. I love you."

Rain thought he heard her say she loved him back, but couldn't be certain because he quickly and quietly hung up the receiver. The slippers shuffled closer and Rain hid on the iron-gated side of the soft drink machine. With any luck, the late-night shuffler was heading to a poker game in Charlie Company. All-night card parties occurred regularly in First Battalion, and rumor had it that "Casino Charlie" hosted some of the best.

But instead of shuffling past, the slippers and their owner turned into the small sallyport and stopped in front of the mechanical vender stoically selling soft drinks. Rain heard the upperclassman mumbling something derogatory about studying all night for a production management test. Then he heard the sound of a coin being fed into the slot that functioned as the vendor's mouth. A mechanical gurgle updated Rain on the coin's progress as it plinked and chinked its way through the machine's internal sorting devices. With a final, dull metallic splash, the coin landed in the machine's belly.

Rain waited for the next coin to take a similar journey, but a different sound reached his ears. The quarter hit the concrete floor and rolled. It appeared at Rain's feet, tapped into his shoe, and died tails up.

Lieutenant Nichols peered around the machine in his standard-issue, red pinstriped MMC bathrobe. Rain grinned sheepishly.

"Henry, what in Gawd's name are you doin' heah standin' by the Coke machine at two in the mornin'?"

"Sir, would you believe guarding First Battalion's carbonated beverages from communist thieves, sir?"

Nichols scratched his head. His tired eyes sat above two puffy, dark pools. "Did Sergeant Sawnay send you down heah? Are you on one of his 'rat missions?'"

Although cadre had ended weeks ago, Sawnay continued to send Bravo freshmen, especially those from his squad, on an occasional rat mission, which was nothing more than some off-the-wall stunt designed to make the rat look like an idiot while at the same time providing a laugh for Sawnay and his fellow upperclassmen. Last week, Sawnay ordered Philip on a rat mission that became an instant classic. Right after lunch, Philip ran back to the battalion and waited in Cadet Captian Paidler's room. As Paidler climbed the stairs, Sawnay cracked the door and told Philip to stand on his head in the middle of the room. Once Paidler entered, Philip serenaded the Bravo Company Commander with an upside-down rendition of "*Happy Birthday*." Paidler burst out laughing, according to Philip, but still gave him five demerits as punishment for having such a poor singing voice.

Rain wished he really was on one of Sawnay's missions, but that wasn't true. One of the first things hammered into a cadet's brain is the creed that a cadet will not lie, cheat, or steal. "Sir, I'm not on one of Sergeant Sawnay's missions, sir."

Nichols smiled. "I'm sure part of your mission is to deny the mission, right?"

Rain scowled and whispered loudly, feigning secrecy, "Sir,

no, sir!" Rain didn't recall *Red Book* rules that disallowed speaking with a deceptive tone. He couldn't believe he might actually wiggle out of this predicament.

Nichols put up both hands and chuckled. "Okay, Henry. I understand. Listen heah, I'm studyin' for a big test tomorrow and plan on being up all night. If you see evidence of any pendin' communist attack, come get me. Otherwise, I'll relieve you of your post around 0500."

Rain snapped to attention and saluted his former cadre platoon leader. "Sir, I'll be here, sir!"

A serious look spread across Nichols's haggard face. He clicked the heels of his slippers and returned Rain's salute. After the machine digested the troublesome quarter, Nichols selected his canned soda and shuffled back to his room.

Rain stood beside that soda machine and guarded against the fictitious communist plot for more than three hours, but the boredom and lack of sleep were a small price to pay versus the prospect of facing severe punishment as a result of "gross poor judgment." As promised, at 5:00, Lieutenant Nichols staggered into the sallyport and relieved Rain of his guard detail. While Rain hurried down the gallery, he heard the faint sound of another canned dose of caffeine dropping through the machine's chute to the small opening at the bottom.

Like a kid on Christmas Eve, Rain barely contained his excitement the day before Catherine's visit. Despite the fact that she still hadn't written him since his daring phone call, he eagerly anticipated her late arrival the next afternoon. He hoped she would make it in time to see him march in parade.

After his last Thursday afternoon class, Rain swung by the post office. Maybe, if he was lucky, his dad had sent him another note with some "insurance" money. With everything he planned to do with Catherine, the extra funds might come in handy.

To start the evening, Rain and Catherine would take a

carriage ride through downtown Natchez before dining at the prestigious Cotton Gin restaurant on High Street. He had also arranged for Catherine to spend two nights at Monmouth, an exclusive bed and breakfast that once served as the former home of Mississippi Governor and MMC President John A. Quitman. Rain estimated the entire weekend would deplete his entire savings, around $300, but Catherine was worth it.

Rain's mailbox fit snugly among the hundreds of other mailboxes that made up the far wall of the post office. Instinctively, he located the square brass door numbered 2028 and entered the spiral lock's combination of five, eight and a half, and six." With the dial still on the six, Rain turned the small, key-like knob to the right, and the tarnished door clicked open. Rain reached inside and a long, thin business envelope tickled his fingers. He pulled the envelope from his box and studied the curious letter. It displayed a Meridian postmark, but no return address.

Rain tore open one side of the envelope and shook out the two-page correspondence, which was written on heavy, expensive stationary by someone with graceful penmanship. Almost immediately, the delicate dips and curls of the cursive handwriting stung his hands.

Monday, October 19

Mr. Henry:

I'll be blunt. Your relationship with our daughter is over.

When you accepted a scholarship to Mississippi Military College, my husband and daughter teamed up to convince me to give you a chance. They said I had no evidence to support my feelings that you were not good enough for our daughter to date. Now, I do.

This past Saturday, Catherine came to me and reiterated her previously denied request to spend the entire weekend of October 23-25 in Natchez. I reminded her that we had agreed she would return to Oxford by midnight on Friday. She then asked to spend the night Friday and return on Saturday. When I demanded to know why, she explained that you had told her attendance at the Rat Dance was mandatory for all freshmen. The doors would be locked by 7:15 and would not open again until 10. Any freshman not present for the entire dance received severe punishment. By the time the dance concluded, she said, it would be impossible for her to drive back to Ole Miss by midnight.

I promised to consider her request, but quite frankly, Mr. Henry, I didn't believe your story. This morning I called MMC, and the assistant to the commandant of cadets informed me that freshman attendance at the Rat Dance was strictly optional. She had never heard of any doors being locked or freshmen receiving punishment for failing to participate.

This afternoon, Dr. Landerson and I drove to Oxford and confronted Catherine with the truth. She tried to cover for you by saying she was the one who had lied. Quite frankly, it sickens me that you have brainwashed our daughter to the point where she would accept responsibility for your devious falsehoods. I won't stand for that sort of behavior, and neither will my husband.

We gave Catherine a simple choice. She could end her relationship with you or be cut off financially. Our daughter may have suffered a temporary lapse in judgment this summer, but she is not unintelligent.

Needless to say, you will need to find another date this Friday. I recommend you consider asking a waitress from a local diner or someone else closer to your own social status.

If necessary, our lawyer is prepared to file restraining orders to legally keep you away from Catherine. Do not test me. I will have you arrested if you try to contact her again.

Mrs. Caroline Landerson

CHAPTER FOURTEEN
DEALING WITH DIAMONDS

Rain folded Mrs. Landerson's letter along its original creases and reinserted it back into its envelope. While he headed to the bathroom across the hall from the MMC post office, his fingers shredded the envelope and its malicious contents as fast as they could tear. Over and over, Rain ripped the paper into smaller and smaller squares until his fingertips turned purple and threatened to bleed beneath the nails. By the time Mrs. Landerson's words of hate swirled into the Natchez sewer system, they had been reduced to the size of confetti. Something in Rain's heart told him Catherine would still come the next day. Logic reminded him that Catherine was an adult, and adults had the freedom to make their own choices. Hope whispered that Catherine loved him more than money or material possessions.

Friday's military obligations of afternoon parade followed by weekend inspection came and went, and Rain's confidence in Catherine remained unshaken, even after Brad and Philip met their dates outside the battalion sallyport and Rain's girlfriend was nowhere to be found. Rain told his friends not to wait up – he and Catherine would rendezvous with them later at the dance.

But by 11:00, almost five hours later, the cold night air chilled his hopes that Catherine would show. By 11:30, the flame of love that had burned so brightly over the summer reached the end of the match and died in a wisp of smoke. With wet eyes and a broken heart, Rain locked his arms by his sides and double-timed back through the sallyport.

The officer of the guard, a Delta Company senior private, stopped Rain halfway through. The guard's sword, dangling from his waist, rattled as he thrust his right arm forward like a railroad crossing gate to block Rain's retreat to his room. Seniors had received their class rings during a ceremony the weekend before, and Rain couldn't help but notice the guard's ring. It hovered on his hand only inches from Rain's chest and demanded Rain's attention. The top of the ring formed the outline of the state of Mississippi and in the middle, a sword and rifle crossed above a mortar shell. Where one would expect, a small diamond, representative of the MMC campus, sparkled as it sat in the southwest portion of the state, positioned by the jeweler with precise geographical accuracy. Like the rest of his classmates, the guard had cut a hole in the white glove over his ring finger. The hole allowed his "Golden Mississippi," the ring's nickname, to jut through like a miniature mountain rising above a sea of clouds. People considered MMC's mammoth ring either majestically magnificent or garishly gross, and one's opinion typically depended on whether he wore the ring or did not. MMC alumni boasted that their rings were more than twice as large as those from other schools for a reason: a cadet's education included lessons gleaned from military discipline and physical conditioning as well as traditional college coursework.

The guard placed his non-ring hand on Rain's right shoulder. "I've been watching you from the guardroom all night, Rat. You got stood up, didn't ya?"

"Sir, yes, sir," Rain mumbled.

"Speak up!" the guard bellowed as he popped Rain in the back of the head. "Maybe if you weren't such a wimp, your date would have been here, instead of gettin' it from some other guy right now!"

Thirty minutes before, Rain would have mauled someone after a comment like that, regardless of the consequences. But at that moment, he had neither the mental strength nor the desire to cause any trouble. Rain simply wanted to pass the roadblock and get to his room.

"Sir, yes, sir!" Rain shouted.

"That's better, Rat," the guard said as he oscillated his right hand, which allowed Rain a better view of the class ring. "Any bitch who stands up a future wearer of the Golden Mississippi *deserves* to get it hard, right Rat?!"

"Sir, yes, sir!" Rain shouted again.

"You want to wear it, don't you?" the guard demanded.

"Sir?"

"The ring, Rat! The Golden Mississippi! Do you want to wear it, or don't ya?"

"Sir, yes, sir!" Rain yelled as loud as he could.

The guard nodded his head. "That's what I thought," he exclaimed through a sinister grin. With the swiftness of a leopard attacking its taller prey, the guard sprang at Rain. A millisecond later, he had Rain bent over double in a headlock. While the senior's thick left arm squeezed Rain's neck like a vice, the right one shoved the outline of Mississippi into the hollow of Rain's cheek.

The attack surprised Rain but he recovered quickly. Over the past few days, he had noticed a sharp increase in the number of freshmen who had experienced mysterious "shaving accidents" covered by band-aids. In truth, the diamond in the class rings caused the cuts. Everyone knew the real reasons for the tiny bandages, including the faculty and administration, but they all chose to look the other way. MMC considered "branding" an unofficial tradition.

Normally, Rain could handle whatever physical and verbal abuse came his way, but here, this night, he drew the line. He'd be damned if some gaudy senior branded him on the same night his heart had been ripped in half. With a left hook, punctuated with knuckles hardened from thousands of Sawnay's "fisted pushups" on the concrete galleries, Rain struck the guard hard in the chest where the two sides of his rib cage met. The senior released his grip and collapsed, breathless, onto the cold floor of the sallyport's entrance. In a single punch, Rain transferred his pain and frustration to the sadistic senior like a bolt of lightning.

"See if wearing that ring can help you breathe, asshole," Rain thought as he hurdled the body of his former tormentor, rounded the corner into Bravo Company, and dashed for the staircase. He returned to his room, without further harassment, and flicked on the light above the sink's vanity mirror. Although Catherine had forever scarred his heart, it functioned well enough to pump blood to the site of the laceration. Using the back of his hand, Rain wiped away the red trickle of blood. He tried licking his wound clean, but his tongue wasn't quite long enough.

Thankfully, fall baseball started the following Monday, and Rain turned his mind from the thoughts of his heartbreaking weekend to his goal of becoming the best player ever to step onto the diamond at Bulldog Park, MMC's baseball stadium. In addition to giving him knuckles of stone, Rain soon discovered that the thousands of pushups he performed during the cadre-training period cured the tendonitis in his right elbow and made it stronger than ever. Within a few days of throwing pain-free, Rain regained the pitching form from his junior year of high school and the stinging wasps returned from hibernation with a vengeance.

But despite how well his arm felt, Rain began to wonder if he had made the right choice of college to advance his baseball career. Thanks to the previous year's losing season, the team's morale was shaken to its core. Last year represented the first sub .500 year in Coach Porter's two-decades-plus career as head baseball coach at MMC. Several upperclassmen recounted gruesome "pride drills" where, after a loss, Coach Porter sat on his lawn chair in centerfield and ran his players from foul pole to foul pole until someone passed out from exhaustion. At first, Rain thought his older teammates were teasing him, but after a few practices, Rain believed their stories. Porter was a mean-spirited tyrant times ten on the baseball field. Rain's mind hoisted a yellow flag when, during the first practice, Porter ordered Rain to abandon his knuckle curve and replace it with Porter's own version of an overhand curveball. When Rain suggested that maybe he could throw both, Porter exploded and loudly proclaimed that he had forgotten more about baseball than Rain would ever hope to know. Rain ran laps the rest of that practice and the entire practice the next day.

Each morning, Porter posted the afternoon workout's itinerary on the locker room wall. After three weeks, as Brad O'Johnovich predicted, "Rain Henry" was never scribbled under the list of drills designed for the outfielders or first basemen. Practices grew more and more monotonous as Rain did nothing but rotate between throwing in the bullpen, fielding bunts from the mound, or working on pick-off moves to the various bases. The occasional highlight came when the pitchers hit fungo, or groundballs, to the infielders. Because Porter used designated hitters, Rain and his fellow hurlers were banned from even thinking about taking batting practice. The other pitchers didn't seem to mind not hitting for themselves, but to Rain, Porter's philosophy raised yet another yellow flag.

During the final week of fall practice, Rain gathered enough courage to approach Coach Porter after a Monday workout. At the end of the day, the freshmen had the responsibility of packing up the practice gear and placing it in the storage shed under the bleachers, a process that Porter personally supervised. Rain had seen the talent in the field and knew he could do more to help the team besides pitch.

The rest of the freshmen started the jog back to the locker room as Porter inventoried the equipment. Rain stepped beside his coach. "Coach Porter, am I gonna get some practice this week at playing first base or somewhere in the outfield?"

Porter frowned, threw his head back, and rubbed his throat as if this exact moment represented the first time he had ever considered the prospect of Rain Henry playing another position. After a few seconds, he looked into the anxious eyes of his prized pitching recruit. "No," he replied as he pushed past Rain and walked toward his car.

Rain hustled in front of his coach. "But, sir. During my recruiting visit this spring, you said..."

Rain never completed his sentence because of the glaring expression that flashed across Chain Porter's weathered face. Rain was about to get caught in the open by a thunderstorm. Porter's dull, gray eyes bulged in their sockets as his splotchy, loose-skinned jowls trembled. "Damn it, Henry, I said no! I'll be the one who makes the decisions on who plays where on my team, not some 'know-it-all' rat! Are we clear on that?" Porter screwed his head and neck to one side as he looked up and waited for Rain's response.

"Yes, sir," Rain replied through clenched teeth. But if anything had become clear, it was that Rain would have a tough time playing baseball for such a closed-minded coach.

Five straight days of scrimmaging started the next day. Porter listed Rain as the starting pitcher for the red team in the first game of the "fall series," as he called it. Porter also listed Jeremy Langford as the red team's catcher. Until then, Rain had only thrown in the bullpen to "catchers" who really weren't catchers at all. They all tried to make the team as freshmen walk-ons, and Porter used them, some of whom had never squatted behind the plate in their lives, to spare his scholarship catchers from absorbing the baseball-sized bruises that resulted as the pitching staff experimented with new pitches. Rain caused his fair share as he tried to control Porter's overhand curve with only moderate success.

After thirty minutes of warm-ups, Porter blew his whistle from the lawn chair where he sat beside the third base line.

"All right, sports fans, let's see what this Henry kid can do. Play ball!"

Rain jogged in from the bullpen and took the mound. The moment had arrived. One of the assistant coaches flipped Langford a ball, and Rain's new catcher hand-carried it to the mound. As Langford offered Rain the baseball with his extended right hand, Rain noticed a distinct gray scar on the webbing between his thumb and index finger. The scar exactly matched the size of a pencil eraser or a bullet from a .22 rifle.

Rain opened his glove, and Langford slammed in the ball. "Henry, I know we ain't never gonna be friends, but we're on the same team now. Old man Porter *thinks* you're a star pitcher, but he *knows* I'm the best catcher on this team. That means we're gonna have to work together, whether we like it or not. I say we call a truce. What do you say?"

Rain snapped back, "I say you shut your mouth and go catch the ball. That is, unless the walk to behind the plate's not too far for you to travel, you lazy racist!"

"Okay, Henry. If that's the way you want it."

"That's the way I want it."

Rain pitched well that day, but he purposely shook off every single first sign Langford gave him. He'd be damned if he ever let that jerk think he knew what Rain wanted to throw. His fastball smoked, and his changeup fluttered, but his overhand curve still needed work. Rain knew he needed to throw it for a strike without "hanging it," baseball lingo for letting a curveball drift into a hitter's power zone without a sharp break.

By the time January rolled around and the team started practicing for their first game, Rain found himself in a tight battle with sophomore Bobby Blakely for the top spot in Porter's rotation. Blakely, a silky-smooth, left-handed sophomore from Frogmore, Louisiana, didn't throw nearly as hard as Rain, but he possessed pinpoint control.

On the morning of February 2, as the team prepared to

board the bus for the late afternoon contest against Coastal Mississippi College in Biloxi, Porter called Rain into his office. "Rain, how do you feel?"

"Pretty good, sir."

The old man smiled. "I want you to know I did a lot of thinking about whether to start you or Blakely today. It was a close decision, but my instinct tells me to go with Blakely because he has a little more experience pitching at this level. Rain, you've got great stuff, so don't let this decision get you down. You're one of the few players on this team with the talent to play pro ball."

The player and coach silently probed each other's eyes for several seconds. Rain seethed, but maintained a poker face. He wanted to start the team's first game worse than anything. If Porter had attempted to give him a compliment with his comment about talent, Rain didn't see it as such. He knew he had the talent to play professional baseball, but that wasn't the point. If Rain had the best stuff on the team, he should start, period. "Will that be all, sir?"

"No, there's one more thing. You'll be the first pitcher to come on in relief, so I want you to be mentally prepared."

Later that afternoon, the MMC Bulldogs found themselves down to the CMC Chanticleers 4-2, when Porter summoned Rain Henry from the bullpen during the top of the sixth. Rain would take over for Blakely in the bottom half of the inning. When their third baseman, Craig Cline, hit a fly ball to the center fielder for the final out in the top half of the inning, Rain confidently strode to the mound.

Rain finished his warm-ups, and Langford fired down to second, narrowly missing Rain's head as he ducked close to the ground. The baseball crisply made its way around the infield before returning to Rain through Cline at third. Rain took a moment to check his fielders. They looked ready, so he climbed the hill and faced his first collegiate hitter.

The leadoff batter, a lefty, bounced Rain's first-pitch fastball weakly on the ground toward short. Toby Phillips made the routine play for the first out. Rain fell behind the second hitter 3-2 before walking him on an overhand curveball. The payoff pitch had been a good one, with a knee-high break, but the umpire called it low. With a runner on first, Rain changed to the stretch. While his right shoe nudged the front edge of the rubber, Butch Candler, Coastal's stocky, right-handed hitting catcher stepped to the plate. He looked like Wayne LeRoy's clone and had a similar batting stance. In the pre-game pitchers' meeting, Porter had delivered the scouting report on Candler: power to all fields, quick hands, and not easily fooled by off-speed pitches. Porter said to pitch him away, away, away, and walk him, if necessary, especially with the bases empty.

Rain checked the runner at first and threw heat. The pitch painted the outside corner, and the umpire called it a strike. Langford relayed Porter's call for the same pitch, and Rain threw another fastball. This time, the pitch crossed a little farther out over the plate and Candler fouled it back. The count was 0-2, and Langford signaled for an ankle-high, overhand curve. Rain disagreed. He wanted Candler to chase his changeup as it fluttered by, just off the outside corner. But Porter had made it clear, time and time again, who made the decisions, and reluctantly, Rain rotated the ball inside his glove until his middle and index fingers sat parallel over the ball's laces.

The runner broke from first as soon as Rain strode for the plate, but there would be no play at second. Rain's curve hung in the strike zone like a bad odor, and Candler blasted it 400-plus feet over the left field fence. With one swing of the bat, the MMC Bulldogs trailed 6-2.

The umpire threw Rain a new ball as Candler crossed the plate to the home crowd cheers. Rain was about to turn and walk off the back of the mound to refocus when he saw Porter waddle out of the dugout. Rain anticipated a well-deserved verbal lashing for hanging an 0-2 pitch. Not wanting to miss the fun, Langford removed his mask behind the plate and trotted to the mound as well. The thought that Porter might pull him from the game never crossed Rain's mind.

Porter reached the mound and held out his hand for the ball. "Damned hanger. Henry, that's the worst curve I've seen in my life. I want you to head back to the bullpen and practice it until the game's over."

Rain's jaw dropped. He couldn't believe Porter intended to take him out of the game. Sure, he had made a mistake, but to yank him after three batters? To add insult to embarrassment, Porter wanted him to go throw again in the bullpen. Rain didn't understand. To make matters worse, Langford did a poor job of hiding his gigantic smirk. With a look of confusion, Rain held out the ball, but didn't place it in his coach's hand. "Sir?"

Porter snatched the baseball. Through gritted teeth, he summarized his request. "I said get the hell off the mound and get your ass to the bullpen."

After Rain's first college pitching performance, his ERA or "earned run average" stood at fifty-four, which statistically meant if he were to pitch an entire nine-inning game, he would surrender fifty-four runs. MMC went on to lose the game against Coastal Mississippi 8-4, and no one felt worse about the outcome than Rain Henry. If he had done his job and pitched effectively, his team could have tied the game and possibly won in extra innings.

Rain performed both better *and* worse on his next opportunity to pitch. The day after their first loss of the season, Porter informed Rain that he would start the following week against tiny Lutheran College in Jackson. Porter must have understood he had damaged Rain's confidence in the Coastal game, because on the trip to Jackson, he and Rain drove together in his car while the rest of the players followed behind on the team bus. The entire trip, Porter explained the importance of mental, pre-game preparation. The two reviewed scouting reports on Lutheran's top four hitters, and by the time they arrived at the field, Rain probably knew

Lutheran's stars' hitting weaknesses better than they did. Coach Porter seemed to really want Rain to succeed this time, and for that, Rain felt truly thankful.

Rain never took the mound that day. When he shut the door of Porter's Pontiac Parisienne, the right index finger of his throwing hand caught on the door latch and ripped wide open. Rain expected Porter to be livid over the freak accident, but he simply laughed and called Rain unlucky. MMC won the game, but whatever bridge existed between Chain Porter and Rain Henry disintegrated that day in Jackson. Although he didn't realize it at the time, Rain had received his first and last invitation to ride with the coach.

The deep cut took three weeks to heal, and over a month passed before Rain pitched again. On March 21, roughly five weeks after the accident, Porter finally handed Rain the ball again against Howard, whose team had stopped in Natchez on its way to Baton Rouge for a weekend series against Southern University. Rain pitched well, but Porter yanked him after Rain's control faltered in the seventh inning. Rain wanted to be happy about his first collegiate win, but his ego wouldn't let him. He had surrendered too many walks. The generous sports writer from the *Natchez Democrat* made Rain's performance sound better than it had actually been.

MMC Pounds Howard

Freshman pitcher Rain Henry picked up his first collegiate win as Mississippi Military College pounded out 20 hits en route to a 17-2 victory over Howard University in a non-conference baseball game at Bulldog Park Thursday afternoon.

The Bulldogs (15-6) have won 14 of their last 16 games. Howard is 11-8.

Henry, a 6-7, 205-pound right-handed pitcher from the Meridian area, allowed five hits and one run while striking out six in seven innings.

In the first inning, the Bulldogs had eight consecutive hits, a walk and a sacrifice fly for eight runs.

All the starters for MMC had at least one hit and an RBI. Craig Cline, who hit a grand slam in the eighth inning, was 3-for-4 with six RBI.

MMC plays host to Rilam College at 3 p.m. today at Bulldog Park. MMC's Bobby Blakely will start.

CHAPTER FIFTEEN
DECISIONS

Despite his victory over Howard University, Rain pitched sparingly the rest of his freshman year. Porter said Rain needed better control of his pitches. Ironically, the more Rain concentrated on trying to throw strikes, the wilder he got. Without the mental change of pace that comes from hitting or playing in the field, Rain overanalyzed everything he did on the mound instead of simply throwing the ball. He wondered if his fingers were spread too wide on his fastball. He debated if he choked his changeup back far enough in his hand. And like a ghost speaking from the back of his mind, Porter's voice constantly hounded him to put more snap in his wrist when he threw the overhand curve. For the first time in his life, Rain's confidence in his pitching diminished to the point that he felt afraid to toe the rubber. Once the ball left his hand, Rain literally had no idea where it would go.

Instead of working hard over the summer to correct the problem, Rain shoved baseball far from his mind. He decided that after a dozen straight summers of playing, he was burned out, pure and simple. Rain felt he needed and deserved a break. Jim Henry didn't try to change his son's mind, but did remind him that without his baseball scholarship, Rain would have to work his way through college.

Rain's strategy seemed to succeed when he rebounded to pitch well during the fall season of his sophomore year. Although Porter no longer listed Rain as one of the staff's aces, the coach did promised Rain significant innings as a middle reliever if he still possessed his rediscovered control in the spring.

But as it had done on the day of that freakish accident Rain's freshman year, bad luck hit again. The day before the Christmas holidays ended and Rain was scheduled to report back to campus, he broke one of Chain Porter's most sacred team rules – he played "pick up" basketball and severely sprained his ankle. Because the sprain affected the same ankle Rain injured his senior year in high school, the doctor strongly advised against putting any sort of physical stress on the joint for a minimum of eight weeks. If Rain failed to heed this advice, the doctor warned, he could expect a greater than fifty percent chance of sustaining permanent ligament damage.

Two days later, on the morning of the first day of regular season practice, Rain hobbled into Coach Porter's office on crutches and timidly explained that he would be sidelined for the next two months. Many teammates recommended he lie, but Rain told Porter the truth about how the injury occurred. MMC had taught him never to lie, cheat, or steal, but if Porter awarded points for honesty, Rain didn't receive any that morning. Porter spun in his chair, snatched a clipboard that hung from a file cabinet and, with a thick black marker, crossed out Rain's name from his roster of players. "Let's see. Rain Henry – out indefinitely," he mumbled before spinning back to his desk and dismissing Rain with a flick of the wrist.

Rain thought baseball practices as a pitcher were boring, but baseball-practices as an injured pitcher took boredom to an unprecedented level. From his last class, which usually ended at 2:30 in the afternoon, until sundown every day,

Rain hobbled to Bulldog Park with his clipboard. For the entire practice, which lasted about four hours, Rain sat on a thin wooden bench at the back of the bullpen and charted pitchers' pitches. Rain got a brief respite from his charting duties during scrimmages, when Porter positioned him high in the bleachers as a "spotter." A spotter tracked the foul balls that flew out of the stadium, over the campus fence, and into the park that ran along Clifton Avenue. With a tiny x, Rain marked the ball's location on a copy of the park's map for later retrieval by an assistant coach.

Despite Rain's excellent ball recovery rate, he never left Porter's doghouse his sophomore year. After his ankle healed, Rain appeared in only six games and pitched a total of 10.1 innings. Although he surrendered only two earned runs and struck out nine hitters in those 10.1 innings, Rain walked an unacceptable fifteen batters. When Rain's confidence sagged lower and lower as the season progressed, he downgraded his dream of playing professional baseball to a desperate desire that Porter would simply renew his scholarship. Otherwise, Rain's cadet career would be finished. His father had already made it clear that without the scholarship, Rain would have to pay his own way, and MMC rules forbid cadets from holding jobs during the school year.

For an entire week after MMC's last game, Rain walked on eggshells. On the eighth day, his campus mailbox contained a memo informing him to meet Porter in his office the following afternoon at 4:00. He felt certain Porter would either cut or rescind his scholarship, and he dreaded the appointment the way an under-performing worker dreads a meeting with the boss during an economic recession.

At 3:50, Rain knocked on the door and Porter shouted for him to come in. Rain entered and discovered Porter in an unexpected, upbeat mood. He leaned back in his plush leather chair and smiled at his former prized pitching recruit. "Have a seat, Rain."

Rain sat across from the man who, with a single decision,

possessed the power to end his tenure at Mississippi Military College. "Thank you, sir."

Porter, still smiling, leaned forward. "Rain, do you like ice cream?"

"Yes, sir."

"Thought so," Porter responded with a twinkle in his eye. He spread a copy of the *Natchez Democrat* on top of his desk. From a hidden location by his feet, Porter produced an extra large ice cream cone covered with a thin, chocolate shell and placed it in the middle of the local newspaper.

Rain guessed one of Porter's assistants had purchased the cone from one of the nearby ice cream parlors on North Canal Street and had hastily rushed it to his boss. A few seconds later, the milky vanilla ice cream, like a thawing prisoner, began escaping from the thin walls of its chocolate jail cell. Soon, the off-white liquid seeped freely through the widening cracks of the dark brown prison and dripped with earnest onto the day's news. Porter said nothing and neither did Rain. They both watched in silence as the cold dessert gradually melted into a sticky mess. After ten minutes, the chocolate shell quietly imploded and collapsed. As soon as it did, Porter rose from his chair. With a single swooping motion, he scooped up the gooey concoction, folded it, and dropped it into his trashcan.

"Know who that ice cream cone represented?" Porter asked.

"No, sir," Rain truthfully replied. He had no idea what his coach intended to accomplish, except for possibly wasting a perfectly good summer treat. He did an excellent job at that for sure.

"It represented you."

"Sir?"

"You. Rain Henry. You're the melting ice cream. I've never seen a player let his talent drip away as much as you have over these last two years. It's a waste. If you don't change your attitude about how you play the game, your baseball career will wind up in the trash, just like that cone." Porter leaned back again in his chair and clasped his hands behind his head. "Do you even care about baseball anymore?"

"Yes, sir," Rain lied for the first time in his cadet career.

"Well, I'm not ready to give up on Rain Henry. Are you?"

"No, sir," Rain said as he shook his head, hoping the double emphasis would help cover his true feelings.

"You gonna play summer ball back in Meridian?"

"I'd planned to, sir," Rain lied again. It had quickly become a habit.

"Good. See that you do. When you come back next year, I want your veins full of piss and vinegar. I want to see that fighting spirit you had back in high school, understood?" Porter jumped to his feet and extended his hand. Both jowls trembled on either side of his lips, which parted like stage curtains revealing the old man's smile.

Rain rose and grabbed the worn, leather mitt with gusto. "Yes, sir. I understand," he replied. He still wasn't sure if he had his scholarship or not, but Rain wanted to get out of Porter's office as quickly as possible. As far as he was concerned, until someone explicitly came out and declared he no longer had a baseball scholarship, Rain would play along as if he still did.

Porter nodded and sat back down in his chair. Rain had almost left the office when he heard Porter's final words chase him out the door. "Don't waste my money again next year, Rain Henry, or you'll be sorry you did, you tall son-of-a-bitch."

In reality, Rain had already decided not to play summer ball before the meeting with Porter. But because he lied and told the old man he planned to play, he made a concerted effort. Teams are always eager for pitching, so Rain didn't have much trouble hooking up with a traveling squad from Meridian's Naval Air Station. Most of his summer teammates were in their twenties and thirties and had played baseball in high school. A few had college experience. The team's captain, a fellow pitcher and aircraft mechanic, made one thing clear from the beginning: they really didn't care if they won or lost. Sure, winning was nice and they played for the love of the game, but most of all, playing baseball gave them a legitimate excuse to get away from their wives and drink lots of beer.

When Rain pitched, the aircraft mechanic let Rain hit for himself instead of using a designated hitter, and baseball became fun again. Rain quickly established his ranking as the team's top pitcher. Two weeks into the season, the team's second baseman received transfer orders to a base in California, and Rain got to invite Railroad to join the roster, an invitation he readily accepted. Reece showed no ill effects from his two-year layoff and soon proved to be one of the team's best hitters and its undisputed slickest fielder.

Halfway through the summer, Rain took over at first base after the regular first baseman wound up in the brig. Apparently, he caught his wife in bed with another man and beat them both to pulp. Unfortunately for him, the other man turned out to be a full-bird colonel visiting from the Pentagon. Rain hated the circumstances that finally put him back on the field as an everyday position player, but he jumped at the opportunity nonetheless. Every turn at bat, Rain tried to crush the ball as if it represented Chain Porter's closed-minded skull. In the last twelve games, Rain hit over .350 and mashed four home runs.

Rain rejoiced that he and one of his best friends were given another chance to play on the same team. He only wished Wayne could have somehow been on the field with them. Then, during one special game, something magical happened. Wayne, who could now walk fairly easily with the assistance of a cane, came to watch them play a game in Meridian. When one of the umpires failed to show, the teams asked if one of the spectators wanted to fill in. Wayne eagerly volunteered, and once again, the three friends took the field together. Of course, he wasn't actually playing, but seeing

Wayne LeRoy actively participating in a baseball game gave Rain goose bumps. When Wayne grinned with laughter after calling Railroad out on a failed attempt to stretch a single into a double, Rain felt the sting of tears that formed in his eyes. Although Reece was clearly out, he played along by arguing the call and kicking some of the infield dirt on Wayne's tennis shoes. By the end of the summer, Rain rediscovered his love for baseball.

Great summers fly by, and the summer between Rain's sophomore and junior years of college proved to be no exception. In the blink of an eye, Reece returned to Princeton and Rain headed back to MMC. Wayne promised to hold down the fort back home, but even he, too, would soon be moving on with his life. After two solid years of intense rehabilitation, he had finally passed the entrance physical for truck driving school. Rain knew that driving an eighteen-wheeler could never compare to piloting a jet, but at least Wayne had found a new professional focal point in his life.

When Rain's third season of fall baseball began at MMC, Rain proudly proclaimed to his coach that he regained his groove over the summer and this would be his breakout year. Rain's competitive swagger returned, and he felt ready to put it to the test. Porter congratulated Rain on his summer successes and his newfound confidence with a firm slap on the back that stung like a slap in the face. With the expression of a mad scientist drooling at another chance to conduct a previously unsuccessful and volatile experiment, Porter made his own proclamation: over the summer, he had decided to turn Rain Henry into the world's tallest sidearm pitcher. With a single sentence, Porter snuffed out the love for baseball Rain had worked so hard to rekindle over the previous three months.

Instead of using an overhand delivery, the method by which Rain had thrown a baseball his entire life, Porter wanted Rain to begin slinging the ball toward the plate with a type of swinging motion where his arm moved nearly parallel to the ground. Rain immediately flashed back to a conversation he once had with Brad O'Johnovich on the first day they met. Porter had tried this experiment before, failed, and in the process, ruined a player's arm forever. Rain knew he had no real alternative if he wanted to keep his scholarship, so reluctantly, he agreed to become Porter's next pitching guinea pig. Although he didn't realize it at the time, Rain Henry mentally quit the MMC baseball team the same day he became a sidearm pitcher.

As one might expect, the freshmen walk-on players experienced an especially brutal time catching Rain Henry in the bullpen that fall season. At first, Rain cringed every time a wayward pitch ricocheted up from the dirt and into an unprotected part of the catcher's body. Soon, however, his mind turned numb, and he stopped hearing the bullpen catchers' sharp cries of pain as they struggled to put leather on Rain's wild pitches. By the end of the fall, Rain became nothing more than an emotionless, minimum wage worker who showed up for the job, did exactly enough to get by, collected his paycheck, then headed home with his head hung low.

By the spring, Rain's passionless play and apathetic attitude left him ostracized by his teammates. Rain didn't blame them for the condescending glares, the jokes they made behind his back, or the fact that the lockers surrounding his sat empty. He even agreed when a non-scholarship starter would complain in the shower, just loud enough for him to hear, about how, "that sorry-ass Henry's gettin' all the scholarship money, and he can't throw a strike to save his life." Had it not been the truth, it would have been easy to blame everything on the lead antagonist, Jeremy Langford, who reveled in Rain's misery with the ecstasy of a swine rolling in a pool of mud on a sultry day. Worst of all, Rain Henry knew he had turned into something he never, ever would have imagined becoming: a coward – but not because his talent and passion for baseball had gradually waned over the last few years. He was a coward for not standing up to Porter and his teammates for the way they shredded his dignity as his struggles worsened. Most of all, he was a coward for not having the courage to quit and walk away from the game, damn the scholarship and the consequences.

The second and third weekends of Rain's junior season, MMC was scheduled to play at Mississippi State and the University of Mississippi, respectively, for the first time in thirty years. Mississippi's recently elected governor, an avid baseball fan and MMC graduate, formally requested the three schools arrange the games to promote "good-natured, intrastate rivalry among Mississippi's top collegiate athletic programs." The athletic directors at State and Ole Miss believed the governor only desired more recruiting exposure for his alma mater, but they complied anyway, because it was the politically correct thing to do.

Had the games occurred two years before, when Rain pitched as a freshman, he would have relished a chance to play against the two major state universities that had snubbed him coming out of high school. Now, as a washed-up junior, he doubted if he would make the travel squad, much less get a chance to see any action on the field. So far, Rain's biggest accomplishment of the young season had come just before MMC's first home game when Porter promoted him to Bulldog Park's chief spotter in a mock ceremony in front of his teammates.

So, as Rain expected, when Porter gathered the team in the locker room after Thursday's practice and called out the twenty names of the players that would make the trip to Starkville the following afternoon, Rain Henry was not one of them. Dutifully, Rain acted disappointed, but secretly welcomed his lack of selection. Rain and his two alcove roommates, Brad and Philip, had already signed up for a weekend pass and planned on spending two nights chasing women and drinking hurricanes in New Orleans. When the meeting broke, Rain cheerfully wished his teammates luck. A few players nodded, but most simply ignored him.

While Rain showered alone in the locker room, he thanked God for his life away from baseball. He felt like a middle-aged man trapped in a loveless marriage to the woman who had once been his childhood sweetheart. Counseling over the summer had helped, but when the sessions ended, both partners fell back into the same old rut. Rain stayed married because he was too scared to end the relationship, and he accepted that. Whatever the weak moral obligations were that tied him to the marriage with strings thinner than human hair, they certainly weren't strong enough to preclude him from beginning to cheat on his wife.

By the spring of his junior year, Rain relished the not-so-secret liaisons that helped fill the void where there had once been seemingly inextinguishable passion for baseball. Rain's academic education quickly became his favorite mistress. She was an innocent librarian with braided, brown hair and big green eyes that smiled back at him through wire-rimmed glasses. Rain first approached her after his feelings for baseball faded in the spring of his freshman year, and she he had ravenously accepted his advances. Their lustful relationship blossomed after Rain received a 4.0 GPA during the last semester of his sophomore year and the first semester of his junior year.

Rain also approached another prospective mistress, the military, at the beginning of his sophomore year, when he had been asked to serve as a cadre corporal under cadre platoon leader Cadet Lieutenant George Sawnay. Rain and the military started out hot, like a five-alarm fire, but cooled quickly when the dark-haired, long-legged beauty began imposing her unending list of regulations on their relationship. As a result, Rain terminated the affair. The domineering diva took the news better than he expected. She had plenty of suitors and luckily, since the two still interacted on a daily basis, Rain maintained a cordial, if not overly friendly, relationship with his former lover.

Rain didn't consider his friendship with Brad and Philip

similar to that of a mistress; they were more like the "single buddies" who, because of the wedding, initially fade into the background only to be rediscovered when the marriage starts to break up. Brad and Philip didn't care that Rain's baseball career had taken a nosedive and because of that, Rain maintained his sanity.

So, while Rain and his two buddies spent the weekend partying with three Tulane coeds they met in a bar on Bourbon Street, his baseball teammates spent the same weekend losing all three games to Mississippi State by a combined score of 36-2. Rain didn't know if they won or lost, and quite honestly didn't care, until he saw the box scores from each game taped on the bulletin board as he dressed for Monday's practice. Underneath, in bold, red letters, Porter had written, "NO NEED FOR GLOVES TODAY. PRIDE DRILL AT 3:30 SHARP. DON'T BE LATE."

Instantly, Rain's apathy turned to anger. He hadn't been a part of the Starkville massacre, so why should he be punished? Rain's conscience, emboldened by the trace amounts of alcohol still circulating in his brain, finally spoke up and told him to quit right then and there. It called him a fool for continuing the charade. When Rain asked his conscience how it proposed to pay for his MMC education without baseball's money, it recommended he apply for an academic scholarship to make up for the loss of the one he had never really earned anyway.

Rain's conscience nearly had him convinced when another voice surfaced. The new, deeper, and more confident voice reminded him that if he decided to leave baseball, it should be on his own terms, and not because he felt too lazy or hung over to run for a few hours. The second voice gave his ailing spirit a small dose of pride and maybe that was why he made the decision to ignore his conscience. Because Rain's mind had been filled with the cobwebs that come from a lack of sleep and forty-eight hours of binge drinking, Rain never identified the owner of the second voice. Only later would he guess that he had most likely heeded the advice of the devil himself.

So, at 3:29, when Chain Porter blew his whistle and gathered his players in the outfield grass behind second base, Rain anxiously stood among them.

"All right, you sons-of-bitches. The rules are simple. I blow the whistle, and you pathetic losers start jogging from the foul line to the imaginary line between those two orange cones in the middle of center field. As soon as you pass the imaginary line, you sprint your asses off to the other foul line. And you better run the whole damn way, or we'll do this again tomorrow." Porter took a moment for his instructions to sink in. "Some of the seniors, who've experienced the fun before, may have told you that you'll run my Pride Drill until someone collapses. They're wrong."

The players nervously murmured and Rain tried to guess what sick twist Porter held up his sleeve.

Porter smiled wide as he dropped the bomb. "We'll run today until the sun goes down or *three* people pass out."

The team let out a collective groan, and Porter scowled as his jowls shook like bowls of jelly. "That's right you lazy losers! You embarrassed me this weekend like I've never been embarrassed before. The flippin' governor even called me last night to complain about your performance. I won't stand for anything like this past weekend to ever happen again, period!" Porter paused as he locked in on somebody in Rain's direction, but Rain didn't think it was him. "There's one more thing. I'm looking at Rain Henry, and I can see in his eyes that he's ready to quit and we ain't even got started yet. If Henry's one of the three that drop, we'll run Pride Drills every day of practice the rest of this week."

With his "pep talk" concluded, Porter blew the whistle, and the MMC baseball team jogged to the outfield foul line on the first-base side of the field. Like a snake, Langford slithered up to Rain and said, "I swear to God I'll kill you if you quit on us, Henry."

"Kiss my ass, Langford," Rain managed to reply before the first whistle blew.

For almost four straight hours, Rain and his estranged teammates jogged to center field and then sprinted to one foul pole and then the other. There were no water breaks and only a few seconds of rest before Porter blew the whistle again. At first, most of the other players threatened Rain as Langford had done when the Pride Drill started. But after the first hour, when they could barely catch their breath and Rain Henry left them in his dust, they mysteriously had nothing to say.

Only two players gave up that day; Rain was not one of them. He and the rest of the team kept running until they could barely see the orange cones in the darkness. Finally, Porter must have gotten hungry, because with three short bursts from his whistle, he motioned the team over and dismissed everyone.

That following Thursday, after practice, Porter announced the players that would go on the road trip to play Ole Miss in Oxford. Rain sat at the back of the locker room, his customary spot, and barely listened as Porter rattled off their names. The girls from Tulane had called on Tuesday night and invited Rain and his roommates back down for another weekend of fun in New Orleans. Rain could hardly wait until they piled into Brad's Bronco the next afternoon and headed south on Highway 61 for "The Big Easy." Their weekend passes had been approved that morning, and mentally, Rain already ran his hands along his date's thighs while she sat in his lap, pounding shooters in a seedy French Quarter bar while a smooth jazz band played in the background.

Porter reached the end of his list, and Rain mentally resurfaced. The last player chosen was usually some starry-eyed freshman who didn't have a chance in hell of playing, but still celebrated as if he had won the biggest prize of his life. Rain always got a kick out of watching the pure bliss caused by Porter merely reading the last selectee's name.

Porter whipped off his glasses and folded them into his shirt pocket. "For this trip, I've decided the last player we'll take along is Rain Henry."

Instantly, more than two-dozen shocked faces frowned and turned to stare directly at Rain. But nobody could have been more shocked than Rain himself. Porter hadn't followed the script, so Rain, the actor, had no idea how to react. He put on a nervous smile and pretended to be flattered.

Porter continued. "State crushed our pitching last weekend, and Ole Miss is ranked higher than they are." He chuckled at his team's reaction. "If things get too bad up in Oxford, we might have to bring in the Satanic Sultan of Sidearm from the bullpen."

Rain's teammates nearly fell off their chairs as they laughed at Porter's clever punch line, and a second later, Rain laughed along with them. So it was a joke, Rain determined with relief. For a moment, Rain worried that Porter really wanted him to go. His blissful weekend wouldn't be spoiled after all.

Twenty minutes later, Rain's heart sank after he finished his shower and began dressing in his duty uniform for dinner. A note, taped on his locker said, "No kidding. You're coming. The bus leaves at 4:00 tomorrow. Consider it a reward for your efforts during Monday's Pride Drill. – Coach Porter."

CHAPTER SIXTEEN SMOKE SIGNAL

Although Rain came, more than once, close to attending the University of Mississippi, he had never actually visited the campus until that Saturday morning when the MMC team bus rolled into the parking lot at Swayze Field. While the bus's brakes released their no-longer-needed air pressure, Rain pondered the differences between his school's campus and the one that beckoned directly outside his window. Rain noticed one difference as soon as he and his teammates entered Ole Miss's campus. Unlike the process at MMC, their bus wasn't stopped at an iron-gated checkpoint manned by cadet guards who would have delightedly interrogated the bus driver. At this school, students, faculty, and visitors flowed completely free of suspicion as easily as the wind. Rain felt like a Cuban ballplayer awed by his first trip to a Western nation, and suddenly, he understood why so many yearned to flee the tiny island nation.

Rain stepped from the bus and joined the other upperclassmen waiting impatiently for the freshmen to unload the team's gear from the luggage compartment. Everyone felt impatient because the early morning air bit cold and sharp on their exposed skin. Rain, along with several other players, rubbed his bare arms in a futile effort to maintain warmth. For what seemed like the millionth time in his life, Rain silently cursed Jeremy Langford, whom Porter had named this year's team captain. Before the team left MMC, the imbecile made the decision for everyone to wear the short-sleeved summer-leave uniforms on the road trip instead of the long-sleeved, and obviously more appropriate, dress-gray uniforms. Rain shook his head as his teeth chattered; Langford lacked any common sense whatsoever. Anybody else would have at least figured out that by the middle of the day, when the temperatures would be suited for summer leave, the team would be dressed in their baseball uniforms.

Finally, the freshmen shouldered the team's gear, and Rain, along with the shivering upperclassmen, moved in to collect their personal tote bags. At the beginning of the trip, each player received a bag in which he packed his glove, cleats, hat, and a neatly pressed baseball uniform.

Like a human pinball, Rain bounced back and forth between the others who pushed and shoved while trying to drag his bag from the ground beneath the belly of the bus. Rain included, they all wanted to head for the heat of the visitor's locker room as quickly as their cold legs could carry them.

Rain had been forced to forfeit a second straight weekend of *bon temps* in New Orleans, but the trip to Oxford almost seemed worthwhile when Craig Cline gave Langford a strong kick in the rear as the team ascended the parking lot's stairs.

"What the hell's that for, Craig?" Langford asked as he rubbed the backside of his gray uniform slacks.

Craig Cline, a senior with the strength of an ox, had started every single game at third base since the beginning of his freshman year. He had been selected all-conference three years in a row, and in Rain's opinion would have made a much better team captain than Jeremy Langford. He represented one of the few on the team that dared to challenge Langford and his position of authority.

"That's for you choosin' summer leave back in Natchez," Craig replied with his husky voice.

At the top of the embankment, Rain and the team turned left on a sidewalk adjacent to a small stretch of road that ran parallel to the right field foul line. They were still officially outside Swayze Field, which, to Rain, seemed more like a well-equipped minor league stadium. Tall light poles surrounded the field and each pole supported its own bank of individual, round lights used for nighttime games. Even the stands, which consisted of alternating red and blue sections of numbered seating, looked well planned and professional. Each seat sat protected from the elements by a gigantic concrete overhang. Trying to compare Bulldog Park to Swayze Field was like comparing a go-cart with a Lamborghini.

A few feet before the team reached the main entrance's gate, Rain heard Langford wolf whistle and point at two beautiful girls walking their direction on a sidewalk that ran along the opposite side of the road.

"Hold on a minute, fellas. I may know these girls," Langford boasted.

The whole team stopped and admired a common sight at Ole Miss, but something never seen on their own campus: two lovely young women out for some early morning exercise.

"You're full of crap, Langford," Craig Cline replied. "How could you know two hot girls like them?"

"One of my old high school buddies goes to school here and plays ball. For years, he's been taggin' this rich bitch that followed him up from Meridian. We all went to high school together." Langford's eyes found and then smiled at Rain, but Rain disappointed him by blankly returning his jab with an expressionless face.

Langford continued, "Listen, Craig. If these girls happen to know this chick, it may help us get into a hot party later tonight. You interested in that?"

Cline shook his head, and his face grew conciliatory. "Okay, Jeremy, okay. I'm always up for hanging out with good lookin' girls," he said with a wide grin.

Sure enough, when the girls got close, Rain saw they both wore Delta Gamma sweatshirts. One had medium-length blond hair while the other's was a rich, cocoa brown. Both looked slim, trim, and flat-out gorgeous.

Langford, seizing the opportunity, stepped forward into the road, removed his white garrison cap, and bowed. His voice dripped with melted cheese. "Ah, hello, lovely ladies. I was wonderin' if you might know a friend a mine."

The girls, now directly across the road, stopped to take a gander at the group of shivering cadets whose white uniforms made them closely resemble a group of ice-cream vendors.

The blonde put both hands on her hips. "I doubt it, private," she said suspiciously.

The team chuckled again, but grew quiet when Langford responded, "I think ya'll are in the same sorority. Her name's Catherine Landerson."

The brunette smiled. "Of course we know Catherine. She's my little sister. How do you know her? Did you go to high school together?"

Langford flashed a toothy grin, like a used car salesman about to close the deal. "That's right. We both went to Pamar Academy back in Meridian. I'm also good friends with her boyfriend, Trip Chadwick. I guess..."

Langford stopped mid-sentence because of the abrupt change in the girls' demeanor. Their faces went from warm and inviting to cold and distrustful as soon as Langford had mentioned Chadwick.

"That tells us all we need to know about you," the blonde said as she and her sorority sister turned with upturned noses and resumed their walk.

Craig Cline stepped forward and yanked Langford back into the rest of the gawking cadets. "Ah, excuse me! Excuse me, ladies!" The girls stopped, but didn't turn. "I have no idea who Trip Chadwick is, but he sounds like a jerk to me." He thrust his arm behind his back and pointed at Langford. "Forget about that idiot; he's just the team's mascot and sometimes his mouth gets him in trouble. The rest of us are some nice guys lookin' for a cool place to hang out later tonight. You wouldn't happen to know about any good parties, would you?"

When the blonde turned to face Cline, Rain saw that her hands were back on her hips. "You boys don't give up, do you? There'll be parties all over campus tonight. Just walk around and you should be able to find one."

Cline had gotten a vague response to his question, but at least the girls had stopped. "I'm sorry, my name's Craig Cline. What's ya'll's?"

"I'm... um... Laurie, and this is..." She looked at her friend for a moment. "Mandy."

"Okay, good. Thanks. Ah, just one more question, Laurie and Mandy. Where are ya'll gonna be partyin' tonight?"

"Why, we'll be partying with you in your room, soldier," the one called Laurie shot back.

"You will?" Cline asked.

"Sure. Where are you staying?"

"At the Hampton Inn up on Highway 7."

"What room number?"

"Two oh eight."

"Okay. Just leave room 208 unlocked. What time's your curfew tonight?"

"Probably ten o'clock."

"Do you have a roommate?"

"Yeah, his name's Steve."

Steve Johnson, MMC's left fielder, stepped forward and shyly waived.

"Good. We want you and Steve to go out and get hammered, so you'll last all night long. When you get back, Mandy and I'll be hiding somewhere in the room. It'll be like a four-person game of sensuous hide and seek."

Rain could scarcely believe what was happening, and apparently neither could the rest of his teammates. Craig basked in the glory as players slapped him on the back and offered their quiet congratulations.

Craig tried to stifle the bulge that grew in his uniform's pants. "Can you give us a clue where you'll be hiding, Laurie," he asked playfully.

"Sure. We'll be easy to find. Go to the bathroom, turn on the shower, and get in. Pour some shampoo into your hand, close your eyes, and start stroking your gearshift. You'll be able to see us, but thank God, we won't have to look at you, jerk!"

Two hours later, Rain still hadn't forgotten about their encounter with Laurie and Mandy. "Wow," he thought as another two runs scored to put MMC down 6-0 in the bottom of the third inning. Not only were the girls at Ole Miss ultra-hot, they were clever and had a sense of humor, too! Now, he knew he made a mistake by choosing MMC.

The next hitter was Trip Chadwick, Ole Miss's All-American right fielder, according to the announcer with the dry voice. Rain yawned and stretched at the far end of the bench while Porter spit tobacco on the concrete floor at the opposite end. In the space between Rain and his coach, a few scrub utility players sat and chewed sunflower seeds. Of the eight pitchers Porter brought on the trip, Rain was listed as number eight on the paper chart posted on the inside wall of the dugout. Beside his name, Porter wrote in parentheses, "Emergency Only." Since he ranked as the pitcher of last resort, Rain held the dubious honor of sitting in the dugout during the game and tracking the pitcher's pitches. The other pitchers, who were more likely to see action, watched the game from the bullpen down the left field line.

As Rain yawned again and shifted the all-too-familiar clipboard that sat on his lap, he watched Chadwick settle into the batter's box. Chadwick had already hit a gap-double on his first at bat and his determined expression made it clear he wanted more. Chadwick had more than grown into his body over the last four years. Two thick, muscular arms bulged from his short-sleeve jersey as Chadwick focused on the MMC pitcher.

Rain readied his pencil as Frank Furman delivered some sort of off-speed pitch. With a sweet and powerful swing, Chadwick launched a home run far over the left field fence. While the crowd cheered as Chadwick circled the bases, Rain half-heartedly colored in the tiny circle next to "changeup" in the column that asked, "type of pitch hit?"

With the score 8-0, Porter rocked back and forth a few times to build up the necessary momentum to pull his wide body off the bench. Once on his feet, he used his finger to extract the dip beneath his lower lip before walking onto the field. The umpire granted his request for time, and Porter motioned toward the bullpen with his left arm. Rain leaned back against the dugout's back wall and put the clipboard and pencil on the bench beside him. With Porter changing pitchers, he'd have a few minutes to ponder what Brad and Philip might be doing down in New Orleans. Rain cursed himself again for running so hard during the Pride Drill.

After relinquishing the ball to Porter, Frank Furman sprinted to the dugout and slammed his glove into the bench. His face looked like a hornet's nest that had been hit with a rock, and Rain thought he might cry any second. Rain watched with disinterest as Porter flipped the baseball to Louis Thorton, the left-handed relief pitcher, and waddled off of the mound. Half way to the dugout, Porter veered and headed right for Rain. Rain snapped to attention and smartly repositioned his clipboard and pencil.

Thorton began his warm-up tosses as Porter reached the lip of the dugout. Rain tried to read the old man's face, but couldn't. With a blank expression, Porter held out his hand. "Give me the clipboard, Henry."

Rain cowered, slowly shaking his head. Maybe Porter had seen him yawn one time too many. "Coach, whatever I did, I'm sorry. I promise to pay better attention."

Porter wiggled his fingers. "Just give me the clipboard."

"But coach, I..."

Though Chain Porter was fat, old, and normally moved slower than a sloth, at times Rain had seen his coach explode with the swiftness of a lion. Before Rain could breathe again, the lion's face hovered inches from his own. "Give me the clipboard!" he screamed.

Rain backed as far as he could against the dugout's wall and handed his coach the clipboard.

"And the pencil, too!" Porter boomed.

As Rain handed Porter the pencil, he hoped he'd get his hand and arm back in one piece. When he retracted the limb back to his side, he felt glad to see everything remained intact.

"Thank you," Porter said and smiled. "Now, get your ass down to the bullpen and warm up. If we go down by a dozen, you're in. It's emergency time." He turned and threw the clipboard and pencil at Furman. "Furman, quit actin' like a baby. You're on chart duty."

Rain, stunned, sat motionless. His clipboard was his shield. Yes, it prevented him from playing, but at the same time, it also protected him from the embarrassment that came from playing. Now, in a single moment, the shield had been yanked away. Rain felt naked. Slowly, his eyes followed Porter as he returned to the opposite side of the dugout and sat down.

Porter exhaled and looked down the bench. "Henry, I said go get loose in the bullpen! If you don't want to pitch, go sit in the locker room or something. Whatever you choose to do, get the hell out of my sight!"

Rain reached down between his legs and under the bench, then pulled out his tote bag. As if a snake might be waiting inside, he cautiously unzipped the bag and took out his glove.

Incredulous stares greeted Rain at the end of his jog to the bullpen. Larry Hutton, the sophomore backup catcher on bullpen duty, asked the question on everyone's mind. "Henry, what the hell are you doing down here? Are you looking for more paper for your clipboard? We ain't got none."

"No, Larry. I'm down here to get loose."

"Are you serious? I can't believe Porter's ready to throw in the towel already."

"Thanks for your vote of confidence. Now, are you gonna get behind the plate, or do I need to go back to the dugout and let Porter know you're down here refusing to catch me?"

"Okay. Jesus, there's no need to do that. Let me put on all my gear. Can you at least try to keep the worm-whackers to a minimum?"

Rain reached down into the five-gallon white bucket and pulled out a ball. He took the bullpen mound as Larry buckled on his chest protector, slid the mask over his face, and ambled behind home plate.

"I'll do my best," Rain offered unreassuringly.

Thorton got out of the third and through the fourth without giving up any runs, but he gave up two solo homers in the fifth inning before retiring the side. When Rain's team came to bat in the top of the sixth, it trailed 10-0. By now Rain's arm felt as limber as a wet noodle. Physically, he was ready to go in, but mentally he prayed he wouldn't be called upon. Today they were playing a doubleheader, which consisted of two seven-inning games. Unless his team scored, which seemed unlikely, if Thorton could record three more outs in the bottom of the sixth without giving up two more runs, Rain wouldn't have to pitch.

Ole Miss's All-American left-hander retired MMC in order, and as Thorton warmed up for the bottom half of the sixth, Rain's hibernating baseball instincts awakened and told him Thorton looked too tired to last through the inning. Sure enough, Thorton surrendered three straight singles, which left the bases loaded with no one out. The next batter blasted a line drive just beyond Craig Cline's diving attempt at third base. Steve Johnson made a strong throw to the plate, but the runner clearly beat Langford's tag. The score was 12-0.

Rain's heart raced and his chest felt like it might burst from the massive quantities of air he forced in and out of his lungs. He expected Porter to pop from the dugout at any moment and wave him into the game. Instead, the PA speakers announced the next hitter, a lefty, who strode to the plate. Rain exhaled the largest sigh of relief in his entire life; Porter had changed his mind. He wanted Thorton to finish the game after all.

Rain sat on the end of the bullpen's bench and stared at his cleats. Now that his mental anxiety had passed, his mind left Oxford and traveled back to New Orleans. After a few seconds of searching, he found Brad and Philip in a dive off Royal Street shucking and sucking twenty-five-cent raw oysters while chugging pints of cold Jax beer. When Rain walked through the door, they both welcomed him with warm embraces and asked the bartender to draw him a pint.

The fantasy broke when Rain felt a baseball bounce off of his right leg. Rain looked up and saw the other pitchers pointing at Porter, who stood on the mound waving at the bullpen like a lighthouse keeper with a broken light trying to save a ship from a hidden reef. Rain grabbed his glove and sprang to his feet. His mind cart-wheeled as he tried to comprehend why Porter had changed his mind.

Larry Hutton leaned against the fence that separated the bullpen from the playing field and shook his head. "Jesus, Henry! Old Porter's gonna have a seizure if you don't get out there in a hurry."

While Rain hustled to the mound, he saw that the bases were loaded, so Porter must have intentionally walked the lefty so Rain could face the right-handed cleanup hitter. Porter stood at the top of the rubber and Langford waited with his customary poor posture at the very front edge of the mound.

Porter looked hurt, like a child who had lost his puppy. "For Christ's sake, Rain. I told you you'd be goin' in when we got down by twelve. Now, could you *please* get your head outta your ass and into the game? I had Thorton walk that guy so you could pitch from the windup." When he flipped Rain the ball, Porter's face grew serious. "I want you to throw strikes. I don't care if these sons-of-bitches hit the ball a mile. No walks, and remember: keep your release point low."

After Porter headed for the dugout, Langford wheeled without a word and lazily sauntered behind the plate. As usual, the back portion of his shirt flopped, untucked, over his pudgy buttocks.

Rain put both feet on the rubber and his heart raced again as he inhaled deeply. He could hear the whispers from the crowd. Most people were more accustomed to seeing a six-foot, eight-inch player – he had grown an inch since his freshman year – on the basketball court instead of on the baseball diamond. When Rain wound up and delivered his first sidearm warm-up pitch, the whispers became "oooh's" and "aaah's." A six-foot, eight-inch sidearm pitcher was even more of a rarity. When the second warm-up pitch bounced five feet in front of home plate and skipped past Langford to the backstop, the "oooh's" and "aaah's" turned into jeering laughter. Rain cringed. He had become nothing more than Porter's freakshow attraction in his own personal circus disguised as the game of baseball. He had reached, without a doubt, the lowest point of his baseball career and quite possibly his life.

The umpire threw Rain a new ball while Langford retrieved the wild pitch. Rain took the opportunity to gather his thoughts behind the mound. He had discovered in the bullpen that if he took some speed off his fastball, he controlled it better. Porter instructed him to throw strikes above all else, so that's what he intended to do. Rain completed his warm-ups without further embarrassment, but threw only at about seventy-five percent of his normal speed. He didn't dare try anything as dangerous as a sidearm curveball or changeup.

While most of the crowd had jeered during Rain's

warm-up, two spectators shifted to the front of their seats and squinted in disbelief. They could hardly believe their eyes. One was Catherine Landerson. She had written Rain a thousand times saying how sorry she was for lying to her parents about the Rat Dance, but she never mailed the letters because whatever she wrote didn't seem adequate. She had planned to disobey her mother and drive down anyway, as she knew Rain must have hoped she would, but her parents made a surprise visit that Friday morning and chaperoned her every move the entire weekend. For the rest of her freshman year, her mother lived in Oxford to make sure Catherine attended her weekly visits with a psychiatrist and took her prescribed medicine. Now that Rain was so physically close, she wanted to run onto the field and tell him those things. She wanted to wrap her arms around his neck and kiss him until her lips went numb. Most of all, she wanted to whisper in his ear, once again, that she'd always love him.

Bob Dennison, a mid-level scout for the New Orleans Crescents, had a different reason for moving to the edge of his seat. Dennison leaned over to his buddy, a scout with the Cardinals, who was there to grade Trip Chadwick. "Hey Kip, did I hear you say earlier that you had a copy of MMC's media guide?"

"Yeah, Bob. You wanna see it?"

"Do you mind?"

"Nah," the other scout replied as he pulled the media guide from his briefcase and passed it to Dennison.

While Dennison flipped through the media guide, the PA system announced, "Ladies and gentlemen, your attention please. Now pitching for the MMC Bulldogs, number twenty-one, Rain Henry."

"Ah, yes. Here he is. I was right." Dennison said out loud as he and read the bio to himself.

> *A veteran performer who has struggled with control problems throughout his collegiate career (38 walks in 33.1 innings and*

24 strikeouts) ... throws a variety of pitches (curve, change, fastball) ... Coach Porter says he needs to improve in his maturity and fighting spirit ... "He will be used as much as his development of control warrants," Porter said. ***Sophomore Season:*** *appeared in six games, starting one contest ... worked 10.1 innings, facing 57 batters ... walked 15 and struck out nine ... had a 1-0 record with a 1.75 ERA.* ***Freshman Season:*** *Appeared in nine games, starting five ... compiled a 1-1 slate with a 6.65 ERA ... walked 23 and struck out 15.* ***High School:*** *A graduate of Jefferson Davis Academy in Vimville (Meridian), MS, where he lettered in baseball, basketball and football.*

"You know this new pitcher?" the other scout asked.

"Yeah, Kip. This kid's from a little town outside Meridian. He was one of my first assignments about four years ago. As a high school junior, this guy threw flames and dominated. He would have been a high draft choice, except he blew out his elbow during his senior season. His fastball went from the low nineties to the low eighties before the doc stopped him from playing. The kid was a helluva athlete and an awesome competitor. He also played first base or in the outfield and could hit." Dennison handed back the media guide. "You know, Kip, despite his arm problems, I urged the Crescents to use a late draft pick on him anyway. He had that kind of potential."

The other scout laughed. "Good thing they didn't take your advice. You might have lost your job." Dennison smiled politely at the joke, and the other scout asked, "Just out of curiosity, did he throw sidearm in high school?"

"No. I guess Porter's done that to him." Dennison shook his head. "Boy, what a waste of talent."

"I'll say. He's trying so hard to get the ball over the plate, he can't be throwing harder than seventy or seventy-five miles an hour."

"I bet you're right. You got your gun on you?"

"Yeah, I got it."

"Turn it on. Let's see how far this kid has crashed."

Rain stood at the bottom of the back of the mound while the announcer introduced Ole Miss's next hitter. "Now batting with the bases loaded, our All-American right fielder, Trrrrrrrrrriiiiiiiiiip Chadwick!"

After his old nemesis settled in, Rain climbed the hill and took the rubber. "Throw strikes, throw strikes, throw strikes," Rain's mind repeated. Langford squatted and stuck his index finger between his legs. Fastball. Rain nodded and began his wind up. He dropped low to the ground and released a "batting-practice" fastball over the heart of the plate. Chadwick swung so hard, he nearly came out of his cleats. The end of his aluminum bat made solid contact and the ball rocketed to Rain's right like it had been shot from a rifle. Luckily for Rain, Chadwick was well in front of the pitch, so the ball left the park foul as it flew high over MMC's bullpen.

Chadwick stepped out of the box and adjusted his top-of-the line batting gloves. Up in the stands, Catherine started to softly cry and Bob Dennison leaned toward the other scout. "You get that one, Kip."

"Nope. It's still warming up. There, okay. I think we're good to go now."

The umpire threw Rain another ball, and Chadwick stepped in again. He mumbled from the right corner of his mouth. "Are you kidding me, Jeremy? Is that all this chump's got?"

Langford chuckled through his facemask as he stuck down his index finger again. "Yep, and here comes the same thing."

Rain delivered again, and this time, Chadwick timed the slow fastball much better. He smashed a towering shot that barely missed being fair as it arched high over the left field foul pole. Rain and everyone else watched with awe as the ball nearly hit the MMC bus, which was parked roughly 450 feet away.

"Foul ball!" the umpire shouted from behind the plate.

"Man, your boy can sure hit for power, Kip," Dennison offered.

"Yeah but I'm not counting this at-bat. I only grade chances against real pitching. That was a sixty-eight mile-per-hour fastball. I know twelve-year-olds that can throw that fast."

"You've got to be kiddin' me!" Dennison exclaimed. "He's gotta be throwing harder than that. I don't believe it. Are you sure that gun's calibrated?"

"Yep. Had it checked out in Memphis before I drove down here. I'll bet you $10 that his next pitch is below seventy, too."

"Sure, I'll take that bet, but you gotta swear your gun's accurate."

"I swear it."

"Okay, you're on."

Rain held another new ball and tried to gather himself before he faced Chadwick again. Maybe he should try to throw a curve. After all, the count was in his favor 0-2. No, he decided, he'd better take his chances with another fastball. There was no telling where the curve might end up – the backstop was as good a guess as any. Langford put down two fingers, but Rain shook him off. He nodded after he got the single finger for the fastball and was about to start his windup, when he read Langford's lips through his mask. Langford had mouthed "fastball." Rain pretended something flew into his eye and stepped off the rubber. He couldn't believe it! Langford told Chadwick what he was about to throw! At that instant, Rain felt a surge of competitive adrenaline course through his body that he hadn't felt in years.

Rain took a deep breath and stretched his arms high to the heavens as he stepped back on the rubber. This time, when Langford flashed the sign for the fastball, Rain smiled as he nodded. Sure enough, as he had done before, Langford tipped off Chadwick. Rain coiled three straight years of frustration into his windup before he released its powerful energy. Instead of coming from the side, Rain's motion carried his arm straight over the top, the same way he had pitched his entire life until Porter made him a side-armed freak show last fall. His right arm discharged the pitch like a cannon. The baseball came so hard and spun so fast, its threads gave it a slight upward movement as it crossed the plate. Rain nearly ejaculated with pleasure as the rising fastball ricocheted off the top of the web on Langford's mitt and struck him squarely in the throat before spinning dead in the batter's box. The ball had already glanced off the mitt when Chadwick swung, making him look like a fool instead of an All-American.

Langford grabbed for his throat before falling like a chopped tree onto his side. His body started convulsing as he desperately tried to breathe but could not . Chadwick, oblivious to his injured "friend," looked around in disbelief. After Porter and the MMC trainer rushed to home plate, the umpire, with a slight grin, reminded Chadwick that he had struck out and pointed him toward the Ole Miss dugout.

The crowd, including Catherine and the two scouts, stood and anxiously stared as the MMC catcher writhed in panicked pain before them. Tears streamed down Catherine's face as she quietly congratulated her former boyfriend, who nonchalantly strutted to the gathering at home plate.

Bob Dennison leaned over and whispered, "I think somebody owes me $10. I know some serious smoke when I see it."

"I don't know," the other scout whispered back. "You may be right about the gun's calibration."

"Why? How fast was it?"

"Ninety-six."

CHAPTER SEVENTEEN
MELTDOWN

Rain wore a look of concern as he approached home plate, but behind the exterior mask, he felt giddy. For the first time in a long time, Rain Henry knew he'd accomplished something worthwhile on the baseball field. With a single pitch, not only had he blow away Chadwick like the good old days, he settled a few scores with Langford as well.

The rest of the MMC infielders gathered at the scene and created what looked like a mini football huddle. They observed the gasping patient with a combination of reverential silence and morbid curiosity, similar to first-year medical students watching their initial ER case. While Langford gradually regulated his breathing, everyone's attention shifted to Rain Henry.

Porter yanked Rain down to a squatting position. "I want an explanation!"

Rain shook his head. "I don't know, Coach. Langford called a fastball and that's what I threw. I guess he just missed it."

Porter stood up and pulled Rain with him. "That's not what I'm talking about. Why didn't you throw the pitch sidearm?"

From the corner of his eye, Rain noticed Langford rise to a sitting position. Unfortunately, he appeared not to be seriously injured.

"I don't know, Coach," Rain answered. "Something inside told me that if I came over the top, I could put enough heat on it to finish 'em off."

Before Porter could respond, Rain heard Langford's raspy voice call out, "Coach."

Porter wheeled. "What is it, Jeremy?" he asked with the tone of a concerned father.

Langford's words sounded rusty, but they sliced through the air like a well-honed knife. "Coach, Henry's lying. He crossed me up. I called for a curveball. That's why I missed it."

With burning eyes, Porter glared at Rain. "Let me get this straight, Henry. Not only did you throw overhand, you intentionally crossed up your catcher?"

Rain glanced around before he answered the accusation poorly disguised as a question. In baseball, intentionally crossing up your catcher compares to sucker punching your mother. Pitch cross-ups occur, but are usually due to a lack of concentration or a misread of signs. A pitcher would only cross up his catcher on purpose if he intended to hurt him. Like a dirty boxer, Langford had seen his chance to deliver a knockout blow below the belt and he had seized it. Rain's baseball career lay on the canvas and he doubted if it would ever rise again. As Rain glanced around the huddle, his teammates' eyes turned icy cold as they awaited Rain's response.

"Coach, that's not true, I don't..."

Porter roared as he cut him off. "Shut up, Henry, just shut the hell up! I want you to get your gear and go sit on the bus! Get off this field and out of this stadium! I'll deal with you back at the hotel!"

"But Coach, this is the first game of a double-header. You want me to sit on the bus for the next three hours?

Couldn't I hang out down in the bullpen and chart pitches or something?" Rain desperately pleaded.

Something snapped in the old man. Porter's eyes rolled in the back of his head. He cocked his right arm and leapt at Rain.

Rain braced for the assault, but the punch never came. When he opened his eyes, he saw that Craig Cline had stepped between them. Cline barely restrained their coach.

Facing Porter, Cline spoke calmly. He sounded like a therapist, and his words were hypnotic. "Coach, you don't wanna do that. It's not necessary. Rain's headed to the bus right now." Cline looked over his shoulder at Rain, who stood motionless and dumbfounded. "You're on your way right now, aren't you, Rain?"

Rain nodded. "Yeah, I'm going." He slowly backed away from the half-circle of salivating wolves that smelled the fresh blood of a wounded animal. If by some chance it wasn't already true, the pack had just officially excommunicated Rain Henry.

When he reached the dugout, Rain pulled his tote bag from under the bench and shoved in his glove. Tears blurred Rain's vision while he zipped the bag shut. Then, without looking back, Rain turned and left. His cleats crackled on the dugout's concrete as his metal spikes tried, unsuccessfully, to gain a foothold in the solid surface. The sound he once loved as a kid, he now cursed because it symbolized his entire collegiate baseball career.

Rain descended the dugout's side stairs and entered the dim tunnel that led to the locker room.

While the trainer helped Langford to the dugout, Porter slowly regained his composure. Craig Cline saved his job and he knew it. If he had struck Henry, MMC would have fired him for sure. There were too many witnesses.

Porter cleared his throat. "All right, everyone back to your position except Craig!" He smiled at his new favorite player. "Craig, didn't you pitch a little in high school?"

"Yes, sir!" Cline grinned back.

"You're our new pitcher."

The umpire tossed a ball to Cline, who gleefully took the mound. Larry Hutton became MMC's new catcher and Porter inserted Troy Benson, a backup infielder, into the game at third.

While Porter and the umpire scribbled the positional changes on their respective scorecards, Cline threw his warm-up pitches. Porter prepared to shuffle back to the dugout when the umpire hesitantly said, "Coach, there's something you should know about what happened."

Porter laughed. "Sir, I'm sure there is, but I'm still a little dizzy from everything. Believe it or not, I've never hit one of my players before, but I came pretty damn close right then. You think it can wait 'till the break between games? I'd like to sit down and clear my head a little."

The umpire nodded. "Sure. No problem."

Bob Dennison hustled down from the stands to the fence adjacent to the visitors' dugout. Catherine, originally seated a few rows behind him, followed.

Porter reached the dugout when Dennison shouted through the fence, "Hey, Coach Porter, could I see you for a second?"

Porter turned. "Who the hell are you?"

Dennison smiled. "I'm Bob Dennison, a scout with the New Orleans Crescents. I promise it'll only be a second."

Porter grumbled under his breath, but headed to the fence anyway. Although he hated dealing with pro scouts, Porter always made a concerted attempt to stay on their good side. If Porter ever got the reputation that pro scouts disliked him, it would make recruiting talented players to MMC even tougher.

"What can I do for you, sir?" Porter asked.

"I've got a quick question about your last pitcher, Rain Henry. How come you took him out of the game after he struck out an All-American with a ninety-six-mile-per-hour fastball?"

Porter bristled. "Sir, not that it's any of your business, but I removed Henry because he threw the ball overhand instead of sidearm. At the same time, he purposely crossed up his catcher and you saw the result. Now, are there any other questions, or can I get back to coaching my team?"

The former MMC third baseman finished his last warm-up toss, and the umpire stood poised to start the game again. "Of course. There's one last thing. You don't mind if I talk to Henry after the game, do you?"

Porter laughed hard enough to make the flab that hung over his belt hurt. The thought of a pro scout wanting to talk to Rain Henry disrupted his equilibrium and he almost fell over. "Be my guest, Mr. Dennison! You won't have to wait until the end of the game. I expect he's headed for the team bus right now. That's where he'll be spending the rest of the afternoon."

Dennison leaned harder against the chain-link fence. "I'm sorry. Did you say Henry's on his way to the bus?"

"That's right! The bus! Good day, Sir." Porter spun, re-entered the dugout, and the umpire pointed at the new MMC pitcher and yelled, "Play ball!"

Rain threw his wadded baseball uniform on the locker room's floor where he anticipated the team's manager would collect it later. And if the manager didn't pick it up after the second game, he really didn't care. He wouldn't need it tomorrow, anyway, because Rain fully expected Porter to drop him off at a bus station later that evening and give him precisely enough money for a one-way ticket to Natchez.

Dressed again like an ice cream salesman in MMC's summer leave uniform, Rain slung his athletic bag over his shoulder and pushed open the locker room door as the home crowd cheered. Craig Cline had given up a bases-clearing double.

On the other side of the door, a medium-sized man wearing jeans and a black turtleneck stood waiting in Rain's path. He wore a navy baseball cap with the initials

NOC stitched in golden thread across the front. A thin but unpretentious smile adorned the man's face, and the outside edges of his green eyes squinted as a result.

The man extended his hand. "Rain, my name's Bob Dennison, and I'm a scout for the Crescents."

Rain shook the scout's hand. "Nice to meet you, Mr. Dennison, but why do you want to talk with me, sir?"

Dennison softly laughed. "Please call me Bob, not 'sir' or 'Mr. Dennison.' I've never been in the military, and I don't plan on signing up anytime soon. Anyway, I'm talking to you because it's my job. The team would probably fire me if they discovered I saw a kid throw a major league fastball and didn't at least introduce myself. Did you know that last pitch you threw by Chadwick crossed the plate at ninety-six?"

"No, sir, I didn't. But what I do know is that pitch banished me to the bus for the rest of the afternoon."

Dennison shook his head. "So Porter told me. Listen, let me at least give you my card." He fished his wallet from his back pocket and produced a weathered business card with frayed edges, which he handed to Rain. "Rain, I saw you pitch back in Vimville during your junior year in high school. You were unbelievable. I don't know what Porter did to screw you up, but I know you've got the talent to play in the major leagues. That last pitch convinced me. No matter what happens after today, if you ever want a tryout with the Crescents, give me a call. I'll either come to you or fly you down to New Orleans. That's my promise as long as I'm with the organization."

Rain rubbed Bob Dennison's business card between his thumb and index finger as the pro scout turned and headed back to the seats. Then, Rain's arm became a mechanical crane that moved the card over the round mouth of an adjacent trash barrel. Slowly, he began to relax the pressure in his fingers that kept the card from mingling with the used paper cups and catsup-stained hot dog wrappers below. But before he let go, something made him pull the card back from the brink of disposal.

The scout was nearly out of sight when Rain shouted, "Hey, Bob!" Dennison turned and Rain asked, "What do you think of the designated hitter rule?"

Bob grinned. "Hate it. I say let the pitchers hit!"

"Good man," Rain thought as he unzipped his bag and dropped in Bob Dennison's business card. The wrong answer would have started the tiny rectangular piece of paper's journey to the local landfill.

Headed for the bus once again, Rain passed the men's restroom and rounded the corner. Suddenly, from out of nowhere, Catherine Landerson sprang. She threw her arms around Rain's neck and sobbing uncontrollably, buried the side of her face in his chest. She held on tight, but with a Herculean effort, Rain managed to unwind Catherine's two arms and push her a safe distance away. She looked awful and deep down, Rain felt a small flicker of pity for the pale, disconcerted creature before him. Giant tears melted away Catherine's face like the visage of a wax mannequin caught in the heat of a museum fire.

"Oh, God, Rain. I'm so sorry about what happened. I'm so sorry," the melting mannequin wailed.

Rain wondered if his day could get any worse. The stitches that held his heart together started to unglue, and he knew he had to get out fast. He rushed past her extended arms, which unsuccessfully tried to block his path. "No need to be sorry, Catherine. You made your choice, now live with it. I have."

Catherine lunged at his legs, trying to tackle him from behind. It was a pathetic attempt, but her effort did momentarily stop his forward momentum. "Rain, please, please, let me explain. My mother, she..."

As Porter had done to him earlier, Rain wheeled and moved to within inches of her face. He grabbed Catherine's wrists and squeezed them tightly together. "No explanation needed, Miss Landerson, or are you and Chadwick already married? And what's this talk about your mother? Did your mother steal all of your pens, stationary, envelopes, and stamps? Somehow, I doubt it."

Catherine's crying intensified, but she managed to blurt out, "Please, Rain. That hurts! I know I should have written, but I didn't. I'm sorry. Please, give me a chance to explain!"

Rain released her wrists. "Pain hurts, doesn't it? But if you think that feels bad, you should try feeling the pain of standing outside a battalion for five straight hours on a cold night, waiting in futility for the person you love to show. Or you should feel the pain of lying in your bed, that same night, knowing your dreams for the future have died. Better yet, you should try feeling the pain of searching your mailbox in vain, every single day, for the letter of explanation that never comes. Those are the kinds of pain you should feel."

Catherine sank to her knees and threw her head back as if the memories of the past would cause her to faint. Eerily, she stopped crying, closed her eyes and mumbled, "Rain, I have felt those pains and many, many more."

"Good. Now you understand why I hope I never see you again."

Rain, once again, headed for the gate. Behind him, the mannequin melted completely, leaving only a pool of unconscious, flesh-colored wax shuddering on the ground.

Rain reached the bus and watched as Cline recorded the third, and final, out of the inning on a long fly ball to deep center. As the teams changed sides, Rain pounded on the bus' locked door. Then it dawned on him: the bus driver had no reason to be inside. He'd be in the stands watching the game.

Rain put his bag on the ground and contemplated his next move. He could either sit or stand by the bus for the next three hours or he could go back to the stadium, find the driver, and borrow the keys. The latter alternative displeased him because the mannequin might attempt another surprise attack.

Then Rain thought of another alternative – why didn't he walk into Oxford and look around? He had plenty of time, and he knew the little downtown square to be only a few blocks away because they had passed it earlier. He could be there and back before Porter would even miss him. Rain touched his back pocket to make sure he had his wallet. Maybe he'd find a bar and have a beer or two. Returning to the bus with a warm buzz would certainly help, especially if Porter decided to verbally assail him on the trip back to the hotel.

Adopting the new plan, Rain left his bag where it lay and headed back toward the parking lot's stairs. This time, instead of turning left to go to the baseball stadium, he took a right toward University Avenue and downtown Oxford.

The second game of the double header began, and as the Ole Miss players took the field in the top of the first, the former home plate umpire decided Porter had forgotten to ask about what he knew. Maybe that was best, he thought. Maybe Porter shouldn't know the truth; it might create even more chaos on a team that had already experienced its fair share for the day. Now serving duty as the third base umpire, he glanced into the MMC dugout at the same time Porter glanced at him. Their paths of vision crossed and Porter remembered their earlier conversation.

Rain reached the downtown square a few minutes after 4: 00, almost exactly the same time Porter waddled out to third base. "My apologies, sir. I forgot you had something to tell me about, you know, what happened last game."

The umpire's shoe scratched at the dirt for a few seconds before he decided Porter had a right to know the truth. "Coach, that tall pitcher of yours wasn't the liar, your catcher was the one who lied."

"Why do you care? What are you, Rain Henry's cousin or something?"

"No, sir. I'm someone who believes people ought to know the truth."

"And how do you know the truth?"

"I heard it with my own ears. He didn't do it on the first pitch, but on the last two, your catcher told the hitter what was coming. On the strikeout pitch, he called another fastball, not a curveball like he told you."

"Damn," Porter mumbled. Suddenly it all made sense. He knew Langford and Henry shared animosities for one another that stretched all the way back through high school. Because he recruited them both, he also remembered that Langford and Ole Miss's Chadwick had played on the same high school team and had been friends. And most importantly, he knew Langford delighted in Rain Henry's failures. Langford was a solid player and Henry was a bust, so Porter typically ignored Langford's transgressions against Henry. But now, Langford crossed the line by lying directly to him. He would have to punish his catcher and offer Rain an apology.

"Thanks, Ump. You may have extended a kid's baseball career and saved me the cost of a one-way bus ticket to Natchez."

When Porter returned to the dugout, he saw Langford, who between games had declared himself fully recovered, swinging a bat. Porter located the felt-tip pen in his back pocket. Laughing, he scratched out Langford's name from the number three slot in starting lineup taped to the dugout's wall.

"Take off the helmet and put the bat down, Langford. You'll be sitting this one out," he said as he wrote in Hutton as his new catcher. He turned to Frank Furman. "Furman, go fetch Henry from the bus. Tell him to get back to the dugout. He's on chart duty again."

At the same time Furman reported that Henry had vanished, leaving only his athletic bag as trace evidence, Rain stood in front of the Lafayette County Courthouse and marveled at its beauty. In the middle of the magnificent and tastefully designed white brick building, three archways led to the courthouse's oversized, wooden double doors. The archways supported a second-level, mini balcony adorned with four majestic columns that stretched to the top of the façade's triangular roof. The balcony appeared to be accessible by two double doors that were almost twice the size of the doors below. At the top of the triangular roof, stone masons had carved two smaller arches into an elegant clock tower. The miniature-domed roof that covered the clock tower, which appeared to be made of copper, had been turned green by years of battling the elements. Back on the ground, Rain read the brass plaque planted in the smartly manicured lawn.

> *The original courthouse was burned in August 1864 by Union troops led by Gen. A. J. Smith. Judge R .A. Hill secured federal funds to construct the present courthouse which was completed and occupied in January, 1872.*

On his way to the front of the courthouse, Rain had walked by the City Grocery, one of Oxford's most famous restaurants. Rain and the other players had eaten there the night before at the special invitation of Shelton Jamison, a minority owner and MMC class of '66 graduate. While the downstairs portion of the building contained the restaurant, Rain remembered that stairs led to a bar on the second level. He hoped the bar would be open as he eagerly retraced his steps back to the restaurant.

When Rain approached, a gentleman in a dark suit opened the door and ushered Rain to the maitre d's stand. The maitre d', an older, distinguished-looking gentleman in a traditional tuxedo eyed the lengthy cadet. "Good afternoon, sir. Will you be joining us for an early dinner?"

Rain pointed at the staircase to the left. "Actually, I'm interested in a beer if the bar's open."

The maitre d' stepped to the side and motioned at the stairs. "The bar opened fifteen minutes ago, sir. Enjoy your beverage."

Once Rain scaled the last step, the bar's main counter materialized against the left wall. What the place lacked in size, it compensated with quaintness. Although multicolored Christmas lights hung stapled along the edges of the ceiling, the atmosphere felt anything but festive. The bar looked as if it had been carved from the middle of a mahogany tree, and the lavish, dark wood cast a somber tone. To Rain's right, in the main section of the small room, a few empty tables and chairs waited patiently in the dim light for customers.

Excluding the bartender, Rain was alone. He sat at a stool positioned at the center of the rectangular counter. On two of the three shelves about ten feet in front of him, tiny spotlights illuminated a cornucopia of liquor and beer bottles. The middle shelf contained no alcoholic beverages. Instead, a few wooden and glass knickknacks surrounded four classic tin lunchboxes from the late 1970s and early 1980s. The Fonz, along with the rest of the cast from TV's *Happy Days* watched Rain through faded paint from the box on the left. The next lunchbox featured Evil Kineval, the famous motorcycle daredevil, who once tried to jump the Grand Canyon – Rain couldn't remember if he had succeeded or failed. The scratched face of actor David Hasselhoff and KIT, the black Firebird from TV's *Knight Rider* adorned the tin box second from the right, and the last lunchbox featured the characters from *Peanuts,* the newspaper comic strip by Charles Schultz.

Like the maitre d', the bartender also wore a tuxedo. Unlike the maitre' d', he didn't wear his tuxedo's jacket, and he seemed more than slightly uncomfortable in his work uniform. His hair looked as white as fresh snow, and Rain guessed the thin man to be in his early to mid-forties.

"Taking a seat at center stage. I like that," the bartender said as he spun a paper napkin on the counter in front of his only customer. "What's with the uniform? You in some branch of the service?"

Rain removed his white garrison cap and put in on the counter beside his napkin. "You're not from Mississippi, are you?"

"Nope. Recently moved here from Texas. Got this job last week, and here I am. So what's with the uniform?"

Rain picked up his garrison cap and pointed to the large

brass insignia on the front that, like the class ring, depicted an outline of the state of Mississippi. "I go to Mississippi Military College. It's down in Natchez."

"What brings you to Oxford?"

"Baseball. MMC – that's what everyone calls it – is playing Ole Miss this weekend."

"You a player?"

Rain hesitated. "Not really. More like the team's unofficial pitching statistician. Or was, I should say. I think I got fired about thirty minutes ago."

"That's too bad," the white-haired bartender offered. For the first time since the conversation started, he looked Rain squarely in the eyes. "What can I getcha to lift your spirits?"

"I'm gonna have a beer. What kind of beer do people from Texas like to drink?"

Rain's conversational counterpart put both hands on the counter and cocked his head to the side. "Oh, they like to drink all kinds. Same as people everywhere." He leaned toward Rain and grinned. "But a man that might've gotten fired needs something stronger than a beer. He needs one of Whitey's special margaritas. You drink margaritas?"

"I've had one or two, but I don't really like them. They reminded me of an extra-tart lime slushy. I wasn't very impressed."

The bartender shook his head, pulled a thick glass from behind the bar, and slammed it down hard on Rain's napkin. "That's what I thought. You haven't had a real margarita until you've had one of my margaritas."

"Let me guess. You must be Whitey."

"Correct presumption, my margarita virgin! What's your name?" Whitey asked before he turned and reached for the necessary ingredients. Whatever they were, his back prevented Rain from seeing them.

"Rain. Look Whitey, I appreciate you trying to expand my drinking horizons, but how much is one of your 'special margaritas,' and what if I don't like it?"

Whitey stopped pouring into his silver shaker and wheeled back to his customer. "This potion is not for the penny pinchers of the world, my dear Rain, but I'll make you a deal. Try it. If you don't like it, it's on the house, and you've lost nothing. If it soothes your soul the way it soothes mine, the first one's half price."

"How much is half price?" Rain asked suspiciously. He was beginning to think he'd run into a con man posing as a bartender.

"Two dollars and fifty cents."

"You want five bucks for one drink?" Rain shockingly asked. "I think I'll stick with a beer, how much are they?"

Whitey confidently resumed pouring. "All beers are two fifty," he said over his shoulder. "So you see, Rain, I'm offering you the experience of a lifetime for the same price as a common beer."

"Wow, the experience of a lifetime for the same price as a beer. How can I pass that up?" Rain said sarcastically. "Fine, I'll try your 'potion,' but I'll tell you up front, I only have twenty bucks in my wallet, so if you're lookin' for some sort of big score, you've got the wrong guy."

With both hands, Whitey used the shaker to mix the alcoholic concoction over his head. "Rain, my good friend, I promise you that after only two of these, your worries will disappear. If you're man enough to finish a third, you'll believe you can conquer the world."

"That's one of the best sales pitches I've ever heard. Bring it on!"

Whitey flipped Rain's glass in the air before he made it disappear behind the counter. It re-emerged with a thick coating of white crystals riding the rim. "I hope you like salt," he said.

"Love it," Rain replied.

Then, again from the mystery area behind the bar, Whitey produced a small scoop of ice and carefully jingled seven or eight thin, square cubes into Rain's glass. The drink finally arrived when Whitey uncapped the shaker and delicately poured its amber-green contents into Rain's glass. The liquid stopped its ascent less than a hair's width below the ring of salt. Whitey had measured everything perfectly and Rain was impressed.

"Presto," the white-haired bartender whispered with arched eyebrows. He spread his arms wide like a magician performing his favorite trick. "One Whitey's special margarita, on the rocks, with salt, at your service."

Rain inspected the drink like a detective searching for a hidden clue. "What's it made out of, Whitey?"

Whitey took his bartender's rag and wiped down the counter. "Sorry, Rain. Can't say. It's a secret, of course. However, I can tell you the best way to drink it. You'll want to take a good lick of that salt and then a solid sip. Don't be afraid to let the mixture dance together for a second or two in your mouth before you send it down the hatch."

Rain did as instructed and as Whitey had described, the elixir seemed to waltz on his tongue before sliding smoothly down his throat. "That's some powerful medicine," Rain muttered to himself. Although Rain had just tasted the strongest drink of his life, the blend was far from overpowering. Instead, it gently warmed the inside of his mouth and the lining of his esophagus like a cozy fire.

"Well?" Whitey eagerly asked.

"Good, damn good."

An hour and a half later, the bar filled with the usual evening crowd. Another, more tenured, bartender joined Whitey behind the counter and Rain moved to the far end of the bar so he could remain Whitey's customer. He sat on a stool beneath a lazily spinning Pabst Blue Ribbon beer sign and sipped his third margarita. Rain's buzz hit halfway through his second drink, and as Whitey had predicted, the troubles he faced earlier in the day soon disappeared like dirt swept under a rug. With a steady hand and a crooked smile, Rain grabbed the liquid broom and kept on sweeping.

Whitey popped two beers for a well-dressed couple and then beamed as he ambled over. "How are you feeling now, my friend?"

"Never felt better," Rain answered with a slight slur before taking another sip.

"You getting hungry?" Whitey asked.

"Nah, I got all the nourishment I need right here." Rain replied contentedly.

"You think you might want another one?"

"No question about it."

"Well, you're not gonna get it unless you eat something. How about I order you some fries from downstairs?"

Rain pulled out his wallet and blinked a few times as he sorted through what remained of his cash. He had only a five-dollar bill, two ones, and the two quarters that sat next to his drink. And he still needed to tip his friend. As if the paper bills were cards at a poker game, Rain spread his money on the counter. "I probably don't have enough. How much are the fries?"

Rain's new friend laughed. "Don't worry about it. They're on me."

At a quarter 'till seven, Rain finished the fries and the last sip of his fourth margarita. Only thin slivers of ice remained at the bottom of his glass and by now, the bar was packed with nicely dressed people who had come upstairs for a quick drink before their tables were ready below. But Rain felt as though he no longer sat in a bar. The dark, noisy room had become a blurry merry-go-round that constantly rotated around him. The people were tigers, lions, and horses that laughed and smiled and flirted and touched one another as they bobbed up and down on invisible poles. The carousel's animals chattered like humans, but their words were unintelligible to Rain's alcohol-soaked brain. Something told Rain the time had come for him to step off the ride and head for the bus before he fell off and wouldn't be able to get back up.

With glassy eyes, Rain stared at what remained of his

money. He didn't want to insult Whitey with a measly $2.50 tip, so he scooped the money off the counter and put it in his garrison cap. After an exaggerated wave of his arms, Whitey hustled over to his shift's original patron.

"My friend, I think you've had enough."

Rain struggled to comprehend what he had just heard. "Whitey," he stammered, "I think I've had enough. I've gotta get off this thing and walk back to my bus." Rain thrust his garrison cap at the bartender. "Thanks for everything. This is for you."

Whitey poured the money into his hand and placed the empty hat back on the counter. "No, thank you, Rain. I've really enjoyed getting to know you over these last few hours. Best of luck with everything."

Rain drunkenly shook his head. "No. The cap's for you, too. It's a gift. I want you to have it. It'll match your hair when you wear it." He thrust the garrison cap again at its intended recipient.

Whitey accepted the white hat. From years of experience, he knew trying to change a drunken person's mind was about as easy as trying to castrate a bull with a plastic knife. He'd tried both before, the latter on a foolish drunken dare that nearly got him stomped to death. Neither could be accomplished quickly, and the harder you tried, the more resistance you usually got. As a new employee, the last thing Whitey needed was for one of his customers to cause a scene at the bar. Besides, he really did like the hat. Maybe he'd ask his boss if he could add it to the other collectibles on the bar's middle shelf. "Okay, then. Thanks again. If you come back next weekend and it's not on my head, hopefully it'll be somewhere up there on the shelf."

Rain stood up and nearly fell before he steadied himself by clumsily grabbing the round stool. "You're welcome. I thought maybe if you didn't want to wear it, you could put it up there on the shelf."

The white-haired bartender exercised a five-minute

break and helped Rain down the stairs and to the sidewalk outside. The chilly night air should have made Rain shiver in his short-sleeved uniform, but the alcohol counteracted the low temperature's normal effect. When Whitey cautiously released his steadying grip, Rain slightly gyrated but seemed to be in no further danger of falling down.

"Are you sure I can't get you a cab?" the bartender asked.

Rain made a hitchhiker's thumb and hooked it awkwardly to his left. "No, thanks. My bus is right around the corner. I'll be fine."

Whitey smiled as he tapped Rain on the side of his right shoulder. He knew Rain would have had a hard time coordinating a handshake. "Take care of yourself, Rain."

"You, too, Whitey," Rain said before stumbling down the sidewalk toward Lamar Boulevard. He vaguely remembered that, somehow, Lamar linked back up with University Avenue, which would take him back to the field.

Forty-five minutes later, Rain reached Swayze field. The stadium was dark and the parking lot deserted. The MMC bus and his tote bag were long gone. However, instead of panicking, the alcohol helped him laugh at his new predicament. "Here I am, Porter!" he screamed at the twinkling stars. "You can't send me back to Natchez if you can't find me, you jackass!"

Unfortunately, the alcoholic euphoria abruptly expired shortly after Rain staggered up to the stadium's main gate. Though physically locked, the gate mentally released a disturbing memory from earlier that day. He peered through the fence and saw the image of his Catherine, shattered, shuddering, and wailing on the concrete. Rain burst into tears.

After several minutes of sobbing, the alcohol in his brain caused another chemical shift, and profound sadness transformed- into sheer determination. Rain had to find Catherine and apologize, even if it took all night.

A few minutes into his fast-paced walk for the center of

Ole Miss's campus, Rain felt his senses sharpen. Rain knew his buzz had definitely begun to abate when he caught a brisk wind that felt like a razor blade as it cut across his face and bare arms.

A quarter of a mile later, Rain headed through The Grove, Ole Miss's park-like center of campus, and found Sorority Row. After passing a few houses, Rain recognized the Delta Gamma House from the golden triangle and upside-down L that hung over its door. The two-story, plantation-style white brick house reminded him of the courthouse he had seen earlier. The architects of both must have strongly admired designs that prominently displayed classic, slender Greek columns. In contrast to the courthouse's four columns, which were restricted to the second level of the middle façade, the six columns on the sorority house stretched nearly the entire length of the building and all the way from porch to rooftop. Unbeknown to Rain, as he walked up the brick sidewalk that led to the long, narrow front porch, a carload of fraternity brothers pulled into a nearby parking space, cut their car's lights, and impatiently waited for their opportunity.

Rain straightened his posture as the sounds from the brass door knocker echoed throughout the inside of the house. He tried to remove his hat, but when his hand couldn't find it on the top of his head, he remembered he had given it to the white-haired bartender as a gift.

After he knocked again, the door opened and Rain recognized the beautiful girl standing before him. It was Mandy, one of the girls Langford and Cline had tried to pick up earlier that day at the stadium. She had also claimed to be Catherine's big sister.

By now, Rain had grown accustomed to icy stares, but Mandy's seemed especially frigid. "Let me guess. Tall, skinny, and in a cadet uniform. You must be Rain Henry."

"Yes, ma'am," Rain formally answered out of habit. "I'm here to apologize to Catherine for what happened earlier today."

Catherine's big sister slowly shook her head and her rich, cocoa colored hair bobbed as it followed the side-to-side movement of her face. "Catherine's not interested in your apology. I recommend you leave right now, before I call the campus police."

Mandy slammed the door in his face. "I think you deserved that one," Rain said to himself as he walked down the porch's stairs. A few dozen feet later, he turned and faced the fortress. With the last bit of courage that remained from his dying buzz, Rain took a deep breath, cupped his hands around his mouth, and yelled at the brick house.

"Catherine, I'm sorry! I'm so very sorry! I hope you know I'll always love you! Always!"

A few seconds passed before Rain saw a ghostly face appear in a second story window. He ran toward it. Sure enough, it was Catherine. She looked as if a vampire had sucked away most of her blood. Tears stained his cheeks as he silently mouthed, "I'm so sorry," over and over.

Catherine nodded, acknowledging his apology, and weakly waved goodbye. Something told Rain it would be the last time he would ever see her and yet somehow, he managed to barely raise the corners of his mouth as he returned her farewell gesture. Then, her face slipped below the windowsill and she was gone for good.

His mission accomplished, Rain turned and headed down the sidewalk in the opposite direction from which he had originally come. As he passed Ole Miss's other sorority houses, he knew not where he headed. Rain soon reached the unlit intersection of Northgate Drive and Sorority Row and stopped. Surrounded by darkness, the feeling of loneliness overwhelmed him, and he sank to his knees. For the first time in his life, he had no idea where to go or what to do next. Something urged Rain to ask for divine guidance so he earnestly began to pray, hoping beyond hope that God was listening and could help him some how, some way.

CHAPTER EIGHTEEN
SO LONG

Trip Chadwick swung the miniature wooden bat hard, but not too hard. He didn't want to commit murder, but he did want to deliver a solid, unforgettable message.

As wood and bone crashed together, the feeling reminded Chadwick of thumping a green melon. "That's for embarrassing me today!" Chadwick seethed. The victim slumped forward and his face landed nose-first on the cracked sidewalk.

One of Chadwick's stout fraternity brothers stepped in. "All right, Trip. You got him back, now let's get out of here."

Chadwick wished his oversized mercenaries would head back to the frat house and leave him alone. He had a good thirty minutes or so of torture planned for Rain Henry. "You guys get outta here," he said as he kicked Rain in the ribs. "I don't need you any more. We're all even."

After the third kick, Willie Reynolds, the largest mercenary, pulled Chadwick off the limp body. The giant from Yazoo City was a starting defensive tackle on the Ole Miss football team. "Trip, there ain't no use kickin' him now. He don't feel nothin'. I warned you against knockin' 'em out first, but you went and done it anyway, and out in the open, too. We all best get goin' before someone comes along and sees what you're doin'."

Chadwick tried to wiggle free, but couldn't. "Let go of me!"

The football player snickered. He agreed to come only because Chadwick promised to forgive the $250 he had borrowed last week. He presumed his two other fraternity brothers worked out similar deals with their house's resident money tree. Willie couldn't think of any frat brothers that considered Chadwick a real friend. The fraternity tolerated him strictly because of his daddy's money. Chadwick's pocket continually bulged from the thick roll of bills he spread around the house like butter at a pancake breakfast. For a while, Willie and a few others in the fraternity enjoyed Chadwick's rich, buttery pancakes, so they pretended to be his friend. But once Chadwick got selected as a pre-season baseball All-American, his already hefty ego ballooned. Now, Willie simply wanted to square his debt and be done with Trip Chadwick. "I'll turn you a loose only if you're gonna come with us; I don't want no guilt from leaving you out here and you windin' up in jail. "

"Fine. I'll come. Give me a second."

Willie released his captive and watched with the others as Chadwick stepped forward, leaned down, and rolled Rain Henry onto his back. Delicately, he rotated Rain's head so it faced him at a slight angle. Satisfied his target lay properly positioned, Chadwick stood and unzipped his pants. "Man, I've waited so long to do something like this," Chadwick muttered with an ear-to-ear grin.

Before he could react, someone pushed Rain into a black room and slammed the door shut. Rain couldn't see a thing. Not even his fingers were visible, even though he waved them inches from-his eyes. Like a toddler afraid of the dark, he panicked from the complete absence of light. Rain desperately searched for either the doorknob or a light switch. He located the doorknob, but it was locked and wouldn't budge. After a few frantic seconds of sliding his hands along the wall, he found a switch and flipped it. Softy, the darkness dissipated as particles of dull light from a low wattage bulb allowed Rain to recognize his surroundings. He stood in his gallery of mental paintings.

With the curiosity of a first-time visitor, Rain approached the four masterpieces and admired their visual compositions. The dried paint, covered by a protective transparent lacquer, felt like lumpy hills and valleys as he ran his fingers over every inch of each painting's uneven surface. Three of the four works of art depicted scenes from Catherine and Rain's first date at Okatibbee Lake: riding in the red Corvette with the wind whipping through their hair, kissing on the peninsula with the sun setting across the water, and making love in the Corvette's passenger seat with the moon shining above. The last painting he touched showed the couple immersed in muddy creek water, warmly embracing under the railroad trestle on the Henry Farm. The paintings represented his most cherished memories and the best moments of his life. The collection was priceless.

But when Rain withdrew his fingers from the bumpy outline of the trestle, loud smashing noises startled him from above. The sounds reminded him of a construction worker breaking cinder blocks with a sledgehammer. He looked up, but had to shield his eyes from the falling debris created by the dozens of fire sprinklers randomly punching through the concrete ceiling. Perhaps a fire had broken out in an upstairs gallery, Rain thought. Certainly, there was no fire here. Whatever was happening had to be a mistake.

The ceiling ran out of space for more sprinklers, and after a brief pause, they began to drip. A few seconds later, the drips became trickles. Because the water appeared odd, Rain cupped his palm and caught a handful of the strange liquid. It was not cool and clear, like water, but warm and yellow instead. Rain dabbed a drop on his tongue and it tasted salty. Perhaps he held a new form of fire retardant, Rain conjectured.

Suddenly, the tiny showerheads spit the mystery fluid full force. The salty solution covered everything, including his beloved paintings. It stung his eyes and squirted directly into the back his mouth, triggering his gag reflex. Stunned and still choking, he watched in horror as the fire retardant ate away his paintings' lacquer coatings. Once the lacquer melted away, he knew the oily paint didn't stand a chance. Rain turned his head toward the ceiling, somehow managed to clear his throat, and screamed for someone to shut off the sprinklers. Either no one heard or no one cared to help him. Rain stripped off his clothes and desperately tried to cover what remained of his cherished works of art. The effort failed. As though he had painted them with cheap watercolors, the vibrant scenes and joyful memories dissolved into yellow-tinged puddles pooled at his feet.

Rain awoke the next morning on a plastic mattress supported by a metal slab chained to the wall of a Lafayette County jail cell. His summer-leave uniform had been replaced with brown corduroy pants and a flannel shirt. Much to his surprise, they fit quite well.

Rain swung his feet over the floor and tried to stand, but the back of his head protested immediately. His skull throbbed from a knot the size of a golf ball. He tried to clear his senses with a deep breath, but dried blood clogged his nostrils. He lightly touched his swollen nose, and it felt misaligned underneath the puffiness. Still, instinct urged him to try standing.

A tall deputy sheriff appeared as Rain struggled to his feet. The big man opened the cell door, rushed to Rain's side, and caught him under the arm. "Take it easy, now. Don't try to do too much too fast."

"What happened?" Rain stammered.

After it became apparent to both men that Rain wouldn't be able to stand, the deputy eased him back onto the mattress. "We're not sure. Last night, Ole Miss campus police found you unconscious."

"Did I pass out?" Rain asked as he rubbed the golf ball protruding from the back of his head.

The deputy's knees cracked as he squatted. Rain saw kindness in his large, round face that sported a mug lightly sprinkled with overnight stubble. "At first, that's what everyone thought. We guessed you broke your nose on the sidewalk, but that didn't explain the lump on the back of your head. When we couldn't find your wallet, we suspected you'd been robbed. Can you remember anything?"

Rain recalled waving goodbye to Catherine at the Delta Gamma House and nothing thereafter. "No, sir."

"Do your remember getting checked out at the emergency room?"

"No, sir, I don't. Where's my uniform?"

The round-faced deputy winced. "Your uniform was pretty bad off. It had yellow streaks everywhere and smelled awful. We figured some dogs had wandered along and mistaken you for a fire hydrant. Anyway, after we got you here, you looked to be about my size, so I went home and brought back some clothes I planned on givin' to the Salvation Army. You're welcome to keep 'em."

Rain more closely inspected the faded flannel shirt and threadbare corduroy pants. They were well worn, but clean. "Thank you, Deputy..."

"Abanathy, but you can call me Robert."

"Thanks, Robert. When can I leave? I'm not under arrest, am I?"

Robert kindheartedly laughed. "You're free to leave whenever you feel up to it." He rose to his full height. "We guessed you were a cadet, but no one realized you might be with the baseball team until the sheriff checked in at midnight and remembered MMC and Ole Miss were playing each other this weekend."

As soon as the deputy said the word "baseball," the

memories of the nightmare that had occurred the day before at Swayze Field stormed back and paralyzed Rain's body. "The baseball team knows I'm in jail?"

"The coach knows, anyway," the deputy answered. "Called him myself. I figured he'd want to know one of his players got robbed, but was safe." Robert rubbed his chin. "Strange thing happened, though. He chose not to come get you last night. He asked me what time the jail opened in the morning, and said he'd stop by then."

The rush of adrenaline cured Rain's headache, soothed the pain from his bruised ribs, and almost overcame his clogged nostrils. Rain wanted to get out of there and get out of there as fast as possible. He didn't know where he'd go, but he did know he'd rather fall into a nest of rattlesnakes than face Coach Porter in his current condition. "What time does the jail open?" Rain asked anxiously.

The deputy checked his watch. "Eight o'clock. I expect they're unlocking the front doors right now."

Ten seconds later, one of the jail's clerks led Chain Porter around the corner. He already wore his baseball uniform. Rain slumped backward against the gray, cinderblock wall as Porter addressed Robert. "You Deputy Abanathy?"

"Yes, sir, I am."

"I thought you told me last night he wasn't under arrest. What's he doin' in this cell?"

"Sorry, Coach. We don't have any beds in the conference room. Why didn't you come get him last night?" Robert fired back.

Porter's jowls shook and his eyes blazed. "I have my reasons — none of which I plan on sharing with you." He turned to Rain. "Get your ass up, Henry. Let's go."

Rain shook his head. "Can't do it."

Porter let out an exasperated sigh, like air rushing out of a blimp. "Why not? Are you hurt too bad?"

"Nope," Rain said casually.

Like a kettle on the stove, Rain heard a slight whistle as

Porter's predictable temper boiled. "So what's your reason, then?" he asked bluntly.

"Yesterday, after you sent me to the bus, this talking donkey came up to me and offered me a ride. I asked him where to, and he said to trust him. The donkey looked trustworthy, and I knew I was a good rider, so I got on. We started off okay, but soon the donkey started actin' stubborn. If I suggested trying even the slightest change in direction, the donkey threatened to buck me off or he tried to bite me. I thought about jumping off the donkey's back several times, but the ground seemed too far down and I knew I'd get hurt if I tried. Finally, after hours of wandering that seemed like years, we reached an ice cream shop and the donkey stopped. Guess where we were?" Rain asked as he turned on his side and faced Porter.

The kettle glowed red from the heat of the stove and the shrill pitch of the whistle indicated that the boiling water grew angrier by the second. "Where?" Porter seethed through gnashed dentures.

"Can you believe it? We were right here in downtown Oxford!" Rain exclaimed. "So this donkey lets me down and tells me to go in and buy an extra-large, chocolate-dipped ice cream cone. When I ask him why, he claims the cone will become a crystal ball that can show me my future. I've ridden this far, so I do as he asks. But when I get outside and offer him the cone, he says I bought the wrong kind of ice cream. When I repeat, verbatim, his previous request, the donkey gets unbelievably angry and calls me a liar. He claims he told me to get an extra-small, plain vanilla cone without the chocolate coating instead of the one that's starting to melt all over my hand." Rain squinted his eyes as he stared at Porter. "Go ahead, ask me what I did next," Rain dared the fat, trembling, old man.

The whistle threatened to deafen anyone within earshot. "I'm waiting, you ungrateful waste of talent."

Rain smiled. "I lifted the donkey's tail, shoved the ice cream cone up its ass, and told him to chill out. Then I ran like hell. I ran away faster than I had ever run before and never looked back." As soon as he blurted the end of his story, Rain covered his ears.

But instead of the whistle exploding, as Rain expected, Porter took a deep breath, nodded his head, and grinned. He reached into his uniform pants' back pocket and pulled out a bus ticket to Natchez, which he tossed in the air. The ticket's thin, flat surface allowed it to slice effortlessly toward the ceiling until it ran out of momentum. Then it tumbled down, end over end, until it landed on the floor by Rain's feet.

"Wonderful parable, Henry. You'll want to tell it again at your expulsion hearing back on campus. And, if by some miracle you're not expelled, I personally guarantee you'll be walkin' tours until you graduate. Whatever happens, you'll never play for Chain Porter again."

Rain nodded. "I never played for you, anyway," he responded indignantly as Porter turned and waddled out.

By 10:00, Rain recovered enough strength to leave the jail under his own power. On the way home after his twelve-hour shift, deputy Robert Abanathy treated Rain to an early lunch before dropping him off at Oxford's bus station. He also gave Rain ten dollars, which he insisted Rain use to buy something to eat when he arrived in Jackson.

"You and that coach must have had one helluva relationship," Robert said as Rain climbed out of the squad car's passenger seat. "If you're ever back in Oxford, I'd love to hear about it."

"I don't plan on returning, Robert, but maybe I'll write a book about it one day. If I do, I promise to send you a copy. Thanks again for your help, including lunch and the loan. I'll get the money back to you in few days."

Rain checked his ticket's itinerary for the tenth time. The bus departed at noon and arrived in Jackson at 5:00. At the Jackson terminal, he would change buses to the one that arrived in Natchez around 9:00 that night. He debated if he should call his father and grandmother now, or wait until he got back to Natchez.

Rain sauntered into the run-down station where a handful of shabbily dressed people of various ages and races waited in rows of dingy, plastic chairs connected by steel rods and bolted to the floor. Rain fit right in with his Salvation Army clothes as he occupied a seat in the middle of an empty row. The worn-out clock, located high on the peeling wall, indicated that he had more than an hour before the bus's scheduled departure. Now would be as good a time as any, Rain thought, as he got up and headed for the pay phone that hung on the opposite side of the waiting area.

Rain's grandmother answered and accepted the collect charges. "What's going on, Rain? Did you know your coach called us first thing this morning? He said you went AWOL from the team yesterday and wound up in jail."

"Relax, Granny. Everything's okay," Rain said as he heard a click on the line. "I'm headed back to Natchez right now. I figure I can be home by two or three tomorrow morning. I'll explain everything then, if ya'll are still awake."

Rain's father spoke up from an extension. "What exactly do you mean?"

"I mean I quit the team and I've decided to drop out of MMC."

A long pause ensued before Rain's father responded. "Son, I suspected the day was coming when you would quit playing baseball, but I can't allow you to drop out of school. Not right now, anyway. Your grandmother and I want you to finish your junior year at a minimum. We'll discuss everything else over the summer. Don't worry about losing your scholarship. We can figure out a way to pay for your senior year. No matter what's happened, you've invested too much time at MMC to give it up on a knee-jerk reaction."

"Dad, I've made up my mind. You have no idea what kind of trouble I'm facing. They'll probably expel me, but even if they don't, I'll be punished for the rest of my cadet career. I can't handle being on restriction that long. It would drive me insane."

Rain's grandmother began crying. "Let him come home, Jim! Please let him come home!"

"Mildred, we already agreed what we'd do if this happened," Jim Henry responded without emotion. "If you can't handle it, hang up your phone." He spoke again to his son. "Rain, if they expel you, then so be it. Otherwise, I want you to finish your junior year. You've got less than three months to go. You're a man now, and a man has to face the consequences of his actions. You can't simply run away and hide when faced with adversity."

Rain couldn't believe what his father was saying. "So you won't let me come home unless I'm expelled. And even though you called me a man, you'd prefer to force me to do something against my will rather than let me make my own decision."

After another long pause, Rain heard his grandmother cry again before a click turned off her sobs.

"That's correct, Son."

Rain bristled. He was done obeying orders from anyone but himself. At that moment, Rain turned his back on his past and focused solely on the future. It would be tough, but he'd survive. He'd teach them all a lesson – nobody dictated terms to Rain Henry.

"Okay, Dad, have it your way. I have only one question before I head back to Natchez. Is Old Blue really mine, or do you own her the way you think you own me?"

"Old Blue's yours and I don't own you, Son. I'm trying to help you make the right decision. I'm sure, one day, you'll thank me for it."

"I've gotta go. My bus is leaving," Rain quibbled.

"Goodbye, Son. Let us know when you get there."

Rain stepped off the bus in downtown Natchez at 9:30. After a fifteen-minute walk, he reached Ellicott Gate, where the cadet guard on duty stopped him as he entered campus. The guard happened to be Rain's former cadre corporal, Mitch Zandon, now a senior cadet lieutenant.

"Jesus, there you are, Rain! General Grimmer wants to see you ASAP. He's waiting for you at Rosalie. I'm supposed to call for relief when you show up and personally escort you down for the meeting." Mitch made a sucking sound with his lips and shook his head. "I don't know what you did in Oxford, but I sure wouldn't want to be in your shoes. Where the hell's your uniform?"

"Back in Oxford and you're right. You wouldn't want to be in my shoes." Rain said as he started walking for First Battalion.

Like a skinny, blond roadblock, Mitch stepped in front of Rain. "Sorry, Rain, but I have my orders. The general didn't say nothin' about you goin' back to your room first."

Rain bent forward. "Mitch, do yourself a favor and get the hell out of my way. I'm in no mood for your silly bravado. I'll only be gone five minutes. It'll take that long for the other guard to get here. Then you can take me to Rosalie and the general. C'mon, didn't we work together on cadre last year?"

Mitch nodded. "You made a damn good corporal."

"Then give me five minutes."

Mitch Zandon moved out of Rain's way. "Five minutes. That's it, Rain. And you owe me one."

"Whatever," Rain responded as he resumed his walk.

Bravo Company held First Battalion guard detail, so Rain knew everyone as he entered the sallyport. They all opened their mouths to address him, but Rain cut them off by saying, "I know, I know. I'm out of uniform, and the general wants to see me ASAP."

Rain climbed the stairwell to the third division and, for the last time, opened the screen door that led to the alcove room he shared with Brad and Philip. They weren't due to report back for another hour, so Rain grabbed a pen from his desk and ripped a piece of blank paper from a spiral notebook. While tears filled his eyes, he wrote his two roommates a short farewell.

Dear Brad and Philip,

Hope ya'll had a blast in New Orleans. As you know, I wish I could have gone with you. Things didn't turn out so well at Ole Miss. I quit the team and got into a little trouble, though I'm not sure which happened first. Anyway, it's a long story and I don't have much time.

Since my dad refused to let me come home, I'm striking out on my own. Wish me luck. I'll need it. You can keep or throw away anything I've left behind.

Thanks for the memories,

Rain

He taped the note onto the mirror above the sink, unlocked the top drawer of his half press, and pulled out the thin box that contained his most cherished letters. From the back part of the drawer, he pulled out the small leather pouch that contained more than $500 in cash. As Rain began to leave, a brown blur from the top shelf of his desk caught his eye. After a short debate, he decided to take his rat stick – it might come in handy if he needed some wood for a fire.

Rain gave a mock salute with his left hand as he and Old Blue zoomed past the two confused guards at Ellicott Gate. In the rearview mirror, the human jumping jacks pleaded for his return. "Now, I'd hate to be in your shoes, Mitch Zandon," Rain said aloud. "Have fun explaining why you disobeyed a direct order from General Grimmer."

Rain followed Broadway until it swung to the left and dead-ended into South Canal Street. He took a right on Canal, then turned west on John R. Junkin Drive, also known as Highway 84. At close to 10:00 on a Sunday night, there wasn't much traffic. Halfway across the Mississippi River Bridge, Rain pulled Old Blue to the side, cut the engine, and flicked on the hazards. His ribs hurt when he leaned over to the passenger side and punched the latch that opened the glove box. His hand located the clear plastic tube, slightly longer than the length of his finger, which contained the glass capsule immersed in the colorless solution. Rain bent the plastic until he felt the internal glass capsule break. The glowstick brightened with life.

From the edge of the bridge's railing, Rain stared for a moment at the MMC campus, situated high on the bluff about a mile upriver to his right. Its tiny, yellow lights twinkled like fallen stars. The bright light in his hand also glowed like a star and Rain felt its desire to join the others. Rain warned the star that it wouldn't fit in, but it still pleaded to become part of the constellation that seductively beckoned from the faraway cliff.

Rain understood. He, too, had once shared the star's desire. With all his might, he heaved the cylindrical tube as far as he could. Rain almost fainted from the pain that punished him as a result of his foolish effort. With overwhelming despair, Rain leaned over the rail and watched helplessly as the dark, swirling waters of the Mississippi River swept the drowning star under the bridge and out of sight.

PART III

CHAPTER NINETEEN
SECOND CHANCES

"Thanks for the ride," Rain said as Wayne eased the truck to a stop beside the front porch of the farmhouse.

"You're welcome," Wayne acknowledged. "I'm excited about the three of us all gettin' together again for dinner tonight, but I'm sorry it's because of what happened with your daddy."

"Yeah, I feel the same way, Wayne. Now, didn't I hear you say you had to hit the road early tomorrow?"

"Pickin' up the load at 7:30 in Jackson. It's gotta be in Phoenix by Thursday afternoon."

"That's what I thought. Go spend some time with little Jack and Stacey. I'll see you in a few hours at Wiedmann's."

"See ya then, Rain."

After his friend drove away, Rain walked around the front of the house to the back and, as he expected, found the rear porch's door unlocked. His father's keys rested in the porcelain change dish on the kitchen counter, the same place he'd kept them for more than thirty years. Rain picked up the keys, deposited them in his pocket, and stepped back outside. He took a deep breath, and the mid-afternoon air pleasantly filled his lungs as he headed to visit his grandmother's grave. She had been the one who brought him back to Mississippi.

Eleven years and nine months after unofficially dropping out of MMC, Rain Henry found himself in his third year as a high school history teacher in Coos Bay, Oregon. He drew a paltry paycheck that mostly went toward the rent he paid on a small wooden house that overlooked the Pacific Ocean. The money that remained barely covered the necessities of life, but he never felt bitter about his circumstances.

Most of the townspeople knew who Rain Henry was, but they didn't know much more. Many considered the tall teacher somewhat of a loner. That was fine with Rain as long as they respected his privacy, which they did. During the week, when not at school, Rain could usually be found at home. Occasionally, he'd make a trip to the antique bookstore on Main Street, where he enjoyed dickering with the owner over the prices of the books he bought. On the weekends, he spent hours exploring the hiking trials that meandered through the Oregon Dunes National Recreation area. He had become an avid naturalist and a voracious reader who relished absorbing his beloved books by the light of a comforting fire during one of the frequent rainstorms that blew in from the Pacific. His life was simple, predictable, stable, and comfortable. He had become complacent, and perhaps, because of this complacency, fate decided to intervene. Rain could never have anticipated the smelling salt that destiny was about to wave under his nose.

The intervention came on the last day before Christmas break, when the boys' basketball coach, who had been battling the flu, fainted in the high school's lunchroom and was rushed by ambulance to the local hospital. That same night, the team was scheduled to play its first game in the annual Coos Who's Holiday Hoops Tournament, and the principal asked Rain if he might be interested in substitute coaching. Because of Rain's height, the principal assumed

Rain had played basketball at some point in his life and would know enough to take the reigns for a game or two. Rain had politely but emphatically declined. Now, as he drove home from school, the principal's invitation dug up the painful athletic memories he hadn't buried as deeply as he'd thought.

Rain pulled in front of his house, turned off the windshield wipers, and killed the engine. While raindrops steadily plinked on the metal exterior of his car, he reconsidered the principal's offer. Rain taught or had taught every player on the team, and he considered each a good kid. The thought of them having to play without a decent coach relit the dormant pilot light of Rain's competitive fire. He decided to take on the task; to hell with the past.

With an invigorating rush of fresh energy and a newfound sense of urgency, Rain opened the car door, put both shoes on the soggy ground, and splashed through the puddles of water that lay in his path as he ran the short distance to the house. After ascending the porch's stairs, he fumbled with his keys before finally unlocking and opening the door. He planned to call the principal as quickly as his legs could carry him to the phone.

Rain froze the instant he saw the intruder. He had long, shaggy hair and was dressed head to toe in a tattered, black leather outfit like some cast-off member of a motorcycle gang. Did he want money? Was he on drugs? Did he have a gun, or would Rain have a chance to fight back? All these questions surged through Rain's mind as the brazen intruder sat in Rain's favorite reading chair and stared back with a broad grin and fiery eyes.

"I've been expecting you, professor," he said wryly. "You know, you really should lock your back door. It almost takes away the fun of breaking into your house."

Somehow, somewhere, Rain recognized the voice. He remained frozen while his mind frantically searched for the dusty folder that would identify his uninvited guest. The intruder began to laugh heartily. "Don't recognize me with the new hairstyle, do you?"

Rain's mind found the folder and opened it. "I know who you are, you crazy-ass hippie from Indiana!" Rain shouted with delight.

In less than a second, Philip Tice had sprung from the chair, and the two men hugged tightly. They held each other for almost a full minute, exchanging slaps on the back like two long-lost brothers. After they separated, Rain took a gander at his former MMC roommate. "What in the world are you doing in Coos Bay, Oregon?"

"I could ask you the same thing."

"I'm a history teacher at the local high school, but I guess you already know that. How about you? Did you join the Hell's Angels or something?"

"You're half right," Philip mused. "I'm an undercover CIA agent working as a liaison with the ATF and DEA. Right now, my team's involved with a wild bunch out of San Francisco that's made a few credible threats against some of our country's top elected officials."

Rain's mind whirred as it tried to calculate the reason for an undercover CIA agent to be in Coos Bay. "So you're up here lookin' for this gang's local chapter?" he asked.

Philip's smile evened. "Nope, I came up here lookin' for you."

"Why?" Rain asked suspiciously.

"Do you remember a certain September night of our freshman year at MMC? The night of The Louisiana Letter Swim?"

"Of course I remember it."

"Then you also remember that if it hadn't been for you, I wouldn't have made it. You gave me a second chance. Without your help, they would have pulled me into that boat and shipped me home, broken and disgraced. Because of what you did, I know one thing's certain: I wouldn't be where I am today with my life and career." Philip deeply sighed before he continued. "You know, it's taken me years to forgive you for running away that night without giving Brad and me the chance to help you. Whatever your punishment might have been, we would have pulled you through. And, not that it matters now, but do you know why General Grimmer wanted to meet with you?"

"No."

"He and Brad's dad planned to push Porter into retirement. Grimmer had heard about what happened during the game. He wanted your side of the story, nothing more, nothing less."

The last thing Rain wanted to do was discuss events in his life that had occurred over ten years before. "Philip, it's great to see you again, but if you tracked me down for a trip down memory lane, you're wasting your time and mine. Don't get me wrong, I've second-guessed what happened at MMC more often than you could ever imagine. And there are definitely times I've missed not knowing what's going on with everyone from my past life, but I can't change what's happened. I can only concern myself with the future."

"That's why I'm here, Rain. To tell you what's going to happen in the very near future, with or without your knowledge or participation. Two days ago, the agency forwarded me an urgent voicemail from one of your hometown friends who claimed to have tracked me down through the MMC alumni association. I used my connections in Washington to find out where you lived, and here I am." The corners of Philip's lips lowered into a frown and he hesitated for a moment. "Rain, your grandmother's losing her battle with breast cancer. Her last wish is to see you before she dies."

The news suffocated Rain's thoughts like a tarpaulin. "My God. Granny's dying?" he eventually mumbled from some distant place.

"I'm afraid so."

"Are you sure she wants to see me?"

Philip put his arm around Rain as his long-lost friend

trembled. "That's what the message said. Rain, this is your second chance. Take it."

"But they've never tried to contact me. Not even now. "

"Did you ever try to contact them?"

"No."

"So who gives a shit? You're even. For God's sake, reunite with your family, and get to your grandmother as quickly as possible. Your friend said there wasn't much time." Philip reached into his leather jacket and produced an airline ticket. "I've already made you a reservation on a red-eye from Portland to Atlanta. Here's the ticket. The connecting flight has you in Meridian by ten o'clock tomorrow morning. Hell, I'll even drive you to Portland, if you'll loan me your car. I think the ride on the back of my bike might get a little wet – I've only got one raincoat."

Rain took the ticket and stared at Philip, who shimmered through moist eyes like a desert mirage, even though he stood less than two feet away. He tried to talk, but nothing came out.

Philip squeezed him tightly. "Don't worry about a thing. I'll let everyone here know what happened. If you decide to stay for a while, give me a call, and I'll personally make sure your affairs are appropriately handled. I'll even have one of my men ship your car to Mississippi, if you decide not to return." He handed Rain a simple business card that listed only Philip's name on the front and had an 800-number scribbled on the back. "Now, promise me you'll go home and rediscover the real Rain Henry, the confident southern boy from Mississippi that everyone loved and believed would one day change the world for the better."

The next day, as the taxicab pulled away, Rain shouldered his duffle bag and stared for an eternity at his childhood home. Twelve years had profoundly weathered the farmhouse's whitewashed wooden slats into tired, gray boards. Along the right side of the house, Rain could see the corner of his granny's garden, which appeared to be irreparably overgrown with weeds.

Rain expected Mackel to explode from the front porch to greet him, but logic tapped him on the shoulder and reminded him that the dog had probably been dead for years. Time changes both man and beast, Rain thought. He shivered from the effects of the cold December wind that exacerbated his nervousness. Carefully, he studied the path that would lead him to the front door of his boyhood home. Although the terrain looked the same as he remembered, he pushed ahead with the deliberate caution of a soldier traversing a field inundated with landmines.

Once he reached the porch, a gaunt man opened the front door and blinked as if an apparition stood before him. Rain noticed the man's left arm still dangled uselessly by his side, but time and neglect had changed everything else. Streaked by rich veins of silver, his brown hair clung greasily to his head. His clothes were ragged to the point that Jim Henry reminded Rain of a homeless man.

Rain's father left the door open as he moved a few steps toward his son. He squinted both eyes and slowly shook his head in disbelief. "I didn't think we'd ever see you again."

Rain gave a slight nod that indicated he had once thought the same thing.

Jim Henry's chin quivered as he extended his functional right hand. "I'm glad you came home, Son."

With tears in his eyes, Rain grasped his father's hand and pulled him into a bear hug. "Me, too, Dad. Me, too."

While Rain stared at his grandmother's headstone, he remembered how she had died the same night of his return. Rain thanked God again for granting him that final opportunity to tell her goodbye and let her know how much he loved her. Although a stroke had robbed Mildred Henry of her speech several months prior to Rain's arrival, her eyes had said all Rain needed to hear: lovingly, they forgave him for leaving, thanked him for returning, and pleaded with him to make things right again with his father. Rain had acknowledged her love, gratitude, and request with a solemn nod and a boyish smile. When Rain's grandmother closed her eyes, Rain watched the pain vanish from her face as she fell into a final, truly restful sleep.

When the time neared to meet Wayne and Railroad for dinner at Wiedmann's, Rain stood and lovingly caressed the top of the granite marker. Surprisingly, he discovered that the rays of the late afternoon sun had warmed the stone the way a grandparent's hand warms the cool fingers of a grandchild.

In 1870, young Felix Wiedmann worked his way from Zurich, Switzerland, to Mobile, Alabama, by cooking steerage passengers' meals onboard an ocean liner. Shortly thereafter, the immigrant heard a tale of a tiny town at the junction where the Mobile and Ohio Railroad intersected the Southern Railroad. The town held the promise of prosperity for entrepreneurs willing to establish new businesses. And so, only a few weeks after stepping foot onto America, Weidmann hopped a train 150 or so miles to the northwest to establish a restaurant in Meridian, Mississippi. The European House, consisting of only four stools, opened that year at the corner of 22nd Avenue and Front Street.

As generations of Weidmann heirs inherited the family business, they eventually changed the name of the restaurant from The European House to Taft and Weidmann's to simply Weidmann's by the 1920s. Today, the restaurant maintains several of the traditions that made it a staple in folklore surrounding Meridian's history. Rain knew that the 1870 Room was as popular as ever for business luncheons, and Weidmann's still offered its famous repeat lunch menus on Tuesdays and Thursdays. Tuesday's special is the "chicken pan pie," and Thursday's menu invites diners to enjoy the "ox-joint surprise."

When Rain walked through the front door, he noticed the crocks of peanut butter and baskets of crackers, yet another Weidmann tradition, placed at each table and along the length of the bar. The most recent tradition began when Weidmann's current owners tweaked its décor to include two television sets that hung from the ceiling against the far wall facing the bar's patrons. The sets enabled the downstairs portion of the restaurant to claim status as a sports bar and tap into a younger clientele on the weekends. While Rain ambled for the long row of barstools, he noted that one TV aired CNN's *Headline News* while the other was tuned to ESPN, the all-sports channel.

At about a quarter of six, Rain settled onto one of the restaurant's bar stools and ordered a soda. He would have preferred a cold beer, but Mississippi's Blue Laws still prohibited the purchase of alcoholic beverages on Sunday. Such was life in the buckle of the Bible Belt, Rain thought as the pony-tailed, twenty-something-year-old bartender delivered his drink.

Rain took a sip and observed the behavior of his server, who stood about two feet beneath the ESPN television and seemed to hang on every word the set's speaker produced. He appeared mesmerized as Peter Gammons, an ESPN baseball analyst, broke down tonight's World Series' pitching match up.

"You follow baseball?" the bartender asked over his shoulder.

"Some," Rain replied. "You?"

"Can't get enough of it," the young man answered as he spun and faced the bar's sole patron. "Who are you pulling for?"

"Who's playin'?" Rain coyly inquired.

The ponytail swished as the bartender shook his head. "Are you kiddin' me? The Crescents and the Yankees! The Crescents are up three games to none and could sweep the series tonight if they win. Not only that, one of the Crescents' star players is a pitcher from right here in Meridian. He was the winning pitcher last night and also won the first game of the series."

"How 'bout that," Rain offered as he sucked on a piece of ice. "Have you ever met this guy or seen him around town?"

The bartender's eyes squinted as they focused on Rain's face. "No, sir, I've never met or seen him, but from what I've seen on TV, he looks a lot like you."

Rain laughed. "I've never been told I resemble a star baseball player, but thanks for the compliment."

Rain's server pulled a flexible hose from behind the counter and punched the button that refilled Rain's glass. "You're welcome. Anyway, this player – Rain Henry's his name – had an unbelievable journey to the big leagues. You wanna hear about it?"

Rain checked his watch. "Can you give me the highlights? I'm supposed to meet some friends in a few minutes for dinner upstairs."

"No problem, sir," the bartender replied as his eyes sparkled. "Rain Henry grew up in Vimville, which is about twelve miles southeast of here. He was a superstar baseball player in high school and accepted a scholarship to play at Mississippi Military College in Natchez, but things didn't work out."

"What do you mean by 'things didn't work out?'" Rain interrupted.

The bartender sighed. "The story in the newspaper didn't really get into a lot of detail. It just mentioned that he left the team and dropped out of school rather than face disciplinary action for going AWOL during a series against Ole Miss."

Rain waved his hand. "Okay, go on. What happened to this guy next?"

"Here's where the details get sketchy. For whatever reason, when he dropped out of school, he decided not to return home to Meridian. Instead, Rain Henry took off out west on his own. Some people think he worked as a ranch hand in Wyoming and Montana. Others believe he made a living as a journeyman carpenter and painter. The author of the article did discover that he graduated with a degree in history from the University of Montana in Missoula about five years ago."

Rain held up his hand. "Wait a minute. So this Rain Henry guy just wandered around the western part of the country as a cowboy or some sort of handyman before he decided to go back to school and earn a degree? What made him decide to do all that?"

"No one knows. People ask him about his past, but he always dodges their questions. You know, he disappeared for over ten years and didn't have contact with anybody back here. Not even his father or grandmother."

Rain shook his head. "What's your name?"

"Thomas."

"Thomas, this whole story sounds pretty far-fetched."

Thomas nodded. "I know, I know. But here's the really unbelievable part. About year ago, Rain Henry was a high school history teacher in Oregon. An old college roommate tracked him down and told him his grandmother was dying from cancer. He catches the next flight back to Meridian, where he arrives just in time to say goodbye before she dies."

"How does he get back into baseball?" Rain interrupted. He was enjoying the game, but didn't want to relive the sadness of his grandmother's passing for the second time in one day.

"The article said he worked with his father on the farm for a few months before he discovered his old baseball glove in the top of a closet. It had been shipped to his house by Mississippi Military College, along with the other personal things he left behind. When Henry blew off the dust and slipped it onto his hand, he found an old business card that a scout from the Crescents had given him years before."

Rain shot up both hands. "Hold on, Thomas. Let me guess. This guy calls the scout, and the scout flies him down to New Orleans for a tryout. After the tryout, the scout signs him on the spot. Spring training starts two weeks later, and the Crescents invite this Rain Henry to attend as a non-roster participant. He pitches so well, the manager not only decides to keep him on the team, he also puts him into the starting rotation. Seven months later, this guy from Meridian's led his team into the World Series after winning over twenty games during the regular season."

"How in the world did you guess all that?" Thomas asked in amazement.

"Thomas, your story sounds like some rejected Hollywood script for a baseball movie that's so syrupy, it'd gag even Kevin Costner. There's no way something like that could ever happen. It's too unbelievable that this Rain Henry simply came out of nowhere to make a major league team after being out of baseball for so long."

The bartender folded his arms. "You're right. Rain Henry didn't make the team right out of spring training. He actually made three starts in the minors before the Crescents called him up when one of their starting pitchers went on the disabled list. And for your information, in two of those minor league games, he pitched no-hitters. Everything else you guessed is true. I swear it."

To Rain's left, the front door opened and he shifted his attention that direction. Railroad held the door as Wayne teeter-tottered into the restaurant. Both wore somber expressions.

Rain extracted a bill from his wallet and dropped it on the bar. "My friends are here. Five will cover the soda, right?"

"Yes, sir," Thomas replied. "You want change?"

"No thanks. That yarn of yours was well worth the extra tip."

Thomas hit a button on the cash register, and the drawer shot open. He placed the five in the appropriate slot under the spring-loaded clip and removed two singles for himself. "Thank you very much, sir. By the way, what's your name?"

"Henry," Rain replied as he headed for his friends.

"Thanks, Henry," The bartender threw after him. "Nice to have met you, and I hope to see you around here again."

"Thanks for coming," Rain declared as he exchanged handshakes with his two childhood friends.

"No problem," Reece Rosenblum replied. "Once you told me Wayne offered to buy us dinner at Weidmann's, nothing could have kept me away."

"That's real funny, Railroad," Wayne said as the three men climbed the stairs to the 1870 Room. "Here I am, the crippled truck driver supportin' a family and the two rich single guys are makin' jokes 'bout me payin' for everythin'."

They reached the hostess stand where a pretty redhead in her early thirties grabbed three leather-bound menus before leading them to a table in the back of the rustic room. The burgundy walls were covered by works of art performed by local artists and photographs of famous patrons.

"You been out with her yet?" Rain asked Railroad after the cute hostess headed back to her station. He had noticed the wink Reece gave her on the way to their table.

"Who? Brenda?"

Rain smiled as they took their seats. "Is that her name?"

"Yeah, but we're just friends. I see her a lot during the week," the town's most eligible bachelor replied.

Wayne pointed to the pictures of Babe Ruth and Jack Dempsey that hung on the wall above their table. "Hey, Rain. When are they gonna put you up there?"

"All they've got to do is give me a call."

Reece opened his menu. "I don't think you'll have to wait much longer. Not too many people can say they've pitched in and won two World Series games their rookie year in the big leagues. But with the experiences you've had, I guess you're a little more seasoned than most rookies." Deciding on his entrée, he lowered the menu. "Rain, if for some reason it goes to seven, do you think they'll hand you the ball?"

The tuxedoed waiter poured three glasses of ice water and shared details of the evening's specials. Rain chose "Gloria's Favorite," which consisted of a grilled Swiss cheese sandwich on rye with shrimp and Buena Vista sauce. "I don't know,

Railroad," Rain replied after placing his order. "That's up to God."

Wayne rubbed his chin. "Has the doc paged you yet sayin' it was okay for us all to go visit him tonight?"

Rain checked his watch. The hands read ten minutes after six. "No, not yet. He said it'd be sometime after six."

Reece took a sip of ice water and his eyes narrowed. "Rain, what if your dad's still in the hospital and the team pressures you to play?"

Rain nodded, indicating he had already considered the possibility. "I don't think they would, but if they did, it wouldn't change my decision to stay. You see, during my ten-plus years of self-imposed exile, I learned some valuable lessons about life that'll stick with me forever. For example, I learned a great deal about true happiness. It's a complicated term with multiple definitions that depend both on the person and the situation. In my opinion, the most important thing anyone can do is to determine his or her own individual definition of the term. And believe it or not, I think wealth or material possessions seldom enter into the equation. I've seen a filthy, fifty-something year-old cowboy, who owned nothing but the clothes on his back and the blankets in his saddlebags, contentedly smile as he slept under an open sky. Meanwhile, the ranch owner, a multimillionaire with forty thousand acres in three states, blows his head off because his trophy wife decides to leave him for a younger man."

"Jesus, that's some pretty heavy stuff. But do you mean to say you wouldn't be truly happy playing in the seventh game of the World Series?" Wayne asked.

"You missed the point, Wayne. For me, right now, true happiness is being here in Meridian and providing comfort to my dad for the last time I'll ever be able to do so. Compared to that, the happiness from playing in the World Series is secondary by a long shot. The key to life, as I see it, is to strike a balance between what you have to do, what you want to do, and what you need to do. The real struggle is to discern which decision falls into what category. When Philip Tice told me about my grandmother's condition and her last wish, I knew I *had* to return home and face my past. When I found that glove in my closet with Bob Dennison's business card, I knew I *needed* to give baseball another chance, despite the odds against me. And when I finally convinced Dennison to give me a shot, I did well because I *wanted* to succeed. Being with my father until the very end is a rare example of something that I feel I have to do, need to do, and want to do. By the way, did I ever tell you guys about the first pitch I threw at the tryout after Dennison flew me down to New Orleans?"

Wayne and Reece shook their heads. "You just called and said everythin' went great and they offered you a contract," Wayne recalled.

Rain squinted. "I've never told anyone about this part until now. Before that first pitch, I trembled at the top of that mound for at least thirty seconds. Dennison wanted my best fastball, and as three scouts focused their separate radar guns on my delivery point, my mind replayed every negative thing that had ever happened in my baseball career. The memories of the sprained ankles, the sore arms, the wild pitches, and the all mental battles I fought with Chain Porter flashed before me as if my life were about to end."

The waiter delivered their appetizers, six giant mushrooms stuffed with crabmeat and coated with a creamy wine sauce, and Rain paused as he used his fork to move one of the delicacies from the silver tray to his appetizer plate. A quick slice with his sharp knife halved the mushroom and its rich contents into two bites, both of which tasted like heaven.

Wayne and Railroad exchanged looks and rolled their eyes.

"C'mon, finish the story! What happened on that first pitch?" Reece demanded.

Rain tapped the pointed edges of his clean fork on his porcelain plate and dabbed the corners of his mouth with his linen napkin. "Boy, I sure do enjoy Weidmann's stuffed mushrooms. Anyway, I'm shaking like a leaf in a windstorm when suddenly it hits me. No matter what happened, it wouldn't really matter if I succeeded or failed at the tryout, because I knew I had just discovered life's most valuable lesson of all: I finally recognized the importance of appreciating the love that comes from family and friends."

"I'm not sure I understood exactly what you're sayin', but it sounded like the biggest load of malarkey I've ever heard," Wayne huffed. "So, what really happened?"

"Yeah," Reece chimed in. "I think you're getting a little soft on us and I'm not sure we shouldn't change the subject. I'm single because I'm married to the law and future political ambitions. Are you single for other reasons and is this your way of telling us something?"

Rain laughed. "I'm serious, guys! Life is about love, plain and simple. I knew you two and my father would always be there for me whether I became a Cy Young winner or a simple farmer praying for a wet spring. If you had listened closely to the story, you might have understood that I was simply trying to calm my nerves. The thought of your love and support did the trick. I love you guys, and I know you love me, too. Anyway, after I relaxed, I reared back and fired that first pitch at ninety-four. As it painted the outside corner, the catcher never even moved his mitt."

"Only ninety-four?" Wayne asked.

"Yeah, I hadn't completely warmed up yet."

Dinner came and went, but not before the three friends took the opportunity to reminisce about their youth. And, over dessert, for the first time since he had become a professional baseball player, Rain got the chance to discuss life as a major leaguer with his two best friends.

"Is the talent level really that much higher?" Railroad inquired.

"Yes and no," Rain answered. "The hitters are bigger, stronger, and more disciplined. They typically won't chase poor pitches unless you've really fooled them. But mentally, you've still got to believe in yourself. You've got to have a stronger belief that you can get the hitter out versus the hitter believing he can hit you. When someone gets a hit, you have to be shocked that they even made contact. Otherwise, it's almost the way a dog can smell fear. You have to be cocky and be able to back it up."

"I guess it don't hurt when you throw in the high nineties," Wayne added.

"No, that doesn't hurt," Rain agreed. "And you knock a guy down every now and then to keep 'em all guessing. Of course, you always claim it was an accident."

"What about the money, Rain?" Wayne asked as he leaned forward. "Do you think it's right for those guys to be paid millions when one of the earrings they wear would buy six months of groceries for the LeRoy family?"

Rain leaned back in his comfortable chair and pondered the question. While he made the league minimum this year, he expected a windfall next year as a free agent.

"Wayne, I think you have to remember that professional ballplayers are simply entertainers making a living proportional to what the market's willing to pay for their services and level of talent. Imagine, if you will, that someone discovered a goldmine in your backyard, but there's a catch: with every second that passes, there's less gold to be mined, because it evaporates. Wouldn't you try to mine as much gold in the shortest amount of time possible?"

"Sure," Wayne agreed.

"That's kind of the way players think. They only have so much talent before they become too old to play at the level the major leagues demand. Believe me, when a team thinks you're over the hill, management won't hesitate to release or trade you. It's sad to see some of these guys treated that way, but ultimately baseball is a business, and businesses rely on success to remain viable. I think most people understand that the best way to succeed or win in business is, more often than not, to hire the most talented workers."

Reece looked disappointed. "You mean no one plays for the love of the game anymore?"

Rain shook his head. "Very few, I think. Some guys, later in their careers, tend to want to play for teams that can help them win a ring and they'll take less money to do so, but you'll find only a handful that play baseball simply because they love the game. Those players are easy to spot because they've stayed with one team their entire career."

"That's sad," Railroad muttered.

"That's not as sad the stories I've heard about how a player won't sign a kid's baseball card 'cause the card company ain't one of his sponsors," Wayne interjected.

"Unfortunately, that kind of stuff happens," Rain acknowledged. "But I think most guys will sign about anything, regardless of which company made it, if you catch them at the right time. They may get a little annoyed if you interrupt their dinner or harass them when they're in public with their families."

"It sounds as though you condone their arrogance," Reece stated in his convincing courtroom voice.

"I don't condone it, but I do understand it. People think fame and fortune is the greatest thing that can ever happen to someone, but it comes at a price. You pay with your privacy; everything you've ever done or ever do is scrutinized under a microscope. Sometimes there's more pressure to perform off the field than on it. I'm wondering right now if there won't be news trucks with reporters waiting to hound me with questions when I get back to the hospital."

The waiter delivered their check and Rain pulled out his wallet.

"What'll you say to 'em?" Wayne asked.

"I don't know. I guess I'll figure that out after I get to the hospital," Rain responded as the vibrating pager shocked the right side of his body. "Looks like that'll be sooner rather than later."

He reached for his cell phone and dialed the number

displayed by the pager. As his two friends watched, Rain uttered a few "okay's" and "I understand's." "I'll be there as soon as I can," he said as he concluded the call, stood up, and hung the phone back on its belt clip.

Wayne and Reece stared intently at their friend. "Rain, is there anything wrong?" Railroad asked.

Calmly, Rain removed a 100-dollar bill from his wallet and slipped it into the leather binder on the table. "That was Dr. Littleton's nurse," he said blankly. "Dad's just had another heart attack."

Rain's friends slumped in their chairs, and Wayne eloquently summed up everyone's feelings with a single word. "Damn," he mumbled as Rain turned and hurried from the restaurant.

CHAPTER TWENTY
THE NINTH INNING

Although Jim Henry survived his second heart attack, everyone knew the next assault would end his life. Even so, Rain and Dr. Littleton decided against re-administering the cocktail of drugs that would induce the medical coma. Instead, they opted to let nature take its course. Rain's father responded to the decision by retreating into a deep sleep that seemed breakable only by a kiss from a fairy princess.

Depending on the circumstances, seventy-two hours can pass by faster than a grandfather winking at a grandchild or as slowly as a snail slithering cross-country. For Rain Henry, the seventy-two hours that connected Sunday evening to the following Wednesday night flowed through his mind like a mixture of both. Rain had Reece check him out of his hotel so he could remain at his father's side while he waited for the inevitable, final tempest. At first, when Rain considered that he was experiencing the last opportunity to see his father alive, time rapidly moved forward, but by Tuesday evening, Rain became eager for situational closure. The fresh tank of adrenaline that carried him through the first forty-eight hours ran dry, and he began to feel anxious as he waited for the arrival of the unavoidable. Again, Rain made peace with the fact that his father was going to die, and now, as though he were inescapably caught in the projected path of an idling hurricane, Rain felt he was as mentally prepared for the onslaught as he could possibly be. He had abandoned the hope that he might have a final chance to speak with his father, so with gnashed teeth and clenched fists, he pleaded with the proverbial storm to stop stalling and hit.

Meanwhile, the passage of seventy-two hours changed the entire complexion of baseball's championship series. Three days ago, the Crescents held a commanding 3-0 series lead over the Yankees, but the Yankees proved, as they had so many times before in their storied history, that they were anything but dead. On Sunday night, the Yankees rallied in the bottom of the ninth inning to win their first game of the series. On Monday afternoon, the re-energized Bronx Bombers crushed the Crescents 12-2 behind determined pitching and six home runs, two of which were hit by third baseman Stan Ludski. Although they still trailed in the series three games to two, momentum had undoubtedly shifted to the team wearing the pinstripe uniforms as the World Series returned to The Big Easy for tonight's game six.

Following his father's second brush with death, Rain had pulled the uncomfortable vinyl and metal chair to the right side of his father's bed, just below the room's tiny window, and, except to use the bathroom, hadn't moved from it since Sunday night. Rain hadn't taken a shower, shaved, combed his hair, or even changed clothes, including his underwear, in three days. He looked as ragged as he felt. Thankfully, hospital security kept away the rabid reporters who congregated in the lobby the way hungry rats converge at a trailer park Dumpster.

Railroad stopped in when he could, but on Monday, his office had been handed an especially complicated hate-crime case that demanded his undivided attention in and out of the courtroom. Wayne, of course, was completely unavailable to help break the monotony because of his trip to Phoenix. Jim Henry's best friend, Mr. Williams, came by every afternoon, but never spoke directly to Rain or his father. Instead, he greeted Rain with a sad-faced nod before silently praying over his dying friend. After a few minutes, his big black eyes filled with tears that dripped to the tiled floor like huge raindrops from a spring cloudburst.

Rain didn't know which visitor his father liked best, but Rain definitely preferred the hospital's assistant marketing director. Catherine, who personally delivered Rain's meals and checked in with hourly precision, watched over and protected them both like an angel of mercy. If Rain needed anything, Catherine made sure he promptly got it. Despite his best efforts to counteract Cupid's spell, in the same seventy-two hours, Rain Henry fell head over heels in love with her all over again. Her daily presence re-ignited the feelings Rain had kept suppressed for so many years.

Now Rain daydreamed as he gazed outside the hospital room's window. Only the last vestige of daylight remained as a cold front's final band of gray showers tiptoed its way through Meridian. While the light rain tapered into a fine mist, he made a solemn promise to himself, once again, that one day Catherine would be his. He didn't know how it would happen or when, but he did know it was only a matter of time.

A raspy but familiar voice broke the silence. "Did I ever tell you the reason why your mother named you Rain?"

Slowly, as though he didn't want to startle away his father's consciousness, Rain rotated his head until he faced his father. Jim Henry looked upon his son with tired, but coddling eyes. Rain began to smile as he shook his head.

Jim Henry coughed as he tried to clear his throat and Rain waited with reverent patience.

"Your mother loved the rain," he continued more smoothly. "Especially in the summer. She'd run through a summer storm and laugh like a child while her hair got wet and her clothes clung to her body. She worshipped the rain and claimed its purity cleansed her soul."

Delicately, Rain put his hand into his father's and held it tightly. "Are you excited about seeing her again?"

Jim Henry managed a grin before he closed his eyes. "I've already seen her, Son. I think it happened when I suffered the second heart attack. I was floating in the sky, and her face appeared in a cloud. She looked as beautiful as the first day we met. When I reached out to touch her, she said it was almost time for us to be together. She reminded me that I still had an important thing to do in this world before I became a part of hers."

Rain raised his eyebrows. "And what's that?"

Rain's father reopened his eyes. "Properly say goodbye, for now, at least, to our son and let you know how much we both love you. You've had a heck of a journey to manhood, but we're so very proud of the man you've become."

"Thanks, Dad. I love you both, too. When you see mom again, please tell her I said thanks for reminding you to come back," Rain said from his heart. "And when you see granny, please tell her hello for me."

"I sure will." After a few blinks around the room, he asked, "What day is it? Is it morning or night?"

"It's Wednesday evening. You've been in the hospital for roughly five days."

Jim Henry thought for a few moments, then asked, "Is the series over?"

"No. Game six starts in about an hour."

"Shouldn't you be the starter?"

Rain grinned, but kept his lips pressed together. After a few seconds, he answered his father's question. "No, Dad. I should be right here with you."

Rain thought his father scowled at his reply, but if he had, it was an extremely subtle reproach.

"Rain, if I were you, I'd be on my way back to New Orleans."

"I don't think you would. You'd be sitting where I am now and holding my hand the way I'm holding yours."

A deep sigh loosened a lump of phlegm, and the resultant cough shook Jim Henry's entire body. "Just remember, Number One, some opportunities in life come around only once," he said with an awkward wink before closing his eyes and slipping back to the world of the unconscious.

Slowly, Rain nodded as he stroked his father's arm. "You're right, Dad. Some opportunities do come around only once in a lifetime."

Shortly after it benevolently allowed Rain and his father a brief goodbye, the hurricane began its methodical march toward shore. It made landfall slightly over twenty-four hours later, but much to Rain's relief, the winds and the rain and the tidal surge were not nearly as violent as he had anticipated. Instead, the physical home of Jim Henry's soul barely shuddered as the tired structure collapsed and released his divine spirit upward toward its final destination. The dreaded storm came and went in less than thirty minutes.

"Time, 7:14 P.M.," Dr. Littleton said quietly as a nurse wrote the official time of death on her chart. Littleton caught Rain's eye. "I don't think he suffered this time around, if that makes you feel any better."

"It does, and I thought the same thing." Rain said as he released his father's hand and stood up from his vinyl chair. Extending his hand to his father's doctor, who stood at the foot of the bed, Rain added, "Listen, I know you did everything you could. Thanks."

Dr. Littleton soberly shook hands. "You're welcome, Rain. Your father fought hard. If only we could have caught this..."

Rain interrupted him. "We can't change the past, Dr. Littleton, but we can learn from our mistakes. My father knew, or should have known, about the dangers of smoking. I'm not saying he deserved to die the way he did, but we all have to make peace with the decisions we make. I'll always love my father and, of course, I'll miss him, but that's the way life works. A person could spend his entire life lamenting about what might have been if only this or that. Instead, I believe it's important to focus on the future and revel in the present while putting the past in its proper prospective."

Littleton acknowledged Rain's comments with a narrow grin. "There'll be some papers to sign, and then you'll be free to go. I'll have one of the nurses bring them by in a few minutes." He dug into the pocket of his white overcoat and handed Rain his business card. "Call or page me if you need anything else. Good luck, Rain."

"You, too, Dr. Littleton," Rain replied as the doctor and his nurse quickly retreated to the hallway.

Catherine, who had been waiting outside the door, entered as soon as the cardiologist and his nurse departed. She hugged Rain and whispered, "Are you okay?"

Rain answered as they disengaged. "Yes. I got to say the things I needed to say last night, and that's all I really wanted."

"I see you have your bags packed. Do you have to go back to New Orleans?"

"I do."

"Right now?"

"I'd like to. After I sign some papers, will you help sneak me out of the hospital and drive me to the airport?"

"Rain Henry, you know I'd do anything for you."

Ten minutes later, like a cat burglar making his clandestine getaway, Rain jumped through the sliding door of Catherine's green minivan and lay as flat as he could across the rear floorboard. Quickly, she drove them out of the doctor's secret parking lot and headed toward 8th Street. When they were a safe distance away from the hospital, Rain scrambled into the front seat, whipped out his cell phone, and hastily dialed a number.

"Charlie Dobbs speaking."

"Charlie, this is Rain Henry. If it's not too much trouble, I'd like you to come get me. I'm on my way to the airport right now."

"Rain Henry!" he exclaimed. "Bob, it's Rain!" Charlie

shouted to his co-pilot. "Rain, Mr. Delacroix had us fly up this morning, just in case you might be able to make it. We'll be ready to go as soon as you get here. How's your father? Is he on his way home from the hospital?"

"Yes, Charlie, he is. Thanks for asking."

"I'm glad everything worked out. We'll see you in a few minutes?"

"I'll be there in about ten."

Before Rain hung up the phone, he heard the plane's engines start singing their high-pitched serenade. Rain felt a rush that made him lightheaded.

"Are you okay?" Catherine asked for the second time in twenty minutes.

"I think so. Everything's happening so fast. It's a little overwhelming."

"Do you think you'll get there in time?"

Rain answered Catherine's question as they turned south from 8th Street onto Highway 11. "It'll be close. The game started almost an hour ago, and it'll probably take me at least an hour to an hour and a half to get to the stadium from here. If I'm lucky, I'll catch the last few innings."

Eight minutes later, Catherine pulled into the loading and unloading zone of Meridian's Regional Airport. Rain hastily grabbed his bags from the back seat and leaned over to offer a temporary goodbye to the girl he had always loved and would forever cherish. Her two sapphires blazed as if they had been dipped in pure alcohol and lit with a match.

"Regardless of what happens tonight, I'll be back first thing tomorrow morning to make arrangements for my father. Catherine, I don't know how I can ever repay you for what you've done over the last several days."

"I do," Catherine whispered as she bent forward and gave Rain a quick peck on the lips. "If your team needs you tonight, you make sure you deliver. I wouldn't expect anything less from the best baseball player ever to come out of Mississippi."

Rain smiled. "You've got yourself a deal. I'll see you tomorrow."

"I'll see you tomorrow," Catherine repeated as Rain closed the car door and hustled into the terminal. "And I'll love you forever," Catherine silently mouthed once Rain disappeared from sight.

This time, Rain remembered to thank both Charlie and Bob before he descended the plane's staircase and jogged to the limousine that waited, engine running, on the tarmac at the New Orleans airport. As soon as Rain sat in the seat and closed the door, the driver sped through tarmac security and headed straight for the exit. Other cars seemed to stand still as they whizzed past, and Rain rechecked his seatbelt to make sure it was properly fastened. After the daring chauffeur turned left onto Airport Boulevard, he mashed the accelerator and weaved in and out of traffic like a racecar driver mounting a final-lap charge to victory. "Glad to have you back, Mr. Henry," the black man calmly offered from the front seat as he swerved to narrowly miss a box van that had unexpectedly changed lanes.

"Glad to be back, and please call me Rain. What's your name?"

"My name's Baxter Breaux, but everyone calls me Bax. I'm Mr. Delacroix's personal driver."

"Bax, you're not trying to kill me are you?"

"No, sir! But Mr. Delacroix did promise me a bonus if I can get you to the stadium in under fifteen minutes."

"And what if we get in an accident?"

"No bonus."

"I understand. Does this car have a radio?"

"Oh, yes, sir! I'm sorry," Bax said as he turned up the radio. "The Crescents is doin' just fine. They's up eight to three goin' inta the bottom of the seventh."

"Maybe they won't need me after all," Rain mumbled as the black Lincoln Town Car shot onto the interstate like a rocket igniting its second stage. Rain leaned his head back into the leather headrest, closed his eyes, and prayed that Bax wouldn't kill them both. At the same time, the radio announcer's voice roared in his ears like the sound of an oncoming freight train. It sounded distinctly similar to the way he remembered it from his childhood.

"Welcome back, baseball fans! This is Bob Costin with Joe 'The Wizard' Merlin calling the seventh game of the World Series live from Jefferson Parish Stadium. With the seventh-inning stretch concluded, this energetic sellout crowd, some 47,000 strong, is back in their seats after a stupendous rendition of 'Take Me Out to the Ballgame' sung by Harry Connick, Jr.

Wizard, the Crescents are six outs away from being the best team in baseball. They've got a five-run lead. Can they hold off the Yankees and bring this city its first professional championship ever?"

"Bob, at the beginning of the game, I had my doubts. When the Crescents lost Rain Henry because of his father's illness, it was almost as though someone took away their lucky rabbit's foot, not to mention one of the best starting pitchers in baseball. After he turned in last Saturday's marvelous performance to give them the 3-0 lead in the series, they looked like a team of destiny."

"How quickly their luck turned, Wizard."

"You're exactly right, Bob. Nothing seemed to go right in their loss the following night. Their defense collapsed, and the three errors they committed led to four unearned runs. Then, to be blown out 12-2 in the next game had to take a toll on their confidence. I have to admit, when they lost last night's pitcher's duel 2-1 and the series evened, I thought the Yankees had them right where they wanted them. But you've got to give this team from New Orleans credit. Tonight, their bats woke up, and their pitching has done well enough to put them in a solid position to win."

"Okay, Wizard. Josh Reynolds, the fifth pitcher of the evening for the Yankees, looks ready. He'll face the heart of the Crescents order: Jeff Roady, Greg Greatwin, and Chip Ford. Wizard, how about the series Greatwin's having?"

"He's been absolutely brilliant, Bob. Four for four tonight, and

flirting with .400 for the series. No question about it: in my opinion, he's the best centerfielder in baseball. He's fast, strong defensively, and hits for both power and average."

"Sounds as though The Wizard likes Greatwin's game. Meanwhile, Roady settles in, and Reynolds delivers the pitch. Roady swings at the fastball and lines a base hit to center. Wizard, even though they're up by five, it looks like the Crescents are calling their AllState agent. They want some additional insurance."

"That's clever, Bob, but you're absolutely correct. A team can never have too big a lead against these Yankees. They're always dangerous, because their lineup is capable of scoring lots of runs in a short amount of time."

"I won't argue with you about that. Now, Greatwin strolls to the plate with a chance to put his team even further out in front. Wizard, Greatwin's always been a leader on this team, but when Henry was unexpectedly forced to leave, he really stepped up, didn't he?"

"Bob, you took the words right out of my mouth. Rain Henry and Greg Greatwin are probably the two closest friends on the team, and what an odd friendship. Greatwin, the perennial all-star who grew up in the inner city of New Orleans, and Henry, the country-boy pitcher from Mississippi who literally came out of nowhere this season. It's almost like Greatwin told his friend 'You go and do what you need to do and I'll keep the ship afloat here.'"

"Greatwin takes a few practice cuts before entering the batter's box. Reynolds, from the stretch, delivers. It's a curveball that crosses the plate low. Wizard, you brought up an interesting point. How exactly did Greg Greatwin and Rain Henry get to be such close friends? Their backgrounds are as different as night and day."

"I had the opportunity to sit down with Greg on Tuesday afternoon. He told me there had been some friction at first, but after they were both selected to the All-Star Game, they got the chance to get to know each other. As a matter of fact, Greatwin claims that it was Henry who suggested a minor adjustment to his stance during an All-Star batting practice. Greatwin tried out the new stance during the game and went two for two. He credits Henry's suggestion for enabling him to better maintain his balance on off-speed pitches."

"Now that's something you don't hear about every day: a pitcher giving a superstar hitter advice that he actually uses."

"Remember, Bob, Rain Henry's no ordinary pitcher at the plate. He won the Silver Slugger Award, which goes to the pitcher with the highest batting average over the course of the season. A .309 average is pretty darned good for a pitcher."

"Wizard, a .309 major league average is pretty darned good for anybody! Okay, now that we've established Rain Henry's prowess with a bat, let's return to our current battle between Greatwin and Reynolds. Reynolds moves into the stretch and checks Roady at first. Here's the pitch. It's a fastball that Greatwin strokes hard on the ground to Vasquez at second. Vasquez flips the ball to Ortiz, the shortstop, who fires over to first for the 4-6-3 double play. Well, Wizard, that proves one thing."

"What's that?"

"Greatwin is human, after all."

"Yes, but he's a human with exceptional speed. He actually made that play close at first when it shouldn't have been."

"So with two outs, the Crescents send their first baseman, Chip Ford, to the plate. Ford's been a solid player throughout the series. Counting his earlier at-bats today, he's hitting .291 for the series with a pair of doubles."

"Bob, Ford's not flashy, he simply does the things that help clubs win. He's a decent hitter with a consistently good glove."

"With no one on base, Reynolds returns to the windup. Here's the pitch. Looked like something off-speed that Ford sends high in the air, but not very deep, toward left center. Chucky Perkins drifts to his right and makes the catch for out number three. With seven in the books, the New Orleans Crescents still lead the New York Yankees 8-3 in game seven of the World Series. We'll be back right after..."

"Hold on a second, Bob. The public relations representative for the Crescents has just handed me a note. I think our audience may want to hear what it says. According to this, Rain Henry has landed in New Orleans and is on his way to the stadium."

"Well, that seems only fitting. He's been a big part of this team's success, and I'm glad to see he'll be around for the celebrations,

provided the Crescents hang on and win this game. Baseball fans, we'll be back with more action and the latest on Rain Henry's pending arrival right after these messages."

"Okay, folks, this is Bob Costin back with Joe 'The Wizard' Merlin calling the seventh game of the World Series live from Jefferson Parish Stadium. We're ready to start the top of the eighth inning, but you may be experiencing some difficulty hearing us. If you are, it's because virtually every man, woman, and child who's cheering for the Crescents is on their feet and screaming at the top of their lungs. Wizard, why do you think they'd do that before the inning's even started?"

"It may have something to do with the fact that an extremely tall pitcher, wearing the number thirteen, has been spotted in the Crescents' dugout."

"That's right, everyone. Rain Henry is not only in the midst of being loudly welcomed home by the fans and mobbed by his teammates, he's actually dressed in his Crescents uniform and appears ready to play. Wizard, do you think there's any chance Henry will see any action in tonight's game?"

"Never say never, but I doubt Henry's even touched a baseball since his last outing. Things would have to go downhill in a hurry for Henry to take the hill. At the same time, I've seen some wacky things happen in the seventh game of a World Series. If the Yankees start coming back, don't be surprised to see Hal Burton pull out all the stops. I guess we'll just have to wait and see what happens."

After the Crescents' reception of their star pitcher caused a lengthy delay, the home plate umpire finally walked over to the dugout and ordered them to take the field. Rain, overcome with the emotion of the moment, slumped onto the bench while several of his teammates, led by Greg Greatwin on his way to center field, urged the crowd to cheer even louder by flapping their arms like gooney birds attempting takeoff. The energy the crowd created was palpable, and Rain nearly hyperventilated when he heard tens of thousands of voices spontaneously begin chanting "Hen-ree! Hen-ree!"

The show of support from the organization, his teammates, and the Crescents fans was unlike anything he could have ever imagined, and would be something he could never possibly forget.

Things settled down when Clyde Jones, the Crescents curly-mustached closer, finished his warm ups and Wally Saxon, the catcher, fired the baseball down to second. As the ball made its way around the infield, Rain looked up at his manager, who stood directly in front of him.

"Rain, if we need it, do you have an out or two in ya?" Burton anxiously inquired.

"Hal, I didn't rush down here to be a spectator. I'll be ready if you need me."

The middle-aged man with the cotton-white hair reached down and put his arm on Rain's shoulder. A close friend of Mr. Delacroix's, he'd been the Crescents manager for more than ten years and his wrinkled face contained a line for every loss he'd suffered, which, up until this year, had been quite a few. "Coming on in relief won't bother you, then?"

"Not a bit."

"Good," Burton said as he removed his hand. "After Jonesy gets 'em out here, I want you to head down to the bullpen. If we get in serious trouble in the top of the ninth, you'll be our man."

Jones retired the side, but not before walking the Yankee leadoff hitter, Jose Vasquez, and then surrendering a monster home run to Stan Ludski. The shot, which landed in the second row of the centerfield upper-deck section of seats, represented Ludski's fifth home run of the series and cut the Crescents lead to 8-5.

Rain, as he had been asked to do, rose from the bench as his teammates returned from the field. When he reached the top of the dugout steps, he paused and waited for Greg Greatwin. Greatwin had unbuttoned the top two buttons of his jersey and Rain could easily make out the centerfielder's thick gold chain as it bounced against the upper portion of his muscular, ebony chest.

As Greatwin got closer, Rain squinted at the reflection of his friend's two-carat diamond earring, which seemed to catch the stadium's lighting, multiply its intensity by a factor of five, and reflect it directly back into Rain's eyes. Greg claimed the jewelry gave him supernatural powers and Rain didn't doubt it. He could run like the wind, and was, hands down, the smoothest player Rain had ever seen play baseball. It seemed as though Michelangelo himself had chiseled Greg Greatwin from a solid block of granite. At thirty-two years of age, he had been a major leaguer for twelve years and an All-Star for the last six. But Rain didn't admire him because of his successful career or his athletic abilities. He admired him because of the money and time he gave back to his hometown community. He was a true role model in every sense of the word. Instead of giving away thousands of dollars each year to support a personal "posse," Greg pooled his money and established a college scholarship fund for inner city youths that served as an escape ladder from the smoldering ruins of the ghettos.

Earlier in the season, when the team announced that it would release Sid Luckman to make a permanent spot on the roster for Rain, Greg had been the first to defend management's controversial action. Luckman, a popular veteran pitcher whose arm troubles necessitated Rain's initial call-up from the minors, tried everything he could to reverse management's decision. Consequently, at first, several of Rain's new teammates resented his presence. They felt Rain hadn't properly "paid his dues" to be with the major league club. But, because of Greg's support and his own stellar success on the mound, most of the team accepted him, and as it so often happens, Sid Luckman was soon forgotten.

"Yo, Rain, where you headed?" Greg asked after he reached the dugout's lip. "I done told ya when you got here to sit back and relax, 'cause the series MVP is gonna carry this team to the championship house!"

"That's awesome, Greg!" Rain exclaimed. "Do you plan on

pitching the last inning from center field, or is Hal gonna let you throw from the mound?"

Greg smirked as he rolled his head back and forth like water sloshing in a bucket. "C'mon, man," he whined. "You know what I'm sayin'."

Rain laughed as he slapped his friend's shoulder. "I'm just kiddin' with you, Greg. Hal wants me down in the bullpen in case Clyde needs some help getting those last three outs."

Greg's face grew rigid, and his happy-go-lucky demeanor vanished. He leaned forward and whispered into Rain's ear. "You be ready, Rain. Clyde threw two innings last night and I think he's worn out."

"I will," Rain promised. As he turned and started the jog down the right field line toward the bullpen, the crowd immediately understood the significance of what was happening and their initial murmurs of surprise quickly became a collective roar of approval.

Twenty-five minutes later, Rain was loose and stood waiting and watching with the rest of the Crescents pitchers and bullpen coaches along the clear Plexiglas wall that separated the pen from the playing field. The Yankees had already scored twice to cut the lead to one measly run. With runners at first and third and nobody out, Jones faced the top of the Yankee batting order and their clutch-hitting shortstop, Jose Vasquez. The previous inning, Vasquez had fouled off almost a dozen pitches before drawing a walk prior to scoring on Ludski's blast.

Burton called in the middle infielders to cut down the tying run at home, instead of having them play back for a possible double play. Rain didn't know exactly what Burton's definition of "serious trouble" was, but if something wasn't done to stem the tide soon, the Crescents would be trailing in the bottom of the ninth with only three outs precariously preventing an embarrassing series defeat. Feeling trapped and helpless, Rain nervously clawed at the bullpen dirt with his cleats while Vasquez stepped to the plate and Jones checked the runners. As the Crescents' pitcher drew his body into the stretch, Vasquez squared to bunt.

"Sacrifice! Move! Move!" Rain screamed through the Plexiglas as the infielders scrambled to cover their fielding assignments. The first and third basemen charged while the second baseman moved rapidly to cover the bag at first. At the same time, the shortstop sprinted toward second base. The Yankees strategy made perfect sense: advance the "go-ahead" runner from first into scoring position, so that Persons and Ludski, the next two hitters in the line up, got a shot at putting the Yankees on top with a base hit. The sacrifice would also keep them out of the double play. But as Rain himself had once done against the all-star team from Meridian, Vasquez tricked the Crescents defenders. A millisecond before the ball crossed home plate, Vasquez pulled the bat back and swung. He barely made contact, but made contact enough to send a soft line drive that lazily drifted over the bag at second toward center field.

Rain watched in slow motion as Johnny Swain, the Crescents shortstop, and Greg Greatwin both pursued the dying baseball as gravity gently pulled it back to earth. The two players were like locomotives on the same track headed for one another at maximum velocity.

"Greg's ball! Greg's ball!" Rain shouted at the top of his lungs while he pounded the see-through wall with both fists. Rain cringed at the mental image of the impending train wreck, which would undoubtedly allow the tying run to score, regardless of whether one of them actually caught the ball in the air or it fell to the ground as a base hit. While the collision drew nearer, Rain quickly glanced at the runner on third. Like Rain, with keen eyes and intense focus, he also watched the play develop. Unlike Rain, he grinned at the possibility of a collision. If that happened, he could walk home uncontested.

At the last possible second, Greg called for the ball and Swain peeled away. Although he made a diving, headfirst lunge, the All-Star center fielder's gallant attempt to catch the ball was in vain. It hit the ground less than an inch in front of his outstretched glove and ricocheted smack dab into his face. The runner on third, who had been ready to tag up, broke for home. Luckily for the Crescents, however, Greg's nose effectively stopped the baseball and Johnny Swain pounced on it a second later. Seeing Swain's quick response, the runner abruptly slammed on the brakes and scrambled back to third. Meanwhile, the other runner, who had been on first, coasted into second because no one covered the bag. Vasquez, another key play to his credit, grinned safely at first. With the bases loaded, the tying run still only ninety feet from home, and nobody out, Rain wondered if trouble got any more serious to Hal Burton.

Apparently, it did not. Hal Burton emerged from the dugout, and with his head hung low, meandered to the mound. While the other pitchers slapped him on the back and showered him with words of encouragement, Rain kept his eyes glued to his manager. Finally, it happened. After a brief meeting with his catcher and his ineffective closer, Hal Burton looked to his bullpen and pointed. When the bullpen coach opened the gate and told Rain, "Go get 'em," the crowd was so quiet, Rain could hear his own heart beating as it frantically pumped a combination of oxygen, glucose, and adrenaline to every cell in his body.

Suddenly, the crowd sounded like 42,186 firecrackers exploding at once. But instead of delivering a quick bang and then fading back to silence, these firecrackers seemed to possess an inexhaustible supply of gunpowder and popped over and over and over again. By the time Rain loped from the bullpen to the mound, the noise level was deafening to the point that Rain could barely hear his own thoughts. He hoped that whatever his skipper and catcher planned to say, they planned to say it loudly.

Burton handed Rain the baseball. "Rain, we wouldn't even have made it to the World Series if you hadn't come along! No matter what happens, I'll never forget what you've meant to this team!"

Rain nodded, and the Crescents manager turned and began his lonely walk back to the dugout as the firecrackers chanted, "Hen-ree! Hen-ree!"

Wally Saxon stood inches away from Rain's ear as he motioned at their departed manager. "I don't know what the hell that 'no matter what happens' crap is all about! I just know the Yankees are in a heap of trouble!"

Rain grinned. "Wall, you remember that pitch I told you I'd been working on for Ludski?" Rain screamed as he asked.

"Hell, yeah!"

"When he comes up, I'm using it on him!"

"Okay, we'll make it four fingers!"

"Okay, let's do it, Wall!"

"Let's do it, Rain!"

Rain completed his eight allowed warm-up pitches and checked his fielders' positioning as they stared back with eyes that pleaded for success and shouted encouragement at the same time. From shallow center field, Greg Greatwin flashed his friend a smile that beamed brighter than a searchlight. Rain acknowledged the smile with a slight nod before turning and climbing the hill.

The crowd reached a fever pitch as Rain straddled the rubber and Chucky Persons, a right-handed hitter, dug in. Rain had owned Persons during his earlier outings in the series. He could remember striking him out at least three times already. Rain received Wall's sign, and as he went into the stretch, his baseball instincts anticipated a daring decision by the Yankees. Sure enough, as he delivered, Rain's peripheral vision caught the runner on third breaking for home. The Yankees were trying to score the tying run with a suicide squeeze.

Once Rain released the fastball, Perkins squared to bunt. Rain's feet were on springs while he waited for Perkins's bat to make contact. Before it did, Rain's fastball rose just enough to turn the would-be ground ball into a soft line drive that drifted up the third base line. Rain grunted as he dove to his right and extended every inch of his lengthy frame at the falling baseball. The ball looked like a scoop of vanilla ice cream as it protruded from the edge of his leather glove, but he had caught it. The runner, for the second time in two pitches, skidded to a halt and tried to sprint back to third base to avoid the double play.

He wouldn't make it. Quick as a cat, Rain rotated and threw from his stomach to Tim Thrash, who had charged in from his position at third, but was able to catch the pass in full stride and beat the Yankee runner back to the bag. The entire stadium shook as Crescents fans jumped up and down, transforming the sound of exploding firecrackers into 42,186 vibrating jet engines screaming at full throttle.

"That's a good start. One pitch and two outs," Rain mumbled after he calmly got up and dusted off the front of the uniform. Thrash called time, and with wild eyes and several ecstatic pumps of his fist, flipped Rain the ball. While Rain headed back to the mound, he smiled at the thought of a certain attorney he knew back in Meridian who had probably jumped to his feet and proudly proclaimed to anyone within earshot, "I taught him that move! He learned that from me!"

While Rain collected himself at the back of the mound, he evaluated the situation. Even though the tying run stood in scoring position at second base and Vasquez, the speedy potential winning run, stood at first, there were two outs now, and only one hitter remained between Rain Henry and the fulfillment of his childhood dream.

"And what a hitter he is," Rain said to himself as he took several deep breaths and watched as Ludski, confidently grinning, strode to the plate. Stanley Ludski was born in the U.S. shortly after his parents emigrated from the former Soviet Union, but to Rain, he appeared to have been bred in a test tube at some clandestine Russian laboratory. The blond third baseman stood nearly as tall as Rain, and his muscles looked like steel implants that rippled with strength beneath the surface of his skin. Ludski reminded him of a classic Eastern-bloc bad guy straight out of a James Bond flick, but instead of making millions as a Hollywood actor, Stan Ludski chose to maul baseballs instead. At only twenty-four years of age, he was not only the strongest player in the league, he was the most feared hitter in all of baseball.

Like fervent Romans pulling for their favorite gladiator, the crowd exuberantly cheered as Rain deeply exhaled and scaled the dirt mountain to oppose the hated beast. If Rain could get ahead in the count, he had a secret sword that he planned on using to mortally wound Ludski. The first pitch would be monumentally important, and he knew Ludski anticipated a fastball.

Rain slid his right foot against the front part of the rubber and leaned forward as Saxon flashed a series of signs. He called for the changeup, and Rain agreed. As Rain straightened into the stretch and gave both runners a final check, he placed his middle three fingers over the top of the baseball and whispered, "Steal me a strike, bandit wasp." Once the grip felt comfortable, Rain slid his left foot toward home and delivered the pitch.

After a powerful stride and gut-wrenching twist of his tree-like trunk, the beast named Ludski swung mightily. The resultant line drive nearly decapitated the Yankee's third base coach. It wasn't pretty, but the pitch served its purpose. The foul ball counted as the first strike and put Rain up 0-1.

The umpire tossed Rain a new ball, and he rubbed it hard with both hands as he walked back to the mound. It was imperative that he could get a good grip on the pitch he would throw next. The last thing he wanted to throw was a wild pitch that would move the tying run to third and the winning run to second.

Rain connected again with the rubber and watched as Saxon ran through the signs. He called a fastball and Rain shook him off. Wally caught on, and when he cycled his fingers through to the "four fingers" pitch, Rain nodded.

This time, Rain checked the runners twice after he brought his body into the stretch position. The key to beating the competition is to keep them off balance, Rain mentally assured himself as he sprang forward at the plate and delivered the sidearm curveball.

The pitch was a beauty and completely caught Ludski by surprise. Disconcerted by Rain's sidearm delivery and the fact that a baseball headed straight for his knees, Ludski bailed out of the box as the pitch broke perfectly over the inside corner of the plate. The umpire called it a strike, and the crowd roared at Rain's trickery. An exuberant Saxon returned the ball to his pitcher, and Rain allowed a chuckle under his breath as he returned to his sacred spot behind the mound. "There you go, Porter, you crazy old bastard. I guess I learned something worthwhile from you after all."

Rain was one pitch away from complete victory. Slowly, he turned and faced Ludski, whose facial expression told Rain that the jab from his secret sword had accomplished its desired effect. Ludski's embarrassment converted his steadfast confidence into undisciplined anger. Rain had masterfully baited the trap, and the time had come to finish off the wounded animal. Rain paused as he savored the moment. All around him, thousands of blurry faces fluttered like leaves rustling in a gentle evening breeze and he mentally journeyed back to the first time he had ever successfully thrown his father's knuckle curve. When Rain returned to the rubber, Wally Saxon didn't call for the pitch, Jim Henry did. Rain couldn't help but smile as he visualized his father behind the plate.

When the ball left his hand, something special mentally clicked. As Rain anxiously watched, the baseball zipped for the mitt like a fastball. Then, as if it understood its mission in shaping Rain Henry's destiny, at the front edge of the plate the baseball surged downward as though an invisible, divine hand spanked it toward the ground.

After Ludski swung on and missed, Rain collapsed to his knees, thrust his head back in exultation and shot both arms into the night sky in exaltation, for he knew whose hand had been responsible for the pitch's big break.

EPILOGUE

I'm older now. As I stand atop the bridge of life and gaze down at the brisk mountain stream rushing below, I'm awed at how the cold water tumbles in, around, and over the rocks beneath me like the passage of time and the memories of my own glory days. Yes, I am older, but I'm also a completely different man from who I was only a few years ago. I've been forever toughened by my past experiences, yet I remain tempered by the thoughts of the exciting adventures that lie ahead.

As for the present, I find myself sitting at my desk and staring at a blank computer screen. "Should I even turn you on today?" I ask the monitor, because sometimes the creative juices flow and sometimes the mind is a desert. When I peer closer at the empty screen, hoping beyond hope that it'll actually respond, I notice my own reflection staring back. The light dusting of snow interspersed among the brown fields of hair at the top of my head serves as another reminder that life is short and time is running out. Soon, other responsibilities will prevent me from writing the conclusion of this novel the way it deserves to be written. I began the book more than six months ago, and the entire process has proven to be an unbelievably difficult exercise in self-discipline and perseverance.

Reluctantly, I reach over and push the round plastic button that sends electrical power to the computer's motherboard and a video signal to my mirror. While the system boots, my wife glides into the room. Throughout it all, she has been patient, loving, and given me the proverbial kick in the pants when I've needed it.

"How's it coming, Sweetie?" she asks as she sits down at the room's other desk.

"Not too well," I respond with a sigh. "Tying this thing up is the hardest part of the entire book. I want to let the reader know what happens to everyone, but I'm not exactly sure how to put it on paper so it makes sense."

My wife gives me an enormous smile. She always seems to have the answers. "Why don't you write a quick synopsis on each character that gives a snapshot of what that character's doing now? Later, once you've written down what you want to include, it should be much easier to put into paragraphs for the final chapter. "

"That's a wonderful idea," I gush.

My wife struggles as she stands back up. "Thank you. Now, while you do that, I'm heading outside to work in the garden. I'll be back in about an hour, and I expect you to take me for a walk when I return."

"Okay, Sweetie," I say. "Just don't overdo it."

"I won't. See you in a little while," she responds before leaving me to finish my assignment.

Eagerly, I use my mouse to double-click on the word processing icon, and the computer's hard drive spins momentarily as it searches for and then opens the program. At the top of the blank page, I type: *SR Characters: Where are they now?*

Rain Henry. Rain's World Series performance catapulted him to fame and fortune beyond belief. He became a free agent the instant he struck out Stan Ludski and almost immediately, the Texas Rangers aggressively pursued his services when their owner figured out that instead of paying $25 million a year to a shortstop, they should have invested in good pitching. But Rain rebuffed their offer of six years for $68 million and re-signed with the Crescents for an additional three years at $7 million per. Though the team from New Orleans reached the playoffs each of those three years, Rain and his teammates were never able to repeat the magic that had made them World Series champions. Three-quarters of the way through the last season of his contract, a torn rotator cuff ended Rain's playing career at age thirty-seven. Today, once again, he's a high-school history teacher and chairman of The Rain Henry Foundation, which donates more than $500,000 annually to children's charities all over the world.

Wayne and Stacey LeRoy. Wayne and Stacey recently welcomed their third child, a second girl, to the family. When Rain Henry purchased Buddy's Athletic emporium shortly after signing his lucrative new contract, Wayne agreed to manage it, which terminated his career as a long-haul truck driver. At twelve years of age, Wayne's son, Jack, is an all-star catcher and pitcher who possesses a hard-core fastball, a stealthy changeup, and a wicked knuckle curve.

Reece Rosenblum. Railroad is in the middle of his first term as Mississippi's first Jewish lieutenant governor. Now living in Jackson, Reece and his newlywed bride, a beautiful and talented civil rights attorney, are expecting their first child.

Catherine Landerson. The day after her twins, Blake and Blair, left for college, Catherine filed for divorce from Trip Chadwick, citing irreconcilable differences. When Catherine remarried a year later, Rain attended the wedding.

While Rain watched as she pledged her devotion to her new husband, he silently prayed that this man, this time, would be truly worthy of her affections.

Cynthia, Chester, and Velma Williams. Cynthia Williams graduated first in her class from Princeton Law School and worked with a Washington firm for several years. Three years ago, she accepted a position as a civil rights attorney in Jackson and moved to Mississippi's capital city. A short time afterward, at a political fund-raising dinner, she "accidentally" bumped into the state's dashing new lieutenant governor. They were married within a year. Two summers ago, to move closer to their daughter and new son-in-law, Mr. and Mrs. Williams, who had inherited the farm from Jim Henry, put the property up for sale. An anonymous buyer from Louisiana purchased the entire estate for $1 million, thus ensuring financial security for Chester and Velma Williams for the rest of their lives. Today, Mr. and Mrs. Williams eagerly await the arrival of their first grandchild.

Brad O'Johnovich. Dr. O'Johnovich is happily married with four kids. Professionally, he's one of his medical practice's senior partners, but still finds time for his duties as chairman of MMC's Board of Visitors. Although he and Rain remain close friends, Brad still hasn't been able to convince his old roommate to donate money to Mississippi Military College.

Philip Tice. No one heard from Philip Tice again. He simply disappeared. In his second season with the Crescents, Rain was in San Francisco for a series against the Giants when he read a small newspaper blurb about four undercover federal officers who were killed in the line of duty. The story mentioned no names because the government denied the incident ever occurred. If the story was true, Rain always wondered if Philip had been one of the four. Rain still held out hope that one day, he'd return home to find the same surprise intruder that had once changed his life forever.

"Whew," I exhale after completing the assignment with fifteen minutes to spare. After clicking the save button, I push back my chair and head to the window that overlooks the garden. My wife is diligently pruning the rose bushes she planted earlier this spring. As she bends over, her pregnant belly nearly scrapes the soft earth. Her pregnancy, at forty years of age, is yet another example that miracles can happen.

"Granny would be proud of the what you've done with her garden, Mrs. Henry," I whisper against the warm pane of glass.

As if she heard my words, Catherine turns her head, and her sapphire eyes lock onto mine. The rays from the late afternoon sun play like young children as they dance through her long golden hair. "I love you, Rain Henry," her lips say before outlining a sensuous smile.

"I love you, too, Catherine," I whisper back.